ONE WOMAN'S FIGHT TO PROTECT CRIME VICTIMS AND EXPOSE CORRUPTION WITHIN THE DISTRICT ATTORNEY'S OFFICE LEADS HER ON A HARROWING AND LIFE-CHANGING JOURNEY.

Bradley's debut novel, *Breach of Trust,* explores the obstacles crime victims face navigating the criminal justice system. When Anne Gardner, a victim assistance program director, learns her boss—the district attorney—has been accused of sexually harassing a young employee, she struggles through uncharted territory. Should she remain silent or risk the career she loves by going public about a powerful elected official?

The harassment allegation—along with evidence that the district attorney's corruption may have enabled a young mother's murder—dredges up painful memories from Anne's past, causes friction in her marriage, and propels her into a moral crisis.

Breach of Trust is a gripping story of corruption, courage, community, and friendship. It's about one woman's profound decision to finally speak out against injustice.

Praise for Breach of Trust

"An absorbing new book filled with heart, wisdom, and a hero you'll cheer on from the opening page!"
—Beverly Willett, author of Disassembly Required: A Memoir of Midlife Resurrection

"Breach of Trust is a page-turner set in the much-publicized and romantic city of Savannah, Georgia. And its subjects—sexual harassment, domestic violence, and governmental corruption before the #metoo movement—are indeed timely. If you're like me, you will be riveted and want to read more."— **Rosemary Daniell, award-winning author of ten books of poetry and prose, including *Fatal Flowers: On Sin, Sex and Suicide in the Deep South*, *Sleeping with Soldiers: In Search of the Macho Man*, and *Secrets of the Zona Rosa: How Writing (and Sisterhood) Can Change Women's Lives***

"*Breach of Trust* is a humdinger of a debut novel. Helen P. Bradley used her insider knowledge as long-time head of Savannah's crime victim advocacy program to create this compelling read about the devastating effect one person's deceit has on the justice system. Despite facing an agonizing moral decision, Anne Gardner—her fully-drawn main character—maintains her zany sense of humor, providing a welcome respite from the novel's mounting tension."— ***Susan Earl, author of We Part to Meet Again***

"These vivid characters navigate life-and-death situations at the mercy of a justice system rife with internal dramas. Bradley—herself a victim advocacy pioneer—has created a gripping, unforgettable story."— ***Dawn Major, author of The Bystanders***

BREACH OF TRUST

Helen P. Bradley

Moonshine Cove Publishing, LLC
Abbeville, South Carolina U.S.A.

Moonshine Cove Edition April 2023

ISBN: 9781952439568

Library of Congress LCCN: 2023906224

Front cover by Ebooklaunch.com
Author photo by Dreamweaver Photography
Interior and back cover design by Moonshine Cove staff

For my mama, the late Martha Wood Pitts,
who taught me the love of the written word

About the Author

Helen P. Bradley grew up in Bethune, South Carolina, and has lived in Savannah, Georgia, all her adult life. She headed Chatham County's nationally-recognized Victim-Witness Assistance Program for twenty-seven years. Before that, she wrote for two daily newspapers. Her essays have been published in magazines and anthologies. She's also written curricula and articles for national and state victim advocacy organizations. She started her own business, Savannah Simple Weddings, where she officiates weddings. She earned her undergraduate degree from Clemson University and her master's degree from Georgia Southern University.

Breach of Trust is her first novel. She lives in Savannah with her husband, teenage grandson, and antisocial rescue cat.

www.helenpbradley.com

Chapter 1

A white moon shimmers over the Atlantic as Anne and Jon sit on the deck of A.J.'s Seafood Restaurant. "A perfect night. Happy anniversary!" Anne says as she raises her Heineken bottle in a toast.

Jon leans closer. "Here's to many more, darlin'."

Anne's cell phone buzzes, and Jon rolls his eyes. "Ignore it."

But Anne can't resist looking. "It's Lisa. She's working at the E.R. tonight. Must be important." She puts the phone to her ear. "Hey, Lisa."

"I hate to bother you after hours," her friend says. "I'm the charge nurse tonight. We've got a pregnant woman whose husband beat her up pretty bad. She has no family here. Can you please come see her?"

"No, I can't. Jon and I are celebrating our anniversary. You know the protocol–call the police and they'll take her to S.A.F.E. Shelter. Where's your social worker anyway?"

"Swamped. Full moon crazy here. I told the victim about the shelter, but she doesn't wanna go. She's anxious to get back to her toddler who's with a neighbor. Anne, you're such a great victim advocate. You can always calm people down and help them think clearly."

Anne avoids eye contact with Jon who's drumming his fingers on the table. "Lisa, you know my program doesn't do 24-hour crisis response. Besides, it will take me nearly thirty minutes to drive from Tybee Island to Savannah."

Lisa talks fast. "I know. But he punched her in the face and stomach. She could lose the baby. We need to monitor her for a while. I'll owe you big time."

"Where's her husband?"

"They've arrested him. Ugh. My pager's going off. Will you come please?"

"Okay, just this once. Bye." Anne clicks off her phone.

"What was that all about?"

"Lisa's freaking out about a domestic violence victim and wants me at the hospital."

"Lisa's a nurse. She shouldn't be freaking out."

"But she is. She has a soft spot for abuse victims. Remember, Lisa encouraged her sister to leave her husband and when she did, he frigging killed her. She's got major guilt."

"I know that, Anne. But it doesn't mean you need to bail on our anniversary, for god's sake. And we just started dinner." Jon stabs his flounder with a fork.

"Hon, would you get me a takeout box?" Anne covers her plate with a napkin.

Jon's blue eyes widen. "Um, I reckon so." He reaches into his pocket for the car keys and slides them across the table. "Good thing we don't live far away since I'll be walking home."

"Oh, darlin', I feel awful for leaving, but Lisa's always been there for me. It's not like I do this all the time, and hopefully, I won't be gone long. I swear I'll make it up to you." She leans over and kisses her husband on the mouth.

Jon scowls. "Anne. I wish you'd stop trying to save everybody."

Chapter 2

It's 10:00 when Anne reaches the hospital parking lot. She texts Lisa, then dashes to the emergency room.

Lisa greets her in the lobby with a hug. "Thanks so much for showing up. Come meet Charisse."

The victim, lying on a bed in one of the small examining rooms, has a bandage covering her left eye and a dark bruise on her right arm. A petite Black woman probably in her twenties, she barely looks up when Lisa introduces them.

After Lisa leaves, Anne sits in the chair beside the bed. "I'm so sorry this happened. You don't deserve to be hurt."

Charisse stares at the ceiling.

"Is there anything I can help you with right now?"

Charisse rubs her baby bump. "No ma'am. I just pray the baby's okay. I've got to get home to my little boy. He's only two."

"He's with a neighbor, right?"

"Yes ma'am. She heard me screaming, called the police, and offered to keep Bernie, Jr. But he needs his mommy. I have to get outta here."

As tears stream down her cheeks, Charisse swings her legs to the side of the bed and wobbles as she tries to stand.

Anne gets up and gently puts her hand on Charisse's shoulder. "You have to stay a little longer to make sure you and the baby are okay."

Charisse groans and leans back into the bed.

"Did your husband hurt Bernie, Jr.?"

Charisse shakes her head. "No. Thank the good Lord."

"You and your son can go to a family violence shelter while you figure things out."

"No need. My husband's in jail."

Anne pours water into a plastic hospital tumbler and hands it to Charisse. "I doubt he'll be there long. It may not be safe to go home."

Charisse takes a sip of water. "He'll probably feel bad and apologize. He'll say it was 'cause he'd been drinking." Her hand shakes as she fiddles with the straw. "Or be super mad 'cause the police came."

"So this isn't the first time he's hurt you?" Anne says softly. *Of course, it isn't. But this time he put you in the hospital.*

Charisse casts her eyes downward.

"Safety is your priority. Is there anyone you can stay with?"

Her voice trembling, she says, "The Army just transferred us to Savannah. I only know the neighbor who has little Bernie. But she has three kids of her own, so I can't ask her."

"Where do you live?"

"On the westside. Oh god, I can't even remember the street address." Her breaths come in short bursts. "It's, uh, it's the Pinewood Apartments." She pauses. "I don't even know how I'll get home!"

"We can call a taxi. In the meantime, is there any family you want to call?"

Charisse shakes her head. "No. My family's in Kentucky, and I don't want my mama to know. Her nerves couldn't take it."

Anne gives her a wallet-sized brochure about developing a safety plan. She explains it's a good idea to have necessary items–medications, important papers, police report, and some clothes–ready in case her husband gets violent again and she needs to leave quickly.

They sit in silence for about an hour as Lisa comes in and out checking her vitals. Despite the flashing lights and annoying beeps on the patient monitor, Charisse eventually dozes off. Anne runs her hand through her shoulder-length brown hair and leans back in the recliner. *I hope Jon isn't too mad.*

Around 2:00 a.m. Lisa returns. "Good news, Charisse. You and the baby are fine. You're going to be bruised and sore for several days so take Advil as you need to for pain." She hands her the discharge papers. "Any questions?"

Charisse glances at the papers. "No, but I just thought of something crazy. I listed my husband as the emergency contact, and he's the reason I'm in the dang hospital. God help me."

Lisa takes her hand and squeezes it. "Please take care of yourself."

Charisse nods. "Thanks. I don't know what I'd have done without you and Miss Anne."

Anne gives Charisse a slip of paper where she's scribbled her cell number and the Victim-Witness Assistance Program number. "We can help you apply for compensation to cover some of the hospital bills, and you can get free counseling. Call if you need anything." Anne helps Charisse into her clothes, calls a taxi, and stays under the covered drive with her until it arrives.

"Get some rest, Charisse," Anne says as she hands fare money to the driver.

"I will. Then I'll be fine."

I sure hope you're right.

Chapter 3

Anne tiptoes into the house at 3:00 a.m. where she finds Jon asleep on the couch. *Is he on the couch because he dozed off there or because he's mad at me? I can't worry about that now. Gotta sleep a few hours.*

A bleary-eyed Anne arrives at the metro police department at 9:30 the next morning. She finds a parking spot in the dirt lot and steps from the car into a pothole. When she wipes the mud off her shoes, she notices she's wearing one navy and one black one. "Oh for the love of Pete," she mutters. *At least the heels are the same height, so I won't wobble like a drunk.*

Inside, the officer behind the glass window looks up from his computer. "Good morning, Anne, you here for rookie training? I'll buzz you through."

"Thanks. You working the front desk now?"

"Yeah, ever since I hurt my back. I'd rather be on patrol. I hate dealing with all the nuts who parade through the front door." He grins. "You excluded, ma'am. I swear, last week a woman showed up insisting Russians were poisoning her through the air conditioner vents."

Anne giggles. "Yikes." A woman walks up beside her, pulls out a crumpled brochure, and hands it to the officer, saying she wants to get a copy of the police report. It's the brochure she'd drafted in 1988 after the Georgia Victim's Bill of Rights went into effect. Hard to believe it's been twenty years since Anne and other victim advocates across the state waged a two-year campaign to get the bill passed.

Inside the training room, the soon-to-be officers are finishing their coffee break. Several years ago, Anne had persuaded the training sergeant to add an extra day to the six-week training course so recruits could learn about social service resources. She pulls up PowerPoint on her laptop and squints at her notes. *Sheesh. I'm only forty-five years old, and my eyes are shot.* She slides on her reading glasses.

The twelve new officers settle into their seats. Anne introduces herself and gives a brief overview of the Victim-Witness Assistance Program. "Soon after taking office two decades ago, District Attorney Martin Clayton established the Victim-Witness Assistance Program in his office. We're advocates–not attorneys–who provide information, support, and assistance to crime victims and witnesses."

She continues, "I want you to think about a time you were a victim or felt victimized."

She pauses for a moment before asking, "Does anyone want to share how you felt afterward?"

A young man in the front row says, "I was mad. Somebody broke out my apartment window while I was on military maneuvers and stole every piece of my electronics."

A dark-skinned woman, who doesn't look old enough to be a police officer, says softly, "I was in shock. I couldn't believe what happened to me."

Anne writes the words anger, shock, and disbelief on the whiteboard. "Anything else?"

"I felt guilty," a woman with curly red hair says.

"Right," Anne says. "Victims often blame themselves and think if only I had done this or hadn't done that, it wouldn't have happened. And that brings up a good point. We–even good people, police officers, victim advocates, and friends–tend to blame victims too. Why do you think that is?"

Silence.

Anne says "If one of you goes to the parking lot to find your car has been broken into–I know that would be weird at the police department, but it could happen–and you come back and tell us, I guarantee someone will ask, 'Were your doors locked?' We like to think we're cautious and if we lock our doors, our cars won't be broken into. But even if your vehicle is locked, someone could still break in."

One guy says, “Yeah, it could happen. Lot of crazies walking around downtown.”

“We tend to blame the victim because it makes us feel safer,” Anne says. “We couldn’t get out of bed every day if we thought the worst. We don’t think someone will break into our home, steal our car, or molest our child. Then the unthinkable happens, and our feeling of safety is shattered.”

A few officers nod.

“Yeah, but some victims do stupid things, almost asking for trouble,” one recruit says. “Like a drug deal gone bad.”

“True. Some victims make bad choices or have committed crimes themselves, but do they deserve to be robbed or killed?” Anne asks. “Does a drunk girl prancing around River Street deserve to be raped?”

A female officer says, “Definitely not.”

Anne scans the room. “What did someone say or do that was helpful after you were victimized?”

“My neighbor replaced my window and changed the locks on my doors,” says the guy whose apartment was burglarized.

A woman in the back raises her hand. “Someone told me it wasn’t my fault. That helped.”

The redhead sighs. “I wish someone had said that to me.”

“My grandma listened to me constantly bitch about what happened,” says a stocky cop.

“Practical assistance, reassuring victims it’s not their fault, and listening are all helpful responses,” Anne says. “We advocates do a lot of listening. One wife of a murder victim repeatedly told me about the murder. She said it helped her process the shock. Most people don’t want to hear about any crime, much less murder.

“Y’all are often the first person a victim will see after a crime, and they may experience any of those emotions. What you say and do is their first impression of the criminal justice system. A seasoned lieutenant once told me two words he initially says to a victim, after securing the scene and checking for injuries, of course. Do you know what those two words are?”

"It's not your fault?" one officer says.

His buddy elbows him and laughs. "That's four words, moron."

Anne says, "The two words are 'I'm sorry.' Police have to ask a lot of questions, and that can make victims feel like criminals. So before he starts, this lieutenant says he's sorry. Simple as that. And usually, the victim relaxes a little."

Anne tells the officers about one of the first victims she helped, an elderly lady whose home was burglarized while she was in Florida.

"A property crime might not seem like that big a deal, but it turned this lady's life upside down. Miss Jones said it was like a death—the death of her way of life, her independence, her old neighborhood where everyone used to know each other.

"When she saw her ransacked house, she was paralyzed with fear and disbelief. A neighbor said a truck had pulled into the driveway and loaded it with her belongings. He thought Miss Jones was moving."

The trainees listen intently.

"We helped Miss Jones get her locks changed. After two men were arrested, we sat with her at the preliminary hearing, kept her informed about court proceedings, and helped her regain a sense of control."

"Eventually, the two bad guys pled guilty, so Miss Jones didn't have to testify in a trial. You can imagine how intimidating that would have been—talking into a microphone in a courtroom full of strangers, including the criminals, a jury, and the judge. The defendants had prior convictions, and the judge sentenced them to five years in prison.

"We helped her write a letter to the parole board protesting early release. When they eventually got out of prison, we notified Miss Jones so she wouldn't be shocked if heaven forbid, she ran into them."

Anne finishes by distributing copies of the victim compensation forms. "Violent crime victims can apply for compensation to help with unreimbursed expenses such as medical, funeral, and counseling costs. Okay, it's time for the next speaker, but I'll be around a few minutes for any questions. Stay safe."

The red-headed woman follows Anne to the back of the room. Ashley is scrawled across her name tag. "I'm going to remember to say I'm sorry. I wish someone had said that to me," she says, blinking back tears.

"I wish someone had, too. That experience has probably made you more empathetic though." Anne's phone beeps. "Excuse me one sec." She reaches into her pocket and clicks it off. But when she looks up, Ashley is already gone.

Chapter 4

Anne rushes outside to catch up with her, but she's nowhere in sight.

As she slides into the car, Anne's cell rings. It's her assistant, Donna. "Don't forget your conference call in ten minutes with Atlanta folks about the statewide training."

"Thanks. I'm on the way."

Before starting the engine, she checks her voicemail and hears Charisse's frantic voice. "Miss Anne, can you please call me right away?"

Anne dials the number but gets a busy signal. *At least she has S.A.F.E. Shelter's number.*

She pulls out of the lot and sees a tour guide leading a walking group into Colonial Cemetery where some seven hundred victims of Savannah's 1820 yellow fever epidemic are buried, along with famous people, such as Declaration of Independence signer Button Gwinnett. Anne likes to tell her out-of-town visitors that after Union troops occupied Savannah on December 24, 1864, the graveyard became a temporary home to several hundred Union soldiers who defaced some of the stone markers, altering birth and death dates. She brags that General Sherman gave President Lincoln the city of Savannah as a Christmas gift because it was too pretty to burn.

She drives the few blocks to the courthouse and gets to her office in time to join the conference call. *Why do they have to ramble on about name tags and notebooks?* She yawns.*I need a nap.* As soon as the hour-long call ends, she dials Charisse who answers on the first ring. "Miss Anne, I need your help. I heard Bernie bonded out, and I'm scared!"

"Where are you?"

"At home." Anne can barely hear her over a screaming child in the background. "My husband probably went straight to work and will be furious if his lieutenant found out. I'm afraid he'll be here soon."

“Did you call S.A.F.E. Shelter?” Anne says.

“Yeah, they’ll have a bed open this afternoon.

“Good. You need to go to the shelter.”

“I don’t have a way to get there. Can you please give me a ride?”

Anne rubs her temple. “Is there a bus stop nearby?”

“No ma’am. And my neighbor’s car is dead. I gotta get out of here.”

The words of the county attorney and her boss reverberate in Anne’s head. They advised her that Victim-Witness staff should not provide transportation because of liability issues. “Charisse, isn’t there anyone you can call?”

Charisse’s response is a loud sob which elicits even louder wails from the toddler.

Anne thinks about Lisa’s sister’s death and that leaving is the most dangerous time. “Okay, Charisse. Just this once. Get your stuff together like meds and whatever Bernie Jr. needs. Give me your address, and I’ll be there as soon as I can. I want to make sure you’re safe tonight.”

“Thank you. Thank you so much.” Charisse says her address in between sniffles.

Anne grabs a granola bar and heads to her car. Traffic is snarled on West Bay Street. Two police cars, an ambulance, and a fire truck block the right lane. *Just my damn luck to get stuck behind a wreck.* When traffic comes to a standstill, Anne rubbernecks and sees a crumpled car beside a tractor-trailer truck. Two EMTs load a stretcher into the back of an ambulance. *Oh my god. I pray everyone’s okay.*

Eventually, a cop directs Anne’s lane of traffic to move ahead, and Anne arrives at Charisse’s cinder block apartment complex. Realizing she parked in front of the wrong building, she walks to the 200 building and knocks on 202-B. Charisse cracks open the door. “Oh, thank goodness. It’s you.” She lifts the chain lock and Anne steps inside. The small apartment is sparsely furnished but neat. “Come on, Bernie, Jr. We’re going for a ride!” Charisse says.

"Yay!" the chubby-faced toddler says. "I go ride." He grabs his teddy bear and a lollipop from the couch. Charisse lifts him into her arms. He pats the deep purple bruise under one of Charisse's eyes. "Mommy got boo-boo."

"How are you feeling, Charisse?" Anne asks, picking up the suitcase by the door. *I sure as hell hope her husband doesn't show up.*

"I've been better. Crap. Gotta find the car seat." She returns from the kitchen with the car seat, and they rush to the car. Charisse installs the seat into the back and buckles her son in it.

"Thanks for getting us," Charisse says, then gasps. "Oh god! That's him!" Pointing to a gray truck pulling into a parking spot about ten spaces over, she crouches down and buries her face in her arms.

"Shh!" Anne says, jerking the car in reverse.

Bernie, Jr. peers out the window to see what all the commotion is about. "Daddy!" Daddy's big truck!"

Charisse whispers, "Hush, baby. Eat your lollipop."

Anne's heart pounds. With sweaty hands, she grips the steering wheel tighter. *Oh dear god. What should I do? What if he has a gun?*

Charisse's husband climbs out of the truck. He's burly and wearing green Army fatigues.

Anne backs out and speeds onto the main road. *When the county attorney talked about liability, I doubt he was thinking about a victim, her child, and me getting shot in my car. Have I lost my ever-loving mind? Jon would probably say yes.*

Chapter 5

Assistant District Attorney Kate Phillips is in Anne's office talking about an upcoming trial. “The victim is terrified of seeing the defendant, and I don't blame her.”

“Mrs. Melton can wait in our witness room until she testifies,” Anne says.

Kate rummages through her folder. “She trusted this jerk at first because he'd done some home repair work for her once before. This time when she offered him a glass of water, he came inside and hit her over the head with a hammer,” Kate's porcelain face flushes pink with anger. “Hurt her bad, stole her jewelry and TV. I want to nail his ass.”

“Oh yeah, I remember discussing this at the multidisciplinary team meeting,” Anne says. “Mrs. Melton reminds me of my mama, trusting everyone. Once Mama hired a house painter because he wore a cross necklace. He took her money and never finished the job.”

“It pisses me off when people take advantage of elders.” Kate pulls a photo of the injured victim from the file and hands it to Anne. “Mrs. Melton hit the corner of the kitchen table as she fell, hence the concussion.”

Anne glances at the picture, grimaces, and hands it back. “Oh God, that's awful. Does he have a prior record?”

“He had a burglary, but it probably wasn't the first time he'd been violent. You know so many seniors are embarrassed to report crimes. They worry their families won't let them live alone anymore.”

“And with the senior population growing so fast, we're going to see more and more crimes against the elderly.”

“Yep.” Kate stands and adjusts the belt around her slim waist. “There's a special place in hell for the punk who hurt Mrs. Melton. If not hell, at least prison. I'm going to the police department right now to talk with the detective to make sure that happens.”

After Kate leaves, Anne thinks about how much she admires Kate's passion. A year ago, Kate heard a nationally-recognized elder abuse prosecutor speak at a conference and was enthralled. She asked her boss if she could focus on prosecuting crimes against the elderly, and Martin Clayton persuaded the county commission to fund the position. Kate created a multi-disciplinary team with representatives from the social services, law enforcement, medical, and prosecution fields. Each week they share information and coordinate efforts to improve the response to elderly victims.

An hour after leaving, Kate calls. "Before I forget, we need to take Harold to lunch for his birthday. When's good for you?"

Anne looks at her calendar. "How about Friday?"

"OK. I'll call Harold to see when he's not in court. And Liz. Can't have a birthday lunch without his old trial partner."

* * *

A few days later, Kate, Anne, and Harold walk to Kate's car in the county garage. There's finally a hint of fall in the air. Harold, still trim at forty-two and a dapper dresser, smiles at Kate. "Nice suit, Kate." She's wearing a navy "lawyer suit" jazzed up with a bright paisley silk blouse and pointed-toed high heels.

"Good gawd, I couldn't walk ten steps in those shoes," Anne says, feeling frumpy in black flats and black dress. *I look like I'm going to a funeral.* She twirls a strand of her hair. *Plus, I need to get this shaggy hair trimmed.*

"Anne, you're so tall, you don't need heels," Harold says.

"Good thing. The oyster shells in this tabby sidewalk are hard enough to walk on." The minute she gets the words out of her mouth, she nearly trips. Harold grabs her elbow to steady her.

"You okay?" he asks.

"Holy cow! I can't even walk in flat shoes."

Kate drives down Chatham Parkway to pick up Liz at juvenile court, and Harold turns to Anne who's sitting in the back seat. "I hope my aunt doesn't see us. Remember last week when we went to State Street Cafe for lunch?"

"Yeah."

"Aunt Sofia was on a trolley tour. She loves to play tourist, even though she lives in Savannah. Anyway, she saw the two of us walking together and called my mama to tell her, 'I think Harold's finally got himself a girlfriend!'"

Anne giggles. "Say what? First of all, it cracks me up that your elderly aunt rides around on a trolley with tourists. And she told your mama what?"

"That night, my sister-in-law called and asked if I was dating anyone. I told her no. She told me what Aunt Sofia said to mama. You know those Italian women like to keep close tabs on their families."

"Well that beats all," Anne says. "You could have plenty of girlfriends. A single, successful attorney and all."

"And ladies like Italian men," Kate chimes in.

Harold's olive skin turns red. "Half Italian. Daddy is from inner city Atlanta."

Anne realizes she's never known Harold to date anyone. She wonders if he might be gay, but Harold doesn't talk much about his personal life.

They arrive at juvenile court where Liz is standing outside. A lanky blonde, she scoots into the back seat of the Volvo station wagon. "Happy birthday, Harold!"

"Thanks! I miss seeing you, Liz."

"You're the one who deserted me, leaving juvey to become a public defender."

"Just for two years though. I thought I could defend juveniles and make a difference. But it was frustrating."

"Thankfully, you're back in the D.A.'s office where you belong."

Kate rolls her eyes and groans. "Good grief, Liz. Why are you wearing pantyhose? It's 2007. Girl, you need to get out of the 80s."

"Listen. I'm from Jesup where everybody wears hose with dresses." She pulls up the dress over her knee to flash more leg.

"Maybe your 90-year-old grandma," Kate drives out of the parking lot, past the barbed-wire enclosed youth detention center, and heads to the Southbridge Golf Club.

The hostess seats them at a table with a view of the well-manicured fairway. The white tablecloths and silverware are a welcome change from their usual downtown lunch spots.

Liz looks at Harold. "Have you been out of the office? I called a couple of times, and you weren't there."

"I was on vacation for a week and stayed home a couple of days with a stomach virus."

"Do anything special on vacation?" Anne asks.

"Not really. Made a quick trip to Atlanta to visit one of my brothers. I've been promising to see his son play in the high school band." He squeezes lemon into his water. "Why don't you girls fill me in on the latest gossip? I never know anything."

"That's because you never come out of your office," Kate says. "You're across the hall from me, but I hardly ever see you."

"Yep, I like to stay under the radar," Harold says, smirking.

Liz tells him about the new hires and office renovations at juvenile court.

Kate fills him in on her upcoming trial, who's dating, and who's getting married or divorced. "Oh y'all, I went to the wedding reception of the century. It was at a friend s parents' home on Modena Island. Champagne flowing everywhere, two bands, and a Brad Pitt look-alike strolling around offering cigars to the men."

"Whoa. That's over the top What does her dad do?" Anne says.

"Retired CEO from some big company. Kellogg's I think. I met the bride in Brooklyn, but her dad retired to Savannah."

"Must have sold a lot of Frosted Flakes," Liz says.

"Anne, why didn't you offer us cigars at your wedding?" Harold asks, peering at her over his glasses.

"Because that didn't quite fit into the budget of this government employee. We built a patio instead of paying for a big wedding."

"Always the practical one," Liz says. "I need to come sit on that patio. So jealous you live at the beach."

"Come visit any time. Moving to Tybee Island was the best thing ever."

Kate says, "Harold, I bet you'll have a fancy wedding when you get married."

"Don't think that's in the near future," Harold mumbles, staring at his menu. "Oh good. Here comes the waitress."

"I don't know what I'm having except key lime pie for dessert," says Liz, a sweetaholic. She even puts Splenda in her wine.

"Remember when you were pregnant, and I gained ten pounds by sympathy eating?" Harold asks Liz.

"Yes, you were a good trial partner," Liz says. "I was starving by ten every morning, and you would go to Sunrise Restaurant to get us both sandwiches and a brownie. Then we'd go to lunch at noon." Liz chuckles.

"Yup," Harold says. "How are your kids, Liz?"

"Growing like weeds."

Kate chimes in, telling everyone her two children–a son and daughter– are fine although eight-year-old Ronan is "apparently aiming to commit all the seven deadly sins. Yesterday I got a note from school saying he stole 75 cents from a kid at lunch. Then lied about it."

"Oh my," Harold says. "And your beautiful daughter?"

"She's okay but in the obnoxious puberty stage. She thinks her dad and I are idiots, and she wants to go live with her godmother in New York. Geez." Kate has close friends in New York where she attended law school and worked for a few years before returning to Savannah to marry her high school sweetheart, Walt Phillips, an engineer at Gulfstream Aerospace. Kate and Anne became close friends, often eating lunch together and taking walks on Saturday mornings.

When their food arrives, Harold bows his head for a silent blessing before drizzling Italian dressing on his salad. "So, is there any talk about who may run for D.A. after our boss retires?"

"I haven't heard much. It's hard to imagine the office without Martin," Kate says. "He's been D.A. for 25 years. Who do you think will run, Harold?"

"I don't know." He lowers his voice. "But between us friends, some people have encouraged me to put my name in the hat."

"Really? That would be great," Liz says. "Go for it."

"Yeah, you'd do well," Kate says. Anne nods.

"It's more than a year before the election. We'll see," Harold says. His phone beeps. He reads the text, his face turning into a scowl. "Oh gosh, a text from my oldest brother. Remember my nephew who lived with me when he was sixteen? He got arrested for possession of heroin last night."

The ladies offer consoling glances.

Harold wrinkles his brow. "Here I was mentoring boys through the juvenile court program, but I couldn't straighten out my own nephew."

"I can't imagine anyone taking in a teenager for a year," Anne says.

The three lawyers launch into a conversation about the new robbery law while non-lawyer Anne tries to follow along.

"We've started a support group for armed robbery victims," Anne interjects. "It's one of the scariest crimes. Just think what it must be like having a gun to your head," pointing her index finger to her tee. "You believe you're going to die."

"Anne, thanks for always reminding us about victims," Kate says. "How was the police rookie class last week?"

"It was a good group this quarter, but I swear, they all look like kids. A few of the guys didn't look old enough to shave much less carry a gun."

"What about that crime spree on the Westside?" Kate asks. They haven't arrested those damn scumbags yet. Maybe one will confess and rat out the others."

Harold grins. "Kate, you don't cuss around your children, do you?"

"Hell no!"

Everyone laughs.

Harold checks his watch. “Better get going. I have a plea hearing at two.”

“Whoa! Is that a Rolex?” Anne asks.

“Yes, I’ve had it for years.”

“I’ve never noticed it,” Anne says.

He smiles. “Well, to be my girlfriend you’re not very observant!”

They pay the tab and pile into Kate’s car.

Harold turns to Liz. “Maybe I'll see you at juvey court this afternoon. I'm supposed to meet one of the young men in the mentor program.”

“You still volunteer?” Anne asks.

“Yes, I’d planned to stop when I left the public defender’s office, but there are a couple of kids I still try to help.”

“Good for you,” Anne says. “Lord knows, boys need strong male role models.”

In front of the juvenile courthouse, Liz gets out of the car. “Enjoyed it, y’all. “

Driving off, Kate rolls down the window and yells, “Hey Liz, there’s a run in your pantyhose.”

Chapter 6

Charisse shifts on the hard wooden bench in the packed courtroom. It's fifteen minutes before the 9:00 a.m. start time.

A woman wearing a name badge approaches her. "Charisse?"

"Yes?"

"Hello. I'm Janine, a victim advocate. You know my boss, Anne Gardner."

Charisse nods and pulls out the crumpled Victim-Witness Assistance brochure Anne had given her at the hospital. "Yes."

Janine sits beside her and says in a hushed tone, "I'll be with you in court this morning and throughout the whole court process. Have you ever been to court before?"

"No."

"As Anne probably told you, today is a preliminary hearing, not a trial. This judge has to decide if there's enough probable cause for the case to continue to State Court."

Charisse scans the courtroom. "Why are all these people here?"

"There are twenty cases on the docket. People are here on their own cases. When yours is called, you'll walk to the front of the courtroom and answer the lawyers' questions."

"Do I sit down like on TV?"

"No, not at this hearing. You and the lawyers will stand up there," Janine says pointing to the front of the room. "There's not a microphone so you'll need to speak loudly and clearly."

"Miss Anne said my husband will be here."

"Yes, the accused has a right to face his accuser."

Charisse doesn't know that six years earlier, Janine had testified in this same courtroom. Her husband was charged with aggravated assault. Janine had told the judge she and the kids had returned home one night after football practice, but her husband thought they had abandoned him. He stabbed her twelve times while the kids hid in the closet. After three surgeries, Janine didn't regain the use of her left hand and has long scars on her back and arms. But she never complains. She went through the criminal justice process with the support of the Victim-Witness Assistance Program, and then her husband was sentenced to prison. A year later, she applied for a job as a victim advocate, and Anne hired her.

Charisse picks at her cuticles. "I haven't seen Bernie in the three weeks I've been at S.A.F.E. Shelter. He'll be furious."

"A deputy will be at the front of the courtroom to make sure everyone is safe. Your job is to tell the truth. If you don't understand a question, say that."

"Okay."

"Has he tried to contact you?"

"He's called my cell a bunch, but I blocked him. My neighbor says he keeps asking about me, but she told him that me and Bernie Jr. were out of town. He probably doesn't believe her though. He knows I don't have any money." Charisse gasps when she looks to the left and sees her husband on the opposite end of the same wooden bench. "Oh my god. There he is." She slouches in the seat and takes deep breaths. About six people are seated between her and Bernie.

Janine whispers, "Is that him in the Army uniform?"

Charisse nods and stares at the floor.

A bailiff appears in the front of the courtroom and raps the floor with his long stick. "All rise. The Family Violence Court of Savannah is now in session, with the Honorable Marguerite Newsome presiding. Remain quiet and turn off all electronic devices."

The black-robed judge takes her place at the elevated bench. The prosecutor and public defender stand behind podiums facing the judge. The two women are about six yards apart. Each has a stack of files.

The bailiff says, "You may be seated. Remain seated until your case is called." The clerk calls the first case. The responding police officer testifies, then the victim. The young woman says her boyfriend chased her with a butcher knife while her six-year-old screamed. "He threw the knife at me, but thank God it didn't hit me or my little girl."

Charisse winces and mumbles to Janine, "I don't ever want my little boy in the middle of a fight."

Next is a mother whose son beat her up when she wouldn't give him money for drugs.

When the clerk calls Charisse's case about forty-five minutes later, she remains frozen in her seat. Janine touches her shoulder and whispers, "You can do this. Just tell the truth. Look at the lawyers, not Bernie."

Charisse makes her way to the front. The lawyers stand in between her and her husband. Charisse's wedding day flashes through her mind–her handsome, broad-shouldered groom in his Army uniform and beret next to her in a simple, long white dress. She held a bouquet of daisies, her favorite flower. Their families looked on from wooden pews in the Army chapel much like people in the courtroom must be staring at them now. *I promised to love him for better or worse. Until death do us part.*

The police officer who responded to the scene is testifying in another courtroom, so the clerk swears in Charisse.

First the prosecutor, then the defense attorney, pepper her with questions. *Where were you on such and such date? Tell the court what happened that night. Who called the police? Were you in fear for your life? Where was your son? Did you receive medical attention?* Head down, Charisse chokes out brief answers.

"Had he ever been violent to you before?" the prosecutor asks.

Charisse pauses, biting her lip. "No."

The judge peers down at Charisse. "Mrs. Butler, you need to speak up."

"Yes, your honor," Charisse says. Her tongue feels thick.

"Please clarify, Mrs. Butler. Do you mean yes ma'am he has been violent in the past?" the judge asks.

"No. I meant, um, what I meant was yes ma'am I would speak up."

"Well, speak up then!" The judge looks at her watch.

Feeling faint, Charisse grabs the railing in front of her. The prosecutor gives her a reassuring nod. "Mrs. Butler, you testified your husband was violent to you, causing you to seek treatment at the hospital and leave the home you share. Are you fearful of further violence from him?"

Charisse glances at Bernie, his hands folded in front of him and his head lowered as if he's praying. He looks like he did when he was a star linebacker on the high school football team. People called him a "gentle giant" back then. Charisse says in a shaky voice, "No, I'm not really scared of him. I want my family back together. That's all."

The prosecutor sighs and closes her file.

The defense attorney clears her throat. "Your honor, the defendant has chosen not to testify, but I'd like to call Officer Butler's commanding officer to the stand."

"Okay, make it brief," the judge says.

The officer is sworn in, and the attorney asks if his subordinate has any record of disciplinary actions. The answer is no. She then asks if he's receiving anger management counseling at the base family advocacy center. He says he is.

"Is that all?" the judge asks. Both attorneys nod.

Judge Newsome peers down at the defendant. "You realize, Officer Butler, these are very serious charges. This could end your military career. I find probable cause to bind this case over to State Court. Meanwhile, I hope you will continue counseling for the sake of your family and your career."

The defense lawyer nudges Bernie who says in a strong voice, "Yes, your honor. I understand, ma'am."

The judge raps her gavel. "Next case!"

Tears trickle down Charisse's cheeks as she walks to the back of the courtroom and sinks into the bench beside Janine.

"You did fine," Janine whispers and hands her a Kleenex. Charisse blows her nose. "Charisse, let's wait here a few minutes until Bernie leaves the building. We don't want to run into him in the hall."

"I don't feel good," Charisse says, holding her stomach.

After Bernie leaves, Charisse rushes to the restroom in the hall and throws up. She splashes cold water on her face and rinses her mouth. When Janine walks in to check on her, Charisse says, "I should never have talked to the police. What if he loses his job? I can't expect everything to be perfect."

Charisse and Janine go upstairs to the Victim-Witness office, where they sit in Janine's cubicle. Janine says, "The S.A.F.E. Shelter advocate said she'd be back shortly to take you back to the shelter. She's in another hearing."

Charisse rubs her belly. "What's going to happen to this baby? To me and little Bernie? I want to go to nursing school, but I probably need a job instead. I finally told my mama about what's going on, and she wants me to come home, but they got their own problems." She twists a paper clip. "Bernie looked kinda pitiful. I could tell that he feels bad for what he did." She stifles a sob while Janine remains silent. "Bernie's my husband. Until death do us part."

Anne walks in. "Hi, Charisse. How did it go?"

Janine shoots her a worried look.

"I dunno, "Charisse says. "But thank god it's over."

Anne hands her a bottle of water and a pack of cheese crackers. "One day at a time. You and your little one are in a safe place now. You're attending a good support group and taking the right steps."

Charisse leans back in the chair and exhales slowly. She looks up at a poster on Janine's wall. It's a picture of a casket with a spray of yellow daisies on top. The caption says: *He beat her dozens of times. She only got flowers once.*

Charisse drops the bottle of water and covers her face with trembling hands.

Chapter 7

A few weeks later, Anne and Jon are snuggled up on the couch after watching *Little Miss Sunshine.* It had been Anne's turn to pick out the movie.

Anne clicks off the DVD. "I loved that movie." She looks at Jon. "And I love you. Thanks for insisting I come home from work at a decent hour." She brushes a popcorn kernel from his upper lip. "And thanks for not raising hell after I skipped out on our anniversary."

Jon nods. "But you're still working too much."

"I know, hon. I'll do better."

"It's Friday night. Time to begin a relaxing weekend."

Before Anne can take another sip of wine, Jon pulls her close and kisses her. "Let's relax in the bedroom."

"Good idea," Anne murmurs as she cups his face in her hands. "Stay-at-home date nights are the best." The romantic moment comes to an abrupt halt when Anne's phone jangles on the coffee table.

"Not now!"

"It won't take but a minute." She taps her phone. "Hello," she says tentatively.

"Hi, Ms. Gardner. This is Tabitha at S.A.F.E. Shelter. I'm calling about Charisse Butler."

"Is something wrong with Charisse?"

"Somehow her husband found out our address and showed up here. He had a dozen roses for her and a happy meal for the little boy. Charisse must have heard his booming voice because she came to the door before I could get rid of him."

"Dang. How did he know your location?"

"I don't know. If she told him, we won't let her back at the shelter. Against the rules. I'm new here, but that's what the house mother said."

"How did he act?"

"Smiling and polite. Typical honeymoon phase of domestic violence. He went back to his truck while she packed her suitcase."

Anne's buoyant mood deflates like a pricked balloon. "Is there something you want me to do?"

"Charisse hasn't answered my calls, but maybe she will from you. I'm worried. I remember how bruised she was when she got here. And her pregnant and all."

Jon stands in front of Anne, his arms crossed.

Anne frowns. "Tabitha, I'm afraid there's not much we can do. It's her choice." *Tabitha better get used to victims returning to their abusers.*

"I know but..."

"All right, I'll try to call her."

"Thanks so much, Anne."

"You're welcome. Bye."

Jon shifts his hands to his hips. "Let me guess. Charisse needs you?"

"I don't know. She left S.A.F.E. Shelter with her sorry-ass husband and Tabitha wants me to call her and..."

Jon interrupts. "And you're going to call her or, even worse, go wrestle her away from her husband?"

"Just a quick call. I doubt she'll answer."

"Suit yourself," Jon says between gritted teeth. He storms out.

"Jon, wait," Anne says as the door shuts in her face. *Dammit. I screwed up a perfectly good evening. Again.*

Chapter 8

Charisse stays in touch with Anne for the next several months, assuring her that things are going well with Bernie at home. Anne is preoccupied with the 2008 election, eager to know who will be the next president as well as the next district attorney.

It's finally November 4th, and the big TVs at Coach's Corner are tuned to the election results. Anne, Kate, and Liz watch the coverage from a booth at the popular sports bar. It's too early to know who will follow George W. Bush to the White House, but that doesn't stop the pundits from rattling on with their predictions.

The three friends are more interested in finding out who their next boss will be: Harold Carter, the Democratic candidate for district attorney, or Republican candidate Frank Evans. Frank is a well-known criminal defense lawyer in private practice. Harold has been an assistant district attorney for ten years with a brief stint in the public defender's office.

"I can't picture Frank as the D.A.," Kate says, sipping on her Merlot. "He's always been on the other side of us in the courtroom."

"I know. I think Harold will win easily," Liz says. "If he does, I hope it doesn't mess up our friendship. It's hard having a buddy suddenly become your boss."

"Nah, I don't think Harold will abandon us," Kate says. "We've all been friends for so long."

"Yeah, he was one of the few non-family members Jon and I invited to our wedding. Some people say it'll be a close race. Frank has worked hard and raised a ton of money. He's from an old Savannah family with lots of connections."

Liz shakes her head. "But Harold has prosecution experienceand would do a great job."

"Whoever wins, I can't imagine our office without Martin Clayton," Kate says. "I know he's ready to retire, but change makes me nervous."

Four middle-aged men in red McCain tee shirts walk in the side door. "Happy election day. Hope you ladies voted the right way," one of them says, pointing to his shirt.

"Oh, we did," Liz says, sipping her frozen margarita. She rolls her eyes at her friends after the men saunter back to a nearby table.

"I bet those die-hard Republicans voted for Frank for D.A. even if they don't know him," Anne says.

"Yep," Kate says. "It's stupid the D.A.'s race is partisan. If someone is a crime victim, we don't ask if they're Republican or Democrat. And although the news shows Harold is leading, the results aren't in yet from the mainly Republican island precincts."

"True. But more Democrats are registered than ever this year. The line was super long at my downtown precinct," Liz adds.

Kate's phone buzzes, and she covers one ear to hear over the noise. After clicking off, she leans across the table. "Hubby's been checking the results from the Chatham County Elections Board. Walt says Harold's ahead by one percentage point."

"Whoa. Can't get any closer than that," Anne says.

After finishing their pizza, the women leave around ten, still not knowing who won the D.A.'s race.

Driving the sixteen miles to Tybee, Anne scans the radio dial looking for a station with local election results but only gets music or national news. Her mind wanders. She thinks about how lucky she's been to have Martin as a boss all these years. He was always open to new ideas and supportive of her and Victim-Witness Assistance.

As soon as she walks in the door, Jon says, "I guess you know who the new D.A. is."

"No. There's a final count?"

"Yup. Harold's going to be your new boss," Jon replies matter-of-factly.

"Wonderful." Anne tosses her pocketbook on a kitchen chair and walks to the TV, squinting to read the small numbers scrolling across the bottom of the screen. Finally, she sees "Chatham County District Attorney: Carter, 53%, Evans, 47%."

A reporter interviews Harold who speaks in a measured tone. "I'm pleased Chatham County voters have spoken. As promised in our campaign, accountability, fairness, and transparency are my priorities."

After the camera pans the cheering crowd behind Harold, there's a close-up of a young blonde reporter. "Chatham County voters have elected Harold Carter to be their next District Attorney. He takes the helm from Martin Clayton on January 6th"

Relieved because someone she knows and likes has been elected, Anne emails Harold: "Congratulations! Proud of you." She hasn't talked with him much lately. She didn't get involved in the campaign, heeding her boss Martin's advice during every election that employees should steer clear of publicly supporting any candidate.

Kicking off her shoes, Anne tells Jon, "I'll come to bed in a few. Wow. A new day is dawning in the D.A.'s Office."

Chapter 9

The next day, Harold's not at the office, but the sixth floor buzzes with nervous chatter about changes that might take place when he comes on board. District Attorney employees serve "at will," so Harold can fire anyone he wants. Some are excited about his victory, others not so much. "He's a control freak," one secretary tells Anne in the break room. "I know. I worked for him for two years."

"I bet he'll hire a lot of young men," says an investigator who had worked with him at juvenile court. "I know you're friends with him, Anne, but Harold's a strange one."

He never seemed sexist to me. But would he prefer a man in my job? Anne clears her throat. "We all need to give him a chance. I've known Harold a long time, and he's a fine person."

Her concern about job security magnifies that night when Harold calls. "Good evening, Anne, how are you?"

"Fine. How are you? Tired, I bet. Congratulations. I'm excited for you. *I need to shut up and find out why he's calling.*

"I'd like to talk with you. Could we meet Friday?"

"Sure. Where?"

"Starbucks on Victory Drive. Nine o'clock."

"Okay," Anne replies. *Wonder why he doesn't want to meet at the Starbucks near the courthouse.*

"I won't be in the office this week, but I'll see you Friday. Good night." Harold hangs up before she can respond.

Anne furrows her brow. "Jon, that was Harold."

"Great," Jon says, continuing to read *Fortune* magazine.

"He wants to meet with me."

"Good."

"Why is that good? He sounded so formal. What if he's going to fire me?"

Jon looks up. "You'll be fine, darlin'. You do a great job, and he knows it. He likes you."

"I guess, but he may have new ideas and new people in mind to implement them. Wonder what he wants to talk about?"

"Don't get yourself all worked up." He holds up his magazine to show Anne what he's reading. "Interesting article about the stock market's plummet."

Anne scans the headline. "That's another reason people in the office are worried about their jobs. The economy sucks." Anne picks up the phone to call Kate but thinks better of it. *No need to get her all hyped up, too.*

Instead, she gathers old newspapers from the basket by the couch and takes them to the recycle bin in the pantry. Seeing flour on the shelf, she thinks, *Hmm. I'll bake something* She looks around the kitchen and sees three overripe bananas on top of the refrigerator. *I'll make banana bread.* She turns to the recipe in the Woman's Club cookbook from her Alabama hometown, finds butter and sugar, and creams them together.

Yelling over the whir of the mixer, Jon says, "What in the world are you doing, Anne? It's nearly eleven."

"Making banana bread. Gotta keep my mind occupied." She slices the mushy bananas, beats two eggs, and adds those to the butter and sugar in the bowl. She dumps in flour, baking soda, and salt. *Oh dang. I was supposed to sift the dry ingredients. Too late now.* She adds vanilla.

Anne looks in the cupboard for a loaf pan but can't find one, so plops down cross-legged on the floor, noisily pulling out pots and pans. "Jon, where is the loaf pan? Actually, we have two. Where ARE they?" she hollers over her shoulder.

"I have no idea."

"Well, I can't bake banana bread without a damn pan."

"That's why I always take out what I need before I start cooking so I know I have everything."

Anne rolls her eyes. "Okay, Mister Organized." She suddenly remembers she keeps the loaf pans in the cabinet above the washing machine. She gets up from the floor, rubbing her stiff knees. Sure enough, the pans are there. She sprays one with Pam, pours in the mixture, and slides the loaf pan into the oven. In minutes, the kitchen smells heavenly and Anne feels calmer. *Hallelujah!*

* * *

Anne arrives at Starbucks early and finds a small table near the window. At nine fifteen she worries she's at the wrong Starbucks and checks her phone, but Harold hasn't texted. Finally, he arrives, saunters over to her, and smiles. "Hi there, Anne. Thanks for meeting me."

No apology for being twenty minutes late? "Good morning, Harold."

They walk to the counter and stand in line at the always crowded Starbucks. Harold orders coffee and a scone. Anne orders hot green tea. *If I get food, I'd probably drop crumbs all over myself.* When they return to the table, Harold blurts out, "So what's the mood in the office?"

"Um, good. Of course, folks are a little nervous. That's to be expected with any change."

"Who's nervous? What are people saying?" His eyes penetrate hers.

Why did I open my big mouth? I'm not going to name the people who are bashing him. "Oh, nothing really. Just wondering what changes you might implement."

Harold dabs his mouth with a napkin. "I guess that's understandable. One of my first decisions will be to name a chief assistant district attorney."

Anne nods.

"One person on my list for second in command is Kate. Do you think she'd be able to step into that position?"

"Kate is super smart and an experienced prosecutor." Anne breathes a sigh of relief. *He's asking my advice rather than telling me I'm fired. Why am I such a worrywart?*

"How do you think she'd handle supervising people?"

"I think she could do that."

Harold mentions two more names as possible chief assistants. Since he doesn't ask her opinion about them, she doesn't offer one. He adds, "I also wanted to discuss the joint federal grant between the Victim-Witness Program, S.A.F.E Shelter, Rape Crisis Center, and Children's Advocacy Center."

Where is he going with this? The three non-profit agencies have shared a big federal grant with Victim-Witness for years and received positive recognition for collaborating.

"Victim-Witness serves the most victims so should be getting most, if not all, of the grant money." He looks at Anne for a response.

She thinks it's a bad idea but tries not to show it.

Harold sips his coffee. "By the way, I've already gotten a gushy letter of congratulations from Carol of the Children's Advocacy Center. I guess she's trying to be nice to me, even though she supported Frank in the campaign." He adjusts his glasses and looks pointedly at Anne.

Anne clears her throat. Carol is her friend, and they have an excellent working relationship. Anne looks down and stirs honey into her tea. After a moment of awkward silence, she says, "Frank served on her board and has been a strong supporter of children's issues. We've always had a good relationship with Carol and her program."

"Well, I'm going to take a hard look to determine if we can get a bigger share of that grant. I have some connections in Atlanta with the agency that distributes the money."

Anne realizes he's made up his mind. *Gosh, maybe some of the comments about him being controlling are true. But he's about to be the head honcho so he can call the shots.*

When he changes the subject, she's relieved. "Anne, I hope you'll help me with my swearing-in ceremony. I plan to invite people to the inauguration and have it in the civic center ballroom. Any suggestions for a caterer?"

"A caterer? Well, not off the top of my head, but I'll think about it."

"And I'll need invitations. Maybe you can draft something for me. And hopefully, Lester's Florist will do the flowers."

Anne hopes her expression doesn't reveal how shocked she is. *Caterer? Invitations? Florist? Does he think he's the president?* She simply says, "Uh, okay."

Harold closes his notepad. "Thanks for meeting with me."

"Sure. By the way, how are your parents doing? Wasn't one of them having medical problems?"

"Yes. Mother is okay, but the doctors can't get Dad's blood pressure under control. I sure wish my family lived closer so they could help out."

Although Harold was born in Atlanta, his family moved to Savannah when he was a kid because his dad got a job at the Union Camp paper mill. With his three brothers living elsewhere, Harold bears the brunt of the responsibility for his aging parents.

They chat for a few more minutes before walking outside. "See you at the office next week," Harold says.

"Okay," Anne says. *Considering I didn't know what to expect from this meeting, I guess it went alright.*

Driving to the office, Anne mulls over their conversation. *Oh lord, I don't want to mess up our good relationship with the other victim service agencies. Harold is making a huge deal about his "inauguration." Martin was sworn in at the judge's office without a big event paid for by taxpayers.*

Anne gets out of her car at the county parking garage and a courthouse employee waves to her. "Hi, Anne, how do you think things will go with your new boss?"

Anne plasters on a fake smile. "Hey there. Just fine." *At least I hope so. But I have a feeling things are going to be very different.*

Chapter 10

As she opens the door to the Civic Center ballroom for Harold's swearing-in ceremony, Anne takes a deep breath. *A new year, a new day for the D.A.'s office. Change can be good.* Some two-hundred people mill about, enjoying the hors d'oeuvres on two long tables covered in white linen. Anne unbuttons her coat and mingles. Right at five, Harold's minister takes the stage and offers a prayer. Superior Court Judge Marcus Adams introduces the man of the hour, ending with "Harold J. Carter is a scholar, a gentleman, exemplary lawyer, and our new district attorney." After a loud round of applause, Harold is sworn in as his mother holds the Bible. He then gives an eloquent speech.

After waiting in the long line to speak to Harold, Anne gives him a hug. "Congratulations, boss."

"Thanks, Anne." He smiles. "Thank goodness the election is over, and we can get down to business. You know Kate is going to be my chief assistant?"

Anne gives a thumbs up. On the drive home to Tybee Island that cold night, the sky's so clear Anne can see the twinkling north star and even the big dipper. When she walks inside their cottage, Jon looks up from his Kindle. "Hey, how'd it go?"

"Nice. Lots of people. Quite fancy. Catered food, flower arrangements, the whole nine yards."

"Really? I guess my tax dollars fed you all well."

"You're always thinking about money. Guess that's why the hospital hired you to work in the finance department. Actually, I was thinking about money too, about how that money could have been put to more practical use. So many victims and witnesses at court don't have money for lunch or bus tickets. I wish we had a fund for that. Oh well. I'm starving."

"You didn't eat at the shindig?"

"Nah. Didn't wanna stand in line or spill food on my dress."

"There's some black bean soup and cornbread on the stove."

"Yum. But first I'm getting into my flannel pajamas."

At the kitchen table, Anne tells Jon more about the evening. "Harold gave a beautiful speech. I'm optimistic."

"As you should be. You like him. I don't know Harold well, but he seems like a nice guy. And smart. A Harvard degree is pretty impressive."

"Yep," Anne says, buttering her cornbread.

"He seems kinda uptight though. At least that's the impression I got at office parties and our wedding."

"I think he's just shy," Anne says.

"Guess the election was tough on him then."

"Probably."

They clean up the dishes and settle in the den to watch an interview with Michelle Obama, the new first lady. Anne yawns as Little Kitty curls up on her lap, purring like a motorboat. "I'm tired, but too hyped to sleep, Let's stay up and watch the eleven o'clock news."

"Okay," Jon says.

Harold's inauguration is the lead story on WTOC. The first clip shows him being sworn in, then cuts to an interview. "Tell us about your plans, Mr. Carter. Any changes you want to implement?"

"Of course, first I'll take inventory of all procedures in place and see what changes may be needed. I promise transparency in everything I do."

"During your campaign, you promised more grassroots involvement from the community, specifically curbing violence among young people. Tell us about that," the reporter says.

"I hope to start a new initiative in the Victim-Witness Assistance Program aimed at reducing recidivism among young men."

Anne leaps up from the couch, causing Little Kitty to tumble to the floor. "Turn up the volume! What did he just say? A new initiative in Victim-Witness? I haven't heard anything about that."

Jon shrugs. "No idea."

Anne scrambles for the remote to turn up the volume. The segment on Harold ends and a blaring car commercial begins.

"Why are these stupid ads so loud?" She trudges back to the kitchen, cuts a hunk of cornbread, and takes a big bite.

Jon follows her. "You're eating that cold?"

"Sure am," Anne says, as crumbs rain onto the counter. "If Harold had this idea throughout the campaign, why didn't he mention it to me? Is he planning to hire someone else? He talked to me about planning his inauguration but not this?"

"Simmer down, sweetie." Jon stretches his arms above his head. "I'm tired. You coming to bed?"

"No, not yet."

"Well, good night. Get some sleep," Jon says, kissing her.

"Oh good lord, you're always so calm. Good night."

On Harold's first day at the helm, he calls a staff meeting. He smiles at the nervous crowd. "Hello, everyone. I know it's been a long time since you all have had a new boss, but no need to fret. Obviously, there will be some changes, but none without serious thought and consideration."

Anne wiggles in her seat, wondering exactly what change he has in mind for her department. As they leave the meeting, two of her staff ask her about what Harold said on the news about Victim-Witness.

"I don't know any details," Anne says.

"He hasn't talked to you about it?"

"No, Harold's real busy. I'm sure we'll talk soon." *At least I hope so, since he's already blabbing to the media about it.*

* * *

A week later, Harold comes into her office. "Got a minute, Anne? I want to tell you about a new program I want to start. Actually, that I want *you* to start."

"Oh?"

"Two of my Harvard classmates are doctors in Chicago. They've started a Violence Intervention Program to assist young men between fifteen and twenty-five who have been victims of violence. Research shows that intense intervention can reduce the likelihood they'll be victims again or commit crimes themselves."

"Interesting. Tell me more."

"I want this up and running right away. As soon as we hire the staff–coordinator, case manager, and investigator–we'll go to Chicago to see their model program."

Anne jots some notes. "Where will we get the money for these new positions?" she asks. "It's the middle of the budget year."

"That's up to you. You need to research grants. You're good at that," Harold says, handing her an email from one of the Harvard doctors with contact info and websites about ten similar programs in the nation. "Don't worry. We'll talk again soon."

"Okay," Anne says, her head spinning. *Does he think I can magically make money appear?*

Chapter 11

After six weeks of frantic work, Anne secures enough money to fund the program for a year. Three positions are advertised. Their first hire is LaShay Thompson for the coordinator position. Anne knows of LaShay's excellent work directing two small non-profits. She and her firefighter husband have twin daughters in kindergarten.

Next, Anne reviews the applications for case manager. One is from Devin Greene who she's seen in Harold's office a few times. She'd heard he was researching violence intervention programs for Harold; Anne found it odd Harold hadn't introduced her to Devin. Her gut told her Harold was grooming him for one of the VIP positions. Sure enough, when she and Harold meet to discuss the case manager position, he pulls out a score sheet he'd created, giving "experience with violence intervention programs" the most points.

"But with only ten VIPS in the nation and none in Georgia, how would anyone locally have that experience?" Anne asks Harold.

"Devin Greene has experience. He's done a lot of research."

All righty then. Why didn't he research finding a grant? I could have used the help. Anne feels her face getting hot and hopes no one notices.

Anne and Harold interview Devin Greene and a young woman with a social work degree. Just as Anne had expected, Harold tells her to offer the job to Devin. He's a good-looking recent college graduate with a degree in public administration. He seems bright and Anne likes him.

Anne pores over ten resumes for the investigator position the County Human Resources Department forwarded to her. All the applicants have law enforcement experience and meet at least the basic criteria. She takes the applications of her top three choices to

Harold's secretary. That afternoon she gets an email from Harold: *Why didn't you send me Jeffrey Williams' application?*

Anne replies: *H.R. didn't send me one from Jeffrey Williams.*

The next day Harold forwards her an email chain where he asked H.R. about Jeffrey's application. The H.R. clerk replied that Jeffrey Williams didn't have enough law enforcement experience, but she would send him all the applications to review.

Harold calls Anne. "I need you to go over to H.R. right away and pick up the additional applications for the investigator position."

On her walk to the administrative courthouse, Anne wonders who this Jeffrey Williams is. *A friend? Son of a friend? Someone who helped with his campaign?*

Back at her office, Anne reads Jeffrey Williams' application. Only 22, he's been working for Savannah-Chatham Metro Police for six months. At Harold's direction, she sets up interviews with Jeffrey and two other candidates.

Harold tells Anne the investigator position will be supervised by program coordinator LaShay and Terry Thomas who's the chief investigator in the D.A.'s office. Since LaShay won't begin for a few weeks, Terry, Harold, and Anne conduct the interviews. Before the first applicant arrives, Anne says, "I don't have any experience hiring or supervising law enforcement types."

"That's why Terry is here," Harold says.

The first person they interview is a military vet who's an investigator with the Hinesville Police Department. The second is a woman who's been a Metro police officer for six years. When Jeffrey Williams walks in, Anne is astonished at how young he looks. *Geez. I must be getting ancient.* Jeffrey's nervous but enthusiastic, saying it's his "dream job" to work with young people. He flashes a winning boyish grin.

After the interviews, Harold looks at Terry and Anne, "So what do you think?"

Terry, who had been in law enforcement for twenty-plus years, peruses his notes. "The woman is certainly qualified, but since the program is targeted toward males, a man would be the best choice. I was impressed with the Army vet."

"True, he has more experience, but he may be set in his ways." Harold says. "What about Jeffrey Williams? He seems eager to learn."

Terry furrows his brows. "But he has almost no experience."

Harold says, "But we can mold him, train him exactly the way we want." He looks at Anne. "What do you think, Anne?"

"As I said, I've never hired a law enforcement person before, and I'm still not quite clear what duties the investigator will have in the Violence Intervention Program."

Harold takes off his glasses and places them on the table. "What are you not clear about? I wrote a job description. Didn't you think Jeffrey was impressive in the interview?"

"Well, yes," Anne says. "He's certainly enthusiastic. I guess with the proper training . . . do you know him?"

"Not really," Harold says. "He and his brother play in the band at my church."

Waving Jeffrey's application in his hand, Terry says, "He's just so green."

Harold doesn't respond. Terry clears his throat, breaking the silence. "But you know I'll follow your direction, boss, and do the best I can to bring him up to speed. You're the D.A."

"Very well, then," Harold says. "Anne, fill out the paperwork to hire Jeffrey."

She returns to her office and signs her name on the personnel action form. Devin, LaShay, and Jeffrey will start work in a few weeks.

Chapter 12

On a busy Wednesday morning, the Victim-Witness Assistance rooms overflow with nervous people waiting their turn to testify in an assault trial. They've already consumed two pots of coffee.

With one of the staff out sick and the others busy, Anne helps answer the phone. She enjoys having personal contact with the people they serve. It's a welcome change from her duties as an administrator.

Anne answers the phone and hears, "Hello, my name is Marie Rossi. I'm calling from Connecticut. Uh, my daughter is a freshman at the Savannah College of Art and Design and . . . " The caller's voice breaks into muffled sobs.

"Ms. Rossi, this is Anne. How can I help?" Anne says softly, then waits for the woman to compose herself.

"Well, my daughter she was, um, sexually assaulted Friday night. My husband and I are taking an afternoon flight to Savannah, but I want to get more information before we get down there."

"I'm so sorry about your daughter, Ms. Rossi. I'm glad you called." Anne scribbles in her Day-timer: "SCAD student rape. Mom from Conn."

"I just can't believe it. We fell in love with your beautiful city when we came for orientation and now...now this."

Anne recalls several other SCAD victims. The bright-eyed, creative kids consider the entire downtown their campus; unfortunately, many aren't aware of the prevalence of crime. And like most teens, they don't heed safety warnings. "Ms. Rossi, what's your daughter's name?"

"Brittney. She's only eighteen. She's my baby."

"Yes ma'am. Did Brittney report this to the police?"

"Yes, and she went to the hospital for the rape exam. The police say they have a suspect. Do you think the police will tell us more about him? My husband spoke with a detective but can't remember his name. And where is the police department? I'm sorry I'm rambling."

"I'm sure the police will talk to you. I'll give you the number for the Special Victims Unit."

"Okay." There's a moment of silence before Ms. Rossi continues. "The police say Brittney was drinking. She was walking back to her dorm alone after leaving a party. We never dreamed something like this could happen. I'm just sick."

"It's not Brittney's fault. No one deserves to be raped," Anne says. "Ms. Rossi, if you have a pen, I'll give you the number to the Special Victims Unit."

"Okay, I'm ready."

After Anne tells her the number, she adds, "There's free counseling available through the Rape Crisis Center."

"I'm not sure she'll want to stay in Savannah."

"I understand."

Anne hears a male voice in the background.

"My husband says we need to leave for the airport soon, and I haven't finished packing. Thanks so much for your help. Can I call you again?"

"Sure. Call any time. My name is Anne Gardner, but Janine is the advocate who'll be your contact person. We'll be here for Brittney every step of the way whether there's an arrest or not."

"Okay, thanks again. Goodbye."

Anne types an email to Janine about the phone conversation.

Anne looks up when Kate walks into her office and plops down in the chair across from her. "Damn it to hell! I need to vent. Harold is breathing down my neck about every little thing."

"I'm sorry," Anne says. "Have you heard anything about the new SCAD rape case?"

"I read a summary on the daily police log, but I don't know specifics."

"The victim's mom just called from Connecticut. Naturally, she's freaked out."

"I'm sure she is. I hope they find the son-of-a-bitch."

"Amen."

Kate's cell beeps, and she looks at her screen. "Sheesh, It's Harold. I've only been gone five minutes." "Hi, Harold. Okay, that's fine." She clicks off her phone. "He wants to meet with me to talk about the new sentencing guidelines. Which we already discussed yesterday, but whatever. I think he's just checking up on me."

"I never realized he could be so controlling," Anne says. "He keeps me off balance. Yesterday he brought me this African violet." She points to the plant on her credenza. "Said his mama grows them. We chatted like we used to before he became the boss."

"Go figure," Kate says. "On a different note, what do you think about this chick Alice likes so much?"

"I haven't met her, but from what Alice says, she sounds nice. She's real artsy like Alice."

"Yeah, I just don't want our friend to get hurt. That last woman she dated was whacky. I hope she protects her heart."

"I think she will. Alice's priority is her baby boy. Can you believe Duncan is already a year old?"

Kate stands. "I still can't believe how that pregnancy came to be—via a sperm donor. And she has more sperm in her freezer, probably right beside the ice cream. Just wow!" Kate stands. "Don't forget the leadership meeting is at two."

"Oh lord, I'm glad you reminded me. I hope it's not another marathon." Harold's leadership meetings involve the various department heads of the D.A.'s Office, including Kate, and Glenn Brinson, the assistant district attorney who supervises the Special Victims Unit. The tedious meetings remind Anne of the grueling times she spent sitting in the hospital waiting room when her dad was in intensive care. Everyone is on edge, certain the clock on the wall is broken because the big black hands move so slowly.

"See you in a bit," Kate says.

Anne eats a sandwich at her desk while reading through a stack of work journals and newsletters. Then she remembers the leadership meeting, grabs her notebook, and rushes down the hall. The long conference table is already full. Harold looks up from the head of the table. "I'm glad you decided to join us, Ms. Gardner."

The clock on the wall says 2:04. *Really? I'm four minutes late. You keep people waiting all the time.* As she sits in the empty chair beside Glenn, she notices his fiery red face. *Is he mad or just hot?* The conference room windows stretch across an entire wall, and the sun penetrates through the blinds

Harold rustles papers. "As I was saying, our first agenda item is security in the D.A.'s office. I think we need a stricter policy about who can enter. People shouldn't be able to wander in. A few weeks ago, I was at my desk, and Dan Donaldson appeared at my office door. That's totally unacceptable."

Anne says, "Dan Donaldson, the court administrator?"

"Yes. He didn't have an appointment. He came by to congratulate me on winning the election, but I don't want anyone popping in unannounced."

What the hell? He has a problem with another court employee stopping by to congratulate him? She glances around the table at the bewildered looks. Since Harold took office three months ago, tension has been thick. No one knows what to expect. Sometimes he's nice and other times a jerk.

Glenn clears his throat. "Of course, the receptionist needs to buzz in the public through the main office. And your secretary is right outside your door to screen your visitors."

"Brenda was away from her desk," Harold says, pushing his glasses up on his nose. "I don't like that people, even court personnel and police, can just traipse all over our office after they get through the front doors. From now on, staff members need to go to the front reception area to escort ALL their visitors to their offices."

"But, boss, it's important that we have a good relationship with the police. They're usually here to see more than one assistant district attorney. We've always encouraged them to come over here to discuss cases, so we shouldn't treat them like the general public. We're on the same team, and I think your policy would seriously hurt morale."

Harold ignores Glenn, looking instead at the chief investigator. "Terry, I need you to draft a memo to the entire staff saying all visitors– including law enforcement–must be escorted by our staff to the appropriate office."

Terry nods. "Yes, sir."

Glenn's face turns a darker shade of crimson as he taps his pen on his notebook and exhales. Across the table, Kate rolls her eyes at Glenn when Harold isn't looking. Anne fans herself with a notepad. *This doesn't make any sense. I bet Glenn wants to punch him in the face. Then Harold will call the police and be glad to let them in the door.*

Moving on to a budget discussion, Harold announces his plans to use funds to redecorate the front reception area and conference room. "Anne, is your friend Rhonda available to help us choose paint colors? She's got a flair for this kind of thing."

"I'll talk to her." Anne jots a note to call Rhonda, who had recently started a small interior decorating business. *I'm glad Harold's got his priorities in order. Decorating the office and throwing a lavish inauguration party. Heavens to Betsy!*

Kate swivels her chair away from Harold and scribbles on her legal pad. Anne reads Kate's notes. Her grocery list is Tylenol at the top. Underneath she had written *We need a new copy machine but Harold's decorating the office? Insanity.* Kate scratches that out.

"And Anne," Harold says. "I'm not satisfied with the direction of the Violence Intervention Program."

Anne blushes as all eyes focus on her. "What do you mean?"

"I need a clear budget projection for next year. Also, you need to get LaShay, Devin, and Jeffrey together with me to discuss measurable outcomes and identify new funding sources, among other matters. It seems none of them is available when I call."

"When would you like to meet?" Anne bites her lip instead of spewing out what she's thinking. *You shouldn't be calling them directly. LaShay is their direct supervisor, and I supervise her. What about chain of command? Is this just an excuse to see Jeffrey and Devin?*

"Check with Brenda about my calendar. Also, your report at last month's meeting was vague. I need a spreadsheet with the exact number of victims being served, their ages, the referral source, and so forth."

"Okay, I'm on it," Anne says in a clear, strong voice. *I'm not going to let him intimidate me.*

"I need a complete report of all VIP activity to date. Can you have that to me by tomorrow morning?"

"Well, I need to talk with LaShay, and they are at a meeting at the hospital this afternoon. I'll get it to you as soon as I can." *What a jerk.*

"Very well, then." Harold retrieves his Blackberry from his jacket pocket, swipes the screen, and texts a message while the others in the room exchange frustrated glances. Anne longs to be home petting Little Kitty. Or cleaning the toilets for that matter.

Harold pulls a Bellsouth bill from a manila folder. "And another thing. It seems there are an inordinate number of long-distance calls being made. Here are copies of the bill for each of you," he says as he hands them out.

The only sound in the room is the shuffling of paper as people flip through the bills.

"Anne, can you justify the calls from your department?" Harold says.

"These calls come from all of my staff, so I have no idea who was called. We have a lot of out-of-town witnesses and victims, so a lot of long-distance calls."

"Some of these calls are quite lengthy."

"Of course, they are!" Anne's voice quivers with anger. "We often talk for a long time with victims. Actually, we usually listen a long time.

That's our job." *Just yesterday, you brought me a plant. Now you're berating me in front of my peers?*

"No need to get defensive, Anne," Harold says in his maddeningly even tone. "I'm trying to be vigilant about our spending. We might need all of the staff to keep phone logs."

Anne's head almost explodes. *Vigilant about spending and nitpicking phone bills, but you're redecorating? Good gawd almighty! We're a governmental agency, not some fancy private law firm. I bet Kate and Glenn are going to go through the roof any minute now.*

Finally, the discussion moves on to buying a computer system, hiring a new public information officer, and other topics thankfully unrelated to her program. *Guess it's my turn to be picked on. Last meeting, he badgered Kate.*

Back in her office after the meeting from hell, Anne tries to clear her mind by checking the news on her computer. When she sees a headline about an Atlanta man who killed his wife and baby, she clicks off. *That's why I don't like to watch the local news at night. I'm always scared I'll hear that one of our victims was killed.*

Janine walks into her office. "I just got off the phone with Charisse. She wants to drop the charges against Bernie."

Anne groans. "So many domestic violence victims say that."

"Yes, but he's seriously intimidating her. I swear I could hear someone breathing in the background. I think he was standing over her. Of course, I told her it's not up to her to drop the charges."

"And her response?"

Janine sits in the chair across from Anne's desk. "She said she's not going to testify against him."

"Damn! And because they're married, she doesn't have to."

Janine nods. "And if she does testify, she'll probably lie and deny he's been abusive."

Anne rubs her throbbing forehead. "A prosecutor's worst nightmare."

"With a toddler and a baby, Charisse has so much on her plate. She sounded defeated," Janine says.

"Charisse can't catch a break."

"I know," Janine says. "She's dreading the trial. Waiting is the worst part."

"The defense has asked for two postponements, probably hoping Charisse would back down. Which is exactly what's happened."Anne pushes back her chair. "Keep me posted, Janine."

Anne searches through her purse for Advil but can't find the bottle. Instead, she settles for a Little Debbie oatmeal cake she finds in her desk drawer.

Needing to vent, she heads to Glenn's office. He's on the phone. She plops in a chair and looks at the family photos that line the wall. The biggest one is of his daughter who plays volleyball at Mercer University. It's an amazing action shot of her spiking the ball with a look of determination and her long blonde hair flying behind her.

After he hangs up, Anne says, "Great picture of your daughter."

"She kicks ass on the volleyball court. Good grades, too. She loves college life."

"Speaking of college, you know anything about the rape of the SCAD student?"

"Not much. The detective said they're following up on leads." He reaches for his coffee thermos on a table piled with videotapes of children interviewed at the Coastal Children's Advocacy Center.

"The victim's parents are coming into town today." Anne picks at her cuticles. "This has been one crummy day."

"Yep." Glenn looks up from the stack of police reports on his desk. "Sorry, the boss jumped all over you at the meeting. I wanted to punch him. And he's making a terrible mistake by not allowing the cops in without escorts. They're going to be pissed, and I don't blame them." As a former cop, Glenn has a great relationship with the police.

"I don't understand why he's being so strict."

"Me either. Why is he so damn paranoid?"

Anne throws up her hands. "I don't have a clue. I hear he moved into a gated community and..."

"Let me guess. The Landings."

"Yep. A friend who lives there says the neighbors never see him. Keeps to himself."

Glenn grunts. "Figures. He's a strange one." His face is still flushed like it was at the meeting. In his early fifties, Glenn has put on weight and his once salt-and-pepper hair is all white. "The boss isn't helping my blood pressure. That's for damn sure."

There's a knock on the door. Startled, Anne leaps up and opens it. She's face to face with a serious-looking Harold. Anne stifles a gasp and hopes her cheeks are not as red as they feel. "Am I interrupting anything?" Harold says, arching his eyebrows. He steps past Anne and stands in front of Glenn's desk.

"Oh no. I was just leaving," Anne says. She brushes past him and scurries down the hall. *How long has he been standing there? Oh crap, did he overhear our conversation?*

Chapter 13

Charisse bounces Baby Alana on her knee while three-year-old Bernie Jr. rolls a truck across the floor. The only place in the courthouse with toys, the witness room in the Victim-Witness Assistance Program office also has a couch, recliner, TV, and magazines.

"Look, Mama!" Bernie Jr. squeals, snot coming out of his nose. "Truck like Daddy's!"

Janine hands Charisse a tissue.

"He's had a cold for three weeks," Charisse says, wiping her little boy's nose

"No fun. They sure are cute kids," Janine says.

"Thanks. These babies are my life." She manages a weak smile and wipes a tear from her cheek. "I don't know why their daddy can't act right. I shouldn't have called the police again 'cause he's gonna be madder than ever. But he hit me in front of the kids, then threatened to take them from me. I was so scared!"

"Of course, you should have called the police. Hitting you is a crime," Janine says.

"I didn't report it right away, but at my ob/gyn check-up, the doctor asked me about the bruise and encouraged me to call the police."

Janine looks Charisse in the eye. "Charisse, you don't deserve to be treated this way. No one does. I'm glad he's in jail so you can come up with a safety plan. Hopefully, he won't get bond. The judge won't take kindly to him being arrested on a second domestic violence charge while his trial for the first one is pending."

"Bernie's freaking out about going to trial," Charisse says. "When he tried to make me promise to drop the charges and I didn't say anything at first, that's when he got crazy mad." Alana whimpers and Charisse pops a pacifier in her mouth. "Why is it taking so long to get to trial? It's been almost a year since he was arrested the first time."

"I know it's frustrating, His attorney got the trial postponed twice. Plus, state court is always backlogged." Janine leans forward. "What brought you here this afternoon?"

"Oh yeah. I'm here because the lady at S.A.F.E. Shelter said I could get a temporary protective order. She's in court now but said you'd help me."

Janine nods. "A TPO can order your husband to move out of the house and not have contact with you. You can also ask for temporary custody and child support."

"I would definitely need child support. My Dollar General job doesn't pay enough for rent, food, and diapers. And my old car guzzles gas."

"Today we'll go to the Superior Court Clerk's Office to get the order, then we see a judge."

"Oh god! In a courtroom? Will Bernie be there?'

"Not today. You just go to the judge's office to ask him to sign the TPO. I'll go with you. Then a hearing is scheduled within thirty days. Your husband can attend that if he chooses."

"Oh lord, do I have to hire an attorney for this TPO thing?"

"No."

Charisse's lips quiver. "You know Bernie's a bigwig in the union. He probably has connections in the court system. And it seems like his daddy has connections everywhere."

"Charisse, you know your job is to tell the truth. And thankfully you got pictures of your injuries." Janine hands her a safety plan brochure. "Do you have this?"

"Yeah, Miss Anne gave me one at the E.R. She said getting away can be a dangerous time."

Janine shudders, remembering how her husband threatened to kill her when he thought she and the kids had left him. "Trust me. It *is* a dangerous time. We want you and your children to be safe. You know him better than anyone else, so you do what's best."

"I thought I knew him. I believed him when he came to the shelter and said he'd changed and would never lay a hand on me again.

That's why I went back to him. Plus, I didn't have enough money to make it on my own." She bites her fingernail. "Now I feel stupid."

"Don't say that, Charisse. You're alive and taking the right steps. You're stronger than you think."

"Miss Janine, every night I pray to God Almighty my husband doesn't kill me. Or take the kids." She hugs Alana close to her chest.

Janine looks at her watch. "Oh my gosh! It's after four. Let's get to the clerk's office before they close."

Charisse grabs Bernie Jr. by the hand, hoists the baby on her hip, and follows Janine to the clerk's office. By the time they get the TPO paperwork, they can't find a judge to sign it. Janine calls Anne. "All the judges are in court or already gone for the day. Charisse has to work tomorrow and can't come back. Could you possibly work your magic and find a judge?"

"Hmm. I'll see what I can do." Anne calls Judge Adams on his personal cell. "Your Honor, I'm so sorry to bother you, but we have a bit of an emergency, and no judges are available. Is there any way you could sign a TPO? It's a volatile situation."

The judge exhales. "I guess so. I'm halfway home, but I'll turn around and meet you in my chambers."

"Judge, I can't thank you enough. Janine and the victim will be waiting for you."

When Janine returns to the office, she gives Anne a thumbs up. "Thanks for helping."

"You're welcome, but I can't make a habit of calling a judge on his cell."

"I know, but Charisse needed that TPO. I have a bad feeling about her husband."

***

Two days later, Janine appears at Anne's office door with Sheila, the family violence prosecutor. "We've got a problem," Janine says. "You have a few minutes?"

"Sure, come on in and have a seat," Anne says.

With her petite frame and high heels, Sheila could be a stand-in for Carrie from *Sex and the City.* But she's a tough and experienced prosecutor. "You're not going to believe this, but Bernie Butler got out on bond."

Anne gives her a quizzical look. "Whoa! What happened?"

Sheila leans forward, her silver bracelets jangling as she gestures. "On Friday when I was off, the defense attorney, defendant's father, *and* Harold met with the judge and got him to set a low bond." Sheila's eyes widen. "Bernie got released Friday night. I am beyond furious!"

Anne shakes her head. "Wait a minute. I can't believe he was out on bond for beating his wife, got arrested for hitting her again, and then got a low bond. And Harold *helped* him?"

"Yup. Our boss, the chief prosecutor, claimed the defendant needed to be released to attend counseling," Sheila says.

Anne slams her fist on the desk. "The D.A.'s office is supposed to protect victims. Why would Harold do that?"

"No clue. But he did. And without talking to me," Sheila says in a shrill voice.

"What the hell?"

"You remember the defendant's dad is some big shot with the International Longshoreman's Association? They supported Harold in his campaign. I think they got to him somehow."

Janine chimes in. "Charisse predicted her father-in-law could pull strings. I called her today to make sure she knew he was out of jail. She knew and fortunately hasn't heard from him."

"Thank God!" Anne says. "But the TPO won't stop him from showing up at her door."

"Exactly. I told her to keep the TPO with her at all times and to call the police if he comes near her."

"Good advice," Anne says, fanning herself with a legal pad.

"Yeah, I reminded her even if he violates the TPO, he still has a right to a hearing, Charisse is scared and real pissed too. She doesn't trust any of us now."

Anne sighs. "I don't blame her. The D.A. helping a bad guy get bond is a new one on me. It's usually defense attorneys we're fighting, not our own colleagues."

Sheila blinks back a tear, then sits up straighter. "If Harold had just talked to me, I would have explained everything. I don't always ask the judge to not grant a bond or set a high bond, but this is a dangerous situation. I checked this guy's criminal record, and he has charges pending in Kentucky from an ex-girlfriend. He's a repeat offender."

Anne grimaces. "I wonder if it would do any good for me to talk to Harold."

Sheila rolls her eyes. "Too friggin' late."

"I'm not a lawyer. And questioning my new boss on his legal decisions is probably a bad idea." She pauses. "But damn it! On behalf of all victims, I need to try so maybe this won't happen again."

Sheila shrugs. "It's useless. As soon as I found out about the new bond, I emailed Harold asking to discuss it with him. He hasn't responded and probably won't." She shakes her head and says in an almost whisper, "I used to love what I do here, but I'm job hunting. Our boss working against us is too stressful. Not to mention unethical." She stands and turns to leave.

"Thanks for letting us vent," Janine says.

"Sorry I couldn't help," Anne says, rifling through her desk for chocolate. *I hate feeling powerless. I guess this is a tad bit like how domestic violence victims feel.*

After they leave, Anne looks out the window at the sun setting over the Talmadge Bridge. The orange ball reminds her of a crayon drawing by her four-year-old grandson Ethan. On her refrigerator door, the picture is of a giant sun with yellow flowers below. But not even sixty-four crayons could do justice to the real thing. The huge sphere appears ready to crash both arches of the bridge which divide Georgia from South Carolina.

Anne takes her pocketbook from a desk drawer, pulls out her keys, and trudges to the elevator. In the lobby, she waves to the night security guard.

"Hey, why so gloomy, Anne?" he asks. "You're done for the day."

"I'm just tired. Have a good night, Curt." Anne tries to sound upbeat, but she feels like one of those homeless, sad-eyed puppies in the Humane Society commercials.

Chapter 14

At home, Anne remembers it's Girls' Night Out. She finds a bag of tortilla chips and a jar of salsa in the pantry and puts them and a Diet Coke in a grocery bag. When Jon walks through the door, she gives him a tight hug.

"Hey 'darlin," he says, loosening his necktie. "Rough day?"

"Awful, but I'm heading to Girls' Night Out."

"That always makes you feel better."

Admiring Ethan's artwork on the refrigerator, she says, "Bad day, but I did see a gorgeous sunset over the bridge. How come you're so late?"

"Remember I told you, I had to stay for training on the hospital's new computer system. Lots of changes lately."

"Oh yeah, I forgot." Anne pecks him on the lips. "See ya, love you."

"Have fun. Tell them I'm sorry I couldn't make it."

"Ha. You weren't invited, Mister."

She drives ten miles inland to Rhonda's house on Wilmington Island. When she arrives, Maggie is pouring herself a glass of wine at the kitchen bar. She peers at Anne. "Hey little sis, you okay? You look beat."

"Oh, just more crap at work." Maggie wraps her arm around Anne's shoulders. Maggie spoils her baby sister; she's always available to help, whether it's with a broken computer, a broken heart, or anything in between.

Rhonda walks in from the patio. "Anne, glad you're here! Special treat tonight. I made margaritas."

Anne pulls out her can of Diet Coke. "Oh, Rhonda, you didn't have to do that. You know it's B.Y.O.B."

"Yeah, but lately you gals in the D.A.'s office look like you need something stronger than soda." She pours a margarita into a salt-rimmed, chilled tumbler and hands it to Anne. "Fix yourself a plate. The rest of our motley crew is already on the patio. Except for Lisa. Haven't seen her in ages. She's always working night shifts at the hospital."

"Oh, before I forget, I'm supposed to ask you about helping Harold with some decorating. I'm sure he won't be a paying client, though."

"Oh well. I don't mind giving him some ideas. Tell him to call me."

"Okay, thanks," Anne says, tasting her drink. "Mm mm. Good."

Maggie hands Anne a plate with chips, salsa, and two brownies. "Here, hon."

"Thanks," Anne says. "I need Girls' Night Out more than ever now. Keeps me semi-sane." Anne loves her friends. They've been getting together for over a decade. Ranging in age from 35 to 62, the group—which one husband calls the Mafia Mamas—has celebrated birthdays, marriages, babies, and promotions. They've consoled each other through bad days, divorces, miscarriages, and parents' deaths. They laugh, cry, gossip, argue about politics, and discuss crime, a popular topic for the mostly courthouse crowd.

Anne, Rhonda, and Maggie join Kate, Liz, and Alice on the patio. Anne sinks into a cushioned wicker chair and props her feet on the coffee table. "Y'all won't believe this." She tells about Harold's part in getting a low bond for Charisse's husband. The others look stunned.

Rubbing the back of her neck, Anne adds, "It's one thing for Harold to treat his employees like crap, but now he's treating victims badly, too. It makes me sick."

Kate throws her hands up in the air. "And you forgot to add he's treating the police like they are our enemies. I don't get it."

As the conversation drifts to other topics, Anne leans back in her chair. Between the soothing whir of the overhead fan and the margarita, she gets drowsy. *I'd like to fall asleep for a long time.*

Chapter 15

Anne grabs her file folder and heads to the conference room where several people have already gathered for the planning meeting for the clergy seminar.

For several years, staff at the Victim-Witness Assistance Program have coordinated with other victim service agencies to host an annual seminar for faith leaders. Most people with problems prefer seeking help from their church or synagogue rather than a governmental agency or non-profit organization. Anne had seen pastors coming to court to support those accused of a crime, and she's familiar with prison ministries. But she's never unerstood why she rarely saw clergy comforting victims.

The idea came to Anne after her staff assisted several families whose children had been molested in a home daycare. The abuser was the brother of the daycare owner. Retired and widowed, Mr. Reynolds entertained the children with games and kept candy in his pockets to reward "good younguns."

Four-year-old Erica told her mom, "Mr. R. touched my pee pee." The horrified mom quizzed her child and called the police the next day. Carol at the Children's Advocacy Center interviewed all the kids at the daycare and four more revealed Mr. R. had touched them inappropriately, too. His arrest set into motion the arduous journey for the victims' families.

Mr. Reynolds belonged to the same church as Erica's family. At the end of a Sunday service, the minister called Mr. Reynolds to the altar. The minister placed his hand on his shoulder and prayed. "Lord Jesus, we surround our dear brother in Christ with your unconditional love. We feel the mighty power of the Holy Spirit offering strength and forgiveness to you as you endure trials and tribulations. We know that only you, our Father, can judge. We bless our brother in Christ. In Jesus' name, we pray. Amen."

Erica's family was stunned. They walked out that day and never returned to the church where they'd married and their two children were baptized. Not once did the pastor speak to them about the allegations or offer solace. They felt like they'd been re-victimized by the very person who should be comforting them.

Eventually, Mr. Reynolds pled guilty and was sentenced to ten years in prison. The daycare closed. Erica's mom began speaking publicly about her family's experience, saying they didn't attend a church for three years but then found a supportive congregation. "I pray no one will ever have to face what our family did. Although it's not easy, I'll continue to speak because it's worth it if my story can encourage one clergy member to respond appropriately to crime victims." She ends by saying that, after counseling, her daughter is doing well.

When Anne received a grant to fund the first clergy seminar, she worried nobody would show up. It was before the sex abuse scandal in the Catholic Church. But fifty faith leaders attended the first seminar, and more than one hundred came each year after that. Several clergy already had crime prevention efforts underway—mentoring and after-school youth programs—but most acknowledged knowing little about victim services or how to best help crime victims. They were eager to learn more.

* * *

Two months later, close to a hundred clergy are seated at large, round tables in a church fellowship hall. Lily Davis, a middle-aged, plump woman with an engaging smile, steps up to the podium and adjusts the microphone. "Good morning. Thank you for being here today."

She holds up a picture of a grinning young man in a maroon graduation cap and gown. "I was told I could never have children. But this is a picture of my miracle baby, my only child, on the day he graduated from college four years ago." She smiles and gingerly places the framed photograph back on the podium and picks up another picture of a man about her son's age. "This is the young man who shot my son five times, twice in the leg and three times in the chest."

She pauses as a hush falls over the room. "My son, Jerome, died in the ambulance on the way to Memorial Hospital on October 2nd three years ago. Alphonso was sentenced to life in prison. I lost a son. Alphonso's mother lost a son too. We both grieve."

Mrs. Davis recounts how late one Friday night, she and her husband were at home watching TV when a knock at the front door startled them. Her husband jumped up from his recliner and pulled back the den curtains. A police car was parked out front. He cracked open the front door and saw two men–one in a police uniform and the other in a suit and tie–approaching the porch.

Mrs. Davis pauses to take a sip of water, then continues. "They introduced themselves as Officer Gonzales and Police Chaplain Richards and asked if they could come in. My father was a police officer, so when I saw those solemn-faced men, I knew something was terribly wrong. My heart sank."

"Inside our den, Officer Gonzales motioned for us to sit down, but we remained standing, frozen. I grabbed my husband's arm and braced for the worst. And the words that tumbled out of the policeman's mouth turned my universe upside down. 'Is Jerome Davis, the manager of a convenience store on MLK Blvd, your son?"

"Yes,' my husband croaked, pointing to the pictures of Jerome on the wall–one of him on a red tricycle wearing a policeman's hat, another of him smiling with silver braces, and a third in his high school baseball uniform. The largest picture was him in his college graduation gown giving the thumbs-up sign.

"The officer told us Jerome was taking the deposit bag to his car when a young man robbed and shot him. Jerome's cause of death was three gunshots to the chest." Mrs. Davis clears her throat as a tear rolls down her cheek. A few sniffles can be heard in the audience.

"The officer shuffled from one foot to the other. I felt sorry for Officer Gonzales. I remembered how daddy hated death notifications.

"The room started spinning, and I fell back onto the couch. The chaplain went to the kitchen and got me a glass of water. I gulped it like my life depended on it.

"It was all so surreal," she continues. "I was too shocked to cry or even speak. I felt like a character in some awful movie. I picked up the phone, but I had no idea who to call."

The seminar attendees lean forward in their chairs, hanging onto every word.

From her seat in the front, Anne notices Mrs. Davis starts breathing harder and clutching the podium with both hands. *Oh dear. I hope she's not having an asthma attack.* "Are you okay?" she mouths.

Mrs. Davis nods yes and continues speaking.

"I couldn't believe–didn't want to believe–that my son's life could end that way." She uses the tissue she'd been clutching to wipe her forehead.

"I do remember the chaplain asking if we wanted him to call anyone. My husband said Pastor Roberson, and within fifteen minutes he and Deacon Jackson were by our side. They've been here for us ever since, even after the casseroles, sympathy cards, and flowers stopped. After a while, friends and co-workers felt uncomfortable talking about Jerome and the murder, but not Pastor Roberson. He's prayed. He's sat with us. He's listened to me tell about that awful night dozens of times. Repeating the story was the only way to make it sink in my brain. Thank God he still listens. Ladies and gentlemen, this kind soul is here today. Please stand up, Pastor Roberson." She points at her pastor who stands for a moment, nodding when the audience applauds.

"We had recently moved here from Detroit, eager to escape that crime-ridden city. My son's college degree was in business. He had a job interview at an insurance company scheduled the week after he was shot. My Jerome had a bright future. He was engaged to a lovely young woman. I was looking forward to being a grandma. But it all ended that October night, and so did the future of the young man who murdered him." She holds up the picture of the perpetrator again.

"I tell you without a doubt that my faith is what has kept me going. My church family and the Victim-Witness Assistance Program staff continue to bless me with comfort and guidance. I wanted to run away–leave Savannah–but I've come to realize this is where I was called to be. My son's death will not be in vain. I'll speak to anyone who will listen about how we can work together, and how we must end this senseless violence.

"I pray every night for the strength to see another day. I also pray every night for Alphonso and his family."

An older man yells out. "Amen! Amen, sistuh. God bless you!"

"In the first few weeks after Jerome's death, I struggled every morning to merely get out of bed. It took a few minutes after waking up to remember the awful reality that my son was dead. Although my legs felt like they had weights strapped to them, I put one foot on the floor and then the other. I had to go on."

She says her first venture out of the house was to church, then the grocery store, and then her job at Dixie Crystals sugar refinery. Eventually, she attended neighborhood watch meetings.

During those initial weeks after the murder, her asthma worsened; the grief choked her lungs, and pain knotted in her stomach like a tight fist. She had occasional good days when she baked pound cakes for church suppers and sang along with the gospel radio station. She jotted notes about what to tell young people about the effects of violence. The mayor asked her to serve on a crime prevention task force. "Even politicians will hush up when you speak," he told her.

A regular at monthly support group meetings for families of homicide victims, she helped organize the annual candlelight vigils.

A few months after her son's death, she insisted on going to the convenience store where Jerome had experienced his last moments on earth. When her husband couldn't talk her out of it, he went with her late one Friday night. Holding hands, they slowly walked around the parking lot full of SCAD students, tourists, and late-night revelers buying sodas, six packs, and cigarettes. She gazed up at the night sky and a bright star above the crescent moon winked down at them. The thought that Jerome might have seen that same star comforted her.

She looks down at her notes for the first time. "I know my life will never be the same. Anne Gardner tells me this is my new normal. I've vowed that Jerome's tragic death will not be in vain. I'll keep speaking and advocating for victims. I can't give up. Jerome wouldn't want me to. And I do believe he's giving me a thumbs up from heaven." She smiles and walks away from the podium to a standing ovation.

Anne holds back tears. Mrs. Davis is one of the strongest and most inspiring people she's ever met.

Anne recalls that after the murder trial ended, the young detective who investigated the case gave Mrs. Davis his cell number, and they remain in touch. He calls her on the anniversary of Jerome's death. When the detective's baby boy was born, Mrs. Davis showed up at Memorial Hospital with a yellow baby blanket she'd crocheted. Mrs. Davis had confided to Anne that even though she was thrilled about his new baby boy, she felt a deep sadness, knowing she'd never hold a grandchild of her own.

Anne's emotionally exhausted after the seminar. Maybe a walk will help clear her mind. She drives to Forsyth Park and changes into socks and Nikes she keeps in her car. As she strolls under the moss-covered oaks past the big fountain, Anne thinks about Mrs. Davis. *I wish I had a fraction of her strength and resilience.*

Chapter 16

"I Gotta Feeling" by the Black-eyed Peas awakens Anne from a deep sleep at 5 a.m. Rubbing her eyes, she presses the off button on the radio alarm. She plants her feet on the floor and shuffles to the closet. Dressing in the dark so she won't disturb Jon, she finds her old Clemson University tee shirt and athletic shorts.

At the Tybee Y, the instructor cranks up the music for the body sculpt class. Her gym buddy Deb high-fives her. "Long time no see, Anne. Glad you're back."

"Yeah, I've been a bum lately, getting up just in time for work," Anne says as she retrieves hand weights from the rack. She finds her usual spot in the back as the young teacher with six-pack abs begins the warm-up. Anne huffs and puffs through the 50-minute workout, exhausted by the time they get to the final stretch, her favorite part.

Back at home, she turns on the shower and enjoys the hot spray on her sweaty body. She reluctantly steps out and towels off. She slips on her robe, pads to the kitchen, and sits across the table from Jon who has a bowl of oatmeal waiting for her. She reads the front section of *The Savannah Morning News* while he peruses the sports section. *Have we become like old married couples who hardly talk to each other?*

"Ugh, another murder yesterday." Anne points to a front-page headline. "Man Killed Near Kayton Homes."

"Yep, that's Savannah these days. Plenty of job security for you." Jon sips his coffee.

"Well, I don't know about that. Harold doesn't seem too pleased with my job performance. He's been criticizing me about the new VIP program. Nothing I do suits him."

"Maybe he's still getting comfortable in his new position."

"But he doesn't have to take it out on me. Or whoever else he happens to be picking on that day," Anne says with a grimace.

After arriving at the courthouse, Anne scrolls through her emails and is surprised to find one from an old Clemson University friend. It's an invitation to the 100th-anniversary celebration of the campus newspaper, *The Tiger*. Although most of her childhood friends had gone to Alabama colleges, Anne chose to attend her dad's alma mater. Majoring in English at a school known for engineering, architecture, and agriculture degrees, she became close with the students and professors in the small English Department. During her sophomore year, she began writing for *The Tiger* and became news editor her senior year. The staff spent hours each week putting together the award-winning college newspaper. After the papers were distributed on Thursday afternoons, they often spent Thursday nights drinking pitchers of cheap draft beer at Sloan Street Taproom, their favorite watering hole.

Memories of days with that tight-knit group come flooding back. She loved writing for the paper. She broke one big story about a 24-year-old "townie" accused of raping a freshman co-ed. *The Greenville News* and other media picked up her article. Rumor was the rapist, a nice-looking guy with blonde hair but sinister eyes, had sexually assaulted other women. This was just the first time he'd been arrested. Anne shivers as she remembers the details.

After the rapist pled guilty, the judge ordered chemical castration instead of prison! Although the judge was known to be harsh, that sentence shocked everyone. The campus was abuzz, especially when Johnny Carson made a crack about it on the *Tonight Show*. Anne got creeped out when a friend warned, "It's a tough sentence, but this rapist isn't locked up. I hope you don't run into him around town because he's gonna be mad you broke the story." Anne kept her eyes peeled. Once she thought she saw him at Lake Hartwell and avoided going there all spring. She heard the victim left the university soon after the crime.

Wow, I haven't thought about that in years. I wonder what happened to the poor girl. I hope she got counseling. Interesting that I ended up working with crime victims. Back then, I had no idea what I wanted to do.

She hoped Dr. Hinchey would attend the celebration. Adviser to *The Tiger* and English prof, he was respected and loved by generations of *Tiger* staffers. Once he told her, "If you ever come in my office, and I'm wearing this Bi-Lo baseball cap, you better not cross me. It means I'm having a bad day and wishing I was bagging groceries at Bi-lo." He usually sported the cap when faced with a mountain of departmental reports or office politics.

Dr. Hinchey reminded her of Henry David Thoreau. In his 50s back then, he lived in a cabin about ten miles from campus in the middle of several acres of tall pine trees. He cherished his cabin mates: Stella the cat, golden retriever Barney, and all the birds and critters on his property. He also loved his students, books on topics from religion to humor, and Clemson baseball. He never missed a home game.

Dr. Hinchey taught the college Sunday school class at Clemson United Methodist Church. Each year he invited the class members to an Easter sunrise service beside a small pond on his land. Afterward, he served fresh-squeezed orange juice, steaming grits, ham biscuits, and strong coffee.

Anne still sends him a card each Christmas and looks forward to reading the newsy letter he sends in return. It always includes a list of books he read that year. He praised author Annie Dillard in the most recent letter. These days he suffers from lung problems and uses an oxygen tank. *Oh yes, I want to go to this reunion. Dr. Hinchey won't be around forever.*

Remembering her college days makes Anne smile. Until she recalls another professor. Dr. Rob Griffin taught journalism and was a tall, bearded man in his late forties. Unlike most profs in the 1970s who wore button-down shirts and neckties, Dr. Griffin usually sported a flannel shirt, blue jeans, and wide brown leather belt with a big silver buckle. Right away Anne pegged him as a rugged renegade. She was captivated by his stories about being a former reporter and editor at the Texas newspaper, *The Austin Statesman.* Wide-eyed and eager to learn everything she could, she didn't mind getting up early her junior year for his lively eight o'clock class.

One of his assignments was to write a restaurant, movie, or album review. She labored for hours on her article about The Old Stone House, a local restaurant known for good country cooking at lunch and fancier weekend evening meals. When she and her buddies scrounged enough money together, they piled into someone's car and went there for Sunday lunch.

When she got her assignment back with a "C" across the top, Anne was crestfallen. Dr. Griffin had scrawled in green ink, "Anne, you need more vivid descriptions. Put us in the setting. See me. Rob."

Anne clenched her fist. *Damn, what's his problem? And good grief, I'd never call him by his first name.*

With only fifteen minutes before her next class, she walked to the front of the room where Dr. Griffin was gathering his notes from the podium.

Anne held up her paper. "Did you want to talk to me about this?"

He smiled. "Yes, Anne. I have some suggestions. Your restaurant review has potential but can be better. Come see me in my office," he said.

"Okay, I have classes most of the day. When would be good?"

"What about 5:00 today?" he said, touching her shoulder in what seemed like a fatherly way.

"Okay. See you then."

She hurried down the hall, nearly bumping into Kevin, the lanky editor of *The Tiger,* who was also in Dr. Griffin's class. Anne thought he was cute and had a little crush on him. "Hey, how did you do on the journalism paper?" she asked.

"A-minus. How 'bout you?"

"Dang, I got a C." She bit her bottom lip.

"Really? What's the deal?" He frowned. "You're not a C kinda student."

"Dunno. I guess I'll find out this afternoon when I go to his office."

"Okay, good luck. You coming to Sloan Street Tap Room tomorrow night?"

"Yep, I'll be there." She hoisted her book bag up on her shoulder. She had four classes in a row, and toting all those books made her slouch. She could hear her Gram say, "Stand up straight and be proud of your height. Look regal, my honey bun."

She could barely pay attention in her next class because she was so absorbed in worrying whether English should be her major if she couldn't even write a decent restaurant review. She pulled it out and read again what she thought was a vivid description of the food–crisp, hot fried chicken, gooey mac and cheese, green beans flavored with ham. She'd even described the long-time waitress. *Not vivid enough? Seriously?*

After her last class, she grabbed a Coke from the vending machine and took it to the amphitheater, killing time before meeting with Dr. Griffin. She sat on the wooden benches built into the side of the hill, a perfect fall day. The trees had turned a brilliant blaze of orange, red, and yellow. She was glad she'd chosen this beautiful campus in the South Carolina foothills. On Friday the amphitheater would be filled with orange-clad students at a pep rally. Saturday was a big game against Maryland. Of course, every football game was big at Clemson. At the stadium in Death Valley, players continued the lucky tradition of touching the big rock at the top of the hill before rushing onto the field. When the band played *Tiger Rag*, the 80,000 fans went wild.

Anne checked her watch and hiked the short distance to Strode Hall which housed the offices of the liberal arts professors. This late in the day, the building was almost empty. She took the elevator to the fifth floor and tapped on Dr. Griffin's door.

"Come in," he said.

Sitting behind a desk cluttered with papers, he smiled. "Hi Anne, have a seat."

She sat on the leather loveseat opposite his desk, the only other piece of furniture except for two tall bookcases. She was sure he could sense her nervousness.

"I haven't eaten at The Old Stone House in a while, Anne, but reading your paper made me hungry to go there again."

"Yes sir, I like their home-style cooking." She tried not to blink her eyes excessively, a nervous habit she had.

When Dr. Griffin stood up slowly, he looked taller than ever. He walked to the front of his desk and leaned against it. His silver belt buckle was at Anne's eye level, only inches away. "You did a great job describing the food, Anne, but when writing features, you need to describe the setting, too. Like that winding, dirt road that leads up to the restaurant." His blue eyes twinkled. Anne gave a halfhearted smile.

"Tell the reader about the outside of the building. Use some comparisons. What does that beautiful stone remind you of? What do you see before you even enter the restaurant?"

"Oh, okay." Anne fumbled with the paper in her hand.

Dr. Griffin sat beside her on the loveseat, and when he used his index finger to point to the first page, his large hand brushed against her small one. Anne worried he could hear her heart pounding like a Sousa band. "See. You describe the meal too soon. You have to put us in this place."

"Yes sir. I understand." Anne stared at her paper, trying to focus on what he was saying instead of the butterflies fluttering in her stomach.

"You're a good writer. I always enjoy your articles in *The Tiger,*" he said, pointing to the latest edition on his desk.

"Thanks. I like writing them." *Oh god! That was a lame thing to say.*

"Yeah, I see you newspaper guys at Sloan Street Taproom. Journalists always like to write and drink. At least I did back in Texas."

The late afternoon sun gleamed through the office window, making Anne sweat.

Dr. Griffin continued, "Rewrite the beginning with more details and turn it in next week. I know you can make this stellar." His hand grazed her knee.

"Yep, I mean yes sir, I'll do that." Anne looked down at her blue jeans. *Was it an accident he touched my knee?*

"Maybe I'll see you at Sloan Street and buy you a real drink, not just that watery beer." When he smiled, she noticed the crinkles around his blue eyes. He reminded her of Kris Kristofferson, her teenage heartthrob. Her parents had even taken her to see him in concert at the Birmingham coliseum.

"Okay, thanks." Anne looked at her hands, the floor, anything to avoid eye contact.

"All right, Anne. See you. Soon, I hope."

When she stood, her papers fluttered to the carpet. *I'm such a spaz!* He leaned down to pick them up, but she grabbed them first and their heads nearly bumped. She walked toward the door, turned the handle, and stepped into the hall, relieved to get away. What had seemed like an hour was probably only fifteen minutes. Embarrassed and excited, her palms were clammy.

On the elevator, she exhaled. *He liked my article and thinks I'm a good writer. Awesome!* She felt like an eighth-grader who had just been noticed by a senior boy. Then her giddiness turned to annoyance. *But he gave me a C. In real life, he's my teacher and an old man to boot. Ugh. I'm confused.* Grateful the elevator was empty, Anne was certain her face was as red as the leaves on the maple trees.

Chapter 17

Anne leaves her Honda in long-term parking at the Savannah airport and makes a note of the deck and space number. It's been a habit since a nightmarish experience in Atlanta where she wandered around for an hour searching for her car, only to discover there were two identical parking decks side by side and she was in the wrong one.

After checking her suitcase, she gets her boarding pass and walks to the main lobby.

"Anne, we're over here," Wanda says, waving her well-manicured hand. Recently hired as public information officer (PIO) for the District Attorney's Office, Wanda exudes confidence and poise. The tall Black woman is perfect for television interviews. Jeffrey is sitting beside her. Anne had suggested LaShay, the coordinator of VIP, come. But Harold insisted she needed to stay in the office to write policies and procedures. In typical Harold fashion, he only told her yesterday that Jeffrey and Devin would also be traveling to Chicago. They will meet with Harold's physician friends at the Illinois Masonic Medical Center to learn about their Violence Intervention Program (VIP).

Anne rolls her overnight case toward them. "Hey, y'all."

Jeffrey, clad in jeans and a polo shirt, rises and shakes Anne's hand. "Hello, Mrs. Gardner," he says with a boyish grin. "I'm excited about learning a lot in Chicago."

"Yes, it should be interesting."

Jeffrey says, "I'm going to get a Coke. Y'all want coffee or anything, Anne?"

"No thanks."

Wanda looks up from her phone. "I'd love a cup of coffee." She hands him a five-dollar bill.

When Jeffrey is out of earshot, Wanda says, "Anne, this is going to be an interesting trip. Two boy-men, Harold, and us."

"You got that right. I still think LaShay should have come." She looks down the concourse. "Harold is late."

Wanda leans in closer. "I need to tell you something. I applied for another job and am one of two finalists. We've been calling back and forth, and I may get a call today, so if I step away from the group, that's why."

"But you've only been here six or seven months."

"I know and it's been the longest seven months of my life. Harold is the strangest person I've ever worked for. He constantly criticizes me and meddles in my work. I've been in public relations for fifteen years, and I know what I'm doing. I don't need him always looking over my shoulder."

"I know what you mean." *Dang, Wanda must think it's really bad if she's already jumping ship.*

"Just between us, I think Harold has a problem with strong women." She raises her eyebrows for emphasis. Anne nods.

When Anne sees Harold and Devin walk up behind Wanda, she changes the subject. "Wanda, you used to live in Chicago, right?"

"Yes for a few years after college. And even though it's 72 degrees in Savannah, I read online there may be snow in Chicago."

Harold joins the two women. "Good morning, ladies."

"Good morning," they reply.

"I'm glad I brought my big overcoat, but I sure hate dragging it around," Anne says. In Savannah's climate, she rarely wears the red wool coat draped across the back of her chair.

"Did you pack my overcoat, Devin?" Harold asks.

"No, it takes up so much room. You'll be fine, sir." Devin is a good-looking man with wide-set brown eyes and a thin mustache. He's wearing a neatly-pressed suit, blue necktie, and polished shoes.

"I hope I'll be fine," Harold says, smiling back at him.

Anne can't believe her ears. *Devin packed Harold's suitcase? And they rode to the airport together? What the hell? Does that mean Devin spent the night at Harold's house?*

Jeffrey returns with Wanda's coffee and his Coke. Wanda whispers to Anne, "I might need something stronger than coffee on this trip."

When the five of them board the plane, Anne's glad she'll have an aisle seat where she can stretch out her long legs. And she's relieved to be sitting next to a stranger, so she won't have to chat with her colleagues. She thumbs through her copy of *The New Yorker,* then picks up a Jodi Picoult novel.

They land in Chicago on schedule and rent a car. With Harold driving and Wanda in the front seat giving directions, Anne is squished in the back between Jeffrey and Devin. Even though the rental car is a tight fit, everyone seems in an upbeat mood. They pass the exit for Wrigley Field. "Where's the Sears Tower?" Anne asks, leaning forward to see between Harold and Wanda. "I've been here once but can't get my bearings."

"We'll see it in a minute," Wanda says. "Our hotel is on the Magnificent Mile. Maybe we'll have time to go to Lake Shore Drive to see Lake Michigan."

When they get out of the car at The Doubletree, a blast of arctic air hits them. "Whoa. I see why they call this the Windy City," Jeffrey says, pulling his jacket tighter.

Harold takes off his scarf and drapes it around Jeffrey's neck. "Here, that oughta keep you warm until we get inside," he says, winking.

Despite the wind, Anne's face feels hot. Jeffrey laughs nervously.

This IS going to be an interesting trip, Anne thinks, shivering more from Harold's actions than the cold weather.

The valet unloads their luggage, and they hurry inside. In the lobby, people chatter about a coming snowstorm. Anne runs her fingers through her tousled hair. *Oh crud, what if we get snowed in and have to stay an extra night?* She inhales and whispers to herself, "This too shall pass," as her mama used to say.

Wanda checks in first, then Anne. When it's Harold's turn, he reminds the registration clerk not to charge state taxes because they're from a government agency.

The clerk nods. "Yes, I have that noted. I hope you enjoy your stay." She hands him his room key and a complimentary bag of chocolate chip cookies. Smiling, she looks behind Harold to Devin and Jeffrey and says. "Which of you gentlemen is next?"

"Oh, they're with me," Harold says, rolling his suitcase toward the elevator as Devin and Jeffrey follow like baby ducks after their mama. Wanda and Anne join them at the elevator.

Anne fiddles with her room key. *What the hell? Why are they staying in the same room when Wanda and I have separate ones? What is this? Rub a dub dub, three men in a tub?*

"Do y'all want us to meet for dinner?" Harold asks.

"Thanks, but I'm getting together with an old friend," Wanda says.

Anne yawns. "Um, I'm tired. Think I'll order room service." *The last thing I wanna do is go out with them.*

Harold shrugs his shoulders. "Guess it'll be just us guys then."

Devin nods, but Jeffrey says, "I may get room service too. I've never done that before."

Harold slaps him on the back. "No way! You're in a big city, and you need to enjoy some big city life!"

Devin narrows his eyes at Harold. "Jeffrey might enjoy some time by himself."

Jeffrey nods. "Yeah, I need to make a few calls and stuff."

Harold shrugs. "Suit yourself."

Anne switches on the light in her eighth-floor room. She changes into sweatpants and a tee shirt. Nibbling on a chocolate chip cookie, she raises the blinds. Outside an American flag flaps ferociously, and people scurry on the sidewalk, their heads bowed against the gusty winds. She sprawls on the bed and flips through a *Chicago Today* magazine she found on the nightstand. She'd brought background material Harold gave her about violence intervention programs but would rather read about Second City, the comedy club where so many great comedians, including John Belushi, got their start.

Anne rubs her lower back, aching from the plane ride and probably stress. She remembers reading in Louise Hay's book, *You Can Heal Your Life,* that back problems indicate a "lack of support." She lies on the carpeted floor and does some yoga positions, and her back begins to loosen up. She sits up and calls Jon.

When she describes the hotel sleeping arrangements, he says, "I can tell you one damn thing I would never stay in the same room with another man on a work trip. And Harold's staying with two guys? Plus, he's their boss, and there's a big age difference. Very strange." He ends the conversation with, "Just remember, darling, you'll be home in two days."

"I miss you," Anne says. "I wish I was walking on the beach right now. Good night, hon."

Anne flips through the TV channels and not seeing anything of interest, she clicks it off. After tossing and turning for at least an hour, she drifts off to sleep.

She gets to the lobby by eight-thirty the next morning. A beaming Wanda appears first. "I got the job!"

Anne hugs her. "Congrats!" *Geez, who will be next?* In a few minutes Harold, Jeffrey, and Devin step off the elevator. Devin and Harold are laughing, but Jeffrey looks solemn. He fingers his tie and sidles up beside Anne. She tries her best not to picture their sleeping arrangements. They pile in the car, and Harold drives through heavy traffic toward the Illinois Masonic Medical Center on the north side of town. When they arrive and walk toward the hospital, she notices everyone is walking fast and not making eye contact. So different from the South where folks saunter like they have all the time in the world.

The Savannah contingent heads to a small conference room. Harold's friend, Dr. Wright, welcomes them and leaves them with two social workers who explain how their program operates. Harold's other classmate, Dr. Morrison, joins them during the mid-morning break. When Devin and Jeffrey are down the hall at the soda machine, Dr. Morrison says, "Harold, I didn't want to say anything in front of Jeffrey, but I don't understand the role of the investigator. I think victims won't respond well to someone with a law enforcement officer connection. There could be trust issues. Our approach is to treat violence as a health issue, not a crime problem."

Harold says, "If we're going to make home visits, I want an investigator present."

"Why? Don't get me wrong, I understand violence and safety issues for staff. We've got two kids in the E.R. right now from a shootout with The Gangsta Disciples. Anyway, consider that you might not need to make home visits; you could meet at a public place near the victim's home or at school. That's what we do."

Harold frowns. "Savannah has a different dynamic than Chicago. I don't think we'll have trust issues between the victims and law enforcement."

Although Anne agrees with the doctor, she knows better than to question her boss. *Why did we come here if Harold isn't going to listen?*

Jeffrey appears at the door and motions for Anne to step into the hall. She excuses herself and Jeffrey whispers, "I have to tell you, um last night..."

Harold appears. "Break time is over. Time to get back inside."

Jeffrey and Anne hustle back inside the conference room like reprimanded children. After about an hour, they tour the hospital. Everyone except Jeffrey asks questions of their hosts.

That night they meet for dinner at a trendy restaurant called The Blackbird. The two physicians are already seated at a table. As the Savannah folks walk past the long bar, Dr. Wright comes over to greet them. "I think you'll enjoy it here. The chef recently received the James Beard culinary award."

"I read about him in Conde Nast," Harold says, taking a chair beside his old college friend. "Chef Peter Kahan, right?"

Anne looks at her boss. *Harold loves to drop names.*

"Yes, exactly!" Dr. Wright says. "And last month he was on the Top Chef TV show. Oh look, there he is talking to the couple in the corner!" Everyone looks toward the famous chef, including Anne who'd never heard of him.

Vicki, one of the social workers, sits next to Anne. She peppers Anne with questions about Savannah. "I've seen pictures of those huge oak trees with that gray moss stuff and that big fountain. What's the name of that park?"

"Forsyth Park. It's just one of our many beautiful spots," Anne says proudly.

After studying the menu, Anne finally decides on a salad and roasted wild salmon. The salad is served in a little basket made of crispy potatoes. It's delicious. *I bet Jon's home eating a peanut butter sandwich. But I'd still rather be with him than here.*

After dinner, Dr. Wright picks up the tab, and they make their way outside where huge snowflakes fall from the dark sky. It reminds Anne of the beautiful pictures in her grandson's book, *The Polar Express.* "Look! Snow! I haven't seen snow in years." Anne is as excited as a little girl unwrapping a new doll on Christmas morning.

Harold shakes Dr. Wright's hand. "We appreciate the dinner and thank you for providing the beautiful snow for us Southerners."

"We aim to please," Dr. Wright says. "But, my goodness, you all are not prepared. Harold, you don't even have on an overcoat."

"I sure don't, do I, Devin?" Harold smirks and pats Devin on the shoulder.

Anne and Wanda exchange knowing glances, but Jeffrey stares down at the snow-covered sidewalk.

Chapter 20
Chapter 18

A couple of days after the Chicago trip, Anne looks at the invitation to *The Tiger* newspaper reunion she'd taped to the refrigerator. Feeling nostalgic, she pulls the 1981 Clemson yearbook from the bookcase, curls up on the couch, and turns to a photo of *The Tiger* staff. Standing on railroad tracks, everyone is wearing goofy hats. Sporting a black fedora, Anne looks like an innocent kid. Next to her is Kevin, the editor who's a lawyer now. A big photo on another page is of Anne pasting up an edition of the newspaper, long before it was done by computers. She's wearing dark brown corduroy pants and a white turtleneck. *Look how skinny I was! Dang, I need to lose at least ten pounds before the reunion. And my hair looked like a Dorothy Hamill cut gone bad!*

The Tiger staffers were a diverse but close-knit clique. They worked in the Student Union building. The space was divided into small offices with electric typewriters and a big communal area with two couches, bean bag chairs, a stereo, TV, and refrigerator. Staffers hung out there even when they weren't working on the weekly edition of the paper–drinking beer, eating junk food, smoking cigarettes, studying, and napping between classes. Some even slept there overnight after too many beers or if they wanted to escape an annoying roommate. Their group had been called "incestuous," and there was always a romance or two brewing.

Anne's excited but nervous about seeing the crowd again. Because of the distance to her alma mater, she'd only been back a few times for football games. Grinning, Anne keeps turning pages as fond memories flood back. She remembers the one-dollar midnight movies where she saw *"Rocky Horror Picture Show"* and danced to *The Time Warp.*

She's never eaten fried mushrooms as delicious as the ones served at Nick's Bar, still an institution in downtown Clemson.

Anne had a blast on a trip to New York City with her art history class. They traveled on a Greyhound bus and stayed in a cheap hotel across from the *New York Times* building. Anne was the only one in the group who took a tour of the building; she was enthralled and decided right then to apply for a newspaper job after graduation.

There's also a photo in the yearbook of The Sloan Street Taproom. The small dark tavern had a long wooden bar, booths against the wall, and Formica tables with plastic red chairs. Anne spent many hours playing Pacman in the adjoining game room where spilled drinks made the carpet squish underfoot. Buddy, the owner, knew the regulars by name, joking and chatting with students and townies alike.

Dr. Griffin showed up at the taproom the night after she'd turned in her revised restaurant review. Surprised to see him, she quickly looked away, wondering why he was on her turf. A little later, when she was returning from the restroom, Dr. Griffin slid off his bar stool and approached her. "There's the writer of the week." He winked. "Your revision of the restaurant review is superb." Anne ducked her head and blushed. *Does he really think I have talent?*

"Hey, remember I promised to buy you a real drink? I know you're not twenty-one yet, but I don't think old Buddy here would mind my treating you to a bourbon and Coke." He pulled out a five-dollar bill from his jeans pocket.

"Thanks," Anne said, "but I'm a beer drinker."

"Okay, then." His face turned crimson, and he returned to his perch at the bar.

Back at her table, Anne gulped her watery beer. One of her friends said, "I think that journalism teacher has the hots for you, Anne."

"Uh, no he doesn't. Geez. He gave me a C on a paper."

"Well, I bet I know how you can get an A," Kevin said.

"Shut up. He's married. And old. Gross."

"Well, I hear he's getting a divorce. And he's looking this way as we speak."

Rolling her eyes, Anne reached across the table to pour herself another glass of beer and knocked over the entire pitcher. "Shit!" she cried, grabbing a bunch of napkins from the metal napkin holder. Buddy sauntered over with a big white towel and mopped up the mess. The others laughed and ordered another pitcher. Anne's tee shirt was soaked. She pulled the fabric away from her body. *No wet tee shirt contest for me.* She looked to see whether Dr. Griffin had seen the commotion, but he was deep in conversation with another professor.

Around midnight, the group paid up and left. They meandered through downtown past Ibrahim's Sporting Goods Store, more bars, and a pizza joint. Fortunately, the campus was within walking distance of downtown. College Avenue was filled with students enjoying Thursday night, the most popular for bar-hopping. Anne and her pals lumbered up the grassy hill to Tillman Hall, the campus landmark with the big clock tower.

Anne lived the furthest from Sloan Street and walked alone on the sidewalk toward her dorm. When someone called her name, she jumped and squinted into the headlights of a black Ford pickup. Dr. Griffin leaned out the window. "Hey Annie, you need a ride?"

"Uh, no I live right there." She pointed to the brick dorm in front of her.

"Okay, see you in the morning." He drove slowly down the hill toward the football stadium.

Did he follow me? How does he know where I live? And did he call me Annie?

Suddenly she felt like she was going to throw up. Her shirt reeked of beer. She stumbled to the dorm and tried to open the double glass doors, but they were locked after midnight. She pressed her face to the glass, but the student desk clerk was nowhere in sight. She pounded the door with her fist, then slumped down on a nearby bench. It seemed like forever before the clerk unlocked the door.

"Anne, you okay? Damn, girl, did you fall in a beer keg?"

"Yep. I mean yep I'm okay. Just tired."

Head throbbing, Anne tiptoed into her dorm room. She brushed her teeth, splashed water on her face, peeled off the icky tee shirt, and fell into her twin bed with her jeans still on. She was out like a light.

The next morning, her roommate Pat tapped her on the shoulder. "Anne, it's seven-thirty. Don't you have an eight o'clock class?"

She opened one eye and mumbled, "Uh, yeah." Her mouth felt like a furry animal had hibernated there. She gulped some water, popped an aspirin, and padded down the hall to the showers. After showering, she felt human again and arrived at Dr. Griffin's class just after eight. The events of the night were sketchy like a blurry TV movie. *Was it a coincidence that Dr. Griffin was driving near my dorm? Surely he doesn't live that close to campus.*

Giving a thumbs up, Dr. Griffin returned her restaurant review with a big "A" scrawled on the top. He had written "Great revision. Vivid description of the setting." Embarrassed by the night before, Anne kept her head down through most of the fifty minutes.

After class, she scooped up her books and stuffed them in her backpack, but Dr. Griffin followed her to the door. "I knew you could do it, Anne," he said.

"Thanks." She scurried to the hall.

The next night, Anne was at her desk in *The Tiger* office copy editing a news article when Kevin appeared. "Hey, Dr. Griffin has a story idea for you. I hope you don't mind me giving him your phone number."

"Huh? What kind of idea?"

"He said it's an investigative piece."

"He sees me in class three times a week. Why does he need my phone number?" Anne picked at the thumb cuticle. *Does he think I like him or something? I mean he is kinda cute but...*

"Beats me. How many inches is it?" Kevin asked, leaning over her desk.

"What?"

"The news story. We don't have a lot of space this week."

"Oh. I'll check and let you know."

When she returned to her dorm, there was a note on the mirror. "Dr. Griffin called. 656-2183."

Anne crawled into bed and dreamed Dr. Griffin took her to eat at The Old Stone House where she choked on a chicken bone. She coughed and sputtered until he did the Heimlich maneuver, wrapping his burly arms around her torso. She woke up feeling jittery. *I am not calling him back.*

The topic of Friday morning's journalism class was investigative reporting. Afterward, Dr. Griffin followed her into the hall. "Hey there, did you get my message?"

"What message?" Anne said, feigning ignorance.

"I think you should do a story about sexual assault on campus. There have been at least three reports this semester, but the campus police have kept them low-key."

Anne perked up. "Really? I've only heard about one."

"I read an article saying there are thousands of unreported rapes on college campuses. And the police often don't fully investigate the ones that are reported."

"Wow! I want to hear more, but I've got another class right now."

"How about I tell you what I know over pizza and beer tonight? I'll meet you at Nick's Bar at five-thirty."

Anne mumbled, "Okay," and then hurried down the hall. The chance to write an investigative piece about an important topic intrigued her. *The Tiger staff should be checking campus police reports every week.*

When she returned to the dorm after her last class, her roommate had her meal ticket in hand. "Ready to go to the cafeteria?"

"No, got some stuff to do for the paper. Go ahead without me."

Anne walked downtown to Nick's. Even though it was still light outside, the bar was dark and almost empty. *I'm glad Dr. Griffin didn't suggest Sloan Street. If my friends saw us, they'd make a big deal out of it.* Her professor stood and waved to her from a back booth, a pitcher of beer and mugs already on the table. His Texas A&M tee shirt was tucked into a pair of tight jeans and that leather belt with the big, silver buckle. "I was beginning to think you were going to stand me up."

"Nope."

He filled her frosty mug. "For my beer-drinking friend." He lifted his glass for a toast.

"Thanks," she said, feeling uncomfortable that he'd bought her a beer. "So what do you know about these sexual assaults?" she asked, trying to sound business-like.

"A colleague said that late one night a couple of weeks ago a girl was walking near faculty housing. These two guys in a Camaro stopped, offered her a ride, and said they knew her roommate. She got in, but they drove to Lake Hartwell instead of taking her home. One of them raped her while the other one watched."

"Oh god. That's awful." Anne covered her mouth with her hand.

"Somehow she ended up on a bench in front of her dorm."

"Did the city police get involved or just campus police?"

"I think it was handled by campus police, but she wasn't able to give a good description because she didn't remember much. She thinks they put something in a drink they gave her in the car."

Like a good reporter, Anne pulled out a pen and small notebook from her pocketbook. "Do you have any names or the date of the incident?"

"No, but you can find out. You're the investigative reporter." Dr. Griffin poured himself another beer. "What kind of pizza you want?"

"Uh, pepperoni and mushroom. No, just pepperoni, but I want some fried mushrooms. They're the best."

Dr. Griffin walked to the bar and placed the order. Back at the booth, he took a swig of beer. "So I see you hanging around with *The Tiger* editor a lot. Y'all dating?"

Anne blushed. "Um, no. Just friends. Can I talk to your friend who knows about the rape?"

"I don't think she'd feel comfortable talking to you because it's mostly hearsay. But I'll ask her."

"Okay, thanks."

"So, Anne, surely a cute coed like you has a main squeeze?"

Why is he getting so personal? Nick brought their pizza and a basket of steaming fried mushrooms. Relieved by the distraction, Anne pulled out a ten-dollar bill from her jeans. "Before I forget, here's money for the food."

"Nope, this is my treat," Dr. Griffin said, patting her hand. "I needed a beer and some good company after today's brutal faculty senate meeting."

Oh shit. Why did he touch my clammy hand? Putting both hands in her lap, Anne asked him about his time as a reporter. His eyes lit up as he chatted non-stop while she ate pizza. Then he sighed. "But I got too old for the crazy hours and pauper's salary, so I went back to Texas A&M and got my doctorate. Taught at a small college in Texas and then got this job at Clemson. My wife didn't want to move here though."

"Oh, what does she do?"

"Well, these days she mainly bitches about me," he laughed. "We're separated."

"Oh." *So Kevin was right. Interesting. Why do I even care?*

"She's visiting family in Texas right now and probably comparing notes with my first wife." He reached for another slice of pizza.

God, he's been married twice? Is he some kind of alcoholic or wife abuser? After they finished the beers and food, Anne said, "I have to go. I need to read some British Lit before tomorrow."

"I prefer American literature–Whitman, Flannery O'Connor, Robert Frost. What about you?" Dr. Griffin asked, his blue eyes twinkling.

"I like Flannery O'Connor, too. Macabre and fascinating." *At least he's not treating me like a kid. He sees me as an investigative reporter and discusses his favorite authors with me. I've always liked hanging around with older people.*

After he paid the tab, he opened the door for her. The rush of crisp air was refreshing. She'd felt a little claustrophobic inside the bar.

"I'll give you a ride," he said, pointing to his truck.

"Oh no. It's a short walk."

"I insist."

"Um, okay. Bennet Dorm."

"Yeah, I know." He opened the passenger door and grabbed her arm to help her up into the truck.

Dang. He does know where I live.

"What kind of music do you like, Annie?"

"Anything except disco. Not really into jazz either." She scooted closer to the passenger door.

He cranked up the truck and turned the radio to a country station. From her perch, Anne looked at the students milling around the sidewalk. They looked so young and immature. *Or maybe I'm the naive one. Why did I get in the truck with him? Oh my God, what if he takes me somewhere and rapes me like that story he just told me?*

He drove to her dorm and stopped. As she reached for the door handle, he leaned across the seat and squeezed her thigh. "Thanks for keeping me company. The day started off crummy but ended up fun, thanks to you." His eyes were glassy.

"Thanks for the pizza, mushrooms, and beer." Anne jumped out of the truck.

"Sure thing, kid."

Why did he call me a kid? And touch my leg? She crossed the street without looking and almost got sideswiped by a guy whizzing by on his 10-speed bike.

* * *

Enough of this trip down memory lane! I haven't thought about this crap with Dr. Griffin in years. Anne slams the thick yearbook shut and when she plunks it on the end table, it knocks over her glass of tea. *Dammit!* She leaps up and grabs paper towels to mop up the mess.

Jon walks in. "Hey, you okay? You look like you've seen a ghost."

"No, just deep in thought." She's not sure why, but she'd never told him about Dr. Griffin. "How was your day?"

"Pretty good." Jon pours himself a glass of water and opens the refrigerator. "What you want for supper?"

"Oh, I dunno. I'm not very hungry. You want a sandwich? We have turkey and cheese."

"I'll fix something later. I need to burn off some stress. Think I'll cut the grass."

"Okay." Anne can't stop thinking about Dr. Griffin. Remembering how she felt about Dr. Griffin reminds her of how Jeffrey acted on the Chicago trip. *At first, I thought I was imagining things, but Jeffrey sure seemed uncomfortable. And Devin and Harold were flirting with each other. What the hell?* Anne pulls out a package of Oreos but remembers her goal to lose ten pounds and returns them to the cupboard.

She calls her sister Maggie, always a good listener. She tells her about the invitation to the Clemson reunion and shares her concern about Jeffrey and Devin.

"That boss of yours is a piece of work. I still can't get over him staying in the same hotel room with two guys. That's just creepy."

"I know. I swear he and Devin seemed like a couple. Meanwhile, Harold's criticizing everything I do."

"Sweetie, I feel so bad for you. Why don't you and Jon come over tomorrow night? I'll cook a pot roast."

"Yum, my favorite comfort food. Maggie, you're the best sistuh ever!" Anne clicks off the phone, pulls out the Oreos again, and gobbles three.

Chapter 19

As soon as she walks into her office the next morning, Anne's phone rings. It's Terry Taylor, the chief investigator for the D.A.'s office. "Hey, Anne. We've got a big problem. Harold's received a letter from the police department saying we owe them $36,000 for hiring Jeffrey."

"What?" Anne thinks she's heard him wrong so turns up the volume on her phone.

"Apparently there's a Georgia law saying a department that hires a law enforcement officer within fifteen months after their mandatory training must reimburse the agency that paid for the training."

"Oh, good grief. I didn't know that."

"Figured you didn't. I had to look it up myself. I guess the intent is to prevent the police from bearing the burden of all the initial costs—training, uniforms, that kinda thing—if an officer leaves right away. One-half of the training, including salary, has to be reimbursed."

"Where will that money come from?" Anne slides her pocketbook into a big desk drawer and pushes it closed with her knee.

"I don't know."

Anne sighs. "Good lord in heaven."

"Jeffrey only worked six months at Metro Police before we hired him."

"I told Harold repeatedly I wasn't familiar with hiring cops."

"I'll give you a copy of the law so you can read it yourself. One of my buddies at Metro told me about it. The boss hasn't told you he got a letter from the police chief?"

"Nope. I'll see him in a little while when we go to a budget meeting together. Maybe he'll tell me then."

"Okay, sorry to start your day with bad news."

"Not your fault. Talk later." She reviews her budget proposal, trying to anticipate any questions the finance staff may have. After a few minutes, she senses someone is nearby and looks up to see Harold standing just outside her door.

"You ready?" he asks.

"Yes." Anne slips her file into her briefcase. They make small talk as they walk the four blocks to the county administrative building and wave at three ladies in Sunday dresses sitting on a bench, offering religious tracts and smiles. Harold points at the engraved plaque on a big rock in one corner of Wright Square. "It's a shame Tomochichi only gets a little plaque. He helped establish the colony of Georgia. "

"I know," Anne says. "I think the Talmadge Bridge should be renamed in honor of him rather than racist Eugene Talmadge. Native Americans get slighted. Let's face it. General Oglethorpe is credited for founding Georgia, but he would have had a rough time without the help of Tomochichi."

Inside the stately granite building on Bull Street, Harold says, "Let's take the stairs instead of the elevator. I've been working so late I don't go to the gym much."

"Sure." Anne can't picture him at the gym. He doesn't have the build of a weightlifter or gym rat. He's actually kind of scrawny.

After the meeting, they walk back to the judicial courthouse. Anne wonders why Harold hasn't mentioned the letter from the police, but her confusion is par for the course these days.

As they reach the courthouse sidewalk, Harold says nonchalantly, "Anne, the police think we owe them money for hiring Jeffrey."

Determined to be cool and collected, Anne says, "Really?"

"Yes. The chief claims we owe them $36,000 because Jeffrey had only worked for them for a short time before we hired him."

"You've got to be kidding me." Anne looks at Harold's matter-of-fact expression. *He's going to drop this bomb on me and just leave it at that?* Anne bites her lower lip.

In the lobby, Anne places her briefcase on the scanner. Harold puts his keys in the blue plastic bowl and walks through. At least he doesn't complain. She's heard him say he shouldn't have to be screened because he's the D.A. But he wants the police to be escorted into his office? Of course, his complaints made him unpopular with the security staff. One of the gentlemen flashes Anne a big smile. "Kinda hot out there today, isn't it?"

"Sure is." She picks up her briefcase off the end of the moving belt. "Harold, what are we going to do about that letter from the chief?"

"Oh I'm not going to worry about it," Harold says as they get on the elevator.

Since they're alone on the elevator, Anne persists. "Well, I'm worried. Jeffrey is my employee."

The elevator door opens, and they step out. Before parting ways, Anne tries again. "Harold, this is going to make me lose sleep. What's the plan?"

"Oh, I'm sure you have a spare $36,000 in your budget." Harold grins before strolling through the double doors into the D.A.'s office.

Anne stands in the middle of the hall, trying to comprehend this bizarre conversation. Her face, even her neck, feels hot. *He's making this my problem when he's the one who insisted on hiring Jeffrey.* She feels like Alice in Wonderland tumbling down the rabbit hole. Everything is getting "curiouser and curiouser."

An assistant prosecutor sees her standing there looking like a lost witness. "Anne, you look befuddled. Do I need to remind you where your office is?"

"Very funny," she says, attempting a smile. Instead of walking to her office, she goes to the end of the hall with the big glass windows to collect her thoughts. The Savannah College of Art and Design student union is across the street. She's fascinated by the two-story, red brick building with both the Star of David and a cross on its top. She'd read that the building was designed in 1909 for Congregation B'nai B'rith Jacob's first synagogue. Later it became the St. Andrews Independent Episcopal Church until its congregation dwindled, and they sold it to SCAD. She watches students unlock their bikes from the rack. A blue coat motions and hollers at a driver going the wrong way on Montgomery Street. A tourist, no doubt.

Anne heads back to her office and finds the copy of the statute Terry had left on her desk. After reading it twice, she realizes his interpretation was correct. *Oh good grief. What happens next?*

She frantically rifles through her file cabinet for a copy of the personnel action form requesting to hire Jeffrey. Harold's signature is nowhere to be found, just hers, which is standard procedure because Jeffrey works in her department. *Great, so the responsibility is on my shoulders, and the police chief will demand the $36,000 from my budget.* She grimaces. *That's the salary for one of my advocates.*

Anne recalls how their Chicago colleagues questioned the need for an investigator. Jeffrey's role is to go to the home or school of the young victims. But Devin and LaShay do that. Harold said the investigator was for home visits in "rough" neighborhoods. Anne surmised the investigator would escort Devin or LaShay. No wonder Jeffrey is confused about his position. Harold doesn't supervise him. LaShay and Terry do, but right from the start, Harold inserted himself in the chain of command,

She returns Jeffrey's file to the drawer and sighs. *New day, new dilemma.*

Two weeks after moving back home from his parents' house, Bernie pops a cork and pours champagne into two glasses. "A toast to Charisse, my beautiful AND smart wife who just got a full nursing scholarship to Savannah Tech!"

"Thanks, babe!" Standing in the kitchen, they clink glasses.

"I'm so proud of you. You're gonna kick ass!"

"I don't know about that, but I'll work hard. I've always dreamed of being a nurse."

"Charisse, we've been through some rough times, and that's all my fault. At first, I was only going to counseling 'cause my commander ordered me to, but I've learned a lot. I swear I'm gonna be the best husband and dad in all of Savannah."

Charisse takes his hand. "I never wanted our family to break up, and I believe you've really changed this time."

"I'm glad you gave me another chance. I did a lot of thinking the last couple of months at my parents' house." He wraps his muscular, tattooed arms around her tiny waist, leans down, and kisses the top of her head. "God, I missed you and the kids. Y'all are my world."

"I missed you too," Charisse whispers. "Speaking of kids, I better make sure they're asleep."

"Okay. I'll put the steaks on the grill and grab a beer. I'm not a champagne kinda guy."

Charisse returns and joins her husband on the small patio. "Both are sound asleep like little angels." Easing into an Adirondack chair, she sips her champagne and watches him grill. *Life is good. I'm going to school, Bernie's home, and he still loves me.*

"You want grilled onions?" Bernie asks.

"Nah, but I'll make us a salad."

"I already did. It's in the fridge."

"Dang, Bernie. They teach you that in counseling too?"

He winks at his wife. "Told you I learned a lot." As he flips the steaks, tantalizing smoke wafts around them. "Tell me that's not one of the best smells known to man."

Charisse lights a candle at the kitchen table as Bernie brings in the ribeyes. They don't talk much, enjoying a rare peaceful meal without toddlers underfoot.

Charisse takes her last bite of steak and puts her hand on top of his. "I appreciate your daddy agreeing to pay for daycare while I go to school."

Bernie pops the top on another Budweiser. "I bet he'll help out more if we need it."

"Actually, my car's been acting up. Hopefully, we can afford to get it fixed."

"Aw, that sucks. I'll get somebody to look at it this week."

Charisse nods and takes a deep breath. "Bernie, I hate to bring it up, but your trial is coming soon. You know I'm not going to testify against you. I hope the D.A. drops the charges."

Bernie cracks his knuckles. "Goddamn it, Charisse, we were having a fine evening. Why did you have to bring up that crap?"

"Oh, babe, I'm sorry. I just know we're both worried. Your attorney is trying to get a good plea deal. It'll be okay."

Bernie stands and slams his beer can on the table. "Subject closed!" He marches to the corner of the living room, lifts the barbell, grunts, and does a few bicep curls.

Knowing he doesn't like dirty plates left on the table, Charisse removes the dishes and rinses them in the sink. *What is wrong with me? Why do I ruin everything?* Hands trembling, she tosses the empty beer cans in the trash and wipes the table. When he drops the barbell on the floor with a loud thud, she jumps. He walks across the room and stares at the framed photos on the wall near the front door. After a minute, he removes one of a grinning Bernie Jr. perched on his shoulders at the beach. Taking a deep breath, he walks over to Charisse who's standing still as a statue.

He points to the photo. "Look, babe, I remember that day at Tybee like it was yesterday. We played in the tidal pool for probably three hours straight, then got ice cream at The Sugar Shack."

"Uh-huh."

"This little dude needs me, right?"

"Of course. And your daughter too."

"Alana's gonna be one soon and hardly even knows her daddy." He lowers his head. "I got a lot of time to make up to her."

Charisse relaxes her shoulders.

Bernie takes both her hands in his. "You believe me when I say I'm not fucking up again, don't you?"

She looks up at her husband, the father of her children, her first and only love. "Yes, Bernie. Yes, I do," she whispers as he grips her hands tighter.

Chapter 21

On a rainy Saturday morning, Anne flips on the light in her walk-in closet and stares at the mess. Unlike Jon's, her closet has shoes, coat hangers, clothes, and socks strewn all over the floor. Every January, she resolves to be more organized, but the vow's forgotten after a month. Hands on hips, she takes stock of the clothes squished together on the rods. *I need order in my life and this closet, but where to start?* She climbs on a step stool to reach the top shelf and, one by one, pulls boxes down.

She sits cross-legged on the carpet, and Little Kitty stretches out beside her. The dust she's already stirred up makes her sneeze. A "De-Clutter Your Life" article in *Real Simple* magazine said to create three piles: Toss, Save, and Maybe. Don't be sentimental. If you haven't used it in a year, get rid of it. *Okay, this sentimental packrat better get busy.*

She rifles through a box of notebooks and papers she wrote for her master's program in public administration a few years before. Into the "toss" pile they go. With a full-time job, it hadn't been easy, but she did it. One of her most important lessons didn't come from the evening lectures or mountains of reading material. It came from a project with a fellow student.

When the professor announced they'd pair up for a research project, a freckle-faced fellow who looked like a teenager walked over to her. "Hey, Ms. Gardner, I'm Rusty McIver. but everybody calls me Coach. I'd like to be your research partner."

She'd heard he was an assistant football coach at Savannah State University and had played linebacker at a small college in Virginia. His muscular neck was almost as wide as his shoulders. Caught off guard by his request, she mumbled, "Okay." He seemed nice, but she'd been hoping to partner with an older student, one experienced in the real work world. *Why did that kid choose me? I hope he doesn't think I'll do all the work.* Still, she agreed to meet him at the college library on Saturday morning.

Wearing athletic shorts and an orange tee shirt about the color of his hair, Coach showed up at the library with a broad grin and eager attitude. He agreed to her suggestion for the topic, "The Media's Influence on Crime Victims." They met weekly for the rest of the semester.

He did the statistics and Anne focused on the writing. After a couple of weeks, she realized they made a good team and her first impression of him being a dumb jock had been wrong. He was studious, mature, and dedicated.

Once when Anne met Coach for a study session in the community room of his dorm–he was the resident assistant for undergrad athletes–she felt as out of place as a rabbi at a Jehovah's Witness meeting. The guys walking past them chuckled and high-fived Coach. One teased him, "Coach, we didn't know you went for older chicks." They all laughed, so Anne did too.

Coach said, "You fools get outta here. We're trying to study."

The night before their final presentation, he called to remind her to dress professionally which Anne found endearing. They aced the research paper and hugged on the last night of class. She hoped they'd have another class together, but he finished his master's degree the next semester, got married, and moved back to Virginia.

* * *

Peering into a big shopping bag that had been shoved in the back of the closet, Anne discovers a collection of caps and hats, including a blue and green baseball cap from a Bahamas cruise. The glossy brochures with pictures of sunny skies, white beaches, and clear waters had enticed them to book a trip.

But what a disappointment! A tropical storm with pounding rain and heavy winds rocked the ship, making her nauseous. The ship was filled with silver-haired retirees, starry-eyed honeymooners, sunburned men with big bellies, and high school seniors who couldn't hold their liquor. Anne dubbed the Carnival Cruise ship a "floating Wal-

Mart." *Another example of things not being what they seem.* She puts all the caps and hats in the toss pile.

In a small box covered in pink hearts, she finds love letters from Jon and a note her mama had written in shaky handwriting after her daddy's sudden death. "Don't worry. I'm fine. All this love is sustaining me. Love, Mama." Anne's eyes well up as a stray marble rolls out from underneath the box. She leans against the wall, remembering something she hadn't thought about in years. When she was eight, she was playing marbles on the back porch when her daddy came in from cutting the grass. She tugged on his pants. "Daddy, what are these swirly things inside this marble? This blue part looks like the sky, and the white is like fluffy clouds. I want to see the middle. Is it soft inside like clouds?"

"You asked me that last week. Let's find out. Follow me." Her dad got a hand saw and vise from the shed. Clutching the marble, Anne followed him to the long cement block on top of two wooden saw horses. With wide-eyed Anne at his side, he placed the marble in the vice and sliced the marble in half. But the inside wasn't soft like clouds after all. She was as sad as when Maggie told her the Easter Bunny wasn't real.

It strikes Anne that people aren't always as they appear. Her boss, who she'd considered a friend and upstanding person, belittles her and others at staff meetings, and, even worse, is making inappropriate advances on young men who work for him. The thought makes her stomach hurt.

Wonder what Daddy would say about my work dilemma? A calm man of few words, he'd been the rock of the family. If one of the four grown children did something he didn't like–date a jerk, buy a way too-expensive car, grow a scraggly beard–his response was, "Well if I had my druthers...but I don't. It'll all work out." He died of a heart attack at age seventy-two, leaving the family devastated.

She was blessed to come from a solid family who provided unconditional love. She hadn't appreciated that until she worked at

Victim-Witness and met many dysfunctional families or heard friends describe painful childhoods with addicted, abusive, or absent parents.

Her next find is the photo album from her parents' 50th wedding anniversary party. About a hundred friends and family members gathered at the church fellowship hall to celebrate the milestone. She looks at the family photo and thinks about how drastically their family has changed. She and one brother are no longer married to their spouses in the picture. Someone once told her you should always put spouses at the end of family photos so it's easy to crop them out.

Anne uses a coat hanger to pry more boxes down from the closet shelf. She pokes something on the far back corner of the shelf. She wiggles the coat hanger at a different angle and a dusting of white powder rains on her head. *What the hell?* It's a box of Arm and Hammer baking soda she put up there Lord-knows-when to keep the closet smelling fresh. A snowy mist covers her, the clothes, the cat, and the floor. Little Kitty's black nose looks like it's been dipped in powdered sugar. "Just frigging great! Now I'm going to have to wash or dry clean all these clothes.". Anne storms out of the closet and into the kitchen for a drink of water. She wipes off her tee shirt and shorts with a dish towel.

"How's it going?" Jon asks.

"Awful. Like my work life." She returns to her task and plops back down on the dirty closet floor. She hears a tap, tap, tap. *Is someone at the door to sell me something? Or maybe save my soul? Either way, Jon can deal with it.* She winces when she tries to stand because her legs are cramped from sitting cross-legged for so long. She realizes the tapping sound's coming from the backyard and peers through the window blinds. A red-headed woodpecker is pecking on the bark of a tall pine tree. Admiring the regal bird for his persistence, Anne wonders if he ever gets tired. *Does all that pounding hurt his beak? Or make him feel powerful? It must take a lot of pecking to find food and establish his territory. I sure don't feel powerful these days.*

She gets a red cowboy hat from the toss pile and puts it on. *Maybe I'll become one of those little old red-hat ladies. Or buy a motorcycle or get a tattoo. I'm tired of being the good girl who does what everybody expects.* She looks at herself in the mirror. *Dammit! I'm gonna be strong like that red-headed woodpecker.* She tosses the hat in the save pile and grins.

Chapter 22

Jeffrey paces in the small VIP office he shares with Devin and LaShay at the hospital. As soon as she hangs up the phone, he tells LaShay, "I can't believe this. Mr. Carter wants me to drive him to Valdosta tomorrow."

"What? Why?"

"To take him to Devin's grandma's funeral."

LaShay scrunches up her face. "Say what?"

"Yes ma'am, that's what he said." Jeffrey shakes his head in disbelief.

"Devin is a new employee, and Harold doesn't even know his grandma. Why would he go to that funeral?"

"I don't know. I mean, maybe he and Devin are close, but why do I have to go?"

"There are a lot of things I don't get about Harold," LaShay says, drumming her fingers on the desk. "Why in the world can't he drive himself? He's not the President, for heaven's sake." She sighs. "Sorry. Inappropriate for me to criticize the boss."

"Look, you'll go with us, right? I mean there are three of us VIP employees–me, you, and Devin. You should go pay your respects too,"

"I have to take the twins to the dentist in the morning, and I've got meetings here all afternoon. Besides, someone has to staff the office."

Looking defeated, Jeffrey plops in the chair. "So I have to drive Mr. Carter across the state by myself?"

"Well, he is the big boss. You'll survive."

A hospital social worker appears at the door. "We have a seventeen-year-old gunshot victim in the E.R. His mama needs support."

"Sure. We'll be glad to help," LaShay says. "What's the name?"

"Here's the intake sheet."

LaShay gets her clipboard, grabs a box of Kleenex, and follows the social worker. The E.R. waiting area is crowded with distraught people, most watching Oprah on the big TV anchored to the wall. A crying toddler chews on a *People* magazine. LaShay waves at Anne's friend, Lisa, talking with another nurse.

The social worker points to a woman sobbing into a cell phone. "That's her."

"My baby, my baby. Lord help me Jesus!" she wails. LaShay walks over and introduces herself.

After an hour of calming the victim and answering her questions, LaShay returns to the office. Jeffrey's on the phone. "Yes, sir. Okay, 7 a.m. I'll be there. Bye."

"Getting your taxi service ready?" LaShay asks.

"Aw man, I don't want to go. You sure you can't come?"

"I wasn't invited. You can handle it."

"Guess I'll go gas up the county car. Seems wrong to be taking this trip on the county taxpayers' dime." He lets out a long sigh. "How's the shooting victim?"

"He's going to make it. Shot in the hip," LaShay says, typing on her laptop. "We'll follow up next week to see how he's doing."

Jeffrey retrieves his cell phone from his desk and slips it into the back pocket of his khaki pants. "Okay, I guess I'll see you Friday."

"Good luck."

"Yes, ma'am, I'll need it. I sure didn't know driving the boss to a funeral was in my job description." He trudges out, closing the door behind him.

After gassing up the car, Jeffrey drives to his girlfriend's house. Kiara is the pretty 22-year-old daughter of the senior pastor at a big church Jeffrey and Harold attend.

Jeffrey tells her about his assignment for the next day. "I can't believe I'm spending the day with my big boss. The guy creeps me out. I mean after that Chicago trip..." His voice trails off.

"I know Daddy doesn't think so, but Harold Carter is a weird dude," Kiara says. "I mean, texting you all the time, asking you to lunch. Not cool."

"The worst was having to stay in the same friggin' hotel room with him in Chicago." Jeffrey pops a rubber band on his wrist. "At least this isn't an overnight trip, but why can't he drive himself?"

"Babe, I have no clue."

"I better get home. Got to get up super early tomorrow. See you later."

Kiara leans forward to kiss her boyfriend on the mouth, but Jeffrey pulls back and kisses her cheek instead. She rolls her eyes, mumbling, "Might as well get kissed by an old lady at church."

***

At ten to seven the next morning, Jeffrey pulls the Crown Vic up to the guard house at The Landings.

"Good morning," the guard says.

"I'm Jeffrey Williams, here to see Mr. Harold Carter," Jeffrey says through the window.

Looking at his clipboard, the guard says, "Mr. Carter's expecting you. Here's your pass." As Jeffrey places the visitor placard on the dashboard, the guard says, "You know where to go, right? You've been here before?"

"No, sir. I've never been here."

"Oh, it must have been someone else. Follow the road to the right about a mile, and you'll see the sign for his street."

"Thanks." *Dang. Someone who looks like me comes to see Harold on the regular? I don't even want to think about that.*

After passing a golf course, Jeffrey pulls into Harold's circular driveway. He cuts off the ignition, takes a deep breath, walks to the front door, and taps the brass knocker.

A smiling Harold opens the door. "Good morning, Jeffrey. Come on in."

"Uh no, that's okay. I'll just wait in the car."

"But I need to print the directions. Come on in."

"I've got the GPS, sir."

Harold opens the door wider, puts his hand on Jeffrey's shoulder, and says, "Come in. It'll just be a minute."

The wall of the spacious front hall is filled with modern artwork. The dark hardwood floors are spotless. Shifting from one foot to the other, Jeffrey puts his hands in his pants pocket and jingles the change. From a family of cops and restaurant workers, he's not used to fancy houses and neighborhoods.

Harold returns from the back of the house, carrying a black leather laptop case.

After they buckle up in the car, Jeffrey drives down the curvy road, passing people jogging and riding golf carts on the paved trail beside the road. After exiting the gate, Jeffrey heads toward I-95 South.

"Glad we're driving this new county car. These Crown Vics are smooth," Harold says.

"Yes, sir, I'm glad I got assigned this one." He turns on the air conditioner to diffuse the scent of Harold's cologne. It's a familiar smell, but he can't place it. "I thought LaShay might come with us, but she couldn't."

"Oh, that's okay. How are things going with her?"

"Fine. Everything is fine." Jeffrey keeps his eyes straight ahead.

After a few minutes of silence, Harold says, "Sometimes I think LaShay isn't always focused on the task at hand. Y'all really need to get VIP up to speed. It's time to have another meeting to discuss lessons learned so far."

"Yes sir." *Doesn't seem right that he's talking about my supervisor.*

"I called Devin last night and told him we were coming."

"Okay."

Harold's cell phone rings. He says, "I'll be out of the office all day but can talk to you about that Monday. Okay, okay. The trial is Monday. Maybe we can talk tonight." He ends the call. "That was Kate. You've met my chief assistant, haven't you? Anyway, she was asking about a murder trial coming up Monday."

"Oh. The one where the guy shot his brother after a fight at a birthday party?"

"Yes, that's the one. Do you want to stop for breakfast?"

"Yeah. I mean yes, sir." Jeffrey fiddles with the CD player.

Near Jesup, they stop at a crowded McDonald's. "What do you want? My treat," Harold says.

"Egg McMuffin and a Powerade."

"Okay. We'll get it to go."

After they climb back in the car. Harold says, "You need to eat TWO Egg McMuffins. We need to fatten you up."

Silence. *Harold is skinnier than I am. Why is he talking about my weight? Not his damn business.*

"What size shirt do you wear anyway?" Harold probes.

"Uh, 14 neck," Jeffrey says, loosening his tie. Perspiration is already trickling from his armpits. Even Axe deodorant won't keep him dry today.

"I know it must be tough working with all those women," Harold says with a smirk. "At least Devin is there. We need more males in victim services."

When Harold gets that look on his face, Jeffrey can't tell if he's smiling or grimacing. Jeffrey clears his throat but doesn't respond.

As Jeffrey merges onto the highway, Harold says, "Tell me what you think about your new job."

"I'm learning. It's interesting so far," Jeffrey says, wondering where this conversation is leading.

"You know I don't much like working with women. Ladies can be so flippant. What about Anne? How are you getting along with her?"

"Okay," Jeffrey says, wishing that LaShay, or anyone for that matter, had taken this trip with them. *Why is he asking about Ms Gardner? Did I make a horrible mistake leaving my Metro Police job? Harold is screwy, and I'm stuck with him all day.*

Harold dabs his mouth with his napkin and sips coffee from the Styrofoam cup, then powers on his laptop.

As they travel west on U.S. 84, Jeffrey's relieved the questions have stopped for a while. His mind wanders from why Harold asked his shirt size to what's happening back at his office.

But Harold starts talking again. "Jeffrey, I noticed you weren't at church Sunday. I missed your guitar playing."

Jeffrey's throat feels as dry as when he did sprints in ninety-five-degree heat during police training. He reaches for the cup of Powerade in the console and takes a swig. "Oh, I couldn't practice last week. I'll be back though." His hand shakes, and he spills a little as he places the cup back in the console. "Shit! Oh, excuse me, sir."

As Harold reaches for his coffee in the console, his hand brushes against Jeffrey's. "You didn't get any on your clothes; you're fine," he says, as he hands Jeffrey a napkin. "You're really good on the guitar. When did you start playing?" Harold peers over his glasses at his young employee.

"When I was thirteen. It's my favorite instrument. I took lessons . . ." His voice trails off as he suddenly remembers where he'd smelled Harold's cologne before. *That's the same cologne Mr. Carl at the Cleveland church wore. I smelled it during guitar lessons. Oh crap.*

"So, Jeffrey, are you still dating Pastor Rob's daughter?"

"Sir?" With his mind still in Cleveland, Jeffrey swerves onto the shoulder before pulling back to his lane.

"Careful now. I was asking if you're still dating Pastor Rob's daughter."

"Yes, Kiara and I still go out," Jeffrey says. His breathing speeds up. *God almighty, he's grilling me. He better not start talking about pleasures of the flesh like Mr. Carl did when I was just a kid!*

Harold grins. "Better be careful. Girls can be trouble. You have a sister, don't you?"

"Yeah, an older sister." *This dude getting into my personal life is pissing me off.* Jeffrey ejects the CD and turns on the radio. "I think there's a good jazz station around here somewhere." He finds it, and Dizzy Gillespie is playing "It's My Way."

"That man can play a horn," Harold says.

"Yeah, my mom has a CD of Dizzy and Stan Getz playing together. It's pretty awesome." As the conversation turns to music, Jeffrey's breathing slows down.

"Speaking of jazz, I have two tickets to the jazz festival next Saturday at the Westin. Would you like to go?"

"Well, uh, I don't think so. I've got to, uh, got to help my mom with an event she's catering Saturday." *God almighty, is he asking me out like on a date?*

"Okay. Maybe another time." Harold checks his cell phone for messages.

Finally, they see the Welcome to Valdosta, Georgia, sign. Jeffrey can't wait to get out of the car. Harold checks his laptop for directions to the church even though the GPS is guiding them. So, he hadn't printed the directions while Jeffrey waited in his house. "Take a right here. We're coming up on Cypress Street where the church is," Harold says.

Damn. There's a sign for Tallahassee. We're almost to Florida, Jeffrey thinks. He turns onto Cypress Street. The Crossing Jordan Baptist Church is on the right. The parking lot is full of cars, including several ones with Valdosta Police emblems on the sides.

Harold says, "You know Devin's dad is a major at the Valdosta Police Department?"

"No, I didn't." Jeffrey parks under a pine tree. They get out of the car and slip on their suit coats despite the oppressive south Georgia humidity.

Standing on the front steps, Devin looks sharp in his black suit, white button-down shirt, and light blue tie. Devin shakes Harold's hand, then Jeffrey's. "Wow. I can't believe y'all came all this way. This means a lot to me."

Devin turns to the older, husky man standing nearby. "Dad, I want you to meet my boss, Mr. Carter, and my co-worker, Jeffrey."

"Pleasure to meet you," Mr. Greene says, shaking their hands. "Thank you for coming today. My son is mighty proud to be working for the District Attorney's Office right out of college."

Inside the crowded church, Jeffrey and Harold sit on a back wooden pew with deep red cushions that match the red carpet. Down front, a middle-aged woman at a grand piano plays "How Great Thou Art" as the Greene family walks down the aisle to two front pews.

The tall, black-robed preacher emerges from a door to the left of the altar and says in a loud, deep voice. "Welcome, friends and family as we celebrate the life of a fine Christian woman who's been called home."

After an hour-long service, pallbearers roll the casket down the aisle, and the family follows. Everyone files slowly out to the piano music of "Shall We Gather at the River?"

Outside, Devin steps away from his family to speak to Harold and Jeffrey again. "Thanks so much for coming. Don't worry about going to the cemetery. It's too hot. But please come by the house. You need a break before you head back to Savannah, and there's tons of food."

Harold nods toward Jeffrey. "Well, we do want to pay our respects. We'll drop by."

Jeffrey clenches his jaw.

Devin points to the program in Harold's hand. "The address is on the back. Folks are already there, so go on and chill out a while."

"Okay, thanks," Harold says. After he and Jeffrey remove their coats and get in the oven-like car, Jeffrey cranks up the a.c. *I can't believe we're going to the house.*

"We're not going to stay long, are we, boss?" Jeffrey asks through gritted teeth. "It's a long drive home."

"No, we won't. But if it gets too late, we'll spend the night at a hotel. My back will be hurting if we drive all the way home tonight," he says nonchalantly. He pulls out his cell phone. "Let me see if I can get us a reservation just in case."

Blood rushes to Jeffrey's face. Between the heat and the thought of spending the night in a motel with Harold again, he worries he might pass out. "Sir, I have to get back. I have to uh...I have something to do early in the morning. I can't stay overnight."

"It's just an idea," Harold says with a slight smile.

Jeffrey fixes his eyes straight ahead at the road, and sweat trickles down his back. He loosens his tie and unbuttons the top button of his shirt. *It's a friggin' insane idea, that's what it is. I drive the man nearly to Florida and now he wants to spend the night in a motel? I can't take this crap anymore!*

Chapter 23

At Devin's family home, women are setting out food on a dining room table already laden with casseroles, fried chicken, pimento cheese sandwiches, and three cakes. One matronly woman says, "Gentlemen, please help yourself. There's plenty."

"Thanks. I'll just have some tea," Harold says. "But I bet Jeffrey wants some food. I was just telling him he needs to fatten up." Harold pats Jeffrey's shoulder.

"Y'all came all the way from Savannah, didn't you?" the woman says. "So nice of you. Let's see." She looks at Harold. "I know you're the district attorney. Is this your son?"

Harold grins. "No ma'am. This is Jeffrey Williams, my employee." Pause. "And traveling companion."

Jeffrey manages a smile, puts food on his plate, heads to the living room sofa, and nibbles. Harold sits beside him. Pretty soon the house fills up with people. Jeffrey tosses his Styrofoam plate in the trash and steps outside for a breath of air. More people there too. Glancing at his watch, he walks back inside. He leans over to Harold, "Boss, isn't it time to get going?"

Harold rises and smooths his tie. "I guess so. I saw Devin come in, so let's tell him farewell." They find Devin in the kitchen. Harold puts his arm around his shoulders. "Devin, we're going to leave now. I tried to talk Jeffrey into spending the night at a hotel here, but my traveling buddy is in a rush."

Devin gives Harold a sideways glance. "I'm sure Jeffrey is eager to get back."

Jeffrey stares at his shoes. "Yeah."

"Thanks for coming," Devin mumbles.

Outside of town, Jeffrey pulls into a Shell station. After pumping gas, he goes to the restroom. As he's washing his hands, the door opens. Harold says, "Why did you leave the door unlocked?"

"I didn't mean to." Jeffrey turns toward the door, but Harold's standing in the doorway with one hand against the door frame.

"Really?" Harold raises one eyebrow and smiles.

Jeffrey ducks under his boss's arm, dashes to the front of the store and paces between the candy aisle and drink coolers. *Dear Lord, get me home and away from this man.* He opens the door to the beer cooler so the cold air can blow on his face. Harold saunters to the car, and Jeffrey reluctantly follows. He grips the steering wheel, his hands still damp because he didn't take time to dry them after Harold startled him.

Back on the two-lane road, Jeffrey turns on the radio. Duke Ellington is singing "Take the A Train." *I wish I was on the A Train. Or anywhere but in this damn car.*

Harold hums along.

Jeffrey hopes his boss can't hear his heart thudding. *Mr. Carter's acting like nothing happened. But I swear he tried to trap me in that bathroom. Or did I imagine it?*

Jeffrey tries to concentrate on the music, counting the beats and listening intently to the horn section. Eventually, his heart returns to normal, and he loosens the grip on the steering wheel.

"Getting tired?" Harold asks. "I saw a sign for a hotel up ahead."

Jeffrey raises his eyebrow. "No. I'm not tired. I have to get home."

"We could take a break tonight and get an early start in the morning."

"No sir. We'll be in Savannah soon."

"Okay, as you please." Harold turns toward Jeffrey. "I really appreciate your driving today."

Jeffrey nods and tries to breathe normally.

As the last pink streaks of the sunset reflect in the rearview mirror, they hear a kerplunk, kerplunk, and the car wobbles.

Harold looks up from his laptop. "Oh dear. Do we have a flat tire?"

Jeffrey swerves to the right shoulder and slams on the brakes, causing him to topple over toward Harold. "Crap. I think so." He jumps out of the car. Sure enough, the back right tire is flat as a pancake. He pops the trunk button. No spare. He stares upward. *Dear God. Is this some kind of cruel joke?*

Jeffrey returns to the car and turns on his cell. "Dammit! No signal out here in the sticks."

Harold pats Jeffrey's thigh. "Don't panic. Looks like we're going to have even more time together."

Chapter 24

Back at the apartment he shares with his brother Dale, Jeffrey heads straight to the CD player and turns on *Boyz II Men.* He removes his tie, shoes, and belt, then collapses on the couch. He texts Kiara. "Hey Babe, I'm finally home from Valdosta."

When she doesn't immediately reply, he goes to the kitchen and roots through the refrigerator, finding two cans of Coke, a half-eaten Subway sandwich, and a carton of Hawaiian punch. *Dang. I thought Dale was going to the grocery store.* He pulls out the punch and pours himself a glass.

He calls his mom. "Hey, mama, I just got home."

"Hey honey, how was it?"

"Pretty awful. Flat tire on the way back."

"Oh no."

"Fortunately, some dude in a pickup came along and gave us one of those small spare tires."

"God bless that good Samaritan!"

"For sure. Mama, you cooking supper?"

"Well, I've got some collards left from last night, and I can fry up some ham and make some cornbread. Does that sound good?"

"Oh, yes ma'am. I'll be right over. You need me to bring anything?"

"Yes. I need a gallon of two percent milk."

"Two percent milk. Gotcha. See you in a few."

Hungry for comfort food, Jeffrey sprints upstairs, and changes into athletic shorts and a Nike tee. He checks himself in the mirror. *I'm gonna eat Mama's cooking because it's good and I'm hungry, not because Mr. Carter said I need to fatten up.*

Driving across town, Jeffrey turns into the parking lot at what the police dubbed the "crack Kroger" on Gwinnett Street, the only grocery store downtown. Its customers include a mix of regular folks, affluent downtowners, SCAD students and, well, crackheads.

The homeless guy pushing a grocery cart in front of the store is a lanky man with yellowed eyes except for his dark pupils. He's drinking something from a bottle in a brown paper bag. Inside, Jeffrey runs into Antonio, an officer he'd worked with at Metro Police. "Hey, man, how goes it?" Antonio says, fist-bumping him.

"Good. What about you? You still at Precinct One?"

"Yep, not working midnights right now, thank God. How's that new job you deserted us for?"

"Not bad. Still learning."

"What's it like working for D.A. Carter? I've seen you with him a few times."

"It's okay. He's kinda weird though."

"Yeah, I hear he's on the down low, likes to surround himself with young men, if you know what I mean. I've heard some stories."

Jeffrey swallows hard and looks around to see if anyone is listening. *Damn. I didn't know there was so much talk about Carter.*

"Why in the world did you leave Metro after only a few months? I mean, that's not right," Antonio says.

"I thought this was a good opportunity. I've got my own county car and everything."

Antonio gives a thumbs up. "Sweet."

"Listen, I gotta go. See you around."

"Take care, man."

Jeffrey heads toward the exit, then remembers he's there to buy milk. He turns around and walks to the dairy section. As soon as he pays and gets in the car, his phone buzzes. A text from Kiara: "Hey Boo, glad you're home. Wanna get pizza?"

"Going to eat @ mama's," he replies.

"U r a mama's boy."

"I'll call you when I get back to apt."

"K."

Jeffrey pulls up to his parents' white two-story house on 38th Street. They moved there from Ohio four years ago. Jeffrey walks inside. "Mama, I'm here!"

Jeffrey finds her in the kitchen and hands her the grocery bag. "Hey Mama, here's your milk."

"Thanks, honey." She reaches inside. "Jeffrey, I specifically said two percent. This is whole milk. I'm trying to get your daddy to watch his weight. Otherwise, he's going to have to buy a new police uniform. His is mighty tight around the middle." Sighing, she slides the milk into the refrigerator.

"Sorry, Ma. Got distracted."

"Well, sit down and let me put this cornbread in the oven. Should be ready in fifteen minutes."

Jeffrey pulls his phone out of his pocket and starts to play Angry Birds, but the ride home from Valdosta crowds his thoughts.

"I declare, you young people sure are attached to those electronics. I don't know who's more addicted, you or your brother. I know that's Mad Birds you're playing. I'd recognize that chirpy music anywhere."

"Angry Birds, Mama, not Mad Birds." Jeffrey swipes the phone screen.

Mrs. Williams uses a wooden spatula to transfer the cornbread mixture from the bowl into a square metal pan. She grabs two potholders from a nail near the stove before sliding the pan into the oven.

"You know, I've had these potholders since you were a kid; I reckon you were eight or nine when you made them at Bible School. Look, you drew a police car on this one. With fabric paint, I guess."

"Uh-huh."

"Put that phone down and tell me about your day." She sits across from him at the kitchen table and gazes at her younger son with a worried look. At 45, Tanya Williams is an attractive woman who has kept her girlish figure. When she's not cooking and serving at Sisters of the New South Restaurant, she sings in the church choir and cooks for all the church potlucks and neighborhood gatherings. Her red velvet cakes are legendary. Her two boys, Jeffrey and Dale, take after her both in appearance and musical ability. The boys' sister, Ayanna, attends nursing school in Augusta and looks like their dad.

"It was a long day," Jeffrey sighs, placing the phone on the kitchen table in front of him. "I dunno, Ma. Mr. Carter freaks me out sometimes."

"Well, he's well respected at church. Didn't you tell us it's a grant-funded position with no guarantee it'll last? Your daddy thinks it was a mistake to take that job since it's not permanent."

"Yes ma'am, but hopefully the grant will get renewed. I know Daddy and Dale are into law enforcement careers, but I wanna do something else. I like the idea of helping youth."

"Well, that's admirable, son. I want you to be happy." She reaches across the table to pat Jeffrey's hand.

Jeffrey's phone vibrates, and he glances down at the screen. "Son of a bitch! A text from Mr. Carter."

"Watch your language, young man." She frowns. "Well, what did he say?"

"He says he left a file in my car and wants me to bring it to him. I hope he doesn't mean to take it to his house. Crap. Spending the entire day with him was enough."

Jeffrey jumps up and sprints to the car. He doesn't even notice the next-door neighbor kids arguing over a little Hot Wheels bike.

"Hey, Jeffrey, wanna play with us?" asks the younger boy. "I can do wheelies. Watch!"

"Not now." Jeffrey unlocks the car and spots the manila, legal-size folder in the back seat. He puts it in the trunk and texts Mr. Carter: *I'll bring it to the office first thing in the morning.*

Jeffrey returns inside to the smell of cornbread and ham frying.

"Where's Daddy?" he asks as his mama dips collards onto a plate.

"He should be along directly. Had to run by church. Being a deacon is more work than he thought."

Jeffrey slathers his cornbread with butter and takes a bite.

"Real good, mama."

"You boys couldn't wait to get your own apartment, but you miss your mama's cooking."

Jeffrey takes a bite of the collards slick with fatback. "Mama, how's Daddy going to lose weight if you keep cooking with grease?"

"I've been cooking like this all my life, and I'm known for my good food. I make healthy eating changes one at a time. Do you like it or not?" She exhales, wipes her hands on her apron, and pours iced tea into the glasses emblazoned with blue Metro Police seals.

Jeffrey checks to see if Mr. Carter replied to his text. Nope. *Oh shit. Did he leave the file on purpose so I'd have to see him?* His hands tremble. When his dad lumbers through the door, Jeffrey's picking at his food.

"Howdy. I sure hope the A.C. is working. Why we wear polyester uniforms in this heat is beyond me." He wipes his brow with the back of his hand and places the day's mail on the counter. He removes his gun holster and loosens his belt. "Hmm, sure smells good in here. I'm starving."

"Pull up a chair, hon," Mrs. Williams says. "Jeffrey was just telling me about his trip to Valdosta."

"No, I wasn't," Jeffrey says, twirling his fork around.

"So son, how'd it go? How's the new job?" his dad asks.

"Okay; it's all okay."

"Well, I know the job title is investigator, but it seems more like social work to me. You went through the police academy and all that training and for what?"

Mrs. Williams clears her throat. "Don't give him a hard time, Sam. He doesn't have to be a policeman if it's not his calling." She glares at her husband with a look that could freeze a puddle on a hot Savannah sidewalk.

"All right, all right. Pass me the collards, son. And eat some yourself. Seems you're getting skinnier every day. You still working out at the gym?"

"I am not getting skinny!" Jeffrey yells, picks up his phone, and darts out the door. The screen door slams behind him. *Mr. Carter, and now Daddy, calling me skinny. Dammit.*

"Good grief. I was just trying to get the boy to eat," Mr. Williams says. "You know I've always thought kids picked on him, called him sissy and rubber band man when he was younger 'cuz he's got no meat on his bones. I'm just trying to help." Mr. Williams pops his knuckles. "Folks at the department been asking me why he left so soon. I don't understand."

"No, you don't understand." Mrs. Williams bites her bottom lip. "He needs to do what he wants. It's hard for young men, especially young Black men, to find themselves." Fingering the potholder, she says, "He's been doing so much better since we left Ohio."

"Yeah. I miss Ohio, but Jeffrey's been thriving in Savannah."

"I know. He's kept up with his music, doing real good playing the guitar in the church band. I thought he was going to quit church altogether after that–well, that so-called youth pastor in Cleveland–put a move on him. Thank the Lord we left. Makes me want to cry just thinking about it." Mrs. Williams puts her face in her hands. "I know I'm supposed to forgive, but it's hard. Lord help me."

"I wanted to slam that stupid-ass pastor into the pews." Her husband pounds his fist on the table. Looking up at his wife, he says in a lower voice, "But that's all in the past. I wish you'd stop bringing it up."

"Fine, just fine!" Mrs. Williams says, her voice quivering. She unties her apron, wads it up, and flings it in the laundry basket near the back door. She stomps upstairs, leaving plates of uneaten food and her husband at the kitchen table.

Mr. Williams throws his hands up in the air and mutters, "I've been home for thirty minutes, and I've already pissed everybody off."

Chapter 25

Jeffrey drives down Montgomery Street early the next morning. He ignores the red "low gas" indicator light so he can get in and out of the courthouse before his boss gets to work. He'd rather be tazed than see the district attorney, but he has to return the file Harold left in his car.

In the county garage, he's relieved the district attorney's reserved space is empty. He parks on a different floor, puts the file under his arm, and walks past a line of people on the sidewalk waiting for the doors to open. He flashes his county employee badge to the security guard outside. Instead of stopping at the snack bar for coffee, he goes to the sixth floor. Kate is unlocking the front door to the D.A.'s office. She has a stack of files in her arms and a big tote bag on her shoulder.

"Hey, Ms. Kate. I have a file here for Mr. Carter."

"Okay, come on in," she says.

"Can I leave this with you?"

"No, just take it to Harold's secretary. I'm meeting witnesses on a case who should be here any minute," she says in that rushed I-have-a-trial-don't-bother-me tone typical for attorneys before big trials.

"Do you need this file?"

Kate glances at the defendant's name on the folder. "Nope, different case." She scurries off in the opposite direction.

Before he can reach the D.A.'s corner office, Jeffrey sees Harold's secretary in the break room. *Sweet!* He walks up and hands her the file like it's a grenade. "Good morning, Brenda. Here's a file for Mr. Carter."

"Okay, thanks." She takes the file and turns to chat with another secretary.

When Jeffrey turns around to leave, Harold's standing right in front of him. Jeffrey's heart starts thumping like a bass drum.

"Well, if it isn't my traveling companion," Harold says with an impish grin. "Did you bring that file?"

"Yes sir. I just gave it to Brenda." Jeffrey attempts to walk past him, but Harold puts a hand on Jeffrey's shoulder.

"Thanks for returning it. I'm glad you're here. Come back to my office." Harold gets a bottle of water from the refrigerator while Jeffrey stands frozen in the middle of the room. *Why in the hell does he want to see me anyway? We just spent all yesterday together.* Jeffrey trails behind Harold like a kid summoned to the principal's office.

"Have a seat," Harold says, motioning to the sofa. He puts his briefcase on the credenza and buzzes Brenda. "Hold my calls please."

"Okay."

Jeffrey perches on the edge of the sofa.

Harold sits on a chair beside the sofa and checks his Blackberry. He looks at Jeffrey. "Thanks for driving me to the funeral yesterday. I think Devin appreciated us being there."

"Yes, sir." Jeffrey stares at a painting on the wall.

"You like that painting?"

"Uh, I dunno."

"I bought it one Sunday afternoon when Omar and I went to an art gallery downtown. It was expensive, but Omar talked me into buying it."

Jeffrey studies the oil painting of an old woman wrapped in a gray and green scarf. Her sad brown eyes seem to stare at him with pity. He mumbles, "Omar?"

"Yes, he was my personal assistant before he got a job in D.C."

"Oh yeah. He was gone before I started." He'd heard people refer to Omar, a muscular young man, as Harold's bodyguard. Rumors were rampant about his relationship with the D.A. and why he left.

"Jeffrey, I may need you to drive me on other out-of-town trips, like to Atlanta. I have a two-day meeting there next week."

Sweat beads form above Jeffrey's lips. *I'm sure hauling the D.A. across the state isn't an allowable expense on the grant that pays my salary. It has nothing to do with helping victims.*

Harold fixes his gaze on Jeffrey and leans closer. "I want to treat you to lunch today as appreciation for driving me yesterday."

"Thanks. But I've got a lot of work to do. Uh, LaShay needs me at the hospital." *How can I get out of this? I could lie and say I have an appointment with a victim.* But instead of saying it, he just swallows hard. His throat is parched.

"Since you can't do lunch, let's run across the street for a quick breakfast. I'm hungry." Harold pulls a granola bar from his coat pocket. "And I don't want this."

"Uh, but..."

Harold pats Jeffrey on the knee. "We'll make it a working meeting. We can discuss VIP."

"But LaShay..." When he slowly gets up from his seat, his legs wobble like a newborn calf.

"No problem. I'll handle LaShay. I'll text her that you'll be in the office by ten. We can't let these women around here control us."

Chapter 26

Per Harold's request, Anne arranged for her interior designer friend Rhonda to meet with him to discuss redecorating the conference room. When Rhonda, the petite, vivacious sixty-year-old, arrives at the office one Friday afternoon, she chats with several staff members. She could strike up a conversation with a fence post. That ability–plus her eye for decor–has made her new business a success. She's agreed to help Harold free of charge. Anne calls Harold to meet them in the conference room.

He arrives a few minutes later and greets Rhonda in the conference room with a smile. "Hello, Rhonda! Good to see you."

"You too, Mister District Attorney!"

Harold hands Rhonda a brochure with paint colors. Rhonda studies the choices. "With all these windows, this room must be sunny all day. You could go with a darker color. Just remember, though, it will look darker with two coats."

Harold follows her as she holds the paint swatches against the wall, and they discuss whether to go with a blue or green. "I think we should replace the carpet too. This looks too institutional," Harold says.

Anne shifts in her seat. *Good grief. What does he want? Persian rugs?*

Rhonda nods. "I suggest muted carpet that blends with the wall color. She holds up a paint swatch. "Harold, you've got good taste. Which color would work best?"

He narrows the paint choices to two shades of blue, then says, "We can think about the carpet another day. What about these blinds? Should we leave them?"

"Definitely. It gets hotter than Hades in here in the afternoon." Rhonda fans herself with the brochure.

Kate walks in and says, "Hi, Rhonda. Sorry to interrupt, but, Harold, I need to talk with you about Marsha's murder trial starting Monday."

Harold peers over his glasses. "Not now."

Kate's eyes glitter with anger. "But Harold, the defense attorney just called Marsha. The defendant may plead guilty; there are some evidentiary problems. But you have to approve the plea first."

Harold turns to Rhonda. "Should the baseboards be white or the same color as the wall?"

Rhonda purses her lips. "White would look nice, but it seems y'all have more important things to talk about. I can come back next week."

Too shocked to utter a word, Anne remains seated at the conference table. *Baseboard color is more important than a murder case? What the holy hell?*

Kate says through gritted teeth, "Harold, we need to let the jury manager know ASAP whether to call in jurors for Monday. And we have to call the victim's family. Marsha and I need to talk with you *now.*"

Anne glances at Kate whose face has turned two shades redder than her auburn hair. *Kate's liable to cuss out Harold right here in front of me, Rhonda, and God himself.*

Harold looks at his Blackberry. "Kate, tell Marsha I'll be there in a few minutes."

Kate spins around, and her high-heeled black pumps click down the hall.

The tension in the room is as thick as early morning fog over the Savannah River. Anne exhales. *If I hadn't been sitting right here, I wouldn't believe it.*

Rhonda says, "All right, Harold. You just give me a call, ya hear? We'll have this place spruced up in no time."

"Thanks, Rhonda. I'll call you."

Rhonda nods. “I better go. I don’t want to get a parking ticket.” She waves goodbye to Harold and walks with Anne back to her office. Rhonda rolls her big blue eyes. “God love a duck, that man is crazy.”

“Yep. Tell me about it.”

Chapter 27

The next week, Anne closes her office door. "Good morning, Jeffrey. What's on your mind?"

Jeffrey clears his throat and sits across from Anne's desk. He'd asked to meet with her to discuss his "situation."

"LaShay said I should talk with you." Long pause. "Ms. Gardner, I'm confused. LaShay is my direct supervisor, and you're her supervisor. Mr. Carter is the big boss." He frowns. "I don't know why Mr. Carter is always calling and asking me to do stuff."

"I know you're used to a strict chain of command at the police department. You're correct that LaShay is who you report to." She turns her head to one side. "What is Mr. Carter asking you to do?"

"Like I had to drive him to a funeral in Valdosta. I didn't know I was supposed to escort him around. That trip was awful."

"How so?" She dreads his answer because LaShay had told her he was upset when he returned.

"He weirded me out the whole day. For one thing, he talked about personal stuff."

"What personal stuff?'

"Said he doesn't like women. He talked about people in the office, asked what I thought about you and LaShay, said he needed to fatten me up, and asked my shirt size."

"Wow. I'm sure that made you uncomfortable." *I need to hear what else he'll say without my leading him.* "Anything else?"

"He wanted to stay at a motel. I mean after Chicago, no way was I gonna do that! I basically begged him for us to go straight home."

Anne's eyes widen. *Harold suggested spending the night in Valdosta?*

"Ms. Gardner, I'm not lying." His words spill out. "We had a flat tire on the way home, and I was scared to death he was gonna insist we stay at a motel. The day after Valdosta, I had to eat breakfast with him. He calls me down to the courthouse sometimes for no good reason. I don't know why 'cause our office is at the hospital."

"Right, and since you've finished your training, you should be at the hospital most of the time."

"Good. Another thing. He texts me after hours."

"About what?"

"To say like good job today or to ask what TV show I'm watching." Jeffrey looks into Anne's eyes. "The main thing is I don't want to go to that conference in California."

Harold had mentioned to Anne a couple of weeks earlier that he, Devin, and Jeffrey could stay in one room in California "to save money." She had done her best to convince him to take LaShay and not the guys, but he hadn't budged. The phone rings. It's Harold. *Oh god, has he been listening outside my door?* "I'll let that go to voice mail," she tells Jeffrey.

When the ringing finally stops, Anne exhales. "Jeffrey, if I have any say in it, you won't have to drive for Mr. Carter. Or go to California," she says, sounding more confident than she feels. "I'll talk with him."

"Thank you so much. I told my mama no way could I go to California. She's worried about me. I've been having stomach problems from stress." Jeffrey pauses, then looks at Anne. "Do you know how I found out about this job opening?"

"No."

"Mr. Carter came to our apartment one morning, and my brother went to the door. I was asleep because I'd worked the midnight shift. My brother woke me up and said some dude he thought was from church wanted to see me."

Anne tries to hide her shock, but she's sure her expression looks like the person in the painting called *The Scream.* "He came to your apartment?"

"Yes ma'am. Mr. Carter told me he was starting this new program and thought I'd be a good fit."

Beyond inappropriate. Anne shudders, picturing Jeffrey—maybe in his underwear— having a conversation with the district attorney. "Had he ever been to your apartment before? How did he know where you lived?"

"I asked him that, but I'm not sure what all he said. I was half asleep. The whole visit freaked me out, although I was pumped about the opportunity. He gave me a job application."

"Really? How did you know Mr. Carter?"

"We go to the same church where I play in the band. I knew he was the district attorney and everything, but I didn't know him personally. I don't even wanna go to church anymore because I don't want to see him."

For the next couple of minutes, there's an awkward silence. Anne waits it out, just like she does with crime victims. Jeffrey opens his mouth as if to say something, then looks down at the floor.

"Anything else you want to tell me, Jeffrey?"

"Yes ma'am. I missed a meeting yesterday called by Investigator Thomas. I'm in trouble, Ms. Gardner."

"Why did you miss the meeting?"

"I'm so stressed. My mind isn't working right. I forgot."

"Things happen, but you can't miss meetings. Try entering them in your phone or whatever helps you remember."

"Okay," he says, staring at the floor. "I gotta tell you, ma'am. I'm real uncomfortable around District Attorney Carter." He jostles his leg. "To be honest, this feels like something that happened to me before." He stops speaking, still looking at the carpet.

"Tell me more, Jeffrey."

"There was this youth pastor in Ohio who started acting like a father figure and, well, uh, well he tried to mess with me." He bites his lip. "I don't want that to happen again," he mumbles. He stands as if the conversation is over, but then sits back down.

Anne has heard dozens of victims talk about sexual abuse, but this is different. This is her employee implying that his boss—and hers—is treating him inappropriately. *Good Lord! I can't believe Jeffrey hasn't resigned.*

Jeffrey leans forward and looks straight at Anne. "I want Mr. Carter to leave me alone. Maybe he thinks he's acting like a mentor or father figure, but I think it's sexual harassment."

The words reverberate in Anne's head. *I need to acknowledge his pain.* "I'm so sorry, Jeffrey." She hesitates before saying, "What would you like me to do?"

"I dunno. Like... uh make it stop. What *can* you do?"

Anne has no idea what to tell him. "I'm not sure, Jeffrey. To be honest, I've never been faced with a situation like this. I'll call Human Resources. Come back in the morning, and I'll update you. Meanwhile, take care of yourself, focus on your work, and tell LaShay or me if there are more problems."

"Thank you, ma'am." He gives her a weak smile before standing and shuffling out the door.

Anne stares out the window at the big cottony clouds drifting across the sky. When she was a kid, she loved naming the shapes they made: Dumbo the Elephant, an angel, or a dog. If only she could return to those carefree days.

Snapping back to reality, she tries to wrap her head around everything Jeffrey told her. *Is he exaggerating? Did I say the right things? What am I going to do now?* Her stomach churns like it did when she rode the roller coaster at Myrtle Beach as a kid.

She pulls out the Chatham County personnel manual and turns to the section labeled "Sexual Harassment - Grievance Procedure." LaShay had told her Jeffrey felt "uncomfortable" around Harold. But to Anne's knowledge, he'd never alleged sexual harassment until today.

Anne underlines this section of the manual:

> If the harasser is a supervisor or superior, the employee may present a written grievance directly to the Human Resources Department within three days of the occurrence. All employees should clearly understand that harassment constitutes failure of personal conduct and is subject

to formal warning and suspension. More serious forms of harassment may result in immediate dismissal for detrimental personal conduct.

She then googles "sexual harassment." After reading several articles, she concludes it's a serious allegation that's hard to prove. She rubs her eyes. *Time for a break.* She goes downstairs to the snack bar and grabs a chicken sandwich and Diet Coke. *Where are the brownies?*

Anne snaps at the snack bar manager. "Charlie, don't tell me you're out of brownies."

"My goodness, Anne, you okay? You're usually so chipper. The brownies are already gone. Here, take a couple of peppermint patties. Maybe they'll make you feel better."

They don't.

Chapter 28

After wolfing down lunch at her desk, Anne goes to the copy room where two staffers are debating who is the best performer on *American Idol.* "Anne, who do you think will win?" one of them asks.

"I haven't been keeping up with it, but I heard one of the finalists is from Savannah." *American Idol* is the last thing on her mind.

She waits until they leave before she hits the copy button. She doesn't want anyone to see she's copying info about sexual harassment.

Back at her desk, she calls H.R. After being told the director is unavailable, she leaves a message for him to call her. "It's very important."

Later that afternoon, Harold appears in her office to "talk about three matters." To Anne's surprise, one of the matters is Jeffrey.

She hasn't had time to figure out how to handle Harold, and now he's in her office. *Dear God! Help me say the right thing. And fast.* She makes a quick decision to frame it as a chain of command issue.

Harold begins, "When I called Jeffrey this morning, he seemed discombobulated. He needs to get it together."

That's the perfect opening for Anne. "As a matter of fact, Jeffrey spoke with me earlier today. He's frustrated because he has too many supervisors–LaShay, the chief investigator, me, you–and he's uncertain about his duties."

Harold gets a deer-in-the-headlights look.

"You have so much on your plate. LaShay and I can handle it from here."

"I want this new program to work," Harold says. "That's why I'm communicating directly with VIP employees."

"But we all need to follow chain of command. Jeffrey's a 22-year-old kid from the police department where they have a strict chain of command."

"I know that," Harold says in a sarcastic tone.

"Jeffrey's confused about his role. Frankly, I'm a bit confused myself. I didn't realize he'd be driving you places. The grant doesn't allow that."

Harold rolls his eyes. "So he complained about going to Valdosta?"

"He said you've also asked him to drive you to Atlanta."

"Yes. He knew all along it was a new position, and the job description would evolve. He was eager to apply."

Anne clears her throat and says in an even tone, "Yes, but didn't you *ask* him to apply?" *I can't believe I said that. He'll deny it.*

To her dismay, he doesn't.

"That's right. I went to his apartment to tell him about the job. He seemed excited about it. I think Jeffrey came to you because he was in trouble for missing a meeting yesterday."

Anne is speechless. *He just admitted he went to Jeffrey's house.*

"Anne, he's scared because he got reprimanded. Jeffrey needs to put on his big boy pants and get his act together. He's acting like a victim."

Anne's eyes widen. *Exactly. He is acting like a victim because he* ***is*** *a victim.* She fans herself with a brochure. "I don't think Jeffrey needs to go on the California trip. He doesn't want to, and it's not necessary."

"What do you mean he doesn't *want* to go? It's not his choice."

"Remember, we discussed this recently. He's already been to Chicago, and it makes more sense for LaShay to go this time. I'm not clear about this trip, anyway. I know you plan to visit the Oakland VIP program, but why are you staying six days?"

"For the National Prosecutors' Association Conference. Jeffrey can help me staff a recruitment booth."

But Jeffrey isn't a prosecutor. I can't justify the expense of him staffing a booth for you when it's not related to his job duties. Anne thinks her head may explode. "No need to spend money sending Jeffrey; you can bring back the information."

"Don't worry," Harold says in a patronizing tone. "You have enough money in your grant. And Jeffrey and I can share a room. If there's one thing my parents taught me, it's how to be frugal."

Anne opens her mouth to speak, but nothing comes out. *Are you out of your ever-loving mind? Your parents taught you to be frugal, so you're going to share a room with a young employee? This is a repeat of Chicago.*

Harold removes his glasses, rubs his eyes, and puts his glasses back on. "And speaking of budgets, you need to get yours on Excel."

Mustering her strength, Anne says in a confident voice, "Okay, I will. But Harold, I think it's best that you not contact Jeffrey directly. If you have a problem or question you can ask me, and I will relay it to LaShay. *I can't believe I just reprimanded my boss. He's so damn calm, and my heart is about to pound out of my chest.*

"Fine. I won't contact him directly, but he better shape up. This could ruin his career. And you don't need to baby him anymore." He glances at his watch and strolls out.

The man is unflappable. Harold had told her he wanted to discuss three matters, but they'd only talked about Jeffrey. That was more than enough.

A few minutes later, an advocate asked Anne's advice about a complicated case. Anne tries to focus but can't. The advocate finally says, "I'll talk to you about this later."

"Okay."

LaShay calls. "Jeffrey's here but real quiet. How was your meeting with him?"

"Toward the end of the conversation, he said he thought Harold's behavior was sexual harassment. I've called H.R. because this is a serious allegation."

"Oh my god! Let me know if there's anything I need to do. And to think I've known Harold for years. He's been to our house for

Christmas parties and Bible study. I never knew he treated employees like this."

"Keep detailed notes about everything and keep me posted. We'll get through this," Anne says, trying to convince herself as much as LaShay.

Since she's spent most of the day dealing with Jeffrey's allegation, Anne's work has piled up. Dealing with financial issues is not her favorite task, but she starts entering budget data into Excel. Thankfully, it doesn't require emotional energy or depend on her for solutions. If she makes a mistake, she can delete it and start over. The figures– income, current expenses, remaining balance–align themselves like soldiers marching across the page in neat little boxes, then magically total in the far right column. The answers are clear and concise, unlike those to the problem Jeffrey had just dumped in her lap.

Chapter 29

That evening, Anne's too antsy to read or watch TV. She joins Jon in the kitchen and asks him if he wants some ice cream.

"No. Too fattening."

"Is that a hint? Are you saying I'm fat? You know I can't resist ice cream, and you're the one who keeps buying it."

"Don't be ridiculous."

She scoops out a big serving of rocky road ice cream, then drowns it in Hershey's syrup. Between bites, she tells Jon about the meeting with Jeffrey and her conversation with Harold.

"Can you believe Harold admitted he drove to Jeffrey's house to tell him about the job opening? It's like the mayor of Savannah showing up here to tell me about a job, all while I'm in my pajamas. Is that weird or am I losing my mind?" Anne takes another bite of ice cream, and syrup drips down her white blouse. She doesn't bother to wipe it off.

"I have never heard of such." Jon shakes his head. "But if my boss told me I had to share a room with him, I'd pay for my own damn room. Grown men just don't sleep in the same room. It's bizarre."

"Bizarre isn't a strong enough word. And now Harold wants Jeffrey to go to California with him. I'll hide Jeffrey in our backyard before I'll let that happen. I've got to protect that boy."

"I know, darlin'. You're trying to do the right thing." He pats her hand.

"Why do you think it's okay for women to share a room but not men? I've stayed in a room with a woman before. Is that sexist?"

Jon shrugs. "I don't know."

After putting her empty ice cream bowl in the dishwasher, she pours herself a glass of Chardonnay, grabs her cell, and heads for the

Adirondack chair on the back patio. Swatting at sand gnats, she calls Maggie who worked for decades in human resources for a large company.

After listening to Anne prattle on, her sister says, "First of all, you march yourself to that H.R. Department first thing in the morning. Be on their doorstep at 8:00 a.m. sharp. Tell them about your conversations with Jeffrey and Harold and ask their advice. Your employee has alleged sexual harassment, and there should be a clear protocol to follow."

"I called H.R., but they never called back."

"That's why you have to go to their office. Another thing, you'd better start documenting every single thing that occurs because you won't be able to remember it all. Take notes every day. I'm serious, Sistuh. You're going to need a record."

"Okay, okay," Anne promises, scribbling notes on the back of an envelope.

"Honey, I'm just telling you this sounds like it's going to be one hell of a mess. At least we're heading to the mountains this weekend where hopefully you can relax. We'll pick you up about one tomorrow. You are taking the afternoon off, aren't you?" Maggie says.

"Oh yeah. See you then. Love you."

"Love you too."

I wonder what Kate will have to say about all this. I could use her insight, and she's Harold's second in command. She punches in Kate's number.

"Kate, you got a minute?"

"Sure, what's up?"

Anne summarizes her conversations with Jeffrey and Harold.

Kate says, "Holy shit, this could be a disaster. I mean sexual harassment accusations against our boss."

"Yeah, tell me about it."

"Anne, you need to be careful. Harold may retaliate against you. You know how he can be nice one day and vengeful the next. Like that time he gave you a flower, then criticized you the next day at the leadership meeting."

"Yeah, LaShay told me she wonders if this is how domestic violence victims feel, always walking on eggshells. Harold keeps us off balance."

"Yep," Kate says.

Anne fishes a sand gnat out of her wine glass. "Ugh! There's a gnat in my wine. Par for the course today," she mumbles and takes another sip anyway.

"Gross. Anne, I'm so sorry for you, Jeffrey, and LaShay. Hell, I feel sorry for all of us. But I guess Harold won't be breathing down my neck for a while. He seems to take turns picking on people. Picking on women I should say. First, it was poor Ellen, that new assistant DA he hired right after taking office. Remember? He treated her like his servant."

"Yep. Then he criticized and micromanaged everything you did. And ever since the Violence Intervention Program started, he's gotten on my case."

"And I thought he liked you, Anne."

"Yeah, so did I. But not lately."

Anne leans her head on the back of the chair. "Kate, why do you think he appointed you chief assistant district attorney and kept me as head of Victim-Witness Assistance? He could have chosen anyone for those positions. I don't understand why he's treating us like we're incompetent."

"I don't know. I'm shocked and just plain sad–that is when I'm not furious." Kate sighs. "I had high hopes and was looking forward to working with him. Remember when we used to go to lunch together? What's happened to him? Was he always like this and we just didn't see it?"

"I can't figure him out." Anne wanders back inside and lies on the couch, the phone still against her ear." I feel a little queasy. Maybe ice cream and wine don't mix."

"We'll talk later, but please keep detailed notes about the Jeffrey drama. This could end up in federal court."

"Federal court?" Anne squeals. "That freaks me out. And Maggie told me the same thing about documenting everything. She said to go in person to H.R. in the morning, but I'll call first." Anne yawns. "I'm exhausted, and I haven't packed for the mountain trip."

"Get some rest, my friend."

"Okay, thanks for listening." Anne clicks off the phone and sees a missed call. It's from Miss Dot, the elderly woman she and Jon take to church every Sunday.

Anne calls her. "Hello, Miss Dot. Sorry I missed your call."

"Hey there. How are you doing, sweetie? How's things at the courthouse?"

"Kinda crazy, but I'm hanging in there."

"Don't let the craziness get the best of you. Life is too short."

"True. I'd appreciate your praying for me about my work situation. I know you've got a direct line to God."

"Of course, I'll pray for you. The good Lord looks out for all of us," Miss Dot says in her shaky voice. "And you know I love you."

"Thank you." Tears well up in Anne's eyes. She's grateful for this kind lady who reminds her there are still good people in the world. "How are you doing, Miss Dot?"

"I'm okay. Still having a time with bad arthritis in my back. Makes it hard to get around, but I manage. I'm 84 years old and thank my loving God every day for waking me up."

"Still doing crossword puzzles?"

"Every day. Listen, one reason I called you was to tell you about my granddaughter. Oh, Anne, she's having a time. That new husband of hers, well, he's not treating her right." Miss Dot's breathing becomes labored. "He can't keep a job, and he shoves her around." She pauses to catch her breath. "He gets real violent when he drinks."

"Oh, Miss Dot, I'm so sorry."

"You know about help for women in these predicaments, don't you?"

"Yes ma'am. The S.A.F.E. Shelter provides a safe place to stay, and they offer free support and counseling even if you're not staying there. I'll give you the number. Do you have a pen?"

"Yes, right here. She might pay me no mind, but at least she'll have the information."

Anne gives her the number.

"I wish she hadn't married that boy," Miss Dot says. "To tell you the truth of the matter, I'd like to stick a bomb up his ass."

Anne can't stifle a giggle. She's never heard Miss Dot talk like that. "I understand, Miss Dot. I feel the same way about a few people."

"Honey, I'm not going to keep you. Always good to hear your voice. Love you and Jon both. And the Lord willing, I'll be sitting on my front porch Sunday waiting for y'all to pick me up for church."

"Yes ma'am. See you then. Love you too." *I can't wait to tell Jon what Miss Dot said. She's got some spunk.*

Anne packs her suitcase, then slides into bed beside Jon who's sound asleep. She ruminates about the day's events and prays silently. "Lord, help me to do the right thing. But for now, Lord, just help me to get some sleep."

Friday morning Anne arrives at work early, calls H.R., and asks for the director. "I need to speak to Mr. Dixon right away."

"Sorry. He's already left for the Memorial Day weekend," his receptionist says.

"I have to talk to someone." Anne's voice cracks." I need to report an allegation of sexual harassment. *This is a huge deal, people. I'm tired of waiting on return calls.*

"Oh, that is important. I'll try to reach Mr. Dixon on his cell."

"Thanks. Please tell him it's urgent. I'll be traveling this afternoon, but I'll have my cell with me at all times. Do you have my cell number?"

"Yes, I do. I'll call Mr. Dixon right away," the receptionist says. "Have a safe holiday weekend, Anne."

"Thanks. You too."

Anne heads to the break room where Jeffrey is pouring himself a cup of coffee. "Hi, Jeffrey, how are you this morning?"

"Okay."

But he seems jumpy. He stirs his coffee so hard it splashes out of his cup. He mops it up with a napkin.

"Jeffrey, I need to talk with you for a minute."

He follows her into her office and remains standing while Anne closes the door behind them.

"Did Investigator Thomas write you up for missing the meeting?" Anne asks.

"Yes ma'am." Jeffrey hangs his head.

"As we discussed yesterday, you have to keep track of meetings."

Jeffrey nods.

"I made you a copy of the personnel manual section that concerns sexual harassment." She hands it to him and says softly, "I need to ask you, has Mr. Carter ever touched you inappropriately?"

Looking at the floor, he shuffles from one foot to the other. "Um, well, um not really."

"Jeffrey, I know this is embarrassing, but you can tell me if he did."

Anne notices Jeffrey's hand trembling, and she's afraid he may spill his coffee again. He mumbles, "No ma'am. He didn't."

"Okay, if you're sure." She pauses a moment. "I'm waiting on a return call from H.R. It's my responsibility to report your allegation."

"Okay, that's fine."

Hmm. I thought he'd be mortified I told anyone. "Also I talked with Mr. Carter, so he shouldn't be calling you directly anymore."

"Good. Thank you, ma'am." Jeffrey looks relieved but then blurts out, "Is Mr. Carter mad about me missing that meeting?"

Dodging the question, Anne says, "We discussed chain of command and how things are going with VIP. Hope you have a good weekend."

"Thanks. You too."

Two hours later, Anne gets a call from Jeffrey. He sounds frantic. "Ms. Gardner, Mr. Carter called and wants to meet with me today. I told him we had a meeting at Savannah State University. He said to come to his office right after that. I guess he's really mad." Jeffrey sounds like a little boy.

Well, son of a bitch. Just yesterday Harold promised me he wouldn't contact Jeffrey. "Meet with Mr. Carter. I don't want you to get in trouble again for missing a meeting."

"Uh, no ma'am. I don't want to."

"I'll tell LaShay to come with you." *Jeffrey probably doesn't trust me after I promised him Harold wouldn't call him. Why in the hell DID Harold call him?*

Beyond furious, Anne kicks over the trash can, spilling its contents onto the carpet. But it doesn't make her feel better. She calls LaShay who says, "Our boss is insane. Didn't he tell you he wouldn't contact Jeffrey?"

"Yes, but now that he has, I don't want to give Harold any reason to reprimand him. LaShay, you need to be with Jeffrey at the courthouse."

"Don't worry. I'll be there for him. Meanwhile, it seems Harold's been calling Devin to ask HIM what's going on with VIP. He should be asking me or you, not my subordinate. I guess Devin and Harold have been having pillow talk."

"LaShay!"

"Well, it's the truth. Devin has mentioned stuff he and Boss Man have discussed. This new program is supposed to focus on victims, but it's impossible with Harold interfering and obsessing about these young hires."

Anne calls H.R. again to see if the receptionist reached Maurice Dixon. Voice mail. *Dammit it to hell. It's already 1:00.*

Jeffrey calls. "I'm on the way to the courthouse now."

"What about LaShay?"

"She's driving over too."

"I'm leaving the office now and will be on the road but call me on my cell if you need me."

"Okay."

After leaving an out-of-office reply on her phone and computer, Anne slings her pocketbook over her shoulder and plasters a smile on her face. “Bye, everybody. Have a fantastic Memorial Day,” she calls out cheerily to her staff as she walks toward the hallway.

The truth is, she’s anything but cheerful. She’s a mess.

Chapter 30

Anne changes into jeans and a tee just before Maggie and Ralph pull into her driveway. Jon's swamped at work and can't go. She leaves a note on the counter reminding him to buy cat food and ends with "See you Monday. Love you."

"I'm ready for some family time," Anne says to her brother-in-law as he lifts her suitcase into the trunk.

Since their parents died, Anne and her three older siblings and their spouses get together at least twice a year. After leaving for college, Anne never had family nearby and was thrilled when Maggie and Ralph retired and bought a house on Wilmington Island, just ten miles from Anne and Jon's Tybee beach cottage.

As they drive up I-95, Anne stretches out in the back and flips through a women's magazine. At 4:00, her cell rings. Jeffrey says, "Ms. Gardner, I'm still waiting to see Mr. Carter."

"What?" Anne sits up straight,

"Yes ma'am. Been here since 2:00. I just ran into my dad in the courthouse." Jeffrey lowers his voice to a whisper. "My dad's really mad Mr. Carter is treating me like this. He said he always knew Mr. Carter was a nutcase."

"Did you remind Mr. Carter's secretary you're still waiting?"

"Yes, ma'am I did. He's in his office. He's playing me for a fool."

"Oh dear." Anne remembers Harold keeping a Superior Court judge, who was there at his request, waiting for forty minutes. She was not amused.

"Is LaShay there with you, Jeffrey?"

"Yes ma'am."

"Good. Try to relax this weekend, Jeffrey."

An hour later, LaShay calls. "I'm driving home now and guess what? Mister District Attorney never did see Jeffrey."

Why would Harold insist Jeffrey come to his office and then not see him? A power play or maybe it was because LaShay was there? "Thankfully, we have a long weekend," Anne tells LaShay. "I hope you can chill out a bit."

She clicks off her phone. *I'm a failure as a supervisor and an advocate. I've been a victim advocate all my adult life, and I can't even help my own employees.* Anne rolls up the magazine and smacks it against the back of Maggie's seat.

Maggie jumps. "Whoa! What's wrong?"

"Unbelievable. Just yesterday, Harold promised me he wouldn't contact Jeffrey, but in less than twenty-four hours he's called him, demanding he go to his office. Then he kept Jeffrey waiting all afternoon and never saw him."

Maggie sticks out her tongue. "That's hateful."

"Meanwhile, H.R. still hasn't called me. This is unreal. More like surreal. I mean I don't know what it is."

"That son of a bitch," Ralph says. "Who's the boss of this Harold Carter anyway?"

"He's elected so his bosses are the voters, the public."

"Well, the public needs to get him out of office," Ralph says.

"I wish it were that simple. He's only eighteen months into a four-year term. The public doesn't know everything that's going on."

"Somebody has to do something," Ralph says as he exits the interstate and pulls into a gas station.

"You got that right. But what?" Anne says. While Ralph fills up, Anne buys a Diet Coke and a Little Debbie oatmeal cream pie, her go-to comfort food in college. Back in the car, she scarfs down the pie and flips through the magazine. *I wish there was an article about dealing with sexual harassment instead of the same old fluff about diets and makeup.*

Ralph takes the exit for Blowing Rock, North Carolina. Homemade signs for "Farmers Market This Saturday" dot the curvy road up the mountain. Black and white cows graze on a grassy hill. A small wooden sign in front of a clapboard church reads, "Jesus Saves!" Anne sighs. *I wish Jesus could save Jeffrey.*

It's dusk when they arrive at Luke and Sharon's cabin. "Hey, baby sisters!" Luke says, wrapping both Anne and Maggie in a bear hug. He helps them take their luggage inside. Anne expected the vacation cabin they recently bought to be rustic, but it has all the comforts of home.

They retreat to the porch, and Sharon brings out a tray of cheese and crackers while Luke uncorks a bottle of wine from a nearby vineyard. Fireflies twinkle in the valley below.

"I haven't seen fireflies in years," Anne says.

"Pesticides are to blame for that," Sharon says.

Anne sighs. "That's sad. I remember when Daddy used to poke holes in mason jar lids for the fireflies we caught."

An hour late, her brother Peter and his wife Deborah arrive from Alabama.

The mountain breeze picks up and the temperature drops. Shivering, Anne pulls her jacket around her shoulders which are starting to relax at last. She leans down to pet Sharon and Luke's beloved Jack Russell terrier, but he scampers away. His soulful brown eyes peer from underneath Sharon's chair.

"You know John Henry is super shy," Sharon says.

"Such a sweet dog," Anne says.

After everyone catches up on family news, it's only 9:30, but Anne is tuckered out. "I'm going to call it a night, y'all," she says. "I'll sleep on the couch." She brushes her teeth and changes into cotton pajamas. She snuggles under a green and brown log cabin quilt, dozes off within minutes, and sleeps better than she has in months.

The next morning Sharon and Deborah go to the farmer's market. The others gather around the kitchen table while Luke flips giant whole-wheat pancakes on the griddle. Spatula in hand, he says, "Anne, give us an update on your work situation."

Recounting the weird events of the last few weeks, Anne chatters like a toddler who's overdosed on Skittles.

"Somebody's got to advise you how to navigate through that quagmire," Luke says.

"I know. I've been trying to reach H.R."

Peter says, "Maggie's the H.R. guru. Maybe she can help."

"I'll do what I can," Maggie says. "I told her to document everything and get direction from her H.R. people. That is if they ever return her call."

Luke puts the pancakes on the table, then rubs Anne's shoulders. "I'm so sorry, Anne. This sucks, and I wish I could help." His life has centered around helping others by fighting legal battles to secure safe working conditions for coal miners, fair housing for low-income tenants, and justice for minorities mistreated by police. Ten years older than Anne, he fixed many of her childhood scraped knees with iodine, a band-aid, and a kiss. If only he could fix the mess she's in now.

Anne says, "Harold's a smart guy, a Harvard graduate. I've thought he might be gay, and I couldn't care less. But he should know better than to harass younger employees."

"He should know better than to harass ANY employees." Luke bangs his fork on the table.

Peter refills the coffee mugs. "Can't the feds or the state get involved?"

Luke says, "There's certainly potential for a harassment allegation under the federal Equal Employment Opportunity Commission."

Anne drizzles syrup on her pancakes. "I feel guilty for agreeing to hire Jeffrey and putting him in this mess. It's turned into a trashy soap opera."

Peter leans over and puts his arm around Anne's shoulder. "Don't blame yourself, Monkey." Ever since Anne was little, her siblings teased her that she was a monkey they'd found in the tree.

Luke asks if Jeffrey has an attorney.

"No, the harassment allegation just came out this week," Anne says.

"Well, he needs one."

The family's reaction validates Anne's feelings that the situation is bonkers. Since working for Harold, she'd started wondering if she was the crazy one.

"Has he always acted this weird?" Peter asks.

"Well, I don't think so. When he got elected, I thought he'd make a great D.A." Anne stares into her tea cup. Her voice softens. "But things have been awful. I haven't felt this upset since Mama died. I'm glad she's not around to see me so stressed."

Maggie looks at her little sister. "Mama used to tell us 'this too shall pass.' Well, it will, honey." The others nod.

"I'm glad we can't get cell phone reception up here," Luke says. "No phone calls for you, Anne."

"I just hope Jeffrey doesn't try to call me."

"You need a break," Luke says.

After breakfast, they hike around the mountain, then stop at the pond below the cabin. After Ralph and Peter catch several trout, they all meander back to the cabin. Sharon and Deborah return and show off their bounty from the farmer's market: strawberries, apples, honey, and fresh loaves of bread. On the porch, Peter strums his guitar and Luke joins him on the harmonica while Maggie and Anne tackle a crossword puzzle.

If only Anne could stay in the mountains with her family forever. *I'll tell Jon we should move here. I could bake apple pies and sell them at the farmer's market. Yes, that's the perfect life.* And then she remembers she's never made an apple pie in her life.

* * *

On Monday morning the family hugs goodbye, promising to see each other at Christmas. Anne gets misty-eyed.

Peter squeezes her extra tight. "Hang in there, Monkey."

Anne stretches her long legs across the back seat as she, Ralph, and Maggie head south.

Do y'all want to stop at that café in Saint George?" Maggie asks a few hours later.

"Oh yeah!" Anne replies.

Ralph parks beside two semis and a police car, always a good indication that there's home cooking. At the buffet, Anne piles macaroni and cheese, lima beans, creamed corn, and a chicken drumstick on her plate. The waitress brings sweet tea.

Sipping her tea, Anne says, "I wish their cabin was closer. I had such a good time. But going back home puts me in a funk again."

"Well, you can't just complain. You have to do something. I know I'm always bossing you around." Maggie says. "But trust me on this. You need to go to the H.R. office in person tomorrow and stand there 'til somebody listens to you. Make a scene if you have to."

They finish lunch and drive home. On Highway 80 close to Tybee, they meet a long line of cars returning from the beach after the holiday weekend. As they step out of the car in Anne's driveway, the humid air feels like a sauna. No more mountain breezes–not even an ocean breeze on Tybee today.

Jon greets them outside, giving Anne a big hug.

"We had the best time. Wish you had come," Anne says, as Jon rolls her suitcase toward their cottage. She crawls into bed at nine. Her stomach churns. Not from the big lunch but from dreading work the next day.

Chapter 31

After a fitful night, Anne is jarred awake by the alarm clock. Scratching her head, she debates going to the Y, then hits the snooze button. When the alarm blares again, she drags herself to the bathroom. In the shower, she prays out loud, "God, help me to do the right thing. I pray for Divine Order. I know you are in charge because I certainly am not." She exhales slowly and feels better.

After toweling off, she slips into her soft, cotton robe. When she peers into the bathroom mirror, she sticks out her tongue. *Oh, my word. I look like hell.* She finds her dark circle eraser in the medicine cabinet and dabs some underneath her eyes. *This damn makeup might work for Ellen DeGeneres but apparently not for me. What a waste of money.*

While she gets dressed, her mind revs into overdrive, reminding her of Fox News political pundits yelling over each other so that you can't understand any of them. Her internal debate makes her head spin. *I used to love my job. But not anymore. It could get better. No way. Not with Harold there. He does act nice sometimes. But I can't take it anymore. I shouldn't give up.*

As soon as she arrives at the courthouse Tuesday, Anne dials H.R. The receptionist says the director will be in a meeting for at least an hour. Anne leaves yet another urgent message. She emails her staff telling them to interrupt her if H.R. calls. *If Maurice Dixon doesn't call by 11:00, I'll walk the four blocks to his office and do what Maggie said: stalk them until someone talks to me.*

At 10:30, Maurice calls. Anne worries Harold might appear in her office while they're talking. "Maurice, hold on one sec. I need to close the door." She closes it and returns to her chair. "I have a serious problem, and I need your advice. What is the protocol when an employee alleges sexual harassment?"

"Is the allegation against a colleague or supervisor?"

"A supervisor," Anne says, annoyed that he seems to have her on speakerphone.

"The employee can submit a written grievance directly to H.R. and can also make an appointment to discuss the matter."

Anne raps her pen on the desk. "I read that in the personnel manual. That's it?"

"For now. Of course, contact me if you have any questions. I'll be glad to help you or the employee."

Thanks for nothing. Anne hangs up the phone, grabs a rubber band, and shoots it across the desk. She begins typing an email to Maggie to tell her she finally talked with the head of H.R. But she stops typing in mid-sentence. A friend who worked for Harold at a previous job was convinced he was reading her emails. Unethical but certainly possible. She deletes the message and calls Jeffrey at the VIP office instead.

"Jeffrey, I talked with Maurice Dixon. I didn't use any names, but I asked him about the procedure for allegations of harassment. He said you could give him a written grievance and make an appointment with him to discuss the matter. It's up to you to decide if you want to do that."

"Okay, then. I will."

Anne is surprised he agrees so quickly. *I bet he has no idea what chain* of *events his accusation may set off. Heck, I don't know myself.*

"How was your weekend?" Anne asks.

"Not good. I didn't go to church. I have a stomach ulcer."

He's so pitiful. I doubt he'll talk to H.R. I shouldn't judge though because I never told anyone about my Clemson professor. "Jeffrey, focus on work today, and let me or LaShay know when you decide to talk to H.R."

"Yes ma'am."

"Is LaShay there? I need to update her."

He transfers her to LaShay, and Anne tells her what's going on.

LaShay speaks softly. "God help us all. I feel terrible for him."

"Me too, but we'll get through this somehow. Call with any updates."

Anne returns to the computer to work on a grant proposal but can't wrap her mind around goals and outcome measurements. She returns some calls, then walks down to Kate's office. Kate's on the phone and gestures for Anne to sit in her comfy visitor chair. Staring out the window, Anne admires the regal spires of St John's Cathedral and the tall Savannah Bank Building, then squints at roofers laying black shingles on top of a Broughton Street store. From her vantage point on the sixth floor, they look like miniature action figures. So do the SCAD students biking to class, rolled-up artwork tucked under their arms.

Kate hangs up and scowls. "Dammit! The police lost the fingerprint files on a burglary case."

"That stinks. Are the girls getting together tonight? It's been a couple of weeks," Anne asks.

"Sounds good to me. Want to come to my house?" She reaches for her red Michael Kors pocketbook and pulls out her lip gloss.

"Good. I'll email the others and pick up pizza."

Kate leans forward and frowns. "You look tired. You okay?"

"Yeah, I guess. Well, not really. Maurice finally returned my call but was basically useless. The entire time I was talking to him I was afraid Harold would show up at my door."

"I'm sorry. Geez, you know this allegation's bound to get out. I'm surprised everyone in the courthouse doesn't know already."

"Yeah, gossip spreads through this place like wildfire." She stands. "I gotta get back to my office." Anne walks down the hall and nearly runs smack into Harold. She nods and tries to rush by him.

Harold turns to face her. "Hey, Miss Anne, why are you in such a hurry?"

"Oh! I have to finish a grant application."

Did he hear me talking to Maurice or Kate? These walls are paper thin. I'm glad I have that meeting at the Children's Advocacy Center today so I can get outta this screwed-up place soon.

The two-story house in midtown is where abused kids are interviewed and receive counseling. Cheerful and child-friendly, the center has a basket of stuffed animals in one corner and pictures of dragons, princesses, and puppies on the yellow walls. On a bookcase, there's a stack of Spider-Man comic books that tell how Spider-Man was abused as a boy. Her long-time friend Carol, the director of the center, holds out a tray of granola bars and bananas. "Want a snack?"

Anne grins. "No thanks. I know you get that stuff from the food bank and keep it way past the expiration date."

They are meeting to revise the child sexual abuse protocol. But Anne stares into the fish tank, mesmerized by the guppies swimming in circles.

"Anne, what do you think about the changes I made on page three?"

"Oh, uh, I'll look at it again. Did you get the email about us going to Kate's tonight?" Anne's cell phone rings. She turns to Carol. "Sorry, but I have to take this."

"Hello." She hears rapid breathing, then Jeffrey talks so fast she can barely understand him.

"Listen, Ms. Gardner, Mr. Carter left me a message. He wants me to come to his office now. It's 4:55 and I'm at the hospital office, and I'm not going downtown. He left me sitting there all Friday afternoon without ever seeing me. That asshole! Excuse me, but it's the truth."

Anne rubs the back of her neck. "Okay, try to calm down. I wonder what he wants." *I shouldn't have told him to calm down. I hate when people say that to me.*

"I have no idea. You told me he wasn't going to call me anymore."

"I know. I'll buzz him to see what he wants. Hang tight."

"No ma'am. I'm leaving at five. No matter what he says, I'm not going to his office."

Anne says goodbye and tosses her cell phone onto the couch. "Damn it. Damn it to hell. I've had it!"

"Anne, what's wrong? Who was that?" Carol asks.

"There are some problems." Anne jiggles her foot.

"What kind of problems?"

"Big ones."

"Anne, tell me about it."

"I could use your professional advice. I'm not going to say names but to make a long story short, someone has alleged sexual harassment against their supervisor."

"Oh gee, that's messy."

"The supervisor has said and done inappropriate things. Keeps calling and texting the victim. The supervisor agreed not to contact the victim again, but now the jerk has demanded to see him again."

"Oh shit." Carol scoots to the edge of her chair.

"Carol, you and I have worked with abuse victims for twenty years, but I can't protect this person. I feel helpless."

"That's a problem for Human Resources."

Anne rolls her eyes. "You would think so."

"Seriously, this is clearly an H.R. issue. I haven't seen you this upset in a long time. I gathered from how stressed you and Kate have been that there were problems, but nothing like this." She reaches into the small refrigerator beside her desk. "Here, have a bottle of water. I wish I had something stronger to offer you."

"I don't know where this will end up, Carol. People probably already know about the allegation. But still, don't mention this to anyone."

"I won't."

Anne retrieves her phone from behind the couch cushions and dials the D.A.'s office, but gets the after-hours recording. "This is the District Attorney's Office. Our offices are closed now but feel free to leave a message, and we will return your call as soon as possible. If this is an emergency, dial 911."

"It *is* a damn emergency!" Anne screams into the phone as the recording starts to repeat itself.

Chapter 32

It was the fall of 1978 when Anne sauntered into *The Tiger* office suite late one afternoon, surprised at how quiet it was. "What's up?" she said to her fellow newspaper staffers.

"Dr. Hinchey's in the hospital!" Roxanne blurted out. The Women's Studies textbook in her lap fell to the floor as she got up from the couch.

"What?" Anne didn't remember their beloved newspaper advisor ever being sick.

"Maybe a stroke," Roxanne said. "Kevin and a couple of others have gone to St Francis Hospital in Greenville. You know he doesn't have family here in Clemson."

"Oh my God! He's only in his late 50s. What happened?"

"We don't know much except an ambulance took him. Kevin said he'd call us the minute he finds anything out." Stunned, Anne tossed her backpack on the big round table and sat down to wait with the others. She tried reading her British Lit assignment but couldn't concentrate. After what seemed like an eternity–but was only an hour–the phone rang and Roxanne answered. After she hung up, she said, "Kevin said Dr. Hinchey did have a stroke but is in stable condition. His sister is on the way from Orangeburg. He asked if we'd feed his pets. The key's under the back doormat."

Two of the guys jumped up to drive to his cabin to tend to Stella the cat and Barney the golden retriever. "Put some food in the bird feeder too," Anne said and handed them Cokes for the road.

Weak but improving, Dr. Hinchey came home three days later. Concerned about his slurred speech, he scheduled speech therapy twice a week. Church members brought him casseroles, books and firewood. "I'm grateful for the help, but I hate being dependent on anyone," he said when Anne called to check on him. "You know I'm a stubborn old mule who's always done everything myself."

"Yes, I know. And you're always doing for others. But once in a while, you need to be able to receive as well as give," Anne told him, sounding like her mama talking to her elderly neighbor. *Hope he's not put off by advice from a nineteen-year-old college kid.*

At *The Tiger* staff meeting the following Sunday night, Kevin said, "Okay guys, Dr. Hinchey's doctor said he needs to take it easy for a while. Dr. Griffin is going to be our adviser for the rest of the semester."

Anne covered her mouth and hoped no one heard her gasp. She didn't know what to think about Dr. Griffin. Just last week when she returned to her dorm, the front desk clerk said, "Hey Anne! I see there's a package here for you. Is it your birthday or something?"

"Nope." Had her mama sent brownies? But there was no postage or return address so it must have been hand-delivered. In her room, she unwrapped a hardback copy of *The Complete Stories of Flannery O'Connor*. A note scribbled inside said, "Hope you don't already have a copy. Cheers! Rob." At first, she was baffled but then remembered telling Dr. Griffin at Nick's Bar that she liked Flannery. *A gift from a professor delivered to my dorm? And he signed it Rob?* She stretched out on her bed, the unopened book on her chest.

She thought about some of the guys she knew, but they were so immature. She'd always gravitated to older people. When she was only eleven, she had a huge crush on her brother's college roommate. Myra, one of her Clemson study buddies, is 40 with a daughter Anne's age. Back in junior high, she'd wished the high schoolers would pay attention to her. *Wonder how old Dr. Griffin is. He actually talks to me about books and authors. That's pretty cool. Good grief. He's old and my professor. I have acne, for goodness sake. He's not interested in me. And I don't want him to be. Or do I?*

She opened the book and turned to O'Connor's *A Good Man is Hard to Find* and smiled at the part about the prissy grandmother whose collars and cuffs were white organdy trimmed with lace. In case of an accident, she wanted anyone who might see her dead to know "she was a lady." And her dress took on more significance as the story drew to a macabre close. Bizarre and vivid. Determined to shake Dr. Griffin from her mind, she closed the book and wrote a letter to her parents.

The next week when she arrived at the Sunday night staff meeting, Dr. Griffin was sitting in the back of the lounge. *Crap. Why is he here?* Dr. Hinchey never came to staff meetings. They met with him weekly in his classroom to critique the previous edition of *The Tiger.* He was available if they needed him, but he encouraged their independence.

When it was her turn to speak as news editor, she rushed through her report, then retreated to the office with the electric typewriters. She wrote an article about the renovations on East Campus, then mulled over story ideas for her American Humor English class. Since it was due the next day, she'd have to hunker down and finish it that night. *Why am I such a procrastinator? At least I can use this electric typewriter instead of the dinky manual in my room.* She started a story about her great Aunt Betty Lou. She described her aunt's purplish hair, red rouge, and jangling bracelet. She wrote that her false teeth clicked when she talked. After the first few paragraphs, Anne wrote in a stream of consciousness, fingers flying across the keys. She wrote about Aunt Betty Lou enlisting her to pluck her eyebrows and chin hairs. Yuck.

A little before midnight, some *Tiger* staffers yelled, "Good night, Anne. Don't forget to lock up." A knock on the door around 1:00 a.m. made Anne jump straight out of her chair. Dr. Griffin opened the door. "Hey, hon, what you doing here so late?"

"Jesus, Mary and Joseph! You scared the heck out of me! What are YOU doing here?" she said. The late-night intruder reeked of beer. His hair was tousled, and his jeans were ripped on one knee.

"After the meeting, I went downstairs to hear the guitar player in the loggia. Then I wandered around outside to clear my head. I saw the light on up here and wanted to see what was going on."

Anne squinted at him. "Dr. Hinchey never comes to our office or staff meetings. You don't have to do that."

"Well, I've got a lot to learn so I thought I'd hang out with you guys some." He sank back in the chair in front of Anne's desk, stretched out his legs, and propped his cowboy boots on her desk. He was making himself way too comfortable. Anne pulled out her last page from the typewriter and placed it on the desk with the rest of her essay.

"What article are you working on?" Dr. Griffin asked, gazing at her desktop.

"This isn't for *The Tiger.* It's an assignment for my American Humor class." She swiveled around in her chair to get the stapler on the credenza behind her and knocked over a stack of old *Tiger* editions and the Associated Press style book.

"Oh yeah, Dr. Steed teaches that class. He's written a couple of funny books himself."

"I know." She returned the papers and book to the credenza.

"I'd love to see what you wrote." Dr. Griffin said. Before she could stop him, he leaned forward, grabbed her essay, and nearly fell off the chair. He put on his glasses and started reading.

Anne's mouth flew open but before she could think of what to say, Dr. Griffin chuckled. "This is funny as hell. I mean, super witty."

"Thanks," Anne said automatically. For a second, she felt proud and flattered, then perturbed again. "Look, Dr. Griffin, it's late. I've got to get some sleep. As you know, I have an 8:00 class with you in the morning." Anne tossed her Coke can in the trash basket and snatched her essay from Dr. Griffin, careful not to touch his hands. When she stapled the pages together, the click reverberated across the quiet room. She stuffed the paper into her backpack and stood to leave.

Dr. Griffin looked at his wristwatch. "Damn. I didn't know it was so late. I've got to get home myself. I'll give you a ride."

"No! I'm fine."

"Listen, it's too late to be wandering around by yourself. I've told you about those attempted rapes on campus. By the way, have you pursued that story?" He stood, stretched his arms above his head, and yawned.

"I've talked with the police and have plans to meet with the Student Affairs Director," Anne said. Her lips quivered. *Why did I stay up here by myself?* She loved the usual swirl of activity and noise–her friends talking, laughing, typing, and listening to the college radio station. She should have left when they did, but she needed quiet to write her essay. Trying to keep her distance from her drunk professor, she backed against the wall and accidentally touched the light switch. The room went pitch black. "Oh, holy crap!" she said, reaching for the switch and turning it back on. Blinking in the glare of the fluorescent lights, Dr. Griffin rubbed his bloodshot eyes with the back of his fists.

Walking through the front office, Anne made her way to the hall elevator, with Dr. Griffin on her heels. He bumped into a trash can and mumbled, "Well, excuse me."

"Oh shit, I forgot to lock the office." She fumbled in her jeans pocket for the key, walked back to the office door, and locked it. Dr. Griffin was holding the elevator door open for her. The stench of beer in the small space was overwhelming. Standing near the front so she could exit quickly, she watched the green number above the door change from 6 to 5. As the elevator dinged for the fourth floor, Dr. Griffin rubbed the front of his body up against her back and butt. *Oh my god! Did he do that on purpose or is he wobbling around because he's wasted?* Anne took a step forward until she was almost pressed against the door. Her heart pounded like The Telltale Heart in Edgar Allen Poe's story. *Why is this stupid elevator so slow?*

Although taller than most girls, Anne felt small and vulnerable. Dr. Griffin was shifting from one foot to the other, but at least he wasn't touching her anymore.

When the elevator door finally opened, she dashed out.

"Annie, I'm walking you home."

"No!" Anne shrieked, hoping someone would hear her and magically appear to rescue her.

"No need to freak out. My truck is close to your drum, I mean dorm. You know my truck is named Betty Lou, just like your purple-haired aunt. Well, it's actually Betty, but close enough."

Anne speed walked through the student union lobby where students watched TV, played ping pong, ate snacks, or studied. But the brown couches and orange bean bag chairs were empty. On the big TV screen in the corner, Johnny Carson was interviewing Jon Belushi.

As they reached the commons area outside, a refreshing cool breeze hit Anne's hot cheeks.

"Brr, it's gotten chilly," Dr. Griffin said, removing his brown leather jacket and draping it and one arm around her shoulders. Leaning down, he nuzzled his rough beard on top of her head. "Ah, sweet Jesus, your hair smells delicious." She elbowed him and hit that damn belt buckle instead of his ribs. The jacket fell to the ground, and her backpack slid down one arm. While he leaned down to pick up his coat, Anne repositioned her backpack and gripped the straps with both hands as if her life depended on it. Then she skedaddled sideways, like a hermit crab, to get out of his reach. She had rolled her eyes when her parents warned her about safety, insisting she never go out at night alone. Ironically, she wasn't alone but still felt as unsafe as she ever had.

She picked up her pace, trying to stay ahead of Dr. Griffin's long strides. The campus was eerily empty and dark this late Sunday evening, actually early Monday morning. Clouds covered all but one sliver of the moon and two tiny white stars. The previous year, students had pushed to install more security lights on campus. Anne made a mental note to do a follow-up story about that.

A voice interrupted the silence. "Hope you get some tonight, Buddy, but you're a little old for her!" Anne looked up and saw a guy with his head out of an upper-level dorm window. With a Budweiser can in one hand and a cigarette in the other, he had a stupid grin on his face.

Dr. Griffin waved at him, but Anne muttered, "Shut up, you idiot!" She silently counted the red bricks of the sidewalk to distract herself.

Although it was a short way to Benet Hall, it seemed to take forever. As Anne walked up the sidewalk in front of her dorm, Dr. Griffin said in a scratchy voice, "Good night, my friend. See you in the morning." She didn't look back or say a word, but she spotted his truck nearby. She shivered, partly from the nippy air and partly from relief that Dr. Griffin was almost out of sight.

Inside the dorm, she ran up two flights of stairs to her room, locked the door, and breathed a sigh of relief. Thank goodness Pat was a sound sleeper. Even though Anne told herself nothing horrible happened, she felt violated. Dr. Griffin had touched her–*gross!*–twice. Even his reading her essay without permission felt like a violation. Now that she was away from the creep, she realized how scared she'd been. Her body was as tense as when she sat in the dentist's chair or watched an intense movie like *Apocalypse Now.* Checking the door again to make sure it was locked, she berated herself. *Did I lead him on? I shouldn't have met him at Nick's Bar and let him drive me home the other night. I'm a complete spaz.*

Grateful to have a sink in the room, she washed her face, brushed her teeth, and dabbed Clearasil on a pimple. She didn't want to walk down the hall to the bathroom for a shower. *I can't go to Dr. Griffin's class in the morning, but I have to go to the same building to turn in my American Humor paper. At least that class is on a different floor.* She put on her soft flannel pajamas and fuzzy pink socks. Taking the stuffed Snoopy from her bed, she sat cross-legged on the closet floor and hugged him to her knees, creating a cocoon. Her breathing slowed, and the events of the last hour blurred in her mind as if she was watching them happen to someone else.

She read over her humor essay again, penciling in a few corrections. Good thing she'd finished it before Dr. Griffin barged in on her because she sure couldn't think of anything humorous now.

Chapter 33

As Anne is driving home from work on Friday, her cell phone rings. The 652 prefix tells her it's from someone at county government. *Ugh.* "Hello."

"Hi, Anne. This is Maurice. I want to give you an update. First, I talked with Jeffrey."

"You did?" Anne clenches her jaw. "You told me you would let me know before you contacted him."

"Calm down, Anne. I just talked with him yesterday. He's obviously upset and vulnerable. I told him we can try to find him a job somewhere else in the county, but it'll be hard. He has very little work experience."

"Exactly. That's why Harold shouldn't have hired him. The D.A.'s chief investigator repeatedly said Jeffrey was too inexperienced. He was only at the police department for six months, barely enough time to be trained."

"Hmm."

"Your employment clerk didn't send us Jeffrey's application initially because he didn't even meet the minimum job qualifications. Harold had to ask her to send Jeffrey's application for us to review. Did you know that?"

"No, I didn't," Maurice mumbles. "I explained to Jeffrey our hands are tied because Harold's an elected official."

"Okay, what else?" Anne says. She clicks her cell into speaker mode and places it in her lap.

"Until things settle down, we're putting Jeffrey on paid administrative leave."

"Oh wow. Beginning when?"

"Monday."

"For how long?" Anne asks.

"That's still to be determined."

Wonder who'll determine that. "And you'll call me after the meeting with Harold, right?"

"Well, I'm going to Atlanta after we meet with–"

"Maurice, please call me on your way to Atlanta. I'll have my cell phone on all evening and will expect to hear from you."

"I'll do my best. We'll also tell Harold he's not to discuss the matter with you. We realize you're in an uncomfortable position."

"That's an understatement. Okay, so let me be clear. Jeffrey will be on administrative leave beginning Monday, and you'll tell Harold he's not to communicate with Jeffrey and not to discuss the situation with me. Correct?"

"Yes."

Anne exhales. On the road ahead the drawbridge above the Intracoastal Waterway rises, and she slows to a stop. She watches the triangular white sails of a boat gliding down the river and wonders where it's going–a pleasure ride, the Florida Keys, or across the ocean? *How I would love to be sailing away to some exotic port.*

"I know this is tough, but it is a personnel matter, so I can't share much." He pauses. "Anne, how many years do you have with the County?"

She clears her throat. "Why do you ask?"

"Do you have enough years to retire?"

Anne is speechless. After a moment, she says, "I have nineteen years with the county, but I'm only forty-five. So, I don't think I can retire now. Anne grips the steering wheel so tight her knuckles turn white. *How dare he suggest I leave the job I love? Well, loved until recently. Does he want me gone because I know too much?*

"Okay, Anne. Let me know if I can do anything for you. Have a good weekend."

"Wait! One more thing, Will you tell Harold about the administrative leave for Jeffrey?"

"Yes. Take care of yourself. Goodbye."

"Bye," Anne says, clicking off her phone and tossing it on the seat beside her. Her head throbs. *I better take care of myself because you H.R. fools aren't doing a damn thing for me. Telling me to calm down and have a good weekend. Dream on.*

The cars ahead of her start to move as the drawbridge slowly lowers, locking back into place like two enormous Legos. In several miles, she crosses the Lazaretto Creek Bridge. *Thank God I'm home.* In her driveway, she digs in her purse for her door key but can't find it. She dumps the contents of her purse on the top of the car. *Dammit! I've gotta go to the bathroom.* She walks to the backyard and checks the back door. Of course, it's locked. After looking in her purse again, she yanks the bedroom window screen until it falls to the ground, then pushes up the unlocked window. She slings off her shoes, stands on a wrought iron chair, and hikes one knee up to the windowsill.

She's startled to hear Jon's voice coming from the driveway. "Anne, what in holy hell are you doing?" he yells.

Anne raises up, bumping her head on the partially-opened window. "What does it look like? Trying to get in the god-danged, stupid house!" She then clambers down from her perch. "I couldn't find my key."

Jon holds up a single key. "I found this on the ground next to your car. I've never understood why you keep it separate from your car key."

Anne glowers at him. "Because I read police reports at work. If you have your house key on the same ring as your car key, someone could steal both at the same time. It happens."

"You worry too much," Jon says, unlocking the door. Anne sprints to the bathroom. Then she changes into a Life is Good tee shirt. *But life ain't so good right now. Harold's about to find out about Jeffrey's allegation. Will Harold retaliate? Fire me? Oh, for the love of all things holy.*

She sits on the couch and calls Maggie to tell her about the conversation with Maurice.

"Wait a minute. He said what? He asked if you could retire?" Maggie says. "I've never worked for the government, but in all my years in H.R. I know suggesting someone should retire is entirely inappropriate."

"Yeah, it freaked me out," Anne says, rubbing the spot on her head she'd bumped on the window.

"H.R. should be fixing the problem, not implying you should retire. Does Maurice think Harold will change his behavior if you're not there?"

"I have no damn clue. It's insane. Listen, I gotta get some supper. Love you."

"Love you too."

Standing at the kitchen bar, Jon rifles through a stack of mail. "I see we haven't won Publisher's Clearinghouse Sweepstakes yet."

"Well, we might need to. Maurice Dixon just asked me when I could retire, and he and the county attorney are talking to Harold on Monday. All hell could break loose."

"Seriously? He asked if you could retire?"

"Yep." Anne storms out the door to feed Little Kitty, then comes back inside to the aroma of Jon frying bacon and eggs, one of their favorite meals. They sit at the kitchen table, and Anne squeezes his hand. "Thanks for cooking, darling." Between bites she says, "I've been beyond stressed for over a year. I can't retire, but maybe I should resign. I'd feel terrible because I want to protect my employees from Harold. Oh god. If I did leave, what would I do? What could I do?"

"I don't know, but you don't want to keep being miserable working for a boss who lies and harasses his employees. I know leaving has been at the back of your mind. Of course, we'd have to figure out finances." He sighs. "Property taxes are going up again."

"They are?"

Jon rolls his eyes. "Yes, Anne. That's the big disadvantage to living at the beach–huge property taxes. Don't you remember we talked about this a couple of weeks ago?"

"No."

Jon's face turns beet red. "I swear you don't hear anything I say anymore. All you think about is work. It's time you start paying attention to what's going on in our marriage."

"What do you mean by that?"

He puts both fists on the edge of the table. "I mean it's exhausting listening to you complain all the time. We never have fun anymore."

Anne fights back tears. "I know, but I've been going through hell at work."

"Well, you're not the only one with problems. I haven't told you, but things are crazy at my job, too."

"Really? What's going on?"

"It's hush-hush, but a new company is about to buy the hospital." He grimaces and reaches for his shoulder.

Anne stands and rubs his shoulders."

"Ouch! Not so hard!"

Anne sits back at the table. "So is the new company good?"

Jon throws up his hands. "I don't know, but everyone's on edge. When a new company takes over, there are always changes and layoffs. I'm worried they'll bring in folks from their corporate finance office. My job could be on the line."

"Why didn't you tell me?"

"Because you're too engrossed in your own drama. Trying to save Jeffrey, every victim, and the whole damn world."

Anne crosses her arms and tilts her head to one side. "In case you forgot, it's my job to help victims."

Jon stands and paces. "Yep, to help them but not be their savior. Like going to the hospital in the middle of the night to see a domestic violence victim. Then risk getting killed by her abusive husband when you went to their apartment. That's over the top. Not to mention against the rules."

"Fine, just fine! So sorry I can't be perfect like you, Mister Rule Follower." Anne picks up her plate, scrapes the eggs into the garbage disposal, and puts her plate in the dishwasher.

"Anne, don't put that dirty plate in the dishwasher. Can't you see the stuff in there is clean?"

"Oh, whatever."

"Of course, you wouldn't know since I'm the one who always cleans the kitchen lately anyway." He grabs a sponge and starts scrubbing the countertop.

Anne yanks the plate out of the dishwasher, sets it on the clean counter, and stalks off. *I would have emptied the dishwasher if he hadn't been so snippy. But I'm sure he'd find some way to criticize that too.*

After pouting in the bedroom for about an hour, Anne returns to the den where Jon's flipping TV channels. They watch *Dateline* in silence. It's an episode about a woman whose banker husband has been accused of poisoning her. Anne thinks *Dateline* doesn't adequately highlight the grief of the victim's family. But before she learns if the husband is found guilty, she dozes off on the couch. She opens one eye when Jon gently pulls a blanket over her before heading to the bedroom.

* * *

Jon and Anne's Saturday morning ritual is meeting their daughter Emma and her two-year-old son, Ethan, for breakfast at Sunrise Restaurant on Wilmington Island. Anne beams when red-headed Ethan runs through the restaurant door yelling, "Hey, Nana!"

"Hey there, buddy! Come give me a big hug!" Anne says, enfolding him in her arms and kissing his freckled cheeks. Ethan clutches his sippy cup and tattered stuffed animal, Lion, whose tail and ears dangle by a few brown threads.

Over pancakes, they catch up on the week's events. Several customers stop by their booth to say hello. They've come to know the Sunrise regulars–the big table of golfers, elderly Miss Eunice and Mister Mac, and a middle-aged lady with spiky blonde hair who arrives with her husband on a Harley. A short, pot-bellied man always walks around to the tables, oohing and ahhing over the kids. Anne suspects he's a child molester and keeps a close eye on him. She's seen him hanging out alone at the mini golf and arcade place, smiling and talking to children there too.

Henry, a native of Indonesia, manages the restaurant. Anne and Jon think he's the nicest guy in the world. Just that spring, he proudly received his U.S. citizenship papers. He walks up to Anne, leans down, and says, "Miz Anne, I need your advice. You see, Miz Anne, one of my cooks, he got DUI. I pay his bail. What does he need to do? Not first DUI."

Anne tells him the cook probably needs an attorney and can call the public defender's office if he can't afford one. "His first court date will probably be soon. Make sure he doesn't miss it."

"Thank you, Miz Anne. I knew you have good advice," he says, flashing a toothy grin.

After Jon pays the bill and grabs a lollipop for Ethan, they tell Emma goodbye. She's happy to go grocery shopping without a toddler in tow. Jon buckles their grandson into the car seat while Anne slides into the front of the Honda.

At the beach, Ethan squeals with delight as he chases seagulls while Anne and Jon collect shells. After about an hour, they convince Ethan–now covered from head to toe in sand– it's time to walk the several blocks back to the house. Sitting cross-legged on the den floor, Anne rolls a Tonka truck back and forth with a tired but grinning Ethan. At long last, stress relief.

But the reprieve is short-lived because Jeffrey calls. "Ms. Gardner, I hate to bother you on the weekend, but I talked with Mr. Dixon in H.R."

"Yes, how did that go?" Anne's surprised she hadn't heard from Jeffrey earlier.

"Alright, I guess. They're going to try to find me another job. I don't want another job. I want this one, but I want Mr. Carter to stay away from me." Anne can relate; she feels the same way.

"Well, they're going to talk to Mr. Carter on Monday so hopefully that will help," Anne says.

"Okay, and am I supposed to come to work Monday?"

"No. Didn't Mr. Dixon tell you that you're on administrative leave?"

"Yes ma'am, he said administrative leave but didn't say when it would begin."

"He told me it starts Monday." Anne rolls her eyes. She doesn't know if she's angry at Maurice for not explaining it clearly or irritated with Jeffrey for being confused and naive. She bites her lip. *Why didn't you ask him when you go on leave? Can't you do anything for yourself?*

"Okay, this is all weird," Jeffrey says.

The rest of the weekend is pretty typical – a trip to Ace Hardware, a drop-off at Goodwill, and a quick stop that night at a friend's birthday party where Anne tries to avoid questions about work. When people mention news stories about resignations in the D.A.'s office, she says, "Yes, lots of changes" and switches the subject.

At church on Sunday morning, Anne silently prays for "Divine Order with all this mess and to do the right thing for everyone involved." The sermon is about forgiveness. Anne squirms. She doesn't feel like forgiving Harold. Thinking of the employees who have already left under his watch, she contemplates whether she'll be next. Leaving her career this early was never her plan, and Jon's uncertain job situation makes things more complicated. She closes her eyes. *Dear God, please give me guidance and patience.*

Chapter 34

Monday is a long day, but Anne keeps busy by updating a PowerPoint on volunteer management she'll present at the state victim advocacy conference. Then she edits the VIP brochure draft, knowing Harold will nitpick it and probably find fault. She waits until four– when he'll be meeting with H.R. and the county attorney–to deliver it to Harold's secretary.

After arriving home, Anne charges her cell phone so she won't miss Maurice's call. She pulls some weeds in the backyard, nibbles on vanilla wafers, and files her fingernails. Finally, a little after seven, Maurice calls. "Hey, I'm on the road. Ted and I talked to Harold and told him to stay away from Jeffrey and not to discuss any of this with you."

"So how did he take it?" Anne tries to imagine the meeting. "What did Harold say?"

"He was quiet. Didn't argue. He's pretty unflappable."

"Did he deny it? Does he know I know about the allegation?" *Maurice probably shouldn't be telling me all this, but hell, it won't hurt to ask.*

"He didn't confirm or deny it. And yes, he knows that Jeffrey reported it to you. But don't worry. We'll take care of you." He pauses. "And one more thing."

Anne sucks in a deep breath.

"Naturally, Jeffrey is under a lot of stress, so we're going to order a psychological evaluation for him."

"What?" Anne holds the phone away from her ear. Surely she heard him wrong.

"It's called a 'fitness for duty' test. We can't have him carrying a weapon if he's not mentally stable."

Anne rubs her temple. "Let me get this straight. Because he accused Harold of harassment, you think Jeffrey's the crazy one?"

"Anne, it's not unusual for law enforcement to undergo this test."

"I don't understand. Jeffrey's already at home on administrative leave."

"We'll let you know before we notify Jeffrey about the test. That's all for now." Maurice says and hangs up.

Her hands shaking, Anne clicks off, then remembers tomorrow is Tuesday, the regular weekly leadership meeting for division heads in the D.A.'s office. *Oh crap. I bet Harold will be in a horrible mood and probably target me because Jeffrey confided in me.* Exhausted and achy, Anne feels like she might be getting sick. But she falls asleep quickly that night and only awakens twice ruminating about work. *God is in charge. God is in charge.* She softly repeats this mantra until she drifts off again.

Tuesday morning, Anne decides to wear her navy suit, hoping it will make her look and feel confident. She adds a strand of pearls to complete the outfit.

Her work phone rings shortly after 8:00. It's Harold. "Well here goes," she says, then picks up the receiver.

"Good morning, Anne, how are you?" Harold sounds upbeat.

"I'm fine," Anne sounds tentative.

"I looked at the VIP brochure, and it really pops. I like the colors you chose."

"Thanks." *Whoa. What's up?*

"Anne, I need to talk with you. When's a good time?"

"Uh, any time."

"Well, come to my office now before things get busy."

"Okay." She hangs up and checks her pearls to make sure the clasp is in the back. On the walk down the hall to his office, she wracks her brain. *What could he want to talk to me about? He likes the brochure, so it's not that. Why is he in such a good mood if they told him about Jeffrey? Of course, Harold's mood and behavior can change in an instant.* Brenda greets her with a smile. "Good morning, Anne. Harold said for you to go on in."

She takes a deep breath and walks into his spacious corner office. Refurbished after his election, it now features a large built-in solid cherry desk and a matching computer table and credenza. Six newly upholstered chairs surround a glass-topped conference table. Copies of *Savannah Magazine* and the book *Sights and Sounds of Savannah Jazz* are arranged on the coffee table in front of a loveseat. Anne shudders thinking of the cost to taxpayers. She sits on one of two straight-backed chairs directly across from Harold's tidy desk. A journalist had once described Harold as "fastidious." The description certainly fits. Harold looks sharp in his starched white shirt, gold cuff links, and red necktie. But behind the expansive desk, he seems small and vulnerable. There have been times she's felt sorry for him, especially when he appeared uncomfortable with new people.

Harold places his manicured hands on top of the desk. "So, I understand Jeffrey has talked to you about some things."

"Yes," Anne says, shifting in the chair. *No sir, we're not going down this road.*

"So, what exactly did he say?"

Anne hesitates. *God, I'm counting on you to help me say the right thing.* "Maurice told me you were not supposed to discuss this with me. I feel very uncomfortable right now." Determined to remain strong, she sits up straighter.

"Well, I just need to know the plan for Jeffrey. What's your understanding?"

Anne wants to scream at her boss and former friend. Instead, she says, "Maurice told me that he explained this to you yesterday afternoon. Didn't you meet with him and Mr. Stevens?"

"Yes, I met with them. I just wasn't clear on everything. That's all." Harold blinks his eyes rapidly. *Oh my God. When I get nervous, I blink my eyes fast too. Or does he do that when he's lying? Because he's definitely lying.*

"Jeffrey is on administrative leave."

"How will that work?" Harold adjusts his shirt collar. "Who determines how long that will be?"

Why is he asking ME this? Exhaling, she says, "Harold, once again, Maurice told me you and I are not to discuss this. If you have questions, talk with him. I'm not supposed to be in the middle." *Yikes! Can't believe I'm feeling so strong.*

Harold turns to face his computer on the credenza behind him. When he pulls up his emails, Anne assumes their conversation is over. She rises halfway out of the chair, and Harold says, "Just a minute."

She sits back down and perches on the edge of the seat. The silence is deafening as Harold continues to face away from her. Anne gazes out the window at the sweeping span of the Talmadge Bridge over the Savannah River and remembers when it broke in the 1980s after being hit by a ship. The tune of "London Bridge is Falling Down" plays in her head.

Harold swivels around. His chair creaks, jarring Anne back to reality. "Anne, I emailed you a few weeks ago instructing you to write a letter to LaShay, Devin, and Jeffrey confirming their employment. Where are those letters?" He gives her a stern look.

Why does he want those letters now? Is he grasping for a shred of control over me? Asshole! "Yes, I got your email, and I replied that I'd never done that for any of my employees. I asked what you wanted me to include in the letters. Remember?" Anne locks eyes with Harold.

"I didn't get a reply from you. The letters should include the date of hire and salary." He wags his finger at her. "Next time you're chatting with Maurice Dixon—as you've apparently done often lately—ask **him** what else to include in the letter."

Son of a... "Okay, I'll call him," Anne says calmly. "I heard Devin moved from Statesboro, so I'll need his new address." Anne can barely contain herself. She literally bites her tongue to keep from yelling, *You know his damn address because he's shacking up with you. Everybody knows. So why would you want me to create a record that Devin's address is the same as yours?* Anne hadn't asked Devin his new address because she didn't want to confirm his living arrangements. Too disturbing. But she remembers when the two of them arrived together at the airport before the Chicago trip and Harold mentioned Devin had packed his suitcase.

"Contact Devin for his new address," Harold says so quietly she can barely hear him.

"Okay, even though it's been over two months since they've been hired, I'll write the letters. What about the other victim advocate I hired at the same time as the VIP employees? Should I write one for her also?"

"Up to you," Harold says. His dark brown eyes pierce her blue eyes.

"Is this a new H.R. policy–these letters of employment?"

"It's something I've always required. You should have done them by now."

Anne stands and buttons her suit jacket. "I'll go write them now." She opens the door and walks past Brenda who has dark circles under her eyes. Anne can't imagine the stress she endures working for Harold.

Brenda says, "Anne, you have a good day."

"Thanks. I sure will," Anne says, with a fake smile plastered on her face. She heads directly to the snack bar and buys a Diet Coke and two Snickers bars.

Chapter 35

The big clock on Tillman Hall chimed eight times as Anne bounded up the Daniel Hall stairs. Breathless by the time she reached Dr. Griffin's classroom, she scooted into a desk at the back of the room.

"Hey, where were you Monday?" the girl beside her whispered. "Dr. Griffin asked about you."

"I was up late the night before writing a paper, and I overslept," Anne cringed inside at the lie. As Dr. Griffin lectured about the importance of being keen observers and noticing details, Anne kept her head down, doodling in her notebook.

Then a young man stormed into the classroom and ran up to Dr. Griffin at the podium. Shaking his index finger in Dr. Griffin's startled face, he yelled, "Look, you bastard, I saw you with my wife the other night! What the hell do you think you're doing?"

Dr. Griffin backed up against the wall, and the man rushed out of the room as fast as he had barged in, slamming the door behind him.

All twenty students squirmed in their desks and murmured. Anne's eyes were as big as moon pies.

"Now I want you to write exactly what you just saw and heard," Dr. Griffin said, grinning. "Keen observation is vital to being a good journalist. Get started." He waits a couple of minutes as the students scribble what they witnessed, then says, "Okay, what you got?"

Still stunned, Anne couldn't even remember what kind of clothes the intruder was wearing. Did he have on glasses? No. Brown hair? Yep. She did remember what he'd yelled, so she jotted that in her notebook. *On a scale of one to ten, my observation skills are about a two. And how frigging weird Dr. Griffin chose that scenario.*

The man, smiling this time, returns to the classroom and high-fives Dr. Griffin.

"Aw man, that was a set-up," a football player said. "I thought we were gonna see a real fight."

"Yeah, it was planned," Dr. Griffin admits with a grin. "This is Dr. Russo from the theater department."

Dr. Griffin asked students to share what they'd written. It was amazing to hear the wildly different descriptions. When it seemed he wasn't going to call on her, Anne breathed a sigh of relief. At the end of class, she scooped up her books and slid out the back door. *Only ten more Dr. Griffin classes are left this semester. But what if he continues as our newspaper adviser?*

Anne found a bench near Tillman Hall where she could wait before her 10:00 appointment with the dean of Student Affairs. She reviewed her notes, scribbling questions to ask about sexual assaults.

Students were already lining up outside the building to buy tickets for Saturday's homecoming game. Giant paper-mache tigers, balloons, and tiger paws were already springing up on Bowman Field. Fraternities and sororities had spent days building elaborate displays for Homecoming weekend. The ones with engineering majors had the edge as their creations rivaled Macy's Day Thanksgiving floats. By Saturday morning, thousands of students, families, and alumni would stroll around, snapping pictures of the colorful creations.

Shortly before ten, Anne walked into Tillman Hall, the historic brick building that housed the offices of the college president, vice president, and dean of student affairs. When she asked to see Ms. Newton, the student employee behind the front desk smiled. "Hey there, she'll be with you in a few minutes." Anne picked up the latest edition of *The Tiger* from the counter and winced at a typo on page two. *Damn, we should have caught that.*

She sat down and rifled through brochures on the table, one about financial aid, another about student government. A blue one caught her eye. "What You Need to Know About Sexual Harassment." She slid it into her backpack.

A smiling Ms. Newton walked into the reception area. "Good morning, Anne. Come on back."

The warm greeting surprised her. Maybe Ms. Newton's secretary hadn't told her what she wanted to talk about. Anne shook her hand and followed her into a paneled office. The dean's desk had a brass statue of a tiger on one side, two notepads in the middle, and pictures of a teenage boy and girl on the other side. The pretty girl looked like her mom–slim, dark hair and deep-set brown eyes.

"Can I get you a cup of coffee?" Ms. Newton motioned to the coffee pot and cups on the credenza.

"No thanks. I really appreciate your time." Anne pulled out her reporter's notebook, feeling as important as a "real" reporter.

Ms. Newton sat in a chair beside Anne. "What can I help you with?"

"I'm doing a news story about recent sexual assaults and attempted assaults on campus. After I wrote the article about the rapist a couple of months ago, I hear there have been other incidents. I couldn't get any info from the campus police, so I hope you can help me."

Ms. Newton's smile vanished. "Well, when a case is under investigation, the police don't release information."

"I understand, but students need to be informed to help them stay safe."

"Absolutely. In fact, we're sponsoring self-defense classes in two weeks. I'll get you a news release soon." She wrote a note on a yellow pad.

Trying not to raise her voice, Anne said, "Ms. Newton, rumors are flying. The women on campus need the truth. I don't want to impede the investigation, but I need basic facts."

"I understand, Anne. But confidentiality is a primary concern. We don't want victims' names to be published."

Ah, so there are victims. And more than one! "It's against our policy to publish victims' names."

"I just want to see the police incident reports to find out when and where the crimes happened and get descriptions of assailants. The police can cross out the victims' names. And I don't need to see the follow-up investigative reports."

"Well, I'll talk to Chief Burns and see what info can be released." Ms. Newton stood up, walked behind her desk, and sat in her leather chair.

Anne cleared her throat and leaned forward. "We just want what is allowed by the Freedom of Information Act. And the incident reports are, by law, supposed to be accessible to the public and the media."

Ms. Newton looked at her watch. "Of course, Anne. It's a busy week, and I've got another appointment coming up. I'll get back to you, I promise." She stood, indicating the meeting was over.

Anne rose too. "My editor is really pushing me on this. Can I hope to hear back from you by Tuesday or Wednesday so I can get something written by our Wednesday night deadline?"

"I think that's possible. Thanks for coming by, Anne. Have a wonderful homecoming!" She smiled, but it looked forced.

"Thank you for your time. I'll look forward to hearing from you next week. Oh, let me give you my phone numbers." Anne jotted down the number to *The Tiger* office and her dorm room, ripped the page from her notebook, and handed it to Ms. Newton.

Anne walked through the lobby and onto the front steps of the building, closing the big wooden door behind her. *Well, that was a bust. She rushed me out when I told her what I wanted. She didn't even ask for my phone number; I had to give it to her. You'd think a woman would understand the importance of notifying co-eds about campus rapes. I guess the college cares more about its public image than safety.* Anne crossed the campus to the library, climbed up the white marble steps, and found the Freedom of Information Act in the journalism section on the second floor. After making two copies, she sat outside on a concrete bench near the reflection pool. Suddenly hungry, she dug in her backpack for a Little Debbie pie.

Nibbling on her snack, she stared at the reflection pool. Water shot up from a fountain in the middle, creating a soothing sound. The warm sun beamed down on her shoulders. She loved this time of year in upstate South Carolina. The air was just chilly enough to wear her suede jacket and boots. *I wish I had a date for Homecoming. Oh well,*

I'll have fun sitting with the gang. Actually, standing with. Everyone in the boisterous student section stands, cheering wildly throughout the entire game and only sitting at half-time.

Her eyelids drooped. She felt like Dorothy falling asleep in the poppy field on her way to see the Wizard of Oz.

"Love those boots, cowgirl!" Dr. Griffin's booming voice startled her.

"Hey," she said, jerking herself upright on the bench. She couldn't believe he was already sitting beside her.

"Love a girl in boots. Probably from my Texas days," he said, tapping his large brown boot against her small one. "Annie, you don't mind if I call you Annie, do you? You look like you could use a nap, hon."

"Yeah. I'm a little tired." She cleared her parched throat and hoped he couldn't hear her heart thudding. She moved her feet away from his.

"Listen, I'm having a cookout at my house after Saturday's game. I'd sure like for you to come. Just barbecue and beer." He flashed a smile.

"Oh thanks, but I have plans."

Silence.

"So you have a date for the big game?" He pulled off his sunglasses, and his smile disappeared. He stared at Anne in a way that made her stomach do a somersault.

Is he angry? "No. I mean yeah," Anne said, flustered. "I mean I'm going with some friends. We're going to a party afterward."

"Oh, you could bring a friend. Here's my address and phone number." He scribbled on the back of a business card. When he slid it into Anne's hand, their fingers touched. "We'll be there 'til late. It'll be more fun if you come. But I'll see you at the Sunday evening *Tiger* meeting." He winked and put back on his sunglasses.

Anne stood. "Okay. See ya." She hoofed it toward her part-time job at the Continuing Education Center, thankful she was walking in the opposite direction from Dr. Griffin. She cringed when she heard him say “nice ass” but didn't dare turn around. She walked around the curved sidewalk and past a trio of small maple trees until she couldn’t see him out of the corner of her eye. Pausing in mid-stride, she took a few deep breaths. *Damn! That man’s for real coming on to me. And not just when he’s drunk.*

For a moment, she considered confiding in Margo, her nice supervisor at her part-time job but thought better of it. *I don’t want anybody to know about this. They’ll think I’m paranoid or exaggerating. There was that math teacher in high school who seriously flirted with a cheerleader, but the girl never complained. Or maybe she liked it. Oh god, I’m in a swivet, as Gram used to say.* She couldn’t wait to get busy at work doing data entry and get her mind off all this madness.

Chapter 36

The Sunday after homecoming, Anne slept until noon. She'd stayed out all Saturday night partying with her newspaper cronies. After a shower, she opened her French book but couldn't concentrate, so she walked to Susie's room. "Hey, wanna walk over to the soccer game?"

"Sure. Too nice to stay inside." Susie put on her shoes and grabbed her jacket. They ambled down to the soccer field and found a sunny spot on the grassy hill where they could sit and watch the game. Even though Anne didn't know the rules of soccer, she enjoyed the fast-paced action and beautiful weather.

"You're mighty quiet," Susie asked. "Something bothering you?"

"No, no." Anne twiddled a blade of grass between her fingers. "Well, yeah, kinda. Dr. Griffin has been getting on my nerves."

"Why? What's the skinny?"

"Basically, he's coming on to me. This week he invited me to a party at his house and acted mad when I said no."

"Hmm. That journalism prof with the beard?"

"Yeah."

"But he's kind of hot, isn't he? And I know you love guys with beards."

Anne gazed across the soccer field. If she'd thought he was hot before, she sure didn't now. "Not **this** guy with a beard."

"Now that you mention it, I remember my sister telling me a journalism professor put the moves on her roommate when they were freshmen."

"Wow, so that was what, like five years ago?" Thoughts raced around Anne's head. *Has Dr. Griffin been here that long? I never thought about him acting like that with other girls. Creepy. Wonder if that girl told anybody?*

Two of their friends appeared with sub sandwiches from a downtown pub called The Study Hall. The college town also had bars named The Library and The Bookstore. The joke was that when parents called, students could say they'd been to The Bookstore or The Library. "Hey y'all," one of the newcomers said. "You saving this grass for anybody?"

"Nope, it's all yours," Anne said, patting the patch of grass beside her. Relieved they'd interrupted the conversation about Dr. Griffin, she said in a chipper voice, "I guess no one wants to stay inside on this pretty day."

After the game, they meandered back to their dorm. Anne got her reporter's notebook and flipped to the week's *Tiger* assignments. She was dreading the evening staff meeting and seeing Dr. Griffin, so she called Kevin, the editor. "Hey, this is Anne. I don't think I'm going to make it tonight. Kinda feel gross after partying so much."

"You won't be the only one hung over at this meeting. We need you, Miss News Editor," Kevin said.

"Nah. I've already assigned news stories and photos. I promise I'll get everything done."

"But we want to hear about your meeting with Ms. Newton."

"Unfortunately, not much to hear. She pretty much blew me off, but I'm not giving up. She says she'll talk with the campus police and call me next week."

"Damn. I hope she does. Okay then, I'll see you for sure in Dr. Griffin's class in the morning. He asks about you when you're not there. Bye kiddo."

Holy cow! Why is he talking to people about me? She can't drop out of Dr. Griffin's required class, but she sure as hell doesn't want to see him at *The Tiger.* The way he glared at her when he thought she had a date for homecoming sent chills down her spine. *What else could he do? Flunk me? Follow me around like a stalker? Or worse?*

Anne curled up on the twin bed with her stuffed Snoopy and returned to her French textbook. After fifteen minutes of conjugating verbs, she picked up her American Humor anthology. She snuggled under the blanket Aunt Betty Lou had crocheted for her as a high school graduation gift. Anne was glad her roommate spent most weekends at her boyfriend's apartment. It was nice to have the tiny room to herself. *I wish I could stay in bed and read and not see a soul for a week.*

The black wall phone jangled. She's not sure why, but she felt nervous about answering it. "Hello?" she said warily.

"Hello, honey. Your daddy and I want to know if you had a good homecoming weekend."

"Hey, Mama. I sure did. And we won."

"We know. We listened to Clemson on the radio with the Auburn game on TV at the same time. By the way, I'm planning Thanksgiving. Anything in particular you want me to cook? We can't wait to have all the family home."

"And I can't wait to go home! Home cooking sounds good. Maybe squash casserole? And can we have red velvet cake for Thanksgiving AND Christmas?"

"Sure, we can. I'll be cooking pound cakes for the Woman's Club bazaar so I'll make one of those too. How are your classes?"

"Good." Anne wrapped the curly black phone cord around her wrist.

"What articles have you written lately for *The Tiger*?"

"Oh, just the usual stuff." Anne was glad they'd never mentioned her story about the rapist that caused such an uproar when the judge sentenced him to chemical castration. She assumed they hadn't heard about it. And she sure wasn't going to worry them by talking about campus assaults or possibly quitting the paper. They knew she loved *The Tiger.*

"We're so proud of you, Anne. It's wonderful you're working part-time and writing at the newspaper. All excellent experiences, but you sound tired. Just don't overdo it or let it get in the way of your studies. Hang on, your daddy wants to say hello. Mind your manners, now."

Anne always smiled when her mama said, "Mind your manners."

"Hello, Peanut," her daddy said. "How's my bonus baby?" Her daddy called her the "bonus baby" because they thought their family was complete with three children. But six years after Maggie was born, along came Anne. As a small child, Anne learned the word "bonus" from the Duz laundry detergent commercials. Each box came with a "bonus," a drinking glass stuffed inside the blue and white powdered detergent. The family still laughs that she'd asked Daddy if she was like that tea glass.

"Hey, Daddy. I'm good. How are you?"

"Fine. Played eighteen holes of golf yesterday. Miss Mary June asked about you at church this morning."

"Oh, sweet."

"You doing okay with money?"

"Yes, sir, this part-time job helps. I'm good 'til Thanksgiving." Anne looked at the calendar on the wall to see how many weeks until the holiday.

"Okay, we better not run up the phone bill. We love you."

"Love you too, Daddy." She hung up, her eyes stinging with tears. Talking to her parents made her long to be a little girl again, not someone who worried about newspaper deadlines, creepy professors, and sexual assaults. She began humming *Sweet Home Alabama.* She felt a lump form in her throat. *I can't wait to go home.*

She collapsed back on the bed. *Mama said not to overdo it. Maybe I'm just stressed from taking on so much. Yep, that could be my excuse for leaving The Tiger.* But she loved her friends there. They were like a family—a screwed-up, wacky one—but a family nonetheless. And she thrived as news editor and reporter. She hadn't joined a sorority, Campus Crusade for Christ, or student government. The newspaper made her feel involved, more than just a kid lost in the shuffle of the big student body. It was a perfect fit. "I like to write and I'm nosy," she'd told the editorial staff when she interviewed for the unpaid job.

But since Dr. Griffin's intrusion into her life, she was discombobulated. Just last week she'd failed a French test and forgotten to turn in her time sheet at her job.

Why does Dr. Griffin have to be such a jerk? And why can't I tell him to go to hell? Why should I change my entire life because of him? She flung her bed pillow across the room and accidentally knocked Snoopy to the floor.

"Because he might give me a bad grade, and I need to keep a good GPA," she muttered.

She leaned down to rescue Snoopy who was sprawled half under her bed amid potato chip crumbs, a hair clip, one dirty sock, and dust balls. "Disgusting!" she mumbled, not knowing whether she meant the mess under her bed, Dr. Griffin, or her screwed-up life.

Chapter 37

The last thing Anne wants to do is talk with the county attorney, Ted Stevens. But she sees his number on her office phone. "Hello, Anne. Ted Stevens here. Just wanted to follow up and see how things are going since we talked to Harold."

"Not good."

"Oh?"

"Ted, I sent you an email about how Harold peppered me with questions about Jeffrey's allegation the very morning after you and Maurice talked to him. Didn't y'all tell Harold to keep me out of the loop?"

"We did."

"When I told Harold that was my understanding, he acted oblivious."

"Good for you for standing up to him."

Anne rolls her eyes. "What's going to happen with Harold?"

"Nothing right now."

"What? Why not?"

"We've determined that while there may have been, uh, some questionable behavior, we haven't seen any actual stepping across the line on Harold's part."

She fans herself with a file folder. "Harold's been accused of sexual harassment. He slept in the same hotel room with two boys and paid their airplane fares with county funds. He calls Jeffrey at home and makes inappropriate comments to him. What else does he have to do, uh, to step across the line as you put it?"

"Anne, calm down. This is a personnel matter, and I'm already saying more than I should. All I can tell you is we gave him quite a stern warning. He ought to be thankful we intervened."

What the holy hell? "Thankful? What do you mean?"

Ted clears his throat. "Who knows where this could be headed if we hadn't stepped in?"

Anne's words come out in a rush. She doesn't care that her office door is open and Harold might walk in any minute. "I don't think this is the first time something like this has happened."

"Do you *think* that or know that?"

Anne hesitates. "I think that because of what several people have told me."

"Anne, you know we can't take action based on rumors. And there are plenty of those."

She bites her fingernail. "It's not just Jeffrey. Are you aware how Devin Greene, the VIP case manager, got selected for the job?"

"No."

"Devin had done some research on violence intervention programs for Harold. Then Harold made up his own criteria for the position giving experience in intervention programs the most points. There are only a few violence intervention programs in the country. Obviously none locally. He cooked the books to hire Devin."

"Hmm."

"Harold didn't include that criterion for the other VIP positions. Tell me that's not fishy."

"Interesting, but that's an H.R. issue. Plus, elected officials aren't required to follow the county's hiring guidelines."

"Whatever. All I know is Devin is another good-looking, young man who Harold pays a lot of attention to."

"Anne, you're a valued county employee, and we want to make sure you get yourself squared away. If you leave, we'll do an exit interview so all this is on the record."

She jumps up and shoves her chair against the back wall. "Oh, so you're expecting *me* to leave?"

"I know what a difficult position you're in. We can even assist you in finding another job, in or outside the government."

She wanted to go through the phone and pummel him.

"Now Anne, I don't want you to do anything precipitous. Keep your head up, girl. Call if you need anything at all."

Anne chokes out a curt, "Okay. Goodbye." She slams down the phone and stomps over to her door, banging it shut. *They're trying to keep me quiet by pushing me out. And Harold can continue to pursue good-looking boys on the job.*

She clenches her teeth, then mimics Ted. "Valued employee. Don't do anything precipitous. Keep your head up, girl." *Did he really say that? What a patronizing jerk!*

Anne kicks her trash can, but it doesn't tip over. She remembers the editor at her first real newspaper job in Alabama. One day he strode into the middle of the newsroom–close to Anne's desk–and kicked a trash can clear across the room. Papers, cigarette butts, and Coke cans flew everywhere as the metal can landed with a thud. The noisy room turned so silent you could hear a pencil drop. The editor was upset because reporters were late on deadline and the printing press belt had broken. What a temper. As a naive, young reporter, she couldn't imagine anyone–especially a boss–acting that way.

But now she can relate.

* * *

Instead of going straight home after work, Anne drives to see Maggie who's planting zinnia seeds near her deck. "Yo, little sistuh, what's up?" Maggie pulls off her gardening gloves and wipes her forehead with the back of her hand.

"What's up is the courthouse is nothing but a snake pit."

"Sit down." Maggie gestures to the wicker patio furniture on the deck. "I'm ready to take a break. These dang gnats are about to eat me alive."

Anne kicks off her sandals by the back steps and sits on a cushioned chair. She picks up the bottle of Skin So Soft from the table beside her and sprays her legs and arms, hoping to fend off the gnats.

"Just in time for happy hour. White or red?"

"I'll just have iced tea. I'm parched."

"You sure?"

"Yep."

Maggie returns with a tumbler of tea and a glass of Chardonnay for herself. "You haven't been home yet?"

"No, Jon is gonna be late. I need to bitch, and you're the unlucky victim. Again." Maggie's fat black cat, Olive, rubs against Anne's legs, and she leans down to scratch behind her ears.

"Don't let Olive get fur all over your nice pants." Maggie sets down her wine glass, picks up the watering can, and steps off the deck to sprinkle the newly planted seeds.

"Nah, this all goes in the wash." Anne tells her sister about her conversation with the county attorney. When she gets to the part where Ted said, "Harold hasn't really stepped across the line," Maggie stops watering, holds the can in mid-air, and spins around to face Anne.

"He said what?"

"You heard correctly."

"First, I'm surprised he said anything about their conversation with Harold."

Anne shrugs. "Why are we surprised at anything anymore?"

"True that," Maggie says. "And second, I'd like to know exactly what Harold has to do to step across the line."

"I asked Ted that same thing." Anne drums her fingers on the arm of the chair.

"Well, do tell!"

"He evaded the question and said they gave him a stern warning. Said Harold should be thankful they intervened because who knows where this might be headed." Anne's face is turning beet red, partly from the late afternoon sun but mostly because she's mad as hell. She takes a swig of tea.

Maggie's eyebrows shoot up. "Thankful they intervened? Good grief." Maggie puts the watering can down and sits next to Anne. "Hon, have you been sleeping? You have circles under your eyes."

Anne looks down. "Not much. The drama never ends."

"I'm so sorry. You need to resign."

"Speaking of which, Ted said they'll find me another job. And for me to keep my head up." Anne sticks out her tongue. "Gag!"

A loud buzz nearly drowns out their conversation and Olive darts under the deck. A yellow helicopter, barely skimming the tree tops, belches out a huge cloud of white smoke.

"What the heck?" Maggie yells.

Anne doesn't know if Maggie's referring to what Ted said or the noise and smoke.

"Oh. It's County Mosquito Control," Anne shouts over the whirring. "I thought a war was starting." She looks up at the helicopter circling the neighborhood. "Well, maybe I can work for Mosquito Control. Should be job security there."

Maggie coughs. "Dang, that thing was flying low. I hope that spray doesn't kill humans, although I can think of a few pesky people I'd like to exterminate."

"Well, it didn't kill us as kids," Anne says. "Remember when we ran out in the road and chased the mosquito truck? Then pranced around in the cloud it left."

"Yeah, I do. Wonder why some adult didn't stop us?"

"Same reason we didn't wear seat belts and parents smoked in the cars, I guess. Different times," Anne says, rubbing her eyes. She leans back in the chair. The helicopter whirs in the distance. *I'm trapped in a poisonous fog at the courthouse just like I was with Dr. Griffin at Clemson. But I know better now. I'm getting myself out of that toxic environment.*

Maggie stands and reaches for Anne's hand. "Come on, Sistuh. Let's go inside."

Chapter 38

Anne is busy proofreading an update of the Victim-Witness brochure when Kate calls. "Hey. Glenn invited us to lunch. How weird is that?"

Glenn has the interpersonal skills of a doorknob. He uses email for most communication. "That way, I don't have to talk to humans who get on my nerves. And ALL people get on my nerves," he's said many times. He gets teased about his "uniform:" khaki pants and a frayed white shirt with a navy tie. He claims he owns two identical shirts and switches them out every other day. For court, he adds a navy blazer. He rarely goes out to lunch and instead stays in his office eating a peanut butter sandwich and an apple. But he's comfortable with Kate and Anne, especially since Harold became their boss. The three of them often huddle in Glenn's office, venting frustrations and sharing advice on how to handle Harold. Although a curmudgeon, Glenn's a good listener.

Anne scrunches her face. "Wow, something big must be going on. What time does he want to go?"

"Can you go now?"

"Sure."

They all meet at the elevator, and Kate jangles her car keys. "I'll drive. Where y'all wanna go?"

"I don't care," Glenn says. "I haven't been out to eat since last year when I took the wife to some fancy schmancy place you suggested for our anniversary."

Kate laughs. "Good grief, I don't know how that sweet lady puts up with you. Was that when you gave her a weed eater as an anniversary gift?" Kate points to Glenn. "You like beef, right? How about we go to Outback?"

Glenn shrugs. "Okay by me. I'm sick of this diet I'm supposed to be on. Haven't lost but three measly pounds."

"You still drinking bourbon and Coke every night?" Kate asks as they get in the car.

"Of course. How do you think I survive?"

Anne leans forward from the back seat. "Glenn, you better stay healthy because we need you."

"Yeah, don't go keeling over on us," Kate says. "And you need to exercise. Bowling once a week doesn't cut it." Kate parallel parks her Volvo station wagon on busy Bay Street as trucks zoom by dangerously close. After Glenn feeds the meter, they go inside and find a table near the window. Kate wastes no time getting to the point. "Okay, Glenn, spill it. Either you're dying of cancer or you're leaving the office."

"That would be the latter."

"I knew it. Damn it! You do have another job, don't you? With two kids in college, you have to be employed," Kate says.

"Yes, Mother, I know that. I'm going to work as a prosecutor in the Brunswick Circuit. It's close enough so we won't have to move."

The waitress appears with water. "Do you know what you'd like?"

They scan the menu and order.

"I feel bad leaving y'all," Glenn says, "but I can't work for that lying sack of shit anymore. I don't want to be a part of his so-called leadership team one minute longer and risk being implicated by his unethical behavior."

Kate nods. "I understand, but I keep hoping things will get better. I don't want to go into private practice. I'm a career prosecutor, but there probably aren't vacancies in other district attorneys' offices." She twirls the straw in her glass of water." You're lucky there was an opening nearby."

"I know. I had to go somewhere. I'm done with a boss who spends money on office renovations and expensive retreats instead of training and salaries. He buddies up to defendants and their families like in that domestic violence case. He treats people like crap."

"I know. Our office's reputation is going downhill fast," Kate says. "You're not the first to leave, and you won't be the last. This all sucks."

Anne stares out the window. *This is so sad. I hope I don't start crying.*

Gritting his teeth, Glenn says, "Harold won't support me on my cases. Hell, it's not even that he won't back me. Most of the time he ignores my emails and calls altogether. And his office escort policy has the cops hating us. I detest that he acts like we're idiots and micromanages us."

Anne sighs.

Glenn continues. "And he flat-out lies. I guess the final straw for me was the Michael Peeples case."

Anne shoots Glenn a quizzical look. "You mean that old guy who works in County Engineering? Pale, tall, and skinny like Ichabod Crane?"

"Yup."

"The man who got beaten up last year by some kid who broke into his apartment?"

"That's the one."

"If I remember right, he punched Mr. Peeples in the face and broke his nose," Anne says. "We helped Mr. Peeples apply for compensation to help cover his medical bills."

"Well, it turns out the boy—he was 17 so not a juvey—was at Peeples' home late that night doing sexual favors for him. And had been for quite a while," Glenn says. "The kid was sick of it and beat the hell out of him. Peeples pressed charges but lied, saying he'd never seen his attacker before. The police got Peeples on tape several times talking to the young man. He wasn't a burglar."

Anne lifts her hand. "Wait. Glenn, what in the world are you talking about?"

"One of the first things I did after Harold got elected was talk to him about charging Peeples with perjury for lying on the witness stand."

Anne drops her fork. "I can't believe this! I didn't know Peeples was prosecuted for perjury."

"That's because he wasn't. Harold sat on it so long that the statute of limitations ran out. I asked him about it repeatedly. The police worked hard making the case against Peeples, and then Harold held up everything."

Kate looks at Anne. "Anne, you know what happened to the young guy who pled guilty to assaulting Peeples, don't you?"

"He had a prior conviction and went to prison, right?"

Kate leans over and whispers, "Yes, and he committed suicide in prison two weeks ago."

"Oh, my word. That's awful!" Anne covers her mouth with her hand. "So you're telling me this young man was basically sexually abused by a much older guy? Then he beat up the dude, pled guilty, and went to prison for it." She pauses. "Then the kid committed suicide, but nothing happened to Peeples. Holy crap. I can't even wrap my head around this."

"Yeah, you can't make this shit up," Glenn says. "And our upstanding District Attorney protected Peeples, the lying scumbag."

"Who's a lying scumbag, Harold or Peeples?" Anne asks, looking around to make sure no one could hear.

"Both of them!" Glenn barks, then bites into his hamburger.

"Glenn, why do you think Harold protected him from perjury charges?" Anne asks.

"I have no friggin' idea."

"Good stars above." Anne pushes aside her half-eaten plate of food. "I can't believe I didn't know about all this."

"You've been so swamped dealing with Harold micromanaging you and VIP, you haven't had time for much else," Kate says.

"That's for sure. What else is going on that I don't know about?"

"No damn telling," Glenn says.

Chapter 39

Anne's about to leave the office when LaShay calls. "Jeffrey called freaking out. He said H.R. wants him to take a psychological test. What the heck?"

"Maurice told me that but promised to let me know before he called Jeffrey," Anne says.

"Maurice told him to go tomorrow for a fitness for duty test, whatever that means. Harold is the psycho one. I can't believe they want to test Jeffrey."

"Me either. I'll call Maurice in the morning. Thanks, LaShay."

Heading home, Anne remembers she needs to stop by Target again. She'd gone there on Monday to buy a Target gift card for Alice's birthday party. She ended up spending $60 on paper products, earrings, and a tee shirt but forgot to buy the gift card.

Inside the store, Anne's immediately sucked in by the racks of discount items in the front. She piles stuff in her cart that she doesn't need–a puzzle for little Ethan, dishcloths, chocolate chip cookies, and three small plastic boxes. Determined to get more organized at home and work, Anne's always buying storage containers. They usually end up sitting around collecting dust before Jon pitches them. Then she scolds him, "I needed those to organize the cabinets."

She heads to the grocery section and picks up buns and the last four packs of Oscar Meyer hot dogs for the upcoming neighborhood party. En route to the checkout counter, she detours to the makeup section. She looks at bottle after bottle of nail polish before deciding on "Optimistic" by Revlon. She pushes her now full cart to an aisle with no line– Checkout and Returns.

"Hello," the cashier says. "Did you find everything you need?"

"Yes, thanks. I want a gift card too."

"Uh oh," the cashier says. "I didn't scan the sale price on these cookies." She nervously re-enters the amount. "It's just my second day on the job." Anne gives her an encouraging smile and notices her name tag readsTasha.

As Tasha fills plastic bags with her finds, Anne says, "Dang. I forgot to bring my reusable tote. I hate using these plastic bags. They're harmful to sea turtles and all sea creatures."

Nevertheless, Anne lugs her many bags to the parking lot and loads them in the trunk. Pulling onto Skidaway Road, she remembers she'd bought hot dogs at Kroger two weeks ago and put them in the freezer for the party. "Dammit. There isn't room for any more in the freezer," she mutters while making a quick U-turn. She parks, grabs the bag of hot dogs, and returns to Tasha's cash register.

Tasha frowns. "Oh no. Did I do something wrong?"

"No, it's my bad. I didn't mean to buy these hot dogs. I remembered I already have a bunch at home in the freezer."

As Anne digs in her purse for the receipt, the shoulder strap breaks and her purse falls to the floor, scattering the contents. "Oh, crap." She bends down and crams stuff back in the purse. She hands a receipt to Tasha who looks at it and scrunches up her face.

"Ma'am, this receipt isn't from today."

"What? Oh, that must be the one from when I was here Monday. Let me find the one from today. I know I put it in my purse." She spies the receipt on the floor and hands it to Tasha. "I'm sorry to be such a pain. I just want to return these hot dogs. I hate wasting food."

"You can return them, but it's our policy to discard returned food."

"What? Please don't throw away the hot dogs. I just bought them. Remember?"

Tasha looks down at her long, blue fingernails. "I remember." She refunds the money for the hot dogs as Anne crosses her arms, determined not to give up.

Meanwhile, a large young woman, with a baby on her hip, walks up behind Anne and announces loudly, "I'm returning this ab reducer. I tell ya it ain't made my belly go down one bit. Just jiggled my flab." She grabs her stomach and demonstrates. "I saw this fool thing on TV and just had to have it." She rolls her brown eyes.

Tasha and Anne look at Ab Reducer Woman who's holding the gadget above her head the same way Olympic athletes display their gold medals after a victory.

Ab Reducer Woman tilts her head toward Anne. "Don't ever buy one of these. And another thing. I think Target started sizing clothes the wrong way. You know I am *not* a size 16!"

"I feel your pain," Anne says. "I've been buying a bigger size myself lately."

Anne looks at the hot dogs on the counter and turns to the cashier. "I can't stand the thought of these hot dogs going to waste."

Tasha glances around and motions to a middle-aged woman wearing the red Target vest.

The employee's tag reads Assistant Manager. She looks at Anne. "May I help you? Is there a problem?"

I'll try a new strategy. "I was in here five minutes ago, and I don't need these hot dogs after all, so can I return them myself to the refrigerator section? They were your last packs. And if I return them, y'all won't get in trouble."

"Sorry. It's against store policy."

"At least let me buy them back, and I'll take them to the Inner City Night Shelter."

The assistant manager stares at Anne. As do the string of customers now lined up behind her.

Tasha looks at Anne and says softly, "Ma'am, it's okay. Please don't be upset." She whisks the bags of hot dogs behind the counter.

Tasha is using the same, soothing voice I use when talking to upset crime victims. She wads up her refunded money and stuffs it in her purse with the broken strap. As she trudges across the parking lot, she sees Ab Reducer Woman buckling her baby in the car seat. Feeling an odd sort of camaraderie, Anne smiles at her. The woman grins and waves back.

Anne drives away and resists stopping at Krispy Kreme even though the "hot doughnuts" sign is flashing. Finally crossing Lazaretto

Creek Bridge, Anne lets her window down and smells the salt air. *Getting to Tybee Island is like being transported to another world.*

She flings open the door to the cottage and plunks the Target bags on the floor. Jon takes one look at her and suggests a walk on the beach. Anne tells him about her Target escapades. He listens patiently. "That poor Tasha," Anne says. "Only her second day on the job, and she has to deal with the likes of me. She must think I'm crazy as a loon. And I am." She stops and tosses a shell into the ocean.

"You do understand why they can't take returned food, right?"

"Of course," Anne snaps. "Everything is out of control at work, and I can't do anything right anywhere, even shop." She walks faster to catch up to Jon, then stops in mid-stride and yells over the sounds of the waves, "Oh good lord, I didn't get the damn Target gift card for Alice. That's why I went to Target for the s*econd* time this week! I told Tasha I wanted a gift card, but she didn't give me one."

"Hon, you can buy a gift card at any drugstore or grocery store."

Anne kicks the sand. "Well, yes. Yes, I can. What in the world is wrong with my brain?"

Chapter 40

Jeffrey finishes his bowl of Cheerios and feels like he's going to throw up. Having barely slept all night, he's as nervous as when he played his first guitar solo at church as a kid. But he knows he has to go to see the psychologist for the test H.R. had ordered. Since being on administrative leave for a week, he's had too much time to think about his crazy work situation. Will Harold Carter will fire him or should he quit? What will happen next?

He finds a bottle of Pepto Bismol in the bathroom medicine cabinet and takes a swig, grimacing at the chalky taste. *It looks like bubble gum, but it sure doesn't taste like it.* After a quick shower, he puts on his khakis with a brown belt and a white polo shirt. He's already sweating.

Sitting on the side of his rumpled twin bed, he slips on brown penny loafers. Raised by a father in the military and law enforcement, he keeps his shoes shined to perfection. His cell phone beeps with a message from Kiara: "Good luck today. Call me after." He wants to call her–or his mama–but knows he'd better get going. He grabs the paper with the shrink's office address and the keys to the Ford Crown Vic off the kitchen table. Although Jeffrey likes the big car with all the bells and whistles, he hates being ribbed by his colleagues. He'd heard the other investigators in the D.A.'s office griping about why "the boss gave the new kid a new car." He's surprised Harold hadn't made him return the car since he's on administrative leave.

Jeffrey switches the radio to 1230 WSOK. A little gospel music is in order. As he approaches Eisenhower Drive, he realizes he's twenty minutes early. Not wanting to arrive a minute before he has to, he cruises around, eventually turning into the Oglethorpe Mall parking lot. He parks in front of Belk and listens to the radio, but the music doesn't blot out the memories of when his mama took him to a counselor when he was a teen.

* * *

Back in Cleveland, Jeffrey and his family were active in a big A.M.E. church. Jeffrey, his brother, and sister rarely missed a Wednesday night youth meeting. They enjoyed cookouts, trips to the skating rink, and the basketball league. But his favorite activity was the youth choir. He started off singing but switched to playing the guitar which soon became his passion.

When he was fourteen, the church hired a youth pastor from Pennsylvania, Carl Freeman. He played piano and guitar and had been a star high school basketball player. In his early 30s, he was tall and lanky with a bright smile worthy of a toothpaste commercial. He'd worked as a middle school band director and church youth pastor. The kids thought he was cool.

By organizing bake sales and car washes, Carl helped the church raise money to buy an electric keyboard and eventually a new sound system. His wife Alicia was an attractive, vivacious woman who helped with the youth group and fundraising efforts. Church members bragged they got "two for one" when they hired Carl because he and Alicia brought new energy to the church, attracting more and more young people to what had been an aging congregation.

One Wednesday night after he'd been there a couple of months, Carl walked outside with Jeffrey to wait on his mom and told Jeffrey, "You have so much musical potential. I'd like to give you private guitar lessons."

"That sounds awesome," Jeffrey said, a shy smile spreading across his face. *He thinks I've got talent. Sweet.* Unlike his siblings, he didn't excel at sports and had begun thinking music was his "calling," as his grandma would say.

When Jeffrey's mom pulled into the parking lot, Carl proposed the guitar lessons to her. "And there won't be any charge," Carl said. "I want to work with Jeffrey the next couple of months. This boy of yours has talent."

"Oh, you think so?" Mrs. Williams beamed at her youngest child who she still spoiled. "Well, if he keeps up his grades, maybe so. Very kind of you to offer. Let me talk it over with his daddy."

"Okay, I'll see you Sunday." Carl winked at Jeffrey.

Jeffrey was about to explode. "Mama, I want to take lessons. That would be so cool. You've heard Mr. Carl play. He rocks. Please, please say yes."

"We'll see, honey," Mrs. Williams said.

"Ah, Ma, none of this 'we'll see' stuff. I can keep my grades up, I promise. Anyways, it's almost summer. I won't have anything to do but sit around and play video games."

After the kids were in bed, Jeffrey eavesdropped and heard his mom tell his dad about Mr. Carl's offer.

His father sighed. "I wish the boy was involved in sports. He needs to build some muscle and backbone."

Standing at the bedroom door, Jeffrey rolled his eyes.

His mom persisted. "He'll only be successful if he has an activity that interests him. He loves music. And it's free."

"Yeah, that part sure sounds good. A cop's salary doesn't leave much room for extras. I'm already worrying about the kids' college tuition."

"He can try the lessons then?"

"Yeah. Guess it can't hurt."

Jeffrey pumped his fists in the air. *Mama always has my back.*

When Jeffrey started the lessons, his guitar playing improved, along with his self-confidence. His parents were impressed that their sullen teenage son was blossoming.

"I knew this was a good idea," Mrs. Williams told her husband one Saturday when the two older kids were engrossed in video games and Jeffrey was practicing the guitar.

"Yeah, it does seem to have brought the boy out of his shell."

As a reward for doing so well, Mr. Carl took Jeffrey to a youth music extravaganza at a mega-church in Dayton.

"I thought Ms. Alicia was coming too," Jeffrey said, climbing into the car for the road trip. Jeffrey rubbed his nose. The sweet smell of Carl's cologne was overpowering.

"She was, but she's not feeling so great. Between me and you, she's expecting a baby. We're so excited! We've been praying for a baby for six years."

"Cool." Jeffrey gave him a thumbs up. "I can't wait to tell Mama."

"Oh, let's wait a couple of more weeks before we share the news."

"Gotcha."

Carl started talking about the "blessings of marriage" and "pleasures of the flesh." As he veered into another lane, he said, "Jeffrey, you don't have a girlfriend, do you?"

"Uh, no sir." Jeffrey turned up the air conditioning vent on his side.

"Bet you've kissed a girl,though," Carl said, looking at Jeffrey and smiling.

Jeffrey looked out the window and didn't respond.

"Well, you're a good-looking young man, so I know there's a girlfriend in your future. And one day you'll be blessed with a wife. Jeffrey, I'm here to mentor you in Godly relationships, not just teach you music. So if you have any questions about girls or even sex, you can ask me."

"Okay," Jeffrey mumbled, feeling his face heat up. *What's up with this dude?*

"Nothing to be embarrassed about, son. Our bodies are vessels of God," Carl said, patting Jeffrey on the knee. "Proverbs 5 says 'Let your manhood be a blessing.'"

Jeffrey's head pounded when he remembered the awkward conversation with his dad a few years back about the birds and the bees. *That was bad enough. But now Mr. Carl? Why can't he just talk about music?*

They finally arrived at the church and enjoyed the awesome concert of praise music and dance. Carl bought two of the featured band's CDs, one for himself and one for Jeffrey. Jeffrey was relieved they listened to the CD on the way home. He'd had enough of Mr. Carl's talking.

During the next few weeks, Carl bought Jeffrey two more CDs, a new capo for his guitar, and a music video. Meanwhile, Jeffrey's mama and some of the church ladies planned a baby shower for Alicia and Carl.

When school got out for the summer, Carl asked Jeffrey to help him around the church a few afternoons a week. Jeffrey updated the membership database, ordered Sunday School books online, and washed the windows of the fellowship hall. He helped Carl with the little kids at Vacation Bible School, accompanying them on the guitar as they sang, "My God is an Awesome God!" and "This Little Light of Mine." Jeffrey tied shoes, played dodgeball, and handed out juice boxes to the eager little ones. As the baby of the family, he relished his role as the big, cool kid. But he didn't like it when his brother teased him and called him "Carl Jr."

One afternoon Jeffrey rode with Mr. Carl to Wal-Mart to buy snacks for the kids. On the way there, Carl said, "Jeffrey, the church can't afford to pay you for your work this summer, but here's $75 for you to spend on whatever you want." He handed him a fistful of cash.

"Nah, you don't have to do that. I'm not old enough to get a summer job. I'd be super bored sitting around the house all day."

"Jeffrey, I insist. We'll swing by the mall first."

"Well, if you're sure. Thanks." Jeffrey was all smiles as he strolled out of the mall with a new pair of Nikes.

At home that evening, his mama immediately noticed his new shoes. Pointing at his feet, she demanded, "Where did you get those, young man?"

"Mr. Carl bought them for me."

"What? Don't lie to me, Jeffrey. Where did you get them?" she asked with her hands on her hips and a "Don't-mess-with-me" look.

"No, Mama, really. It's for me helping out this summer."

"You take them off your feet right now and give them back. If I wanted you to have expensive shoes, I'd buy them myself."

"But Mama!"

"He's already giving you free guitar lessons. That's more than enough. Now do not argue with me."

Jeffrey stormed up to his room and slammed the door behind him, then hit his fist against the back of the door. His brother Dale walked in. "Whaddup?"

"Nothing."

"Whoa, it's my room too. Hey, where did you get those new kicks?" Dale asked.

"None of your business. Move on."

"Okay, chill. I don't know what your deal is. You ought to be playing basketball with your friends instead of hanging around with Mr. Carl so much. I'm not the only one who thinks it's weird how you spend so much time with him."

Jeffrey unlaced the Nikes and slung them against the wall. They knocked over his guitar leaning in the corner, making a huge racket.

"Holy crap, dude!" Dale bolted out of the bedroom, shaking his head.

Jeffrey didn't go to guitar lessons or youth group the following night, telling his mama his stomach hurt. She didn't bring up the subject of the shoes again but she inspected his room and closet. She was afraid he'd stolen the shoes to trade for drugs like a work colleague's son had done. She breathed a sigh of relief when she found only CDs, dirty socks, sheet music, and an empty Coke can.

The following week, a nervous Jeffrey went to music lessons. He dreaded returning the shoes so, without saying anything, he put them on the floor near Mr. Carl's desk and sat in the chair beside the desk. *Please don't let there be any talk about girlfriends or sex.*

"Hey Jeffrey, glad you're feeling better," Mr. Carl said. "Let me get the music for today." He reached into the bottom drawer and pulled out a music book. Jeffrey's eyes widened when two pictures of naked teenage boys fell to the floor. Then one of a woman sprawled out face down on a king-sized bed.

Mr. Carl quickly stuffed the pictures of the boys back in the drawer but held out the one of the woman. "Now look what beauty there is right there. Yes sir. As a matter of fact, I'll be glad to show you more. You have God-given sexual urges and sometimes you need help to release your tension." Mr. Carl rolled his chair closer to Jeffrey so their knees touched.

"Uh, can we start the lesson now?" Jeffrey managed to croak out.

"Sure, but you've been really tense lately. Time to relax." He brushed his hand across Jeffrey's thigh and up underneath his athletic shorts. "I can show you some relaxation techniques. When I was a boy, my uncle taught me some things I'd like to share with you about stress relief. I understand what it's like for your hormones to flame up like Moses' burning bush. It's natural. You know I want to be a father figure to you."

Jeffrey stood, his heart thudding. He wanted to run, but he also wanted to stay. He sat back down and placed his guitar across his lap, covering his bare thighs. "A father figure? I have a dad." *Mr. Carl is frigging insane. Have I done something to lead him on? Holy crap.*

Mr. Carl acted like nothing had happened. "Okay, Jeffrey. Let's see. Which song do you want to practice first? The one for the altar call?"

"Uh, yeah."

Jeffrey fumbled through the lesson, fingers trembling and hands shaking as he struggled to remember the chord changes. *I hope Mama gets here soon. I feel sick.*

Thankfully, Mr. Carl didn't do or say anything else strange for the rest of the lesson or for the next three weeks. Jeffrey began to feel comfortable again and wondered if he had imagined the super weird interaction with Mr. Carl. He tried to erase the fuzzy memory every time it popped into his head.

One Wednesday toward the end of summer, his mom said she'd pick him up after his guitar lesson and then they'd go visit his grandma in the hospital. After practicing for almost an hour with Mr. Carl, Jeffrey put his guitar back in the case and stood to leave.

Mr. Carl stood too. "You've made amazing progress this summer, Jeffrey. You've grown as a musician and a man." Mr. Carl reached out his arms and hugged Jeffrey, then began rubbing his legs, groin, and chest back and forth against Jeffrey.

Jeffrey's mind became a blur. He felt like he'd left his body and was watching this happen from across the room. Mr. Carl's cologne overpowered him, making him gag. Then his mind snapped back to reality. *What the hell is he doing? I've gotta get away. But it kind of feels good. What's wrong with me?* He tried to back away, but Mr. Carl had a firm grip around his shoulders.

"Ah, sweet Jesus, there's nothing I admire more than a young, talented musician," Mr. Carl groaned, as he reached inside the elastic waistband of Jeffrey's shorts. His breath was warm against Jeffrey's face.

Jeffrey felt himself getting hard and suddenly froze. *Oh shit, does this mean I'm gay? This can't be happening.* Not knowing what to do with his hands, he plastered them to his side like a soldier at attention.

At that moment, Dale opened the door. "Bro, Mama is waiting... hey, what's going on? What are you doing? Get away from my brother!" he screamed at Mr. Carl.

"Oh hi, Dale," Mr. Carl said and quickly released Jeffrey. "I was just telling your brother what a stellar guitar player he's become. Don't you think?" he said, smiling nervously.

Dale grabbed Jeffrey's arm. "Jeffrey, let's go. Get away from this freak. I mean it."

Jeffrey picked up his guitar case and followed his big brother. When his capo fell out of his pocket, he didn't stop to pick it up.

The next few months were a hazy nightmare. After Dale told their mama what he'd seen, Jeffrey's parents peppered him with questions and, of course, forbade him from guitar lessons and youth group. His daddy called a cousin who'd belonged to the Pennsylvania church where Mr. Carl had served and asked if he'd ever heard about him messing with boys.

The cousin told him, "There were some allegations by a couple of the teenage boys. But nothing they could prove. You never know what kids will say these days."

When Mr. Williams pressed for more information, the cousin admitted, "After a lot of rumblings from the congregation, the deacons finally told Carl to apply for a job elsewhere and said they'd give him a good recommendation. But I'm telling you, Carl did a lot of good things for our church. Our new youth pastor isn't half as good."

Jeffrey's dad approached a church elder about Carl's unseemly behavior with his son, and all hell broke loose. One deacon blamed Jeffrey, saying he was gay and going against God's will. Another said Jeffrey was "lying about Carl to cover up his own sins." Rumors ran wild.

Although some of the congregation sided with Carl, one woman told Mrs. Williams, "My nephew was a member at the church where Carl worked in Pennsylvania. After my nephew went away to college, he admitted Carl had, well, touched him and all. Lord, it pains me to even say this, but I thought you should know." She patted Mrs. Williams on the hand. "I'm praying for your family. Our God is in charge."

The deacons had a private meeting with Carl to discuss the allegations. Carl and Alicia remained at the church. Jeffrey's family did not.

Jeffrey's mama insisted on taking Jeffrey to a counselor. He went three times but barely talked. Mr. Williams' blood pressure skyrocketed, and his wife worried he would physically harm Carl. She convinced him to apply for a job at the metro police department in Savannah, her hometown. She'd been homesick ever since she had followed her then-military husband to Ohio.

Jeffrey felt guilty for causing all the drama and insisted it was no big deal. He blamed himself for uprooting his family. But when the Allied moving van drove up in their yard, he was relieved to be moving far, far away from Cleveland.

* * *

Now, eight years later, Jeffrey leaves the mall parking lot and turns the Crown Vic into the driveway of the office complex in Savannah, the city he'd been so happy to escape to as a teen. He spots the sign that says "Dr. Laura Fisher." After parking the car and unbuckling his seat belt, he steps out and throws up on the grass. Wiping his lips with a tissue, he pops a piece of peppermint gum in his mouth and trudges inside.

Chapter 41

Jeffrey takes a deep breath and opens the door to Dr. Fisher's office. He's relieved there's no one inside the waiting room. Dr. Fisher's receptionist smiles and points to the sign-in clipboard on the counter. He sits on a leather chair in the corner, flips through a *Savannah Magazine*, then picks up a copy of *Law Enforcement Today.* His eyes dart around the room; he can't concentrate on reading. A few minutes later, a petite woman with hair pulled back in a ponytail opens the waiting room door and says, "Hi, Jeffrey. I'm Laura Fisher. Come on back."

Let's get this over with. He stands and shakes her hand, trying his best to appear professional and calm, even though he just threw up in her parking lot.

Jeffrey follows Dr. Fisher down a hallway and into her office. A bookcase against one wall is filled with books. A green plant sits on the top shelf between two funky pieces of pottery.

"Have a seat wherever you like," Dr. Fisher says, gesturing with her hand.

In tan khaki pants, a flowing blouse, and brown Birkenstocks, Dr. Fisher reminds Jeffrey of the counselor he'd seen a few times in Ohio. *Granola girls. I guess most shrinks are hippies.*

Dr. Fisher pulls two bottles of water from a small refrigerator. "Would you like one?"

"Yes ma'am," he says, reaching for a bottle. Jeffrey sits in a chair across from Dr. Fisher and focuses on a painting on the wall behind her. It shows the ocean and sea oats blowing across sand dunes.

"My sister painted that. She knows I'm a beach bum at heart."

"Nice." He takes a swig of water, thankful to get the bad taste out of his mouth.

"Okay, Jeffrey. Thanks for coming and for being on time. Do you know why you're here?"

"Uh, my supervisor told me to come," he mutters.

"Right, you've been referred to me by the County Human Resources Department." She glances at the file folder in her lap, then leans forward and says softly, "Before we get started, I want to say I'm sorry you're going through such a stressful time."

Jeffrey remembers Anne Gardner telling his rookie police class the first thing to say to a crime victim is, "I'm sorry." And she'd mentioned it's also helpful to offer them water. *Hmm, guess that makes me a victim.*

"I've been asked to do what's called a fitness for duty evaluation." She pauses and looks at Jeffrey who stares at his shiny brown shoes.

"Your employer wants to make sure you're able to perform your job safely and effectively," she continues. "You're not here today as punishment but for me to assess your current ability to carry out your duties as an investigator with the Violence Intervention Program. I did say that right–Violence Intervention Program?" She glances at the front of the file.

"Yes ma'am." Jeffrey twists a paper clip he found on the end table. Beads of perspiration form on his forehead. *Look lady, I'm not the crazy one. It's Harold Carter who's nuts. And if I'm the victim, why am I getting blamed?* But he holds his tongue and places the cold water bottle against his temple. *It's not Dr. Fisher's fault. She's just doing her job.*

"Jeffrey, I want to be clear. This is not a counseling session. You may decide to see a counselor to confidentially discuss your situation. I'm the psychologist who does the evaluation. The information I receive, both in writing and through our discussion, will be given to your employer. I've done many of these evaluations for law enforcement officers."

Jeffrey's throat is so parched he can barely speak. He gulps some water and croaks out, "Uh-huh." He could refuse to take the test, walk out her door, and probably get fired. *But if I do that, the D.A. wins.*

His other option is to stay strong, go through with this stupid evaluation, and stick with his accusation against Harold Carter. He jostles his leg.

"Do you remember taking a psychological evaluation before joining the police department?" Dr. Fisher asks.

"Yes ma'am."

"Was that your first job after college?"

"Yes ma'am." Jeffrey focuses on a small framed photo on Dr. Fisher's desk of her hugging a golden retriever.

"And how long were you with Metro before you were hired as an investigator in the Violence Intervention Program?"

"About six months." A soothing hum comes from a small gadget on top of the refrigerator. *I guess that's one of those white noise machines. Maybe I need one to help me sleep.*

"Okay, this test is similar to the one you took before getting hired as a police officer. This one is called the Minnesota Multiphasic Personality Inventory–MMPI for short. It's a fancy title for a bunch of true/false questions. There are no right or wrong answers. Some of the questions seem ridiculous, but it's a standardized test that's been used for decades. The exam's purpose is to answer two questions: Does the employee have psychological problems and can the employee perform their job in a safe and effective manner? There's a computerized version and a written version. I can administer it either way."

A siren wails outside, and they both look toward the window. Jeffrey knows it's a fire engine, not a police car, but he won't be surprised if he hears a cop car next. They both sit quietly until the siren fades into the distance.

One of his first calls at Metro was a domestic violence dispute. The boyfriend had started a kitchen fire by throwing a pan of grease at his girlfriend. Fortunately she ducked and wasn't injured. It was the third time they'd responded to that apartment in two months. Jeffrey had been disgusted with the woman for not leaving the first time.

Dr. Fisher pulls a paper from her file. "Before we proceed, I need you to sign a form called an informed consent. It means you understand you're here for an evaluation, and the results will be provided to your employer. Do you have any questions?"

Jeffrey takes the paper, his hand trembling. "No ma'am. I don't think so." Dr. Fisher hands him a pen and Jeffrey signs his name.

Dr. Fisher looks at her watch. "Jeffrey, would you rather take the test on the computer or with paper and pencil?"

"Uh, on the computer I guess." Jeffrey stands and rubs his sweaty palms on his pants legs. *Thank god the talking part is over.* His foot has gone to sleep, and his neck feels tight like when he uses the pull-down weight machine at the gym. He hasn't felt up to going there in weeks. Wiggling his foot to get the circulation going, he follows Dr. Fisher out the door. She points out the restroom at the end of the hall. "Feel free to take a break now or whenever you want."

They go into a windowless office with a chair in front of a metal desk with a computer on it. A jar of peppermints and a box of Kleenex are on a small table in the corner. Dr. Fisher logs on. "It's self-explanatory. You click 'start' and type in your name and social security number. Then begin answering the questions by clicking true or false. If you want to change an answer, click the 'change my answer' button. If you have any problems, dial 0 on the phone and either the receptionist or I will come help. Any questions?"

"No ma'am." Jeffrey sits down as Dr. Fisher closes the door behind her. He unwraps a peppermint and pops it in his mouth. *I'm gonna do this fast and get the hell out of here.*

He scrolls to question one. *Every time I move I have pain.* False.

I wish I could be as happy as others seem to be. He clicks true.

Once in a while, I think of things too bad to talk about. He clicks false, then changes his answer to true after remembering the youth minister in Ohio. *Gross. I wish I could delete that crap from my brain.*

The questions on the screen seem endless, and after a while, Jeffrey gives up trying to guess which answers will make him "fit for duty."

I can't believe I'm taking this dumb test. Maybe I am crazy. Maybe I caused all these problems myself. I could move to Atlanta, join my cousin's band, and forget all this bull.

The next question is, "*I like Popular Mechanics magazine.*" *Say what?* He reads the question again. *This is insane.* He clicks false. Then true. Then false again. *Who cares?*

I have thoughts of suicide. True. Jeffrey stares at the computer screen. *Just once in a while when my brain goes into overdrive.*

Before long, he's up to question 32:*I know who is responsible for most of my troubles.* He clicks true. *Damn right I know. It's Harold Carter, District Attorney of Chatham County.* His mind wanders back to the trip to Chicago when he had to share a hotel room with his boss, then to when he walked in on him at the gas station restroom. *Why did I ever apply for this job? My career is ruined.*

His stomach churns, but he plows through until he answers all the questions and clicks *submit.* He heads back to the waiting room, relieved to be done.

* * *

Dr. Fisher reviews Jeffrey's file again. It lists Jeffrey's age as twenty-two, but he looks even younger. His sad brown eyes remind her of her dog's expression when she saw him at the pound. Whatever the results of today's evaluation, she hopes he will see a therapist. *He looked so vulnerable. I can't imagine the stress he's under.* Although she's done many evaluations, she's never evaluated someone who's accused a powerful public official of sexual harassment.

Chapter 42

For the first time in five years, Clemson was hosting the S.C. Collegiate Newspaper Awards Ceremony, and they wanted to make a good impression on their fellow student journalists. A large cooler filled with beer sat on the floor where *Tiger* staffers were folding programs for the event. They sang along to Jimmy Buffet's "Margaritaville" blaring from the stereo.

Kevin popped open a Budweiser can. "Anne, want a beer? You seem so uptight lately."

Anne shook her head. "Nah, I'm not in the mood for beer. But Jimmy Buffet makes me want a frozen margarita."

"Well, I can make that happen," Dr. Griffin's voice boomed from the doorway. "I have the ingredients, and I bet somebody around here has a blender."

Anne looked up from folding and saw her professor. *Why is he here? He's like a damn boomerang. Always coming back.*

"I have a blender in my room," Cathy said. "Y'all want me to go get it?"

"Uh, no, that's okay," Anne said. "We've got plenty to drink."

Cathy headed to the door. "But you just said you wanted a margarita. Hey, it's five o'clock somewhere, and we're not gonna make it to Sloan Street Taproom tonight. I'll be back in a few."

"Excellent. I'll go get the rest," Dr. Griffin said, following Cathy to the elevator.

Kevin took a drag on his cigarette. "Dr. Hinchey would freak out if he found out our advisor was making us drinks, but it's actually pretty cool."

"It is not cool," Anne said. "I wish Dr. Hinchey was back. He trusted us to get everything done. He didn't show up at our meetings or look over our shoulders. And he sure didn't ply us with liquor."

Anne reached in the cooler and dug out a Budweiser. "Think I will have a beer." She wiped off the ice with her hand and took a swig before returning to folding programs.

"Good. You need it, my friend," Kevin said. "Just because Dr. G. has the hots for you is no reason to get all bent out of shape."

Anne's face flushed bright pink. "He does *not* have the hots for me. He's just an old geezer who drinks too much."

Anne placed a stack of programs in a box, took a few swigs of beer, and walked over to the big trash can. Before she could toss her beer can, someone yelled, "Hey, no need to waste perfectly good beer."

Anne set the can on the table. "Help yourself. Y'all have this under control. I'm going to study."

"Study what?" someone else asked.

"Astronomy," Anne said.

"But there's no test tomorrow." Kevin frowned.

"There might be a pop quiz, and I got a C on the last one. It's supposed to be an easy elective, and I'm screwing it up. Holler if you need me to do anything before the banquet. See you tomorrow night."

Roxanne, the quiet girl with long braids and wire-rimmed glasses, put her hand on Anne's shoulder. "You okay?"

"Yeah, I'm fine. It's just my GPA is going to suffer if I don't get my act together." Anne liked sweet Roxanne whose dream was to move to New Zealand after college to raise sheep and write poetry.

Anne scooped up her books and headed toward the elevator. She felt queasy remembering Dr. Griffin rubbing his body against hers and breathing hot beer breath on her neck. She never told a soul about that creepy incident. A terrible thought popped into her head. *Oh my god, what if Dr. Griffin got on the elevator with Cathy and groped her? I shouldn't have let them leave together. At least he's not drunk—yet.*

Kevin called out, "Anne, don't go. We've still got to make the signs and, more importantly, I need you to help me write whatever I'm supposed to say at the beginning of this shindig."

"You can handle that. I'm outta here."

"All right, kiddo. Take it easy, okay?"

"Sure thing."

The big clock on Tillman Tower chimed five times as Anne walked back to her dorm. *I miss Dr. Hinchey.* When she'd talked with him last week, he assured her he was recovering well, but the doctor still wanted him to rest.

In her room, Anne put off studying and looked through her closet for something to wear to the banquet. She didn't have many nice clothes at school, but everyone would be dressed up for the awards gala. She pulled out the little black dress her mama had insisted she bring. She removed it from the hanger and laid it across her bed.

Anne took off her jeans and shirt, then slipped the dress over her head, and looked in the full-length mirror. *Looks fine. A little low-cut though.* She had never thought the neckline was too low before, but lately, she'd become hyper-aware of her body. She found a safety pin in her desk drawer and tried to pin the neckline, but it didn't look right. The dress was loose on her frame. She had lost weight–definitely the freshman fifteen she gained last year. She hadn't had much of an appetite lately. And since she didn't want to run into Dr. Griffin, she hadn't been drinking beer at Sloan Street Tap Room.

She found her one pair of dressy shoes–fortunately black–in the back of the closet and wiped off the dust with a paper towel.

She rummaged through her jewelry box for the silver and turquoise necklace her mom had brought back from Albuquerque. Anne loved jewelry but seldom wore any. The only exception was the opal ring her parents gave her for Christmas when she was sixteen. It was a family joke. They'd decided not to exchange gifts that year but to use the money to do something for others instead. She and her parents had bought presents for a family whose house had burned; her older siblings also did good deeds. Anne was the only one who opened a present that Christmas morning. Her mama said, "We already had this ring for you." Her siblings teased her mercilessly. "You got a gift because you're the baby. Spoiled rotten."

Anne smiled, remembering that Christmas. She hung the black dress back in the closet and placed the turquoise necklace on her desk. *Okay, I'm all set for tomorrow night. Guess I'll study astronomy now.*

The next evening, Anne finished dressing and looked in the mirror one last time. She always wore foundation to cover up the blemishes that popped up out of nowhere, but this time she also dabbed on lipstick and mascara, then hurried outside where she'd agreed to meet a few *Tiger* buddies. As they strolled the short distance to the banquet, she admired the white dogwood flowers and inhaled the scent of honeysuckle so sweet it was almost overwhelming. *It's going to be a good night.*

Inside the banquet room, Anne ran into a high school friend who attended the University of South Carolina, and they hugged. "Hey girl, you look great,' Amanda said. "You're so skinny!"

"Awesome to see you! I didn't know you worked for the USC newspaper."

"I changed my major to journalism last semester and I love it. Do you get home to Alabama much?"

"All holidays for sure, and my parents visit here once in a while," Anne said. Kevin tapped on the microphone. Anne said goodbye to Amanda, then sat at one of two round tables near the podium reserved for *The Tiger* staff. Thank goodness Dr. Griffin was at a different table. He waved at her, but she quickly looked the other way. *That weirdo is not going to ruin this big night, dammit.* Anne nibbled a few green beans and took one bite of the rubbery chicken. Finally, it was time for the award announcements. *The Tiger* won awards for Best Editorial, Best News Story, and Best Overall College Newspaper. The Clemson students erupted into thunderous applause. Anne squealed and hugged her friends. When Kevin strutted back to the table with the three plaques, flashbulbs popped all over the room. "Let the celebration begin," he said, yanking off his tie.

Anne raised her glass to Kevin. "I guess those all-nighters have paid off. We deserve this. I wish Dr. Hinchey were here. Is someone going to call him?"

"I will," Roxanne said.

Most of the banquet-goers stayed afterward to enjoy kegs of beer. Anne downed her first cup and held it out for Kevin to pour a second. The lively deejay from WSBF, the campus radio station, coaxed people to dance. Anne, beer in hand, joined the crowd on the floor. She hadn't felt that happy in a long time.

But when two big arms reached around her waist from behind, she jumped. Dr. Griffin said, "Congratulations! So proud of y'all."

"Thanks," she said, untangling herself from his grip. *What the hell?* She made her way to the corner to refill her cup and darted outside for fresh air. She leaned against a tree and sipped her beer.

After a few minutes, she felt better and went back inside to join the crowd dancing to "Brick House" by The Commodores. When the music changed to a slow dance, Dr. Griffin appeared beside her. "Hey there, my favorite journalist, dance with me."

She tried to walk past him, but her ankle turned and she stumbled into his big chest instead. "I hate these stupid heels!"

"I got you. Don't worry. You look great in heels," he whispered in her ear as he put a hand behind her back to steady her. The next few minutes were a blur. Was she spinning or was it the disco ball above her head that made her feel that way? Afraid she may vomit, she stumbled to the bathroom and splashed cold water on her face. That helped. She braced herself against the porcelain sink for a couple of minutes. *Why did I drink so fast? I've got to focus. Actually, I've got to get the hell out of here.*

When she walked out of the restroom, Dr. Griffin was waiting with a cup of water. "Here, drink this. I don't want Dr. Hinchey finding out you got drunk. He wouldn't approve."

She snatched the cup from his hand and pushed her way through the crowd. He followed her and touched her shoulder. "Looks like you're done celebrating. Let me walk you to your dorm. I want to make sure you're safe."

"No!" she yelled and pushed him away. "I don't want you to walk me back. Not now. Not ever. Get away." She spotted Roxanne in a chair near the door. Somehow, she had the presence of mind to walk over to her and yell above the music, "Roxanne, would you please, could you please walk back to room, uh my dorm, with me?"

Roxanne, in a vintage tie-dyed dress, nodded. "Sure thing. I don't wanna hang around any longer anyway. Too many people. Let's get out of here."

"Dr. Griffin is gross. Seriously gross."

"I saw him following you around."

"Oh shit, just shit. What else did you see? I mean what do you, um really think, I mean..."

"Let's focus on getting you home." They headed back to the dorm, arm in arm, as the loud chirping of cicadas filled the night air.

Anne pointed up at the glittering stars. "Look! A disco ball like at the dance. The dance we had to leave," Anne muttered, kicking a pebble across the sidewalk.

How quickly a perfect night had turned into a terrible nightmare.

Chapter 43

Anne boils water for rotini, then slices zucchini, squash, and fat, juicy tomatoes from Davis Produce. She pours olive oil into the frying pan and adds the veggies. As they sauté, she grabs a loaf of garlic bread from the freezer and turns on the oven.

Little Kitty rubs against her leg. "So how was your day, Little Kitty? Maybe you won't be so lonely if I quit work and spend more time at home." Anne's stomach tightens as she contemplates what she would do at home all day. With Little Kitty at her heels, she trudges to the bedroom and changes into a comfy yellow sundress. The oven beeps, and she returns to the kitchen and slides the pan of bread into the oven.

Jon walks in. "Hey, what smells so good?"

"I'm cooking." She stirs the veggies. "And I may do it more often. Paula Deen won't have anything on me."

Jon grins and says nothing as Anne tears lettuce for a salad.

"You know, maybe I should think about leaving Victim-Witness. I'd have to figure out what my new normal would be though. I thought it would be years–decades–before I left my career." She sits at the table with Jon.

"Don't make any rash decisions. I've still got some financial stuff to figure out."

"I know. I know." She pokes the rotini with her fork. "This pasta is gummy. I put some butter in the water so it wouldn't stick, but I guess I cooked it too long. Ugh." She shoves the pasta around on her plate.

"If you put salt in it, the pasta won't stick." He slides his plate across the table. "The salad will be enough for me."

Anne sticks out her tongue. *Good grief. Does he know everything? Fine. He can do all the cooking.*

Anne scrapes the remaining globs of pasta into the garbage disposal, sits on the couch, and logs onto her laptop. She googles sexual harassment.

Jon picks up his keys. "Wanna ride with me to IGA? We're out of coffee."

"Nah. I'm researching sexual harassment again. I've got to help Jeffrey."

"Human Resources is supposed to be helping him."

"Yeah, but you know how unreliable they are. They made Jeffrey get a psych evaluation when they should have sent Harold. Oh, we need bread."

"Okay. Anything else?"

"Maybe coffee," Anne says, staring at the computer screen.

"Uh, that's why I'm going." Jon shakes his head. "Back shortly." As his car pulls out of the driveway, Anne's phone rings.

"Hey, it's Kate. You in the middle of supper?"

No, we just finished. What's up?"

"I heard the County Commission is in an uproar about the harassment allegation against Harold. They have the authority to call in the Georgia Bureau of Investigation to investigate. So do the superior court judges."

"That would be great." Anne sits up straight on the couch.

"But so far no one is planning to do that."

"Why the heck not?"

"That takes guts, and they don't have any."

"It infuriates me that no one is doing anything."

"I know," Kate says. "I guess they think it would look bad to ask for an investigation of the district attorney. I hate politics. They're supposed to discuss it before Friday's commission meeting. It'll be behind closed doors because it's a personnel matter."

"Thanks for the info. I'm going to call my Commissioner right now. Talk later."

When Reggie Lawson answers, Anne says "Hi, Reggie, this is Anne Gardner. I hate to bother you at night, but I understand y'all are considering whether to ask the GBI to investigate Harold Carter. I'm calling to encourage you to do so."

"Well, I don't know. There's really nothing that can be done. He's an elected official."

Anne's sure steam is coming out of her ears. "I'm so tired of that excuse. Can't he somehow be held accountable?" She'd heard through the grapevine Reggie was displeased with the D.A. Surely he'd be in favor of taking some action.

"Unless he's convicted of a crime, it's up to the voters to decide his fate."

"I don't understand. He's accused of sexual harassment. He hires young men for jobs they are not qualified for. He spends taxpayers' money like it grows on trees. People are leaving his office in droves. Speaking of which, did you know Glenn Brinson tendered his resignation? He's an excellent prosecutor with lots of experience. We need him."

"I heard that."

"Reggie, I realize you're probably not supposed to say much, but I need to know what's going on. I won't reveal my source."

"Well, off the record, three women who interviewed for Jeffrey Williams' position are filing a civil suit, saying they are more qualified. Jeffrey Williams may file a suit too. You may have to give depositions."

"Oh lord."

"Anne, I know it's tough, but I hear you may be getting out of there. Might be the best thing for you."

"What?" Anne's tone is shrill. "Who's spreading that rumor? I mean even if I do resign, the rest of the office will continue to suffer. She clenches her fist. *I just told Jon I wanted to quit, but I haven't told anybody in county government.* "Reggie, I need to stay to protect my employees from Harold. You have no idea how bad it is. And it won't get better unless something is done."

"Well, we've been advised against calling in the GBI. We'll discuss it at Friday's meeting and see what happens."

"Who advised against it?"

"Ted Stevens, the county attorney, doesn't think involving the GBI is the best course of action."

"I'd like to know what *is* the best course of action."

"Anne, you'll get through this."

Anne wants to scream. Instead, she says, "Okay. Thank you." She clicks off the phone. *What did I thank him for?* Rote politeness is part of her Southern upbringing, but it's holding her back. She puts both hands on her pounding forehead. "Everybody's a wimp, including me," she says to no one. "How does he know what's best for me?"

Jon walks in, plastic grocery bags in each hand.

"I hate everybody who works for county government," Anne says, leaping up. "And why didn't you take our reusable bags? Those plastic bags last forever and end up in giant landfills. Or gagging fish in the ocean."

"Good grief. What's happened now?"

"Nothing's happened. And that's what's going to happen. A big fat nada. The county commission could call in the GBI to investigate Harold, but they probably won't. And I'm gonna have to give a damn deposition–with Harold present I'm sure–for three applicants who say they were discriminated against and..."

"Slow down. I lost you. What three applicants?" Jon plunks the bags on the kitchen table and puts away the groceries.

"Three women who applied for Jeffrey's position are claiming gender discrimination. They say they are more qualified, which is probably true. Dammit, I'm the one who signed the personnel action form hiring him. I'll look like a fool."

"Listen, Harold told you to hire Jeffrey. Think about it. You advise witnesses every day to tell the truth so that's what you'll do in a deposition. Anne, maybe you do need to get out of that mess. You're way too stressed. It's hurting you, and frankly, our marriage."

"What? Of course, I'm stressed! But with a lawsuit pending, I'll be stuck in the middle of all this foolishness anyway. I confronted Harold about Jeffrey, but that didn't stop the harassment. And Jeffrey may sue

Harold." She wrings her hands. "I'll just have to tell people about all this until somebody pays attention." She slams her laptop closed.

***

At the small, wooden desk in her Clemson dorm room, Anne read the brochure she'd picked up from the Student Affairs office. The glossy cover said, "What To Do If You Have Been Sexually Harassed." She flipped to the inside of the trifold. *"Sexual harassment is often unreported, but you don't have to tolerate unwanted sexual advances."* It said to trust your instincts and not blame yourself. Also that you can confront the harasser, report it to a supervisor or Human Resources, or consult an attorney. *"If you're in an educational institution, you may speak to a counselor for guidance."*

Chewing on her fingernails, Anne read the brochure twice. *Oh right, like I'm going to tell someone. Confront my professor in a required class? Who would believe me? I'm a 19-year-old kid, and he's a popular prof. And our damn newspaper adviser. And when that girl reported her supervisor at the cafeteria for harassment, the response was, "Boys will be boys."*

Small print at the bottom of the brochure said: *More information can be found in Title IX of Educational Amendments of 1972 and Title VII of the Civil Rights Act of 1964.* She sighed. *I should research that.* She glanced around the small dorm room and thought how childish it looked–the poster of red poppies in a grassy field, her stuffed Snoopy dog on her gingham bedspread. She'd always thought of herself as mature, but right then she felt like a kid. She just wanted to make good grades, drink beer, listen to Rod Stewart albums, and giggle with her girlfriends.

Her shoulders ached. *I need to quit The Tiger or report Dr. Griffin. Or both. My Tiger buddies think I have a crush on him. They'll think I'm paranoid and bat shit crazy if I accuse him.* She crumpled the brochure and stuffed it into her desk drawer, then switched on the radio. Gloria Gaynor was belting out "I Will Survive." She liked that song, but the line about "lay down and die" grated on her nerves. *Doesn't she know it should be* ***lie*** *down and die, not* ***lay*** *down and die*? Her English teacher mama had drilled into her the correct usage of lie and lay. *Oh dear god, who cares? I've got bigger things to worry about. Like my own survival.*

Chapter 44

At Jon's suggestion, Anne takes a vacation day. So on a balmy Wednesday, she strolls along the beach as waves crash against the shore and a breeze whips her hair. Remembering family trips to Gulf Shores as a kid, she longs for a sno-cone. *Yeah, I could start a sno-cone business at Tybee. Surely that would be a less stressful job.*

As the sun starts to burn her shoulders, she returns home, stretches out on the couch, and dives into a Mary Kay Andrews paperback. Twenty pages in, her eyelids droop. She props the book on her chest and snoozes. When the phone rings–she vows to change the annoying Irish jig ring tone–she leaps up and the book falls to the floor. She sees the call is from Harold. *Dammit. I'm not answering.*

Pacing around the room, phone in hand, she listens to the message: "Anne, call me. It's important. About Jeffrey."

What now? I'm not calling back. I'm really not.

But of course, she does. "Harold, you called? You know it's my day off."

"Um, it's about Jeffrey." Harold's voice cracks. "He's in the hospital."

"What in the world? Why?"

Harold clears his throat. "He tried to commit suicide last night."

"Oh my god. Is he okay?" Anne feels like someone punched her in the stomach.

"I think so."

"Well, is he or isn't he?"

"Yeah. He took a lot of pills. He's at Memorial. His mother called the D.A.'s office this morning. With LaShay on vacation and you taking off at the last minute, I took the call."

"I'll get to the hospital as soon as I can." She jumps in the shower to rinse off the sand, then throws on some clothes. On the 25-minute drive to Savannah, her mind races. *When was the last time I talked to Jeffrey? Was it after the psych evaluation? No, I didn't talk to him then. LaShay did say he called her afterward and sounded very down.* Anne eases up on the accelerator when she sees a police car just past the Bull River Bridge. *I should have stayed in touch while he's been on this forced leave, but if he was suicidal, wouldn't the therapist have done something? I hate Harold for driving this kid over the edge. And I hate myself for not helping him.*

At the next stop light, she calls Lisa. "Hey, you working E.R. today?"

"Yes."

"Good. Is Jeffrey Williams there?"

"Anne, you know I can't tell you. HIPPA."

"I know, but he's my employee and attempted suicide last night. Is he okay?"

"I'll see you when you get here, hon," Lisa says and clicks off.

Anne can't find a parking place near theE.R. so she parks on a nearby residential street. She sprints the two blocks to the hospital. Catching her breath inside, she heads straight to the woman behind the glass window. "I'm here to see Jeffrey Williams."

"Are you family?"

"No, I work with him. I mean, I'm his supervisor. I'm Anne Gardner."

The woman taps computer keys. "We don't have a Mr. Williams in the E.R."

Oh my god! Is he in ICU? Or dead? She leans closer to the window. "Where is he?"

"I'm sorry. I'm not authorized to release any information."

Anne steps back, nearly bumping into the woman behind her. She calls Lisa's cell, but it goes to voice mail. She calls Donna at the office for Jeffrey's emergency contact number. As she's scribbling the number, Lisa comes through the double doors behind the receptionist.

"Hey, Anne," Lisa gives her a quick hug.

"Hey. Where is Jeffrey?"

"I wish I could tell you, but you know I can't."

"Lisa, please."

Lisa twists a strand of blonde hair back into her ponytail. "I can tell you in general terms that the protocol after a suicide attempt is for patients to be transferred to the med psych unit." She points toward the Waters Avenue side of the hospital campus.

"Thanks," Anne says and rushes outside. She texts Mrs. Williams: *This is Anne Gardner. I'm at the hospital outside the E.R. I'm so sorry. How is Jeffrey?*

In a few minutes, Mrs. Williams texts back. *Please meet me in the parking lot outside the psych unit.*

Anne walks across the parking lot and a woman she assumes is Jeffrey's mother approaches her. "Mrs. Williams?"

"Yes, I'm Jeffrey's mother," the woman says and offers her hand.

"Mrs. Williams, I'm sorry to meet under these circumstances. How is Jeffrey?"

"He's better now. They pumped his stomach because he took a bunch of pills. I still can't believe it. It's like a bad nightmare." Her eyes brim with tears. An ambulance speeds by, lights flashing and sirens blaring.

"I'm glad he's okay," Anne says over the noise.

"He's embarrassed and pitiful now."

What can I say to ease this woman's pain? "I'm so sorry," she says softly.

"Thanks. Jeffrey's brother found him passed out on the couch early this morning. He left a note saying he was sorry, but he couldn't take it anymore. I'm just praising God that my baby boy is alive."

Anne takes both of Mrs. Williams' trembling hands in hers, and their eyes meet. *Strange how a crisis can bond people in a matter of minutes.*

"My husband was right, Ms. Gardner. Jeffrey should have never gone to work in the D.A.'s office. Jeffrey told me a little about how Harold Carter had been stressing him out. I don't know why they put him on administrative leave. And then ordered him to take that stupid psychological test, like he was crazy. I knew things were bad, but I didn't know it was this bad."

"Me either."

"And do you know Mr. Carter had the nerve to ask to see Jeffrey this morning? I didn't allow that."

Anne shifts from one foot to the other. "I hope I'm not intruding by coming here."

"No. It's fine. Jeffrey thinks a lot of you and LaShay." Mrs. Williams pulls a tissue out of her pants pocket and dabs her red eyes. "Jeffrey's resting now. I guess from that tranquilizer they gave him."

"I'm praying for Jeffrey and your family. If there's anything you need, please call me. Day or night. I mean it." Anne presses a business card into her hand. "Mrs. Williams, I'm gonna do my best to make sure everyone knows how dangerous Harold Carter is."

"Really? I hope you can. But he's the D.A. How will you do that, Mrs. Gardner?"

"I'm not sure, but I'll find a way."

Chapter 45

When Anne sees the sign that says, "Clemson, Next Exit," she moves into the right lane. She's in no rush to arrive at the Lake Hartwell house her friends had rented for the weekend. *Oh gosh, was coming to this reunion a good idea? I haven't seen most of these people in twenty years.* She grips the steering wheel with sweaty hands. *Will we still have anything in common? What will we talk about? Will they think I look old and fat?*

Driving through the small college town, she notices several new apartment buildings on East Campus. Much nicer student housing than the Shoeboxes she lived in. She pulls into the agriculture center. Folks come from miles around to buy their ice cream, milkshakes, and blue cheese. She can't wait to have a scoop of homemade peach ice cream.

She orders a cone from the young co-ed behind the counter and sits at a small round table outside on the patio. The creamy ice cream is filled with chunks of juicy peaches. *Why is Georgia called the peach state? South Carolina grows more, and they taste better.*

After she finishes, she strolls around the quiet campus. It feels like a furnace is blowing hot air from the sidewalk. Even upstate South Carolina is brutal in the summer. She takes a sip from her water bottle. She passes her first dorm–one of the high-rises–and the jock dorm across the way. Everything was so new and overwhelming when she came here as a freshman, a small-town girl from a tiny high school. She'd been homesick and worried that she'd be lost at a big university. But she made good friends, liked most of her classes, and found her passion her sophomore year when she joined *The Tiger* staff.

She sits on a bench under a shade tree outside Daniel Hall where all her liberal arts classes had been. She hopes Dr. Hinchey will attend the reunion. Thank goodness Dr. Griffin won't be there. She'd heard he was teaching at a different college.

During the two semesters when Dr. Hinchey was sick and Dr. Griffin became the faculty advisor, her life turned miserable. Now she realizes she was a victim of sexual harassment. Years ago, she'd sat with Kevin on this same bench late one afternoon.

* * *

"I guess you've heard I'm leaving a semester early to do an internship at *The Greenville News,"* Kevin said, pulling out a pack of Winstons from his shirt pocket.

"Wow. No, I hadn't heard. I've been out of the loop."

"Yeah, I noticed. You've been blowing us off."

Anne wrinkled her nose. "Oh, just a lot of classes."

"Come on now. You're only taking twelve hours this semester. Give me the skinny."

"I'm ready for Dr. Hinchey to come back," Anne mumbled, kicking a pebble across the sidewalk.

Kevin nodded. "Yeah, I think we all are."

"Dr. Griffin has been getting on my nerves, that's for sure." *Should I tell him more or will I sound whiny?*

"I've been asking you what was wrong, but I laid off 'cause you always clammed up. You quit going out with us Thursday nights. You won't return my calls, and you're hardly ever in *The Tiger* office anymore. We're worried."

Anne swallowed hard. It was true. She'd been doing her job as news editor, but she'd stopped socializing with the gang. "I figure y'all would think I was exaggerating if I told you how much he freaks me out."

"Aw, man. This sucks. Especially since I want to nominate you to be chief editor next semester while I'm gone."

"What?" She leans back. " No, not me."

Kevin put his hand on her shoulder. "Just think about it. You'd be great."

"Listen, Kevin. Actually, I've been thinking about quitting the paper altogether."

"Hold on, girlie! Don't go spazing out on me." He took a drag on his cigarette.

Anne wondered whether to tell him about her encounters with Dr. Griffin–the groping, gifts, calls, and unwanted information about his marriage. She knew keeping it bottled inside wasn't healthy. She'd lost weight, her grades had plummeted, and she'd made excuses to avoid seeing her friends.

But all she said was, "I think I'll have one of those cigarettes." He pulled the pack out of his pocket again and lit a cigarette before handing it to her. Her hand shook as she took it.

"Look, kiddo. Do I need to kick his ass? Because I can sure as hell do that."

"That might be a good idea," she said with a half-hearted smile. "But he's a professor, and we're just lowly students. He's got the power."

"Shit. Here comes the asshole now," Kevin muttered as Dr. Griffin ambled toward them, a thick journalism textbook under his arm.

"Hey there, you two. How's it going?" Dr. Griffin said, smiling down at them. "Kevin, I hope you're talking this gal into taking over your position as editor."

Kevin looked up. "Uh, no, we're just talking about, uh, a research paper that's due."

Dr. Griffin pointed to Anne. "What's a nice girl like you doing smoking?"

Anne coughed and looked the other way, wishing he would get out of her face. "I gotta get going."

She and Kevin stood simultaneously.

"Okay. Anne, please consider the editor position. I'll help you any way I can," Dr. Griffin said as he turned to leave.

When they were out of earshot, Kevin said, "Yeah, I bet he would. Anne, let's go to The Esso Club and have a beer. It'll just be townies there, no one you know. And I'm buying."

* * *

Adult Anne shakes her head to banish those old memories and focus on the reunion. After wandering around campus, she drives downtown and stops at Judge Keller's Store to buy tee shirts for herself and her grandson. Then she drives the ten miles to the lake house someone had found online. The front yard is filled with cars and trucks all sporting Clemson bumper stickers. *Well, here goes.* She checks herself in the rearview mirror. *Damn these crow's feet.* She'll bring in her suitcase later. Walking toward the backyard, she hears laughter and then finds about a dozen people gathered on the large deck facing the lake. There's a redwood bench along one side and chairs and a picnic table in the middle.

"Anne, you made it." Kevin greets her with a hug and smooch on the cheek. After more hugs and high-fives, she heads to the kitchen. Just like their college days, the refrigerator is filled with beer. She helps herself to a Miller Light. A tall guy wearing an apron is arranging a tray of yummy-looking snacks. "Shane, is that you?"

"Yep, the one and only. I've prepared these delicacies for you wacky people. Shrimp tacos are my specialty. Or maybe you'd like a cucumber sandwich, recipe compliments of my late Grandma Sally." Shane beams.

"Yum. Thanks." Anne finds a paper plate on the crowded kitchen counter and puts two tacos on it.

"Did I hear you live in Charlotte now, Shane?"

"Yep, sure do. This small-town boy now loves city life, except for the insane traffic, of course."

"What do you do there?"

"I work for an interior design firm. Those rich ladies love me more than their husbands and plastic surgeons." He laughs and balances a tray on one hand above his shoulder. "Let's go feed these old people."

Anne grabs a stack of napkins and follows him to the deck. She sits in an Adirondack chair beside Roxanne. Her friend hasn't changed a bit–braided hair, flowing gauzy shirt, and Birkenstocks. "I was hoping you'd be here, Roxanne. So, are you raising sheep in New Zealand?"

She laughs. "Nope, just three sons in the wilds of Oregon. Raising sheep would be easier."

Most gathered on the patio have thicker middles and sprinkles of gray hair; otherwise, they look the same as when they pulled all-nighters putting the paper together. They show family photos on their phones and catch up on their lives.

Diane gets teary-eyed telling about the recent death of her mother. Anne is shocked to learn that Diane, who they'd dubbed "Wild Child," is now a Presbyterian minister.

Roxanne whispers to Anne, "You know Kevin's wife died in a car crash five years ago?"

"Oh my gosh. I didn't know. How awful."

As night falls and stars begin to shimmer over the black lake, the drinks and conversation flow more freely. Everyone is buzzed, but not enough to accept Shane's invitation to skinny dip in the pool.

Munching on a taco, Anne asks, "So is Dr. Hinchey coming tomorrow?"

"Yep, he promised to come even though he's not in the greatest health," Roxanne says. "By the way, whatever happened to Dr. Griffin?"

Anne's shoulders tense.

"Y'all didn't hear?" Shane asks as he tightens the beach towel around his waist. "He got canned after four or five girls accused him of sexual harassment. It happened a few years after I graduated. I heard he came to class smashed a few times too. That cowboy was quite the asshole."

Anne sloshes her drink on her shirt. Shane gives her his towel that she uses to dab on the spill. Thankfully, he has on swim trunks.

"Of course, the higher-ups tried to keep it quiet, but at least he's gone. Went to North Dakota or some god-forsaken place."

Anne retreats to the bathroom. *So, I wasn't crazy. And I wasn't the only one.* She finds a washcloth, rinses it with cold water, and presses it to her forehead. A wave of guilt washes over her. *I should have reported him. Then he wouldn't have bothered those other girls.* She sits on the edge of the tub and tries to stop trembling.

After a few minutes, she hears a rap on the door, and Roxanne walks in. "Anne, you okay?"

"Yeah, I'm fine. I can't drink like I did in the old days. I mean I hardly ever drink now. Just a glass of wine here and there."

"Shane and Diane have made a delicious dinner for us–pasta primavera, salad, homemade bread, and chocolate something. I remember you love chocolate, right?"

Anne winces. "Oh yeah. But not now. Y'all go ahead. I'm going to get my suitcase and change clothes."

"Okay. I'll walk you to your car."

Anne's words tumble out. 'Roxanne, did you know Dr. Griffin, well–he, uh, he put the move on me big time? I should have reported it. I feel so bad for those other girls. No telling how many others he victimized. What a sicko."

Roxanne puts her arm around Anne as they walk outside to get the suitcase. "Listen, sweetie, we were just kids. I'm sorry you went through that."

Anne's eyes fill with tears. She remembers when Roxanne walked her back to her dorm after the newspaper awards banquet.

After a couple of minutes, Anne stands straighter, wipes her eyes with the back of her hand, and clears her throat. "I can tell you one damn thing. My current boss has been accused of sexual harassment, and I'm not going to let him get away with it like I did with Dr. Griffin. I've got to make things right this time. I mean, I work in the criminal justice system and that system needs to live up to its name."

"Good for you, my friend." They walk back to the house, arm in arm, with the chirping of cicadas filling the night air.

Chapter 46

On the drive back from Clemson, Anne mulls over the weekend. *I feel horrible for those other girls Dr. Griffin harassed. Now I've got to deal with Harold.*

She turns off the radio to concentrate. *How can I keep my promise to Jeffrey's mom to expose Harold? God, please help me.* She notices the low fuel light on the dashboard, so she takes the next exit. After refueling the car, she refuels herself with a Diet Coke and cheese crackers before hitting the interstate again.

It's dusk when she arrives home. She gives Jon a bear hug and holds onto him.

"Welcome home, darlin'. You okay?" he asks.

With her head buried in his shoulder, she says, "Yeah, just tired from driving and too much deep thinking."

"I'll bring in your suitcase. Why don't you take a shower? That'd make you feel better."

After a shower, Anne stretches out on the couch and gives Jon a rundown of the weekend. She doesn't mention Dr. Griffin, though. She's not sure why, but she's never told Jon about the harassment in college. Her phone buzzes. "It's Charisse."

"Anne, for the love of Pete, it's Sunday night and you're exhausted. Don't answer that. You can talk with her tomorrow."

Anne stares at her phone. "Wonder what she wants?"

"I have no idea but she doesn't need to be calling you."

"But what if..."

Jon shakes his head. "You're not her personal 24-hour crisis line."

"I guess you're right. She knows S.A.F.E. Shelter's crisis number." Anne swipes "Ignore call."

Anne crawls into bed. It doesn't take her long to fall into a deep sleep. She dreams she's strolling through a forest, with the afternoon sun slanting through a thicket of tall pines. *It's beautiful, but how am I going to get home?* Darkness descends, and all she hears are her pounding heart and the cries of a whippoorwill. Hoping to find her way out of the woods, she sprints down a long, dirt road until her legs ache. At a fork in the road, she recalls her mama reading her Robert Frost poem *The Road Not Taken.* Will she take the road less traveled?

Anne fumbles for the beeping alarm clock on her bedside table and turns it off. *Ugh. Monday morning.* She forces herself to roll out of bed.

At the office, she works on a grant proposal for a couple of hours, then returns Charisse's call but gets no answer. Harold strolls in and makes himself comfortable in the chair across from her desk.

"Good morning, Anne." He looks serious, but Anne never knows how to interpret his expressions.

"Hello." Anne feels the muscles in her back tighten. *What fresh hell am I going to face today?*

"Have you received the results from Jeffrey's psychological evaluation?"

"No, not yet."

"How's he doing since he got out of the hospital? I sent him a get well card and left a couple of phone messages, but he hasn't responded."

No surprise there. "Harold, you know you're not supposed to contact him or discuss him with me, either," Anne says through gritted teeth. She feels like screaming, *A get-well card? As in get well from the suicide attempt I provoked?*

"I hope he'll be okay," Harold says softly.

Anne nods. *He seems concerned about Jeffrey. Strange.*

Harold stands. "Let me know if you hear from him."

Anne narrows her eyes at him as he walks out. *Like hell I will.*

Chapter 47

"Isn't the feature about the Tybee bomb on tonight's 11:00 news?" Anne asks as she rearranges spice jars in the kitchen cupboard.

"Yeah," Jon says. "Hope we can stay awake." He's hunched over the kitchen table with a calculator and spreadsheet. "This is worrisome. Hospital income is way down."

"Why's that?"

"Delays in getting Medicare reimbursements, for one thing."

"Oh." Anne tosses a jar in the trash. "Nutmeg from 1990. Gotta go."

She joins Jon at the table, opens the newspaper, and tackles the word jumble. "Geez. Can this be right? The word is penis?"

Jon laughs. "What's on your mind?"

Anne erases her answer. "Never mind. I think it starts with an 'S.'"

Jon puts down his calculator and jots down the letters. "I bet it's spine."

Just before 11 o'clock, Jon clicks on the TV so they can watch the 50th-anniversary story of the nuclear bomb lost in the waters off Tybee. The reporter says, "During a practice exercise in 1958, the Air Force lost a 7,600-pound bomb when an F-86 fighter plane collided with the B-47 carrying the bomb. No one was injured, but the bomb was never found."

"Oh lord, a nuclear bomb is lurking just off our coast," Anne says, pointing to the window. "Is it emitting radiation?"

As if he heard her, Tybee Island Mayor Jason Buelterman appears on the screen. "Extensive research indicates there are no safety concerns."

The reporter holds up a tee shirt that says "Tybee Bomb Squad" and continues, "Five decades later, local businesses are making the best of this unusual situation by selling shirts and caps emblazoned with these words."

"Only on Tybee," Jon says, chuckling.

Anne heads toward the kitchen but turns around when she hears the TV anchor say, "Breaking news! Police are investigating a homicide on Savannah's westside. Neighbors called 911 after hearing several gunshots. Police arrived on the scene around nine p.m. and found a young woman dead in her apartment." The anchor looks at his notes. "Police are not releasing the victim's name until family members have been notified. We have our crime reporter on the scene now."

Outside a cinder block apartment complex, a reporter interviews a middle-aged woman. Anne drops her pencil and leans closer to the TV. The woman says, "I've lived in these apartments for six years. We've had some break-ins and stuff but never a murder. We're all pretty shook up."

Anne grabs the remote and turns up the volume. *Oh my god, that looks like Charisse's apartment complex. Or is it? Were there bushes out front?* She looks at Jon. "Whenever I hear the victim's a woman, I assume it's a family violence victim we've worked with."

"Now hon, don't jump to conclusions."

Anne paces around the den. "Jon, you know what I'm thinking, don't you?"

He groans. "No, but I'm sure you're about to tell me."

Anne digs her fingernails into her palms. "It kinda looks like Charisse's apartment building. What if the dead woman *is* Charisse?"

"You have no way of knowing that. I thought you said that couple was doing better."

"Yeah. They're back together. Charisse called me a few weeks ago to tell me she'd started nursing school. She sounded so happy."

"See. No need to worry."

"Yeah, but she admitted Bernie is super jealous. He accused her of cheating on him when she didn't come home right after class a couple of times. He gets mad if she's even a few minutes late getting home. Even wants her to quit school."

Jon frowns. "Oh."

"I swear Bernie's more volatile than that damn Tybee bomb!" Anne picks up her phone, sits on the sofa, and calls Charisse. "Damn. No answer. Remember she called last night, and I didn't answer? When I returned her call today, I got her voice mail and left a message."

"You've been way too involved with Charisse. Seems like you've crossed professional boundaries."

Anne glares at her husband. "I do *not* need you lecturing me about professional boundaries. You work with numbers all day. I work with people. There's a big difference."

He holds up his hand. "Okay, okay. I'm just worried about you. All the stress with Jeffrey and Harold. Plus, Charisse. It's taking a toll on you."

"I'm fine," Anne says, leaping up. "I'm calling Lisa. If she's working the E.R., she'll know who was shot." She calls Lisa and leaves a message. "Call me as soon as you can. It's important."

"If you're so concerned, call the police."

"I'm not going to bother them. They're probably still at the scene."

Jon takes off his glasses and yawns. "Okay, I'm hitting the hay. Please don't stay up all night."

"Okay." Anne stands in front of the TV, flipping channels. *Oh dear god, why did I listen to Jon and not answer her call last night? I pray she's okay."*

She calls Charisse and gets her voicemail again. "Hi, Charisse, this is Anne Gardner. Sorry I missed your call last night. Call me. Please."

Chapter 48

After tossing and turning all night on the couch, Anne gets up before daylight. She's at work by 7:15 and makes a beeline to Glenn's office. "Hey, know anything about last night's homicide?"

"Which one?" he grunts.

"Victim was a woman on the Westside. There was another one?"

"Yeah, a 19-year-old guy was killed on 34th Street a little after midnight."

"I hope I'm wrong, but I'm worried the woman is Charisse Butler who we've worked with a lot. Her husband's trial is next week."

Glenn calls the police and puts the phone on speaker. "Hey, it's Glenn at the D.A.'s office. Any homicide detectives there?"

"Hey. Detective Kelly here."

"Y'all got a name on the woman killed last night?"

Papers rustle in the background. "Um, black female, age 27. Charisse Butler. Family lives out of town, but they've been notified."

Anne gasps. "Oh my god!"

Glenn motions for Anne to be quiet. "Y'all got any lead, Kelly?"

"They're questioning the husband. Military guy. He's been arrested for domestics before."

"Yeah, and his trial is next week."

"Well, the victim won't be testifying. Somebody made sure of that."

"Yup. Will you email me the report?"

"Sure."

Anne drops into the chair across from Glenn. *Oh, Jesus, I should have answered Charisse's call. She was probably pleading for help.* "Please tell me the kids weren't home."

"We'll know in a minute when we see the report."

"I wonder what Harold will say about this," Anne says. "He finagled a low bond for her husband, and now she's dead. I still can't believe our boss did that."

"Nothing surprises me anymore. It's one reason I'm leaving. I wish the media would get wind of all that." He looks at the computer. "Here's the report."

Anne gets up to read the screen. "Oh my god. The kids were home, in their bedroom."

"I wonder what they saw or heard. Think they'll make good witnesses?"

"No. One's a baby. The older one–Bernie, Jr.–is only three."

"Is he verbal?"

"Yes."

"Then hopefully the police will set up a forensic interview at the children's advocacy center."

Anne scowls. "Could you please stop thinking like a prosecutor for one minute? The kid's mother was just murdered."

"I AM a prosecutor, and I want someone to nail this guy's sorry ass."

Anne reads the rest of the report. "It says her husband called 911 and reeked of alcohol when police arrived." Anne shudders. "Oh my god, they found her on the kitchen floor in a pool of blood." She puts her hand over her mouth. "I feel sick."

"Take it easy, Anne. Hmm. Report says husband was still at the scene when they arrived."

"Yeah, and he told them it was an accident. Lying dirtbag. I better go tell Janine to contact Charisse's parents about our services."

"I'll let you know if I find out anything else. I know this sucks for you. Y'all worked with that victim a lot." He pauses. "Want some coffee?" He reaches into his desk drawer and pulls out a Snickers bar. "Or candy?"

"No thanks."

Anne walks down the hall on autopilot and hears, "Good morning, Anne. Why so glum?" It's Harold.

Anne's eyes meet his. "Bernie Butler's' wife was murdered last night."

He arches his eyebrows. "Oh?"

Oh? Is that all he can friggin' say? Anne brushes past Harold.

"Wait, Anne. The military couple?"

Anne clenches her teeth and turns to face him. "Yes, the Army couple. You remember them, don't you? You and the father convinced the judge to lower the husband's bond the first time he was arrested for assaulting his wife."

Two employees stroll by and say good morning. Harold smiles and nods at them, before he looks back at Anne. "Yes. I remember," he says in a monotone.

Does he have no feelings at all? Anne turns away and walks to the bathroom. She splashes cold water on her hot cheeks. *I hate myself. And Jon for talking me out of calling her. Gotta get myself together. Breathe.*

She walks straight to Janine's cubicle. Janine says, "Guess you heard?"

"Yeah, when I saw last night's news, I was afraid it was Charisse."

"Tabitha just called and told me. The folks at S.A.F.E. Shelter are devastated. They thought things were going better for the Butlers."

"Me too." Anne pounds her fist on the desk. "Damn it, Charisse did all the right things, reporting it, getting counseling, going to the shelter."

"I do wonder if Charisse would be alive if she hadn't reported the abuse. The court system is so slow, and it can't work miracles."

"We'll never know," Anne says.

"Tabitha said even though this is the sixth domestic homicide this year, this is the first S.A.F.E. Shelter client who's been killed in a long time."

"I have to tell you something." Anne clears her throat. "Charisse called me Sunday night, and I didn't answer. I feel horrible."

"Anne, you can't blame yourself. You're not the police."

"I called her back Monday, but got her voice mail." Anne's voice breaks. "Lord, my heart hurts for those children."

"I hope Charisse's parents get custody. I'm gathering materials for them. I want them to know the compensation fund covers funeral expenses and counseling for the family."

"Good." Anne puts her hand on Janine's shoulder. She knows this must bring back painful memories of Janine's own abuse. "Listen. This is tough on all of us. I'm here if you need someone to talk to."

Janine exhales. "Okay."

Anne walks to her office, calls Jon, and tells him.

"Oh darling," he says. "I'm so sorry."

"Me too." Exhausted, Anne somehow muddles through the rest of the day.

Glenn calls at five-thirty. "Thought you'd want to know they picked up that bastard Butler and hauled him off to jail for murdering his wife."

Chapter 49

Curled up on the couch at home, Anne sobs into a pillow. *What good am I? I can't protect my employees. I can't protect victims. My husband is sick of me.*

She doesn't hear Jon walk in. He sits beside her, hugs her, and places a carton of Publix chocolate chip cookies on the coffee table. "Hey sweetie."

"Hey." Anne sits up and blows her nose.

"Want a cookie?"

"No thanks." She leans her head on his shoulder. "I feel terrible. I wish I had answered Charisse's call."

"Hon, you can't dwell on that. She has, I mean had, lots of resources."

"Yeah, but I still feel awful."

"Don't beat yourself up. It's–"

"I know. I know. But I've gotta do something. I mean something about Harold. He not only harasses employees, but he also got Charisse's husband out on bond, and now Charisse is dead."

Jon punches the back of the couch. "I wanna knock the shit out of Harold."

"Me too. Today was the last straw. He acted so nonchalant when I told him Charisse had been murdered. Does that man have any conscience at all?"

"Apparently not."

Anne cries softly.

Jon strokes her hair. "What is it, hon? What else has Harold done?"

"Well, it's not just Harold and Charisse." She bites her lower lip. "I need to tell you something else. Something I've never told you."

"Okay. What is it?"

Anne wipes her eyes. "When I was a Clemson student, a professor sexually harassed me. I didn't tell anyone how bad it was. At the newspaper reunion, I found out he harassed other girls before he was finally fired. If I'd spoken out, I might have saved them from the misery I went through."

Jon stands. "Oh god, Anne. I'm sorry. What did that creep do?"

"I mean he didn't rape me or anything," Anne says, her voice cracking. "But when he became our newspaper advisor, he put the moves on me. Made me real uncomfortable. My entire sophomore year was horrible."

Jon paces. "That bastard. Tell me everything."

"He was always following me around." She closes her eyes. "And uh, one night when he was sloppy drunk, he groped me on an elevator. Stuff like that."

Jon's face reddens. "Wow. How come you never told me?"

"I don't know. For years I did a good job burying the memories, but this mess with Jeffrey brought it all back."

Jon kicks Little Kitty's squeaky toy mouse across the floor. "Back then people might not have believed you anyway. This does help explain why you're always trying to protect everybody else."

"I still feel guilty for not reporting it. I quit the newspaper for a while but eventually went back when our regular advisor returned from sick leave. But it wasn't the same. It's like a part of me was missing; I couldn't get my groove back."

Little Kitty returns with the mouse and drops it at Jon's feet. Jon tosses it across the room. "You're not responsible for what that jerk did and you're not responsible for what Harold's done."

"No, but I am responsible for *my* actions. I didn't speak out in college, but I have to now."

"What do you mean?" Jon asks, heading for the refrigerator. "I'm getting a beer. You want wine?"

"No."

Back in the den, Jon pops the top on his Bud Light and takes a swig.

"I did a lot of thinking on the drive home from Clemson but couldn't decide what to do about Harold, but now I know." She pauses. "I'm going to the media."

Jon's mouth drops open. "What?"

Anne hugs the couch pillow, now damp with her tears. "Yep. I want to spill all. Tell them Harold harassed Jeffrey and helped a violent defendant get a low bond."

"Slow down. They already know about Jeffrey's allegation."

"They need to know more."

"Like what?" Jon asks.

"They don't know the graphic details about the Chicago and Valdosta trips or that Harold personally delivered the application to Jeffrey."

"Won't that embarrass Jeffrey? I thought he was pretty shaky these days."

"Of course, I'll make sure to get permission from Jeffrey and his mom. I told her I'd try to stop Harold from victimizing others, and I've got to keep my word. Plus, Jeffrey's already filed a lawsuit that's public, but it's pretty weak. Not many details. I'm not hopeful the lawsuit will be enough to stop Harold's behavior."

Jon sits beside her and puts his hand on top of hers. "Hon, I know you're upset, but you need to think about this. You know Harold will retaliate. He might fire you. Are you prepared for that?"

Anne blinks rapidly. "Guess I have to be. Or I could quit before he fires me."

"Think about it, Anne. You'd be seen as a whistleblower, and that could make it hard to find another job."

Anne looks away.

"Look, this is a lot to process. We need to review our finances. I doubt you're old enough to get a pension. I'm not sure we could comfortably live on one income."

"It's not like we haven't discussed my leaving."

"I know. Leaving is one thing, but going public? Whoa. Can't he sue you for slander?"

"We'll never know."

"You need to talk to an attorney before making a rash decision. I'll go with you."

"Attorneys are expensive, and you're always worrying about money. And if I do see a lawyer, I can go by myself."

Jon exhales loudly.

"I'll see what Kate thinks about my getting a lawyer," Anne says.

"Oh great," Jon yells. "You're going to talk to Kate? You don't trust my judgment at all, do you?"

"Don't make this about you, Jon. It's my decision."

"Here's the thing. This probably isn't the time to bring it up, but there are rumors of layoffs at the hospital."

Anne stands. "What? Why haven't you told me?"

"I didn't want to add to your stress."

"Well, don't keep secrets from me, for god's sake."

Jon crushes his beer can. "Seems like we've both been keeping secrets."

Chapter 50

Anne does her best to focus on work but is relieved when Kate comes in around noon. "It's Chick-fil-A day downstairs, and I grabbed two sandwiches. Want one?"

"Sure."

Kate hands her a sandwich and settles into a chair. "The prelim has been scheduled for Bernie Butler."

"I assume our boss hasn't helped him get out of jail again?"

"No, thank God. How ya doing, my friend?"

"I'm okay. Close the door."

Kate reaches over and pushes it shut. "Oh, this sounds serious. What's up?"

"I'm going to tell the media everything about Harold," Anne whispers.

Kate yells, "What? Are you crazy?"

"Shh."

"Harold will go ballistic."

"I'm well aware of that."

"He could fire you. He IS your boss."

Anne takes a sip from her water bottle. "I know that too. But enough is enough. Look. I had a college prof who sexually harassed me. At the reunion, I found out he did the same thing to other women. I feel guilty now for not telling anyone."

"That's awful, but you shouldn't blame yourself."

"Well, I do, and I'm not making that mistake again."

"But people already know about the allegations against Harold."

"Exactly. And they haven't done a damn thing. It's time for the public–the voters–to know, but no one will go on the record. I'll tell the media about Harold helping get a low bond for Charisse's husband."

"What does Jon have to say about this?"

"Not happy. He thinks I need to talk to a lawyer."

Kate scoots to the edge of her chair. "I agree. Harold might be able to sue you for defamation. I'll get you the names of a couple of employment attorneys. Oh Anne, please think long and hard before you do something you may regret."

"We'll see. That's enough about my insane life. How was your weekend?"

"Busy. Two soccer games and a school project." Kate looks at her watch. "Time for my probation hearing." She stands and brushes the crumbs from her skirt. "Anne, please promise me you won't rush into anything. And why have you only eaten two bites of your sandwich?"

"Not hungry."

"You've lost weight, haven't you?"

"Yeah."

"Well, you gotta eat. You know I'll go with you to the attorney's office if you want."

"Thanks, but I'm a big girl. You and Jon both think I'm incompetent."

Kate shakes her head. Oh Anne, of course not. We'll talk soon."

* * *

Three days later, Anne gets home early and turns on the TV. Dr. Phil is confronting a woman about meddling in her grown daughter's business. "Your daughter seems mature and wise. Don't smother her," he says. *Sounds familiar. I'm tired of Jon and Kate hovering and telling me what to do.*

Jon arrives home and sits beside Anne on the couch. "Hey, hon. How did the meeting with the attorney go?"

"Fine."

"What did he say?"

"Basically for public figures like the D.A., there's a higher standard to prove in libel suits than for private citizens. Public figures must prove actual malice."

"Hmm. What does actual malice mean in the legal sense?"

"It's when someone lies, on purpose, to hurt another person."

"Well, Harold sure can't prove you lied."

"Right. I also asked about whistleblowers." She looks at her notes. "The law protects whistleblowers unless the info provided is false or with willful disregard for its truth."

Jon gives a thumbs up. "Sounds like you're protected."

"Yes, except that Georgia is an at-will state, meaning employers can fire someone for any reason, no reason, or even a bad reason. But I knew that."

Jon nods.

"I'm still thinking of resigning before he has a chance to fire me. I would hate to have that on my work history."

"Exactly. Hon, I've been doing a lot of figuring. We can make it if we sell the house and move into a small place in Savannah where property taxes aren't so outrageous. And you'd need to get a job soon. Of course, that's all iffy because the economy hasn't recovered from the recession. The housing market is still slow, and not many places are hiring."

"Oh, Jon, I can't think about all that now. I need to focus on talking to the TV reporter."

"Are you sure you want to go public with all this?"

"Yes, I'm sure." Anne puts her head on his shoulder. "Thanks for being patient with me. I know I've been a little intense lately."

Jon grins. "That's putting it mildly."

Chapter 51

While sitting in the H.R. waiting room, Anne cleans out her purse, throwing out expired coupons, grocery receipts, and gum wrappers. Then she looks down and counts the dirty spots on the carpet.

At last, Maurice opens the door. "Hello, Anne. Come on in," he says. She follows him into his office and sits across from his desk.

Maurice straightens his red necktie. "What can I do for you today, Anne?"

Seriously? No apology for making me wait even though I had an appointment. She sits erect in the chair. "Let me get right to the point, Maurice. You asked me recently if I could retire. I want to find out what benefits I'm entitled to if I retire or resign."

Maurice clicks on his computer. "Give me a minute to review your records."

"I checked the personnel manual, but there wasn't anything that applies to my situation." She spies a Downtown Rotary Club plaque on the wall behind his desk. It's the same downtown chapter as Harold. *Just great.*

Maurice looks up from the screen. "I'm sorry, but it seems you're not eligible for a pension."

"How can that be? I've worked for the county for twenty years."

"True. But you're not fifty-five years old yet."

Anne bites her lower lip. "Oh. What about health insurance?"

"No. Sorry."

Damn. Jon won't like this. She can't think of what else to ask, so she reaches for her purse hanging on the arm of the chair.

Maurice clears his throat. "Before you leave, tell me how Jeffrey Williams is doing. I heard he was hospitalized recently. I'm concerned."

Anne feels her face flush. *If you actually gave a damn about Jeffrey, you wouldn't have put him on administrative leave and forced him to take a psych test.* "As you know, he's still on administrative leave. How long can he expect that to last?"

Maurice rubs his chin. "I'm not certain. We've referred him to a counselor at the Employee Assistance Program. I'm sure he's under a lot of stress."

"Of course he is. And speaking of stress, I want to make sure my insurance covers a few therapy sessions for me."

"Sure. We can set you up with the EAP."

"No, I want to see a counselor I choose," Anne says. "I think the county's EAP is a little too close to all this drama with Harold and Jeffrey."

"It would have to be a provider in our network. There aren't many on that list."

Before she can reply, there's a loud knock on the door, and Ted Stevens, the county attorney, saunters in. *How unprofessional! H.R. matters are supposed to be confidential.*

"Hello, Anne. How are things going with you?"

What a stupid question. "Not good, Ted. I'm between a rock and a hard place. My employee accused my boss of sexual harassment." She stands and looks at Maurice. "I'll be waiting on your call about the counselor."

Ted follows her to the waiting area.

Why is he following me? She turns and leers at him.

"I know you're in a precarious position, Anne. But don't you worry, young lady. You've been an exemplary county employee for a long time. If you leave your position, we'll take good care of you." He pats her shoulder.

Anne steps back. "Exactly how do you plan to do that, Ted?"

"We'll help you find another job, inside or outside of county government."

Anne tilts her head. "Oh really? I haven't decided if I'm going to leave."

"Of course, do what's in your best interest," Ted says in a father-knows-best voice.

She'd like to knock the glasses off his ruddy face. Instead, Anne says–more confidently than she feels–"I'll tell you one thing that's best for me. I need to see a counselor because of all the anxiety I'm experiencing because of this–she makes air quotes with her fingers–precarious situation as you call it. And insurance needs to pay even if my counselor isn't in the network."

"Sounds reasonable."

"Maurice told me it wasn't."

"Surely, he can work something out."

As Anne turns to leave, Ted steps in front of her and opens the door. "Anne, things will fall into place."

"Uh-huh," she mutters, walks into the hall, and stomps down the two flights of stairs. Outside the main door, a wall of stifling heat smacks her in the face. *Why did I tell that busybody I wanted to see a counselor? I'm gonna take the long way back. I can't face the office yet.* She walks slowly to Chippewa Square and slumps onto a park bench. *Forrest Gump was right. Life IS like a box of chocolates. You never know what you're gonna get. Who would have thought I'd leave a career I love because my employee accused my boss of sexual harassment?*

A group of giggling Girl Scouts in matching green shirts skip past. *I wonder what kind of crap they may face one day. I hope they won't have to deal with a bunch of patronizing men.*

Anne sees her pastor walking up the steps of First Baptist Church. She crosses the sidewalk and yells, "Matt, I need to talk with you."

He turns and waves. "Hi, Anne. Let's go inside where it's cool."

She follows Matt into the empty sanctuary, and he gestures for her to sit beside him in a pew.

"What's going on, Anne?"

Anne blurts outs, "Oh, Matt, I'm a wreck."

"I'm sorry. Tell me about it."

"Okay, I know you'll keep this confidential."

Matt nods. "Of course."

Anne tells him about Jeffrey's allegations and attempted suicide.

"Oh, Anne, that's awful. I'm so sorry."

"Plus, when Jeffrey told me about Harold, he said it brought back memories of being sexually abused as a kid by a pastor in Ohio."

Matt groans. "Oh, good heavens."

"Yeah, it's awful, especially since the county staff are treating Jeffrey like he's the bad guy."

Matt lowers his head. "God bless that young man."

"Since Harold's an elected official, the county bigwigs say there isn't much they can do." She sits upright. "But *I* can do something. I'm going to speak out and tell the truth about Harold. I want him gone so he can't hurt anyone else."

"That takes courage. Of course, you want to do what's right but be prepared that things may not go exactly as you want. I'll pray for divine guidance as you navigate these troubled waters."

"And I haven't even told you the worst part." But she can't find the words to tell him about Charisse's death. Instead, she puts her head in her hands and weeps.

Matt hands her a tissue and sits quietly for several minutes. "It's all right. You can tell me when you're ready."

She looks up. "Okay, but not now."

"Anne, it's hard to believe during chaotic times, but remember: God is in charge. Always is. Would you like to pray?"

"Yes," she says as tears roll down her cheeks.

After Matt's beautiful prayer, Anne wipes her eyes and breathes easier. "I better get back to the courthouse."

They stand. "Anne, you'll be in my prayers. I'm always here for you. Call or come by any time."

She hugs him. "Thank you, Matt. Thank you so much."

Ambling back through Chippewa Square, she sees a homeless man she's seen many times before sitting on a bench under a live oak. Spanish moss cascading from the tree's low branches frames his face. She wonders if he has a family, whether he's had a meal or shower recently, and if he's happy. She nods at him. He reaches for his beat-up guitar, strums a few chords, and in a lovely baritone sings, "Amazing grace! How sweet the sound that saved a wretch like me."

Anne's shoulders soften, and she feels a smile coming on. She applauds and drops a dollar in his guitar case.

He flashes her a toothless grin. "Thank you, ma'am. Have a blessed day."

You have no idea how much I appreciate your saying that.

Chapter 52

After getting permission from Jeffrey and his mother, Anne calls Melissa at WTOC. The reporter seems thrilled she wants to talk with her.

"Let's don't meet at the courthouse, though," Anne says. "Not much privacy there."

Melissa suggests the TV station.

Anne's nerves are on edge, so the week crawls by. She calls her hairdresser, who doesn't have an available appointment, so Anne colors her hair, then gasps when she sees the results. *I look like Morticia Adams.* She washes it three times to try to get the color out. No luck. For the next few days, she barely eats or sleeps. On the morning of the interview, she wakes up feeling like there's a lead stone in her belly. *Am I doing the right thing? Oh well, I can't back out now.*

As she leaves the house, Jon gives her an extra hug. "I know you'll do fine, hon."

Anne parks in WTOC's lot and prays: "God, please give me the wisdom to say the right thing and to keep my mouth shut when necessary." She reminds herself what she tells witnesses before they testify or talk to the media: "Take your time, and if you don't understand a question, ask for clarification."

Melissa greets her in the lobby. "Hi, Anne. Thanks so much for coming." She blinks. "You okay? You look tired."

Anne musters a halfhearted smile. "Oh, I'm fine. Just a lot going on." They walk to the conference room where Anne sits across the table from Melissa and accepts a bottle of water.

"Anne, I've heard lots of rumors about the D.A., but so far no one has been willing to talk on camera. You understand this interview is on the record, right?"

"Yes. I'll be honest. I'm a little nervous being the first one to speak out."

"I understand. And remember, we agreed this is an exclusive, meaning that you won't talk to the other stations?"

"Yes, I've always trusted you, Melissa. Please let me know before it airs."

Melissa clips a mic to Anne's lapel. "Of course. It'll probably be at least a week because our editors and attorney want to review the piece. It's a huge deal when an employee accuses the elected district attorney of sexual harassment."

A middle-aged guy with thick glasses walks in carrying a tripod and camera. Melissa says, "Anne, you remember Butch?"

"Sure. How's it going, Butch?"

"Good," he says.

"Butch will tape our entire interview," Melissa says. "Of course, I'll edit it a lot and will only use sound bites. For now, just think of this as a conversation between the two of us. Let me know if you need a break, more water, or anything."

Anne attempts a laugh. "Oh gosh, how long will this last? It sounds like an interrogation."

"Not long. I know this must be hard for you, so take your time. Any questions before we start taping?"

Anne shakes her head.

Melissa turns to Butch. "Ready to roll?"

He gives her a thumbs up.

Melissa looks at Anne, "Anne, is Jeffrey Williams your employee?"

"Yes."

"I read the lawsuit Mr. Williams filed against District Attorney Harold Carter, but it's pretty vague. That's why I'm doing this investigative piece. The lawsuit alleges unusual circumstances regarding Mr. Williams' hiring. Specifically, it claims the district attorney personally delivered a job application to Mr. Williams' apartment. Do you know anything about that?"

"Both Mr. Williams and Mr. Carter told me."

"Mr. Carter told you that?"

"Yes."

"Interesting. So Mr. Carter knew him before he was hired?" Melissa asks.

"Sort of. They attend the same church."

Melissa looks at her notes. "I heard another lawsuit's been filed by three women who claim they were more qualified."

"That's correct."

"Okay, but let's focus on Jeffrey Williams' lawsuit. Did you participate in interviewing and hiring Mr. Williams?"

"Yes." Anne feels sweat beads form above her upper lip.

"Just to clarify, you were technically the person who hired Mr. Williams, right?"

Anne squirms. "Yes, but Mr. Carter instructed me to sign the H.R. forms to hire Mr. Williams."

"Anne, I have to get it on the record. Did Jeffrey Williams ever allege to you that District Attorney Harold Carter sexually harassed him?"

"Yes."

"What did Mr. Williams tell you exactly?"

"Well, um, I can't quote him word for word."

"Okay then. Anne, did you observe first-hand inappropriate behavior on the part of Mr. Carter?"

Anne bites her bottom lip, then takes a sip of water from the bottle she's been clutching with a death grip. "I did."

"Tell me about that."

Anne clears her throat. *Well, here goes.* "One of the most disturbing things was when several of us went to Chicago to visit a violence intervention program similar to ours." She lowers her eyes and mumbles, "Mr. Carter arranged for Mr. Williams and another young male employee to stay with him in his hotel room."

Melissa looks up, eyes wide. "Did you say three men shared one hotel room? And can you please speak more clearly so the mic can pick it up?"

Anne feels sweat trickle down her back. *This is so embarrassing for Jeffrey. I hope he doesn't regret giving me permission to do this interview.* "Yes. Mr. Carter, Mr. Williams, and another male employee shared one hotel room."

Anne hears Butch stifle a gasp.

Anne talks fast. "I know it's hard to believe. Wanda and I each had our separate rooms and then..." *I need to slow down. I've done dozens of TV interviews, but this is no ordinary interview.*

Melissa holds up her hand. "Wait. Wanda? The public information officer who resigned?"

"Right."

Melissa writes in her notebook. "Do you think she would speak to me? I'd like another source to confirm the sleeping arrangements in Chicago."

"You could ask. She's in Atlanta now."

"Do you know for a fact the three men shared a room?"

"I just know that when we checked in at the hotel, Wanda and I both heard Mr. Carter tell the clerk the two young men would stay in his room. Jeffrey seemed uncomfortable during the whole trip, but he didn't tell me any details."

"Would Mr. Williams be willing to talk to me?"

"Probably not since there's a pending lawsuit." *Oh lord, Melissa better not presure Jeffrey.*

"I heard Jeffrey Williams was hospitalized recently."

Anne doesn't respond.

"Were there other unusual or inappropriate things you can tell us regarding the D.A.'s conduct with Mr. Williams?"

"A couple of months ago, Mr. Carter had Mr. Williams drive him to a funeral in Valdosta. Jeffrey, um Mr. Williams, told me afterward he was uncomfortable because Mr. Carter asked him personal questions and suggested they spend the night at a hotel instead of driving back that day as planned."

"So did they stay at a hotel together on the Valdosta trip?"

"No, not after Jeffrey protested."

"What kind of personal questions did Mr. Carter ask?"

"I wasn't there, but Mr. Williams told me that Mr. Carter asked if he liked girls, whether he had a girlfriend, and made comments about his weight, asked about his supervisor. Stuff like that." Anne pauses to catch her breath. "Sorry I'm rambling, but so much has happened."

Melissa exhales. "That's an understatement. What else can you tell me about Mr. Carter?"

Anne closes her eyes for a moment.

"Take your time, Anne. If you need a break, we can stop taping for a few minutes."

Anne takes another sip of water. "No, I'm okay."

"Tell me what you did when Mr. Williams alleged sexual harassment."

"I followed protocol and reported the harassment allegation to the County H.R. Department."

"What was their response?"

"They put Jeffrey on administrative leave and made him take a psychological test."

"Why a psych test?"

"It's called a 'fitness for duty' test to make sure he's mentally stable to carry a gun."

"Hmm, never heard of that. Did Mr. Carter receive any disciplinary action?"

"That's a personnel matter so I don't know for sure, but my understanding was he was given a verbal reprimand."

"Anne, the suit alleges inappropriate touching. What do you know about that?"

"Nothing really. Mr. Williams didn't tell me about any physical contact." *It's hot as hell in here.*

"Hmm. What else do I need to know? I don't want to leave out anything important."

Anne's pulse quickens. "Melissa, I want to tell you something off the record. It's not related to the harassment suit."

Melissa leans back in her chair and nods at Butch. "Okay, Butch, pause the taping."

"You know about the recent domestic homicide on the Westside?"

"The young mother shot by her husband? Yeah, we covered that story. Why do you ask?"

"The victim's husband had been arrested for domestic violence before, and Mr. Carter intervened and recommended that the judge set a low bond for him."

Melissa leans across the table. "What? Isn't that the defense attorney's job?"

"You might want to research Mr. Carter's campaign donations. The defendant's father was a big contributor."

Melissa scribbles a note. "Wow. You've given me a lot of info. I've got my work cut out for me."

Anne rubs her clammy palms together. *Oh god, what have I set into motion? Did I reveal too much?* "Look. I'm not saying Harold pulled the trigger, but Charisse Butler is dead, and I don't think the criminal justice system served her well." *Myself included.* She brushes away a tear.

"How could I confirm Harold talked to the judge?"

"That'll be tough. Bond hearings aren't usually recorded."

Melissa puts down her pen. "Anne, what else can you tell me?"

"Nothing. I've probably said more than enough." Her stomach is in knots. "Can we stop now?"

Melissa nods. "Sure."

Butch gathers his gear as Anne fumbles to detach her mic. Melissa gets up and helps her. "Anne, are you afraid there will be repercussions for your telling me all this?"

"Probably, but it's a risk I have to take. I agreed to this interview for three reasons. First, the public needs to know the truth about their elected officials. And I hope there will be consequences so Mr. Carter won't victimize again. Plus, if Mr. Carter *has* harassed others, I hope they'll come forward after they see your story."

"Anne, I appreciate your candor and courage."

"Well, Jeffrey Williams is the brave one."

"Yes, indeed. Anne, you know I'll have to allow the district attorney to comment about the info you shared today."

"Yeah, I know you have to get both sides of the story. I used to be a newspaper reporter back in the day."

Melissa closes her notebook. "If you think of anything else, call me. I'll give you a heads up before it airs."

"Please do. It's important I tell Jeffrey before the story runs."

After saying goodbye, Anne walks outside into the blinding sun. She climbs into the stifling car, puts on her sunglasses, and stares into space. She calls her office to say she's taking a sick day. After several minutes, she starts the ignition and turns on the air conditioner full blast. Tears of both relief and apprehension flow uncontrollably. *Whew! I did it. I told the truth. Now I have to be ready for what comes next.*

Chapter 53

Anne's tires squeal when she slams on brakes, coming dangerously close to the truck ahead of her on the Bull River Bridge. Lost in a daze, she hadn't noticed the truck slow down for a bicyclist. *Pay attention, Anne, before you kill yourself or somebody else.*

At home, she goes straight to the shower and scrubs herself with a loofah. As the hot water pelts her body, more tears roll down her cheeks.

Jon comes home and finds her sprawled across the bed. "Darlin', are you okay? I've been trying to call you. You weren't at work, and you didn't answer your cell."

"I must've left it in the car." Anne sits up and rubs her eyes. "What time is it?"

"Noon. I drove home for lunch because I was worried. How did the interview go?"

"Okay I guess." Anne sighs. "I did what I had to do, but Harold is gonna fire me for sure."

"You knew that was a possibility. When will they air it?"

"After the editors and lawyer review it. I need to type my resignation letter."

"Since you're not getting pension or benefits, we need to do some serious financial planning."

"Fine. You've said that. But even if I have to dig ditches, I'm leaving."

"Let's get something to eat." Jon reaches for her hand and helps her off the bed.

In the kitchen, Jon says, "What you want for lunch?"

Anne wrinkles her nose. "I'm not hungry."

He pours her a glass of water. "Okay, but drink something. Or maybe you need a glass of wine?" He chuckles.

"Not this early."

Jon sits, but Anne grabs a sponge and scrubs the countertops with a vengeance. "Do you really think we'll be okay with money? What if the stock market gets worse, and we lose all our savings?"

"Slow down, Anne. The recession isn't over, so I don't know what the markets will do. But at least I can add you to my insurance plan. That is, if I don't get laid off. If you don't get a good-paying job soon, we'll definitely have to sell our house."

"Don't say that. Tybee is my happy place. But if quitting this job means leaving the beach, I guess I'll have to deal. I can't work for a boss who helped an abuser get out of jail. A boss who intimidates young male employees."

"I know. Why don't you sit down?"

"I'm too hyped up, but I guess we do need to eat." She tosses the sponge into the sink, then peers into the freezer. "Gawd, these fish sticks have been in here since Jesus was a baby." She throws the box in the trash can. "But this pizza is fine." She turns the oven to preheat.

Jon has the good sense to stay quiet while they wait for the oven to heat. When the timer buzzes, Anne slides the pizza onto the top rack.

"I can make us a salad," Jon says.

"Nah."

"Have you told anyone about your decision to resign?"

She removes the pizza. "Not yet. I don't want anyone else to find out before I tell my staff. But I'm gonna call Maggie." She slices the pizza. "Do you know in Italy it's rude to pick up a pizza slice? They eat it with a fork and knife."

"Yes, you told me after you and Maggie came back from Italy."

"They serve wine with every meal, too. Like we serve water."

"Uh-huh."

"Speaking of wine, I think I will have a glass," Anne says. She finds and opens a bottle of Riesling in the refrigerator and pours herself some.

Outside the kitchen window, a sparrow and a bluebird flit around. "Look!" Anne says. "They both want to build a nest in the bluebird house. Mama loved bluebirds."

Jon reaches for the binoculars on the window sill. "Yep, they're jockeying for position."

"Every time I see a sparrow I think of the spiritual "His Eyes are on the Sparrow." That song gives me chills." She sips her wine. "I need to remember if God looks after sparrows, he'll take care of Charisse's children. I've been praying for those precious babies."

Jon puts his hand on her shoulder.

In between bites of pizza, Anne says, "How can Italians eat all that pizza and pastries and drink wine and not get fat? Maggie and I didn't see one fat person there."

"I dunno. Seems like I've read something about that, but I can't remember."

"Maybe because they walk so much." Anne wipes her mouth with the paper towel Jon had put next to her plate. "We need to start using cloth napkins instead of paper ones. Gotta save the trees. But would we waste more water by washing the cloth ones?"

Jon stands. "I think we have bigger things to worry about right now. I have to get back to work. Get some rest, okay? You've barely slept all week."

"Okay." She pecks him on the lips.

After he leaves, she sits cross-legged on the couch and calls Maggie. "Okay, Sistuh. I'm done. I'm turning in my resignation."

"Hallelujah! I've been worried about you."

"I know you'll be happy not to have to listen to my drama every day. You've been a saint, Maggie."

"I wish I could have helped more. I still can't believe how screwed up those H.R. idiots have been. I'm so relieved you're getting out of there. How was your TV interview?"

"Okay. Glad it's over."

"I bet."

"I'm going to miss so many people at the courthouse. I've spent most of my waking hours there for twenty years. I think about all the victims we've helped, the laws we've changed, and the people I've met across the country who are passionate about victims' rights. It's going to be hard."

"Yes, it will. But you can still have lunch with your buddies. And Girls' Night Out."

"I know, but it won't be the same." Anne puts her wine glass on the coffee table. "I'm about to crash. This must be what it's like to be bipolar. I had crazy energy after Jon came home for lunch. Now, I'm exhausted. Talk later. Love you."

"Love you, too."

Anne stares at the bookcase. Surely one of these books must hold the answers to the questions swirling in her head. *Am I insane for spilling all to the media? Is leaving a sign of weakness or strength? And what now?*

She tilts her head and reads the book spines. She treasures *Sonnets from the Portuguese* by Elizabeth Barrett Browning. Anne gingerly touches the now-tattered book her mama bought with her first paycheck as a teacher. She's grateful her mother had passed down this book along with her love of the written word.

There's Pat Conroy's *Prince of Tides.* She and Jon have read every one of Conroy's books. When Anne met Conroy at a book festival, she mentioned she had a copy of *The Boo,* his little-known first book about a beloved Citadel professor. Conroy scowled. "Oh my god, please throw that in the fireplace. Awful writing." Anne pulls out *You Can Heal Your Life* by Louise Hay, Anne Lamott's *Bird by Bird,* and Kahlil Gibran's *The Prophet.*

She chuckles when she sees *I Like You, Hospitality Under the Influence,* a hilarious book about cooking and entertaining by Amy Sedaris. She opens it to the section titled "The Unexpected Guest" where Amy writes you need to be prepared to come up with excuses like, 'I'd love for you to stay, but they're fumigating for rats," or "I found a spider sack."

She lays the book on the floor with the others, then reaches for her beautifully-illustrated copy of *Winnie the Pooh.* She loves Pooh, Piglet, and even grumpy Eeyore who reminds her of Glenn at work. One picture shows chubby Pooh with half his furry face stuck in the hunny pot. When she reads about Pooh saying how lucky he is to have something that makes saying goodbye so hard, she cries herself to sleep right there on the couch, the Pooh book on her chest, and Little Kitty curled up at her feet.

Chapter 54

Anne arrives at the restaurant before LaShay and asks for the table in the back corner. The place is abuzz with lunch customers, mostly staff from Memorial Hospital across the street, where the Violence Intervention Program office is located. Anne's glad to be away from downtown and the courthouse crowd.

She orders water for herself and LaShay. *This is really happening if I'm telling LaShay I'm leaving. Why am I sweating? The AC is full blast.*

To distract herself, she glances around. That couple at the table in front of her–are they father and daughter or has the woman had plastic surgery? Hard to tell these days. The balding man's name badge reads "Dr. Caulder, Neurology Dept." The woman wears a sleeveless coral dress with a string of pearls, ala Jackie Kennedy. Her arms are as toned as the models in *Fitness* magazine. Anne looks down at her arms. *Dang. I lift weights at the gym, but my arms still jiggle like Jell-O.*

LaShay texts to say she's running late, giving Anne a few more minutes to escape into the world of those around her. She listens to the couple discuss a trip to New York. The woman's lips are tightly pressed together, and her husband says, "I don't know if I can take that much time off from work. Maybe you and the kids could go."

"But this could be a fun trip for just the two of us," the woman says.

Ah. Marital problems. The wife thinks a romantic getaway could be good for them. Plastic surgery and vacations are nice, but money can't buy happiness. Good thing since I'm about to be without a salary.

The couple finishes their lunch in silence as Anne mulls over their future. *Stop eavesdropping. Why am I engrossed in their lives when I need to figure out my own? I've always had a vivid imagination.* She remembers getting emotional on a plane filled with young soldiers headed to Kuwait. They looked like kids. One woman clutched a teddy bear.

Another time she got teary-eyed at the Atlanta airport after seeing two boys–probably eight and ten–crying and hugging their daddy goodbye before they boarded a plane to St. Louis. She imagined an entire scenario: their parents were divorced, and the boys had spent a few summer weeks visiting their dad in Atlanta. They'd probably squealed on every ride at Six Flags, cheered at a Braves game, and eaten ice cream every day. But all that wasn't enough to erase the painful reality of their parents living half a continent apart. The dad waved his final goodbye and blended into the sea of humanity rushing to their tearful goodbyes and happy reunions.

Anne snaps back into reality when the waitress brings a basket of bread.

The server puts two menus on the table. "Our special today is a crab cake sandwich with homestyle fries."

"Okay. My friend will be here in a minute."

LaShay arrives. "Sorry, I'm late. We had a meeting with the E.R. nurses, and it went longer than I expected. Lisa says hello."

"No worries. I've been people-watching."

LaShay butters a piece of bread. "What's new?"

Anne swallows hard. "Well, I might as well tell you because I want you to hear it from me first. I'm resigning. I hate to leave you, but I'm not being much help anyway." She puts down her water glass. "I'm giving my notice to Harold tomorrow."

LaShay's mouth falls open. "Oh my God. This isn't fair. Harold is driving off all the good people." She throws her hands up in the air. "We all need to leave. I feel like yelling 'Fire!' so we can all escape."

Anne smiles. "And your handsome firefighter husband could rescue us."

"Sounds good to me. Honestly, Anne, I don't know how you've survived eighteen months working for that man."

Anne leans closer to LaShay. "I also need to tell you that I talked to WTOC about Harold and confirmed the allegations in Jeffrey's lawsuit. They're doing a big investigative piece."

"Wow. I don't know what to say."

The waitress returns, and they both order cobb salads.

When their food arrives, LaShay pushes hers around on her plate. "I'm glad for you, Anne. Remember when Harold's first public information officer–I forgot her name–left after eight months? She said she'd never worked for anyone like Harold in her life and was going to pray for everybody left."

"Yes, Wanda." Anne puts her hand on LaShay's shoulder. "Somehow it's all going to work out."

LaShay tries to smile. "I guess so. I'll miss you."

They hug goodbye after and Anne drives back to the courthouse, feeling guilty for deserting LaShay but relieved to be leaving. She returns to her office and tells Donna, her long-time assistant, the news. "I was afraid this was coming," Donna says. "Is it really that bad?" She pauses a second. "Never mind. I know it is."

In bed that night, Anne rehearses what she'll say to Harold and tries to guess his reaction. But after tossing and turning for a while, she realizes she doesn't care.

She dreams she's a baby snuggled in her mama's lap. They're swinging on a wooden swing in the backyard. Red juice dribbles down their chins as they nibble strawberries from a brown pottery bowl. They watch a bluebird fly out of a dogwood tree and soar overhead until it's just a blue speck against the orange sunrise.

Anne hates it when the alarm buzzes her awake.

She remembers the last birthday card she received from her mama. "When you were a baby, I'd take you to the backyard early in the morning to feed you. Birds were chirping, and the sun was beginning to rise. Each Spring when I hear birds sing, I think of our special early morning ritual. I love you."

Anne pads to the kitchen. Jon gives her a bear hug and says, "Good luck, darlin'. You can do this."

She gives him a thumbs up. "Yes, I can." After he leaves, she thinks how great it will be not to dread going to work every day. No more walking on eggshells around Harold. *I'm ready to get off the roller coaster.* She's never liked the white-knuckle ride anyway. As a teen, she was the one who waited on the sidewalk, holding purses while her friends braved the terrifying Scream Machine at Myrtle Beach.

Anne steps outside and breathes deeply. *I love this salt air.* She recalls that the word Tybee comes from the Native American word for salt. A neighbor riding by on her bike waves to Anne. *If we have to move, I'll miss the heck out of this place. Am I ruining our lives?*

Instead of her usual route down President Street Extension, she travels Victory Drive, so she can swing by Krispy Kreme to buy doughnuts for the staff meeting. She admires the palm trees standing guard in the median in honor of the casualties from World War I. On either side of the road, gray moss sways like a ghostly decoration on huge oak trees.

She plans to tell Harold first, then her staff at the ten-thirty meeting. As soon as she gets to the office, she emails Harold, "I need to talk with you today. When is good for you?" She hopes he won't ignore her email like he often does.

When Donna sees the green and white box of doughnuts, she says, "That's not going to make the staff meeting any easier."

A couple of minutes later, Anne receives Harold's reply: "You can come to my office now."

Anne types: "I'll be right over." With her resignation letter in her notebook, she walks down the hall to Harold's office. Brenda is away from her desk, so Anne taps on Harold's door. Even though he's expecting her, she knows better than to walk right in.

"Come in," he says.

Imagining there's a string from the top of her head to the ceiling like her yoga teacher instructs, Anne stands tall and goes in. "Good morning, Harold."

"Hello, Miss Anne."

When he calls her "Miss Anne," it usually means he's in a good mood. She sits on the chair in front of his desk and says what she's rehearsed for days. "Harold, I've been working at Victim-Witness for twenty years. My anniversary is this summer. I've decided to resign. My last day will be in two weeks." She hands him the letter and thinks, *When he sees my TV interview, he'll probably escort me out immediately.*

Harold gets a deer-in-the-headlights look. As he puts the letter down, Anne notices his hand is trembling. For a moment, she feels sorry for him.

"Anne, I've known you a long time. I can tell by your voice this is not something you want to do."

Anne does a double take. *What in the world is he talking about?*

Before she can reply, he says, "Why would you want to leave?"

Seriously? Is he kidding? "Um, Harold, it's time. I've been here many years and, uh, work has become stressful. I want to pursue other things."

"You need to think about this, Anne."

If only he knew how much I have thought about it. He seems genuinely stunned. Is he that out of touch with reality? For the life of me, I can't figure him out.

Brenda's voice comes over his phone speaker. "Mr. Carter, you have a call from Devin. Want me to put him through?"

Harold's knee bounces up and down. "No. I have someone in my office."

"Oh, sorry. I'll take a message."

Adrenaline shoots through Anne's body. She scoots to the edge of the chair and looks Harold in the eye. "Harold, I can't work here any longer. Jeffrey has accused you of sexual harassment, and you were told not to discuss that allegation with me. But you continue to ask me questions about it. That puts me in a horrible position. I believed you when you said you wouldn't contact Jeffrey, but you did anyway. I don't know how to work in an environment where trust has been broken. And I don't think you trust me or LaShay to run the Violence

Intervention Program because apparently, you communicate with Devin instead of us."

Suddenly, Harold's eyes dart around the room. Anne can't tell if he's angry or shocked or both.

I hadn't planned to say all this, but I need to speak the truth. Anne clears her throat. "The stress is too much for me. I had high hopes we could work well together, but things haven't gone well. It seems like I can't do anything to please you. I feel like you treat women poorly. And after all the years we've known each other, that both saddens and surprises me." She pauses and exhales slowly, amazed at how calm she feels. "I'll work closely with Donna to make sure there's a smooth transition."

After a moment of awkward silence, Anne realizes Harold isn't going to respond. She pulls her notebook close to her chest and stands.

Behind the large desk, Harold looks small. He puts a pencil behind his ear and says in a barely audible voice, "Very well then."

Rather than going to her office, she bounds down the six flights of stairs to the snack bar. *I deserve a Snickers bar. Maybe two.* She can't remember exactly what she just said to Harold, but it feels like a load of bricks has been lifted off of her shoulders. *Harold can't hurt me now. At least I hope not.*

She bites into the Snicker and savors the caramel and chocolate goodness.

Chapter 55

The late morning sun heats up the conference room as Victim-Witness staff members gather for their Thursday morning meeting. Anne sets a box of doughnuts and a stack of napkins in the middle of the table. "First, I want to congratulate y'all. Our program submitted more victim compensation applications in the last six months than any other jurisdiction in the state, even Atlanta." She gives a thumbs up. "Good job, everybody."

Anne covers a couple of routine items, checking them off her list. They discuss an upcoming trial and volunteer appreciation luncheon. Anne clears her throat. "I have an announcement. I've been at Victim-Witness for twenty years, and it's time for me to leave. I gave Harold my resignation letter this morning."

The room falls quiet, and Anne inhales slowly before saying, "My last day will be in two weeks. As you know, victim advocacy has been my passion, and y'all are like family." She looks around the room at her ten employees. Everyone but Donna and LaShay look stunned. "I'll miss every one of you. But I know you'll continue to make this the best Victim-Witness Program in the state, heck, in the nation." Waiting for someone to speak, Anne shifts in her chair.

Janine breaks the silence. "I'm not surprised. We know you've been going through hell, but it's gonna take a while for this to sink in."

Donna pipes up. "Anne, you'll have more time to enjoy your grandson now."

"But what about us?" Tara asks. She reaches for a doughnut. "If you brought these Krispy Kremes to soften the blow, it's not working." She laughs nervously.

"I thought a little sugar would help us all," Anne says. She takes a sip of water. "Okay guys, anything else?"

Janine says, "No, I think that's quite enough."

Anne gathers her papers. "No sad faces. Y'all are gonna be fine. Now eat those doughnuts." She escapes to her office. *Thank God that's over.* She types an email to the entire D.A.'s staff about her resignation.

Kate appears in her office five minutes later. "When you told me yesterday you were gonna resign, I didn't realize it would be today. Girl, when you make up your mind, you don't mess around. Guess I'm one of the last survivors. Not for long though."

"You'll find the right job and..." Anne answers her ringing phone.

"Hi, Anne, it's Melissa at WTOC. I heard about your announcement. This means we can run our exclusive piece tonight. We'll lead with your resignation and then clips of your interview will explain why you're leaving. Perfect timing."

"Sheesh, Melissa. How did you find out so fast?"

"I got a couple of phone calls from folks in the D.A.'s office."

"You're airing the story tonight?"

"Yep. And I'm giving you a heads up first just like I promised."

Perspiration beads on Anne's upper lip. "Uh, okay."

"When you shared so much in the interview, I figured you'd have to resign. Proud of you. Listen, I gotta go. My editor's hollering for me."

"Okay, Melissa. Bye."

Anne hangs up. "I can't believe WTOC found out so fast."

"You know how news travels around this place," Kate says. "There's already a blurb on the *Savannah Morning News* website."

"Seriously?" Anne pulls up the website. Reading the black words on the white screen makes it real: *Another Shake-up in the D.A.'s Office: Victim-Witness Director Resigns.* "Guess this is really happening," she mumbles.

Kate stands and smooths her skirt. "It is. Well, I've gotta go to an elder abuse meeting. Catch you later."

Ugh. Now I need to call Jeffrey. I feel guilty leaving him in this mess. Jeffrey answers after three rings.

"Hi, Jeffrey. It's Anne Gardner. Hope you're okay. I want to let you know I announced my resignation at today's staff meeting."

"Really? Aw, man. Ms. Gardner, I'm sorry it's come to this. I never expected the District Attorney's Office to be so screwed up."

"I'm leaving in two weeks. LaShay will still be your direct supervisor. You focus on taking care of yourself. I'm sorry your job here has been so difficult. And Jeffrey, another thing. That big story about Harold runs tonight on WTOC's six o'clock news."

"Tonight? The one where you told them about what I said about Mr. Carter?'

"Yes." *I hope he's not regretting giving me permission.*

"Um, okay, I guess that means everybody will be talking about me for real now."

"Jeffrey, I would have never done the interview without your permission. And they already reported on the lawsuit."

"Um, yeah. I mean yes, ma'am. I better go tell mama."

"Okay. Take care."

The next two hours are a blur. It seems like everybody on the sixth floor pops in Anne's office to offer hugs and kind words. When they ask what's next for her, she forces a smile and says, "Not sure. Maybe I'll be a greeter at Wal-Mart or sell sno-cones at the beach."

At 5:15, Anne closes her door and gazes out the window at a ship passing under The Talmadge Bridge. *Heavens to Betsy. What a day.*

Chapter 56

Anne pounds her fist on the steering wheel. Traffic is at a standstill at the railroad crossing on President Street Extension. "Dammit! I've got to get home to see the news." *All hell is about to break lose.*

The train goes forward, backs up, then inches forward again. It's five-twenty. After nearly ten minutes, the cars move again just as Etta James sings "At Last" on the radio. Anne speeds toward Tybee, hoping no police are nearby. *At last! At last, I'm getting out of this hell. At last, I'm speaking my truth.*

When she finally gets home at 5:55, Jon hugs her. "How did your big day go?"

"Can't talk now. My interview is on the 6:00 news. Turn on the TV!"

"Tonight?" He grabs the remote and clicks it on. Anne stands beside him, puts her hand on his shoulder, and kicks off her shoes.

News anchor Sonny Dixon looks solemn. "Today we learned another employee is leaving the district attorney's office. This time it's long-time Victim-Witness Director Anne Gardner. Recently our Melissa Parker did an exclusive interview with Gardner who discussed sexual harassment allegations against Chatham County District Attorney Harold Carter."

Anne gulps a breath of air. "Turn it up!" A thunder clap booms, and the TV flickers off. "What in tarnation?"

After a few seconds, the TV flashed back on. There's a shot of Melissa in front of the courthouse. "An employee has accused the Chatham County District Attorney of sexual harassment. Victim-Witness Director Anne Gardner shared more details about Carter's alleged inappropriate behavior with her employee."

Anne squeezes Jon's shoulder when she hears herself say, "For one thing, he arranged accommodations so two young male employees shared a hotel room with him on a business trip. Another time, he suggested an employee spend the night in a hotel room with him, but the employee didn't. He's been accused of inappropriate touching." In the next clip, Anne is saying, "He personally delivered a job application to a young man who was then hired, even though other applicants were far more qualified."

Melissa is back on the screen. "According to Gardner, these are just a few examples of Carter's improper behavior. The District Attorney and the employee who accused him of harassment both declined to comment, citing a pending lawsuit. We also contacted the county's director of human resources who said he can't discuss personnel matters. Gardner wanted me to make it clear she granted the interview with the permission of the alleged harassment victim."

Jon says, "I figured Harold wouldn't show his face."

Melissa continues, "I did talk to a former employee of the district attorney who asked not to be identified. She called Carter's behavior bizarre and said he has a disdain for women. Since Carter took office eighteen months ago, there's been a mass exodus from his leadership team, In fact, Anne Gardner submitted her resignation today after twenty years as director of the Victim-Witness Assistance Program. Back to you, Sonny."

"Melissa, I know you'll follow this developing story and bring us updates as you learn them," Dixon says, before introducing the next story.

Anne turns down the volume on the TV. "So I'm the only one who spoke on camera? Did I make a fool of myself?"

"No," Jon says softly. "You did fine. I'm glad Harold didn't go on camera. He could have ripped you apart, claiming you're just a disgruntled employee. You have to be prepared for what he'll do now."

"Melissa told me he didn't return her call until yesterday. He was in Atlanta earlier in the week."

"Last time I checked, they have phone service in Atlanta."

Anne heads to the kitchen, pours herself a glass of iced tea and takes a big swig.

Jon follows her. "Your phone is going to ring any minute. I'm telling you, Harold is probably going ballistic." Jon shakes his head. "You wanna eat something?"

Anne rubs her stomach. "Ugh, no."

Sure enough, Anne's phone rings and they both jump. Luckily, it's just Kate. "Hey, what did you think?" Anne says immediately.

"I think you're a hero, Anne, and I'm glad you're getting the hell out of the office."

"The supposed big investigative piece was so short," Anne says. "I talked to Melissa a long time."

"You know they only do sound bites," Kate says.

"Yeah. She didn't mention Harold requesting a low bond for Charisse's husband."

"That's probably hard to verify."

"Oh gosh, I hope I did the right thing."

"Anne, don't look back now. This is what you wanted to do. I'm glad you spoke out."

"Thanks, my friend."

"Gotta go. The kids are demanding dinner."

"Okay. Bye."

After taking calls from Maggie, Lisa, and two nosy neighbors, Anne paces the kitchen floor, tea glass in one hand and cell phone in the other. "I wish Harold would call so I could get it over with. I feel like I'm gonna throw up."

"You need to eat," Jon says,

"Nah, although come to think of it, I haven't eaten all day. Except for Snickers bars. Jon, will my interview do any good? Or did I come across as a disgruntled employee? Once I leave, Harold can't hurt me. Or can he?"

"That remains to be seen."

Chapter 57

Meanwhile across town, Jeffrey clicks the remote. "C'mon, mama. It's almost six o'clock."

Mrs. Williams appears from the kitchen just as her husband lumbers in through the front door. "Hey, hon,' she says. "The story about Jeffrey and the D.A. is about to be on the news."

Mr. Williams removes his gun belt and hangs it in the hall closet before stretching out on the recliner. "I sure hope y'all don't regret agreeing to do this interview."

"Shush, the truth needs to be told," his wife says. "Anyway, it's too late now."

Jeffrey and his mom sit on the edge of the couch. When Melissa mentions the sleeping arrangements in Chicago, Jeffrey pops his knuckles. "Oh, shit." Bug-eyed, he watches the rest of the story in silence. When his mom puts out her hand to stop his jiggling knee, he pushes it away.

After the segment ends, Jeffrey clicks off the remote. "Ms. Gardner is smart to get out of there. No telling what Crazy-Ass-Carter will do now." He looks at his mother. "You think he'll fire me?"

"I don't know," Mrs. Williams says. "He didn't when you filed the lawsuit."

"I'm sure Carter's attorney advised him not to fire Jeffrey with a pending lawsuit," Mr. Williams says. "But that won't stop him from making Jeffrey's life pure hell."

Jeffrey nods. "Probably a good thing I'm on administrative leave." He answers his beeping cell. "Hey, Kiara, what'd you think?"

"Your business is out there now for the world to see, that's for sure. It's embarrassing."

"They didn't say my name."

"But everyone will know it's you."

"Yeah, it sucks. You wanna come over? Mama's cooking."

"Nope. I'm ready for you to spend some time alone with ME."

"Babe, I'll come by after band practice tomorrow."

"Okay, Jeffrey. Whatever." She clicks off.

Jeffrey retreats to his room, slams the door, and grabs his old guitar from the closet. His palms sweating, he sits on the side of the bed and bangs out a random tune, playing the same riff over and over. After twenty minutes of furious playing, he stands and looks at himself in the mirror above the dresser. He sees dark circles under his eyes from lack of sleep. *Dude, you gotta get yourself together.* He fumbles with the pick and softly strums his guitar, this time with focus. *I'm gonna write a song about this pain. Country musicians do it all the time. Time to get serious about my music.* He plays for almost an hour, letting his mind drift and his nerves calm down.

Mrs. Williams knocks on the door. "Son, supper's ready."

Jeffrey puts down his guitar and follows her downstairs. At the table, his mother offers a blessing and serves Jeffrey's plate, then his father's.

Jeffrey picks up his fork, then puts it down again. "You know Antonio has been asking me to come to Atlanta to play with his band."

"Yes," his mother says. "Your cousin seems to be doing well there."

"And I could too. I'm done with this job, this town, all this crap."

Mr. Williams looks at his son. "You know most musicians don't make enough to pay the bills."

Jeffrey sits up straighter. "Well, Antonio does. He said I could room with him and split the rent. I'm calling him tonight."

Mrs. Williams puts her hand on his shoulder. "You're a grown man, Jeffrey. Do what's best for you. We'll support you in your decision. She looks pointedly at her husband. Right honey?"

Mr. Williams mumbles, "Hmm."

After supper, Jeffrey calls Anne. "Hey, Ms. Gardner. I saw the news. I'm glad you spoke out. And I hope Mr. Carter gets what's coming to him."

"Me too."

"I've made a decision. I'm gonna follow my dream to become a full-time musician. I wanna get a gig with my cousin in Atlanta. Maybe write some of my own music."

"That's wonderful, Jeffrey! I'll be the first in line to buy your CD."

"Yes ma'am, that's a deal."

"I hope you'll stay in touch. Don't forget me when you become a big star. Bye now." *Maybe he'll be okay after all. Criminal justice doesn't seem to be his thing.* She closes her eyes. *Looks like it's time for me to find a new dream, too.*

Chapter 58

The next morning, Anne wakes up with a headache that's still pounding when she gets to the courthouse. An attorney sidles up to her on the sidewalk. "Saw you on the news last night. You're ballsy. Crazy maybe, but definitely ballsy."

Anne manages a weak smile.

At the security desk, one of the bluecoats whispers, "I'm glad somebody's telling the truth around here. I've always thought there was something weird about that D.A."

Anne nods and heads to the elevator, where an older woman wearing a juror sticker taps her on the shoulder. "Aren't you the lady I saw on the news last night?"

"Yes ma'am," Anne says, wishing she could become invisible.

When she reaches her office, Anne closes the door. She checks her email and phone for a message from Harold. Nothing yet. *This could be my last day here. I'm sure Harold doesn't want me around another minute.* Rooting through her desk for personal items to take home, she finds a granola bar and wolfs it down. Her stomach churns. She calls Donna. "Have you seen Harold?"

"I saw him getting coffee earlier."

"Did he say anything about the news? Did he look mad?"

"Nope. Didn't mention it. I can't ever read his moods though."

"Hmm. Surprised he hasn't raked me over the coals yet."

"The day is young," Donna says "I'm praying for you."

"Thanks."

Periodically checking her email, Anne packs some belongings in a box. A few minutes before lunch an email from Harold pops up on her screen. "Come to my office."

Anne replies, "Okay." *Here goes. Be prepared for anything.* She takes a sip from her water bottle and heads down the hall, convinced everyone's staring at her.

Harold's door is open. When Anne knocks on the door, he says, "Come in."

Anne steps in. He's typing on his computer, his back to Anne.

"Harold?"

He swivels in his chair to face her. "Have a seat, Anne," he says with a deadpan stare.

She sits on a chair across from his desk and waits for the inevitable explosion. But there's only silence. *Breathe. Just breathe.*

Harold smirks. "Is there anything you want to tell me, Anne?"

She feels like a six-year-old who's broken the cookie jar. "Um, no."

Harold looks at her over his glasses. "I heard about your TV interview."

Anne blinks rapidly.

"I just sent one of our investigators to WTOC to pick up a copy of the tape since I missed the news last night. Maybe we can watch it together."

Anne's mouth drops open. *What in God's name?*

"Now I know why you resigned. Because of your exclusive TV interview." He pauses. "You do realize this is insubordination, not to mention libelous."

Anne's throat is so dry, she doesn't know if she can speak, but manages to whisper, "Do you want me to go ahead and leave today?"

"Not necessary. You wouldn't want to miss the going-away party I've planned for you next Friday," he says, smiling.

Chapter 59

Anne's last week at the office is a blur. She spends many hours with Donna, who Harold will probably appoint as interim director, although he hasn't said that. He emails assignments to Anne daily. Some of his requests are reasonable and some are not, such as completing a five-year plan for the Violence Intervention Program and producing a public service announcement for TV.

The final straw comes at four o'clock on Tuesday. He walks into her office with a manila envelope and plunks it on the edge of her desk. "This is a request for a proposal from the Department of Justice. The Violence Intervention Program meets the criteria for the grant."

Anne looks at the envelope and frowns.

Harold remains standing. "They'll award funds to five communities in the nation that will serve as models. Since there are no other violence intervention programs in the Southeast, I think we have a chance to fund a new employee."

Anne clenches her jaw. "Harold, there's no way I can get that done. Friday is my last day."

"I'm well aware Friday is your last day, so you better get started." He straightens his necktie. "I assume you'll be seeking other employment. You wouldn't want a bad reference from me for not performing your duties, now would you?" He walks out, leaving Anne with her mouth open.

Hands trembling, she tosses the envelope on the credenza. *No way in hell I'll tackle that, and he's not going to give me a good reference anyway.*

* * *

When Anne gets in her car Friday morning, it's already warm and humid. She's been driving to the courthouse for two decades and can't fathom what it will feel like next week when she doesn't.

Turning onto State Street, she sees a once sleepy downtown with empty storefronts transformed into a bustling area filled with shops, restaurants, and people everywhere.

Anne admires the beauty of her adopted city. At Wright Square, Bradley Lock and Key is on her right. An old, dusty place piled with junk, Bradley's was a quirky institution long before downtown was hip. The first time she went there, she was startled by a colorful parrot perched on the counter who squawked, "Hello, hello, welcome." Mr. Houdini Bradley or an old black gentleman with a toothless grin made copies of keys for $1.50.

She winces when she gets to Telfair Square. The building to her left, named for Girl Scout founder Juliette Gordon Low, is ugly as sin. Dubbed the "bathroom building" by locals because of its tile exterior, it's the only federal building in the nation named for a woman. How did it ever pass the Historic Review Board? The saving graces on the square are the historic Trinity United Methodist Church and stately Telfair Museum. The city's squares are breathtaking in early spring when azaleas burst forth in majestic shades of cotton candy pink.

I will not cry. Good grief. It's not like I won't be able to come downtown anymore.

Anne also knows the darker side of the city, stories not found in glossy tour brochures or on slick websites. She knows about the couple from Ohio who was robbed and shot while walking back to their bed and breakfast after dinner at The Olde Pink House restaurant. The man is now paralyzed. She remembers the college student who was raped and left for dead behind an abandoned home on Barnard Street. Amazingly she survived and is now a passionate advocate for sexual assault victims in north Georgia.

An elderly man was robbed one August afternoon and for two months refused to leave his non-air-conditioned apartment even in the sweltering heat. A prostitute was whacked in the head with a baseball bat in a lane on the west side of the city. Long after the headlines had faded and the public had forgotten, Anne's Victim-Witness staff of paid and volunteer workers helped these victims and their families.

Anne feels a lump in her throat as she thinks of the many people she's come to know and love at her office. There's Fred, the 80-year-old retired lawyer who volunteers every Thursday to talk with victims after preliminary hearings. He also writes and performs funny songs at the annual volunteer luncheons. Jan and Kristin, volunteers for two decades, have become Anne's dear friends. Of course, Kate was one of the early college interns, many of whom went on to become lawyers, social workers, and doctors.

At the courthouse garage, she gives herself a pep talk before getting out of the car. *I can do this. I'll smile and breathe. If Harold does something weird at the party, it confirms I made the right decision.* To avoid seeing people on the elevator, she hikes the six flights of stairs. Breathless, she walks into her office and groans. *Still so much packing to do.* She rolls her chair toward the windowsill, removes family pictures, and places them in a box on the floor. She leaves the red bumper sticker that reads "Justice for all, even the victims." *I sure hope there can be justice for Jeffrey.* Part of her wants to throw everything away to make a new beginning while another part of her wants to cling to it forever.

Kate walks in and sees Anne leaning over a stack of boxes. "Yo, Anne, need some help?"

"Yes, please! You love to clean, and I hate it."

Kate kicks off her heels and slides a chair in front of the credenza. She tosses and organizes while Anne tackles the file cabinet.

"Kate, I'm nervous about my farewell party this afternoon. Do you think Harold will embarrass me in front of everybody?"

"I have no idea. Just plaster a smile on your face and get through whatever happens. At five today, you'll be done with this god-forsaken place!"

"Yup. Thank God Harold has been in Atlanta the last couple of days. Even though he's been emailing me orders, at least I didn't have to see him."

Just before three, Anne arrives in the big jury assembly room and sees Jon, Maggie, and Ralph going inside. Jon pecks her on the cheek.

She accepts hugs and well wishes from dozens of current and former volunteers, police officers, victims, and courthouse cronies. All the while, she's keeping her eyes peeled for Harold, but he's nowhere in sight. Donna takes the microphone and asks everyone to be seated. Anne joins Jon, Maggie, and Ralph on the front row. Trying to keep it together as she hears people say kind words about her, Anne squeezes Jon's hand. The first victim she ever helped speaks first, then Carol of the Coastal Children's Advocacy Center takes the mic. Anne's eyes well up when Carol says "I know Anne's parents are looking down from heaven, so proud of their daughter."

Jon whispers to Anne, "Is Harold going to be a no-show?"

"I hope so."

Her former boss, D.A. Martin Clayton, Jr., speaks next and admits, "At first I wasn't in favor of creating a victim assistance program in the D.A.'s office. I didn't want a bunch of red-eyed zealots running around looking over our shoulders and telling us lawyers what to do. As it turns out, starting the program was the best professional decision I made because of the enormous help it provides to our citizens who are victimized. And hiring Anne was another wise decision."

Anne cranes her neck looking for Harold and sees him saunter through the back door and stand behind the last row of seats. Jon squeezes her clammy hand harder.

Donna calls Harold to the front. Stone-faced, he strolls to the podium and adjusts the mic. "Good afternoon, ladies and gentlemen." He clears his throat. "Words rarely fail me, but this is one of those occasions where I'm not sure what to say. Hmm. Anne has certainly made a name for herself." He smiles smugly at Anne. "Right, Anne?"

Anne puts her hand over her mouth to stifle a gasp. The room is deathly quiet.

"She's known to be outspoken, particularly as of late. She's certainly been enjoying the media spotlight the last couple of weeks. But no need to discuss all that at today's gathering. My task is to present a gift from the county human resources department." He looks under the podium and then nods at Anne. "Anne, come on up."

Anne manages to walk the several yards to Harold. He presents her with the standard gift for departing employees, an ugly lamp with the county logo on its black lampshade. "So Anne, I guess this is farewell," he says, his voice flat.

Anne feels dozens of eyes staring at her as she mumbles, "Thank you. Thank you so much." Her face is on fire as she returns to her seat. Maggie puts her arm around her and whispers, "Hang in there, Sissy."

Harold finds an empty seat across the aisle from Anne.

The final speaker is Mrs. Davis whose son was killed at a convenience store. While she's talking, Harold slips out the back. Anne's relieved he's leaving, but others shake their heads, astonished he was rude enough to walk out in the middle of Mrs. Davis' talk. After Mrs. Davis leaves the podium, she walks to Anne, leans down and hugs her neck, and places a beautifully wrapped gift in her lap. "Open it later, sweetie," she says.

Holding back tears, Anne can only nod.

After the speeches, people mingle and enjoy the refreshments her staff had made. *Thank goodness county funds weren't used to have it catered.* On auto-pilot, she smiles, shakes hands, and chats with folks, some she hasn't seen in years.

At five, Jon tells Maggie and Ralph: "I'll ride home with Anne. See you guys tomorrow."

Anne and Jon gather up the flowers and gifts. Jon carries the bulky lamp and says, "Guess we can sell this on E-bay."

"Shh," Anne admonishes him, looking around to make sure no one's overheard.

As they drive toward Tybee, the tide is high under the Bull River Bridge. "Is there a full moon tonight?" Anne asks.

"No, it will be a new moon."

"That seems appropriate. Definitely a new phase for me." Anne leans her head against the passenger window and stares at dark clouds moving east. "It could have been a lot worse. I was scared to death about what Harold would say."

"Yes, you're lucky. Just try to relax now."

She stretches out her long legs. "I feel like I've been run over by a bulldozer."

Jon pats her knee. They ride the rest of the way in silence.

At home, she wants to be alone with her thoughts; she changes into shorts and a tee shirt. "I'm going for a walk," she calls over her shoulder to Jon, who's unloading her farewell gifts and boxes of belongings from the car. She walks the two blocks to the beach. At the end of the wooden walkway, she pauses and gazes out at the ocean. *No more Victim-Witness Assistance. Dear God, please give me strength to see the possibilities in the next chapter of my life. And please help me forgive Harold one day. But I'm not ready for that now.*

She kicks off her flip-flops and walks slowly, her head down. A triangular black speck catches her eye, and she picks it up. A shark's tooth! She hasn't found one of those in forever. Maybe it's a sign of good luck. She can't wait to show it to her grandson Ethan.

I wish I could talk to Mama right now. I need her positive attitude. Right after being diagnosed with cancer, her mother said, "I didn't fall apart when your daddy died suddenly, and I'm not going to fall apart now. We have to accept what comes next in life."

The wind picks up and big raindrops begin to fall from the darkening sky. She hurries home.

She leaves her wet flip-flops on the door mat, goes inside, and hears the shower running. After pouring herself a glass of iced tea, she sits at the kitchen table and looks inside one of the gift bags. It's a giant box of chocolate peppermint patties from Charlie, the manager of the courthouse snack bar. She smiles; he knows how much she loves chocolate.

She unwraps the gift from Lily Davis and finds a silver, heart-shaped music box engraved with: *Life isn't about waiting for the storm to pass. It's about learning to dance in the rain. Love, Lily Davis.* Anne lifts the top, and it plays "Somewhere Over the Rainbow," one of her favorite songs. Tears streaming down her cheeks, she carefully places the music box on the table.

She looks at the stack of boxes from her office and shakes her head. How can three cardboard cartons that once held copy paper be large enough to hold two decades of memories?

Chapter 60

A month after resigning, Anne still wakes up at five a.m. every day. One morning, after tossing and turning for thirty minutes, she climbs out of bed and shuffles down the hall and out the door in search of the paper. Squinting in the dark, she sees the headlights of the newspaper lady's red Chevy truck turn onto her street and hears the thud of the newspaper as it hits her driveway. Perfect timing.

Anne walks barefoot to the end of the driveway, and the little truck backs up and stops in front of her. Leaning her head out the window, the gray-haired black lady says, "I'm proud of you."

Anne mumbles, "Oh? What for?" Although Anne's waved to her many times, they've never talked.

"I'm glad you got away from that district attorney."

"Yeah, me too," Anne says, bending over to pick up the newspaper.

"We don't need anybody up in that courthouse acting all crazy. Ain't nobody got time for that."

Suddenly, Anne feels wide awake. "Yes, ma'am! You're right. And the thing is, Harold and I used to be friends. He came to my wedding." Anne remembers when she, Jon, and their families were lining up at the side door of the church before the ceremony. Harold was late and got in line with the family. Anne laughed when she told Harold, "You're welcome to walk with the family, but guests are entering through the front door."

Anne nods at the newspaper carrier. "You're right. I couldn't deal with his dishonesty and the way he treated people, especially women."

"Reckon after he got elected, that power went straight to his head. Shameful," the woman says, clucking her teeth like Anne's Gram used to when Anne's brothers came shirtless to the kitchen table.

"He's a smart man, but I can't figure him out," Anne says to her new confidante.

"Wasn't it your employee who accused him of sexual harassment?"

"Sure was."

"Lordy mercy. We need us a new district attorney." She puts the truck in gear and waves to Anne. "All right, Ms. Gardner, you have a blessed day."

Anne watches the tail lights disappear down the street. *I guess she read about me in the newspaper or saw me on TV. I hope I gave her a good tip last Christmas.*

In the kitchen, Anne finds her reading glasses and sinks into a chair. The front-page headline says, "Another Departure in D.A.'s Office: Kate Phillips Resigns." *Ah, that's probably what sparked the paper lady's comments.* Anne knew Kate was leaving, but seeing it in print makes her sad. *Kate's a career prosecutor who's going to work as a real estate attorney. She should be prosecuting criminals and helping victims. That's her passion.*

The article recounts other recent departures from the D.A.'s leadership team. Five of eight have resigned in the last six months. The public information officer was first, then Glenn Brinson. Last month, Harold's chief investigator began a new job in Macon, commuting the two hours so as not to uproot his family. The article also mentions Anne's resignation.

The story lists several other long-time employees–not on the leadership team–who have left as well, including Anne's friend Alice, a new mom who quit without another job after Harold belittled her.

An article about a shooting near Waters Avenue reports the sixteen-year-old victim is in serious condition. *I hope someone told the family about victim compensation. I need to stop thinking like that. It's not my job anymore.*

Anne scours the classifieds. *Truck driver, nurse, electrician.* Not jobs for her. She'd applied at a temporary agency as an office worker to make some money and maybe get her foot in the door somewhere.

But they haven't called her. Since the recession, people are getting laid off instead of hired.

She turns to the real estate section and sees the listing for their Tybee house. She lets out a long sigh. *We need the money, but I'm in no rush to leave Tybee. With the market the way it is, it probably won't sell any time soon.*

She gets up and studies the YMCA class schedule on the refrigerator. She'll try nine a.m. kickboxing. It's only eight, so she stirs up pancake batter and pours two big spoonfuls into the skillet. Jon could eat pancakes for every meal. As he walks into the kitchen, she puts her arms around him. "Guess what? I'm cooking pancakes for you."

"Thanks, but I've got to leave now. The new owners have a meeting to discuss the hospital's financial status and long-range strategic plans. Sounds like torture, right?" Jon plants a kiss on her cheek and heads out.

I feel like a useless bum. Jon's working long hours at a demanding job, while I'm just making stupid pancakes. She flips the pancakes with the spatula, only to see the bottoms are burnt. She scrapes them into the garbage disposal, flips it on, and lets out a guttural scream, which is masked by the roar of the disposal until she turns it off. When she and the disposal become quiet, Little Kitty stares up at her with unblinking green eyes. Anne pats her head. "Don't be scared. Sometimes a girl has gotta spew out some anger." Seeming to agree, Little Kitty tilts her head and meows loudly.

Anne turns on the TV but doesn't want to hear about deaths in Afghanistan, the failing economy, and hurricane season. She mutes the TV. *I'll work the crossword puzzle to keep my mind from turning to mush.* She grabs a pencil and sprawls on the couch with the paper. *One across River in Missouri, five letters.* No idea. She scans a few more clues and can only solve two. She tosses the paper on the floor and checks her phone to see if anyone has called about a job or the house. No messages. She stomps back to the bedroom and dresses for the gym.

In the YMCA parking lot, one of her early morning workout buddies is already leaving. "Good morning, girl. What you doing here so late?"

"Hi, Erin. I'm gonna try the nine o'clock kickboxing class."

"Oh, that's right. You're a lady of leisure now."

Anne scrunches up her face. "Yeah." She hates being called that. Being unemployed makes her feel as lost as Moses and the Jews wandering the desert.

"Good luck, Anne. There's a bunch of young skinny blondes with ponytails in that class." Erin rolls her eyes. "See ya. Some of us have to get to work."

Anne can't think of a snappy comeback, so she goes inside to the aerobics room. Sure enough, it's packed with–damn it–a bunch of young chicks with ponytails. Though not all blonde, they sure are skinny and they seem to know each other. She overhears snippets of conversations about tennis, carpool lines, and protein smoothies. *Ugh, these are not my people.* Finding a spot in the back between two chicks in neon, tight-fitting tops, and running shorts, she feels frumpy in her big tee shirt and baggy shorts and longs for her early-morning class of middle-aged working women. An hour later, saturated in sweat, she's proud to have survived but vows not to return. *Since I'm still waking up early, I might as well keep going to the five-thirty a.m. class with my peeps.*

She drives home, showers, and dresses for her hair appointment.

At the salon, Ginger drapes a black cape around her. "Hey there, lady of leisure!"

Anne wants to scream. Instead, she says, "Hopefully not for long. I'm looking for a job."

"Tough time to be job hunting. Hope you find something."

"Yeah. Our property taxes are due next month."

Ginger runs her hands through Anne's hair. "You want the usual today? Trim and touch up those gray roots?"

"No, I don't want the usual." Anne stares at her shoulder-length, mousy-brown hair in the mirror. "I want something sassy. Yeah, short and sassy. And how about some red highlights?"

"Wow, girlfriend. You're feeling wild today. You sure? You mean a lot shorter and maybe auburn highlights?"

"Yep. Surprise me. I'm ready for a change." Usually not a risk taker, Anne's tired of being predictable. Years ago, after her daddy died unexpectedly, she told a friend she was going to have a nervous breakdown. Her friend grinned. "I bet you'll schedule it in your Day-timer."

Ginger clips the cape tighter around Anne's neck. "Did you bring pictures of what you have in mind?"

"Nope. I just decided. Create a new me."

"All right. This is going to be fun. Let me go mix up some color."

Two hours later, Anne has a new look. She shakes her head. The short bob looks chic. But she's taken aback by the color. "Oh my. I've heard blondes have more fun. I hope redheads do too."

"I like the highlights," Ginger says. "It's different, but heck, you're entering a new phase in life. Good to change things up once in a while." As the finishing touch, Ginger dabs a bit of gel into her hair to make it shine.

After a stop at the post office, Anne goes home and rushes to the bathroom mirror. She looks at her reflection and tosses her head from side to side. "I like it, but what will Jon think?" she asks Little Kitty who ignores her.

In the kitchen, she rifles through the mail. There's an official-looking envelope from Barbara Jones-Myers, the attorney representing Jeffrey in his sexual harassment suit. She rips it open and sees a subpoena for a deposition in the matter of Jeffrey Williams versus Harold Carter. *Damn. Will I ever get away from this crap?* The phone rings, and she rushes to answer it, hoping it's about a job possibility.

"Hello," Anne says.

"Hello, neighbor. We're calling about your extended car warranty."

Anne clicks the "end" button, which isn't nearly as cathartic as slamming down a phone receiver used to be. She fans through the mail again. A travel brochure for Aruba with a glossy cover says, "Everyone is happy, always happy on this island." *I should book the next flight.* She leaves it on the counter to show Jon.

She secures the subpoena on the refrigerator with a magnet. *But I don't want to see this damn thing every time I walk into the kitchen.* She yanks it down and stuffs it into the junk drawer already crowded with rubber bands, Scotch tape, scissors, ketchup packets, and two defunct phone chargers. When she tries to close the drawer, it sticks. Cursing, she wiggles her hand toward the back and discovers the cause of the jam—a gingerbread man Christmas ornament with a crack across his neck that she's been meaning to repair for months. She maneuvers him out of the drawer, blows out a long sigh, and snaps off his little head. When she whacks him against the counter, his feet fall to the floor. She gathers up the body parts, holds them in her cupped hands, and tosses the mutilated, once-smiling gingerbread man into the trash can.

Whew! Who knew smashing things could feel so good?

Chapter 61

A bolt of lightning flashes, and it begins to pour as Anne parks in the Victorian District. Huddling under her umbrella, she dodges puddles on her way to the front door. A small brass plaque reads: "Barbara Jones-Myers, Attorney at Law."

Anne shakes her umbrella and hangs it on a coat rack near the door. The waiting room is sparsely furnished with two wooden chairs, a love seat, and a coffee table. She wonders why Jeffrey chose this attorney who's fairly new to the practice of law. *Is she the best person to represent Jeffrey in a lawsuit against an elected official?* Anne's courthouse friends had been more blunt. "She's dumb as a rock," one said. "The other side will make mincemeat of her," another said.

The receptionist smiles. "You here for the four o'clock deposition?"

"Yes."

"It's right this way. Follow me."

In the conference room, Jeffrey and Ms. Jones-Myers–a short, young woman with cropped blonde hair–sit at an oval conference table. Ms. Jones-Myers stands. "Good afternoon, Ms. Gardner. Have a seat."

Anne sits beside Jeffrey who looks like a scared kid awaiting his fate in the principal's office. "Hello, Jeffrey."

"Hey, Ms. Gardner. I like your hair."

Anne smiles. "Thanks. Decided to get a new look."

To Anne's relief, there's no sign of Harold. A man, probably sixty or so, stands and shakes her hand. "I'm Wade Smith from Atlanta. I've been appointed by the Attorney General's Office to represent District Attorney Harold Carter."

Anne musters a smile and a firm handshake. *Ah yes. Because Harold is a state employee, our tax money is paying you to represent him.*

In the corner of the room, a woman sitting behind a small table fiddles with a recording device. "Hello, I'm Gwen, the court reporter. I'll be recording all of today's proceedings."

"Nice to meet you. I'm Anne Gardner."

She silences her cell phone and slides it into her pocketbook. *Why did I wear this suit? I'm already sweating. Harold is the one who should be nervous, but he's not even here.*

Across the table from her, Mr. Smith looks at his watch and then checks his cell. After a few minutes of awkward small talk, Mr. Smith says, "It appears Mr. Carter has been delayed. I suggest we go ahead and get started."

Typical Harold. Couldn't be on time for a deposition in his own damn case.

Ms. Jones-Meyers clears her throat. "Okay, then. I appreciate you all coming to this deposition in the matter of Jeffrey Williams versus Harold Carter."

Nodding at Anne, Ms. Jones-Meyers says, "Ms. Gardner, Mr. Smith, and I will each have some questions for you. Please take your time and speak loud enough for the court reporter."

"All right." Anne rolls her chair closer to the conference table and folds her hands in her lap. *Let's get this over with.* Ms. Jones-Meyers asks her to raise her right hand, swears her in, then asks the usual questions: name, address, work status, and how she knows the plaintiff and defendant.

"Now please state for the record the relationship between Mr. Carter and Mr. Williams," Ms. Jones-Meyers says.

Anne blushes. *OMG! Does she mean a sexual relationship? That's a heck of a way to begin.* But she collects her thoughts and answers, "Mr. Williams is an employee of the district attorney's office, and Mr. Carter is the district attorney. Mr. Carter is–I mean was–my supervisor. Mr. Williams worked in my department."

"Has it ever come to your attention that Mr. Williams has been or is currently uncomfortable around Mr. Carter?"

"Yes."

"When and how did that come to your attention?"

"Mr. Williams' supervisor informed me about two months after Mr. Williams was hired. And later, Mr. Williams himself told me."

"And who is his supervisor?" the attorney asks, without looking up from her notes.

"LaShay Thompson."

Maybe it's adrenaline, but Anne feels a surge of energy and confidence. *Yeah, let's get this on record in the courts.*

"What exactly did Ms. Thompson tell you?"

Anne's voice gets stronger. "She said Mr. Williams felt uncomfortable because Mr. Carter was calling and texting him after hours. Mr. Williams felt the D.A. should follow chain of command and not contact him directly."

The door to the conference room opens, and the district attorney himself walks in, looking self-important as usual. He shakes his attorney's hand and sits beside him, directly across from Anne. He offers no explanation or apology for his tardiness. His leather briefcase thuds as he drops it to the floor. Anne keeps her eyes on Ms. Jones-Meyers.

"Let's see. You were saying Mr. Williams felt uncomfortable when Mr. Carter contacted him directly, right? Can you be more specific?"

"Mr. Carter invited him to lunch and sometimes called him at home to chat. He felt extremely nervous when, uh, Mr. Carter made him drive him to Valdosta for a funeral." Anne pauses when she notices Harold whispering to his attorney.

Anne clears her throat. "He said Mr. Carter asked personal questions on the drive to Valdosta."

"Go on," Ms. Jones-Myers says. "What kind of personal questions?"

"Mr. Carter asked about his girlfriend, and his shirt size, and Mr. Carter told him he needed to fatten him up. He asked if he likes his supervisors. Things like that."

"Did Mr. Williams tell you that or did he tell Ms. Thompson?"

"He told Ms. Thompson first, then he told me."

"Were there other occasions in which Mr. Carter, I mean Mr. Williams, felt uncomfortable around the D.A.?"

Good grief. She can't even get the names right. "Yes. He got extremely upset a few weeks later when the district attorney wanted him to attend a conference in California and stay in the same hotel room with him." Anne feels Harold's piercing eyes on her. Her underarms feel damp, but she doesn't take off her jacket. *I'm not going to let Harold see me sweat.* "Jeffrey had already shared a hotel room with Mr. Carter and another young man on a trip to Chicago."

Mr. Smith looks at his client with raised eyebrows. Harold continues staring at Anne. Jeffrey jostles his right leg.

Ms. Jones-Meyers thumbs through her file and retrieves a piece of paper. "Did Jeffrey Williams ever tell you the district attorney sexually harassed him?"

Mr. Smith interjects. "That's a leading question."

"Okay, what specific words did he use to describe Mr. Carter's behavior?"

"He said it felt like sexual harassment," Anne says.

"Did he use those exact words, sexual harassment?" Ms. Jones-Meyers says.

"Yes."

"When did he say that?"

"May 26th of this year."

"How do you remember the specific date?"

"That day is forever etched in my mind. Plus, my sister told me to start taking notes."

"Your sister?"

"Um, yes, uh, my sister gave me that advice. She, well, she used to work in H.R. at a company in Alabama and..." *Oh god, I'm starting to ramble.*

"Ms. Gardner, do you have copies of those notes with you today?" Mr. Smith asks.

"No, I don't."

"That request for documents was attached to your subpoena. I'm sure you can get them to Ms. Jones-Meyers, correct?"

"Yes sir," Anne says.

Ms. Jones-Meyers continues. "So on May 26th, what did you do after Mr. Williams alleged sexual harassment?"

Anne explains all she did after the allegation.

After a few more questions, it's Harold's attorney's turn. In a soft voice, Mr. Smith says, "Ms. Gardner, you first learned Mr. Williams was uncomfortable when his supervisor told you. Is that correct?"

"Yes sir."

"Did you document that conversation in writing or otherwise?"

"No."

"Did you discuss it with H.R.?"

Anne fiddles with the opal ring she got for Christmas as a teen. "Um, not at that time. Not until Mr. Williams talked with me on May 26th."

"Did you ever discuss this matter with Mr. Carter, who was your boss?"

"Yes. I told Mr. Carter that Jeffrey felt uncomfortable around him and asked him to please stop calling and texting him. Oh, and to stop inviting him to lunch."

"Hmm. You did? How did Mr. Carter respond?"

"He said he would stop."

"Okay and then–"

Anne interrupts. "But Mr. Carter didn't stop contacting him."

Harold passes a note to Mr. Smith who glances at it and continues. "Okay. Ms. Gardner, when Mr. Williams alleged sexual harassment, had anything unusual occurred the previous day?"

"Um, what do you mean?"

"Isn't it true that Mr. Williams was reprimanded by the D.A.'s chief investigator the day before?"

"Yes." Anne twirls a strand of hair. *Uh oh.*

"What was the nature of the reprimand?"

"It was for missing a meeting at the courthouse. Excuse me, but may I have a drink of water?" She fans herself with her notepad and wishes someone would open the door to the hallway.

"Of course," Ms. Jones-Myers says and buzzes the receptionist who brings in several bottles of water.

Anne opens one and takes a swig. She feels better, even though sweat beads are forming behind her knees.

Mr. Smith smiles, and Anne notices his clear blue eyes. "I needed a drink of water myself. Take your time, Ms. Gardner, and let me know when you're ready to continue." Anne had heard through the courthouse grapevine that he wasn't thrilled about being appointed to represent Mr. Carter but, as is ethically required, would do his best to defend him.

Anne swallows hard. "I'm ready."

"Okay, Ms. Gardner, we'll proceed. Did Jeffrey, uh, Mr. Williams, ever state to you Mr. Carter had touched him in an inappropriate manner?"

"No." Anne sees Jeffrey slumped in his chair, and her heart breaks. She can't imagine how difficult this must be for him. *This is awful for Jeffrey, and he's only listening. What if he has to testify in a courtroom full of people?*

Mr. Smith writes on his pad before asking, "Did Mr. Williams ever allege that Mr. Carter asked him to engage in any sexual activity?"

"No."

"Have you discussed this alleged harassment with others?"

"Um..."

"Isn't it true you did an extensive interview with WTOC news about this allegation, even though it had not–and still has not– been investigated and certainly not proven?"

Anne digs her fingernails into her palm. "Yes."

Ms. Jones-Meyers says, "Excuse me, may I interject here?"

"If it's relevant," Mr. Smith says.

Ms. Jones-Meyers looks at Anne. "Were you concerned Mr. Carter would take action against you– even fire you–for talking to the media?"

Anne nods. "Yes, I was concerned. As you know, I resigned."

Mr. Smith leans forward, both hands on the conference table. "Yes, we're aware of that, Ms. Gardner. But Mr. Carter did **not** take action against you or fire you, did he?"

"No, but–"

"Answer yes or no, Ms. Gardner. After you went public with scathing allegations against the district attorney, did he fire you?"

"No sir."

"Thank you. I believe those are all the questions I have for now."

Anne exhales and leans back in her seat. She mulls over her answers and wonders how she did.

Ms. Jones-Meyers thanks everyone for attending. It's five-fifteen, and Anne stands first, looks at Jeffrey, and says, "You take care of yourself now."

"Yes, ma'am. You too."

Chapter 62

Anne dashes outside. The downpour is over, and it's cooler. She drives several blocks north to Victory Drive. *Dammit, I forgot my umbrella, but I'm not going back.* Too late, she realizes she should have avoided Victory Drive because it often floods, particularly at high tide. Worried her Honda might stall, she stays in the middle lane and putters along. As she approaches the end of Daffin Park, she sees two stranded cars and a chubby, unhappy-looking policeman directing traffic around them. At that moment, her engine sputters, wheezes, and dies. *Shit! Make that **three** cars flooded at the intersection.* She sits in her car, unsure if she should get out or wait for the policeman to come over. She jumps when she hears a tap on the window. She lowers her window and a young man wearing a diamond stud in his left ear and an Atlanta Braves cap says, "Sorry. I didn't mean to scare you. I can push your car to the edge of the road before some fool slams into you."

"Thank you," Anne says as the rush-hour traffic sloshes by.

"Put it in neutral."

Anne nods and takes a good look at him. "Rasheed, is that you?"

"Yes." He leans down. "And you're the Victim-Witness lady? Ms. Gainey?"

"Gardner. Anne Gardner. Good to see you." After his younger brother was robbed and murdered while working at Subway, Rasheed attended monthly support group meetings at Victim-Witness and the annual candlelight vigils. *Didn't he have a son?*

Rasheed pushes her car and directs traffic to go around her until the policeman comes over. The cop looks under the hood and pronounces the verdict. "Flooded. Need to call a tow truck."

Well, duh. "I'll call Triple A."

"I'll stay with you 'til they come," Rasheed says.

"Oh that's sweet, but seriously, you don't have to. But do tell me how you're doing. And you have a son, right?"

Rasheed pulls his phone from his jeans pocket and shows her a picture of a grinning kid in a Ninja Turtle tee shirt.

"Cute! How old is he?"

"Turned four last week. I named him after my brother, you know."

"Aw. He's lucky to have you as a daddy."

Rasheed's smile spreads across his face. "Thanks, Ms. Gardner. I manage the Auto Care on Whitemarsh. Drop by sometime. You be careful now."

"Okay. I'll have them tow my Honda there now. Thank you, Rasheed. I hope to see you around but not on a flooded street next time."

"Sounds good. We'll take care of you at the shop." He grins before returning to his truck at the corner gas station.

Goose bumps pop up on Anne's arm. She feels a surge of emotions: gratitude she knows such a fine person as Rasheed, sadness because his brother was murdered, and relief the deposition is over.

She calls Jon to explain her predicament and to ask him to pick her up at Auto Care. The tow truck arrives thirty minutes later, and the burly driver hooks her car to the back. She hikes up her skirt and climbs into the cab of the truck.

"I hope you don't get dirty on this seat," he says.

"Trust me. That's the least of my worries."

As they approach the Thunderbolt Bridge, the driver points at the windshield. "Well, I'll be damned!"

Anne looks up at a rainbow stretching across the eastern sky. "Oh wow. I haven't seen a rainbow in years." Her mama had taught her to say Roy G. Biv to remember the colors in order: red, orange, yellow, green, blue, indigo, violet. *There they all are, created with God's giant paintbrushes.*

"Rainbows are good luck, you know," the driver says, a plug of tobacco in his left cheek.

"I know. They're a sign of hope and just what I needed today."

Chapter 63

The following week, Anne picks up Papa Murphy's pizza for Girls' Night Out. She's eager to get together with friends.

Anne is the first to arrive at Kate's and is greeted by Bailey, a sweet Labrador mix who jumps up to sniff the pizza boxes, almost knocking them out of her hands.

Kate's son ushers Bailey the dog outside.

Kate smiles. "Hey, lady! Glad you're here. Feels like I haven't seen you in forever."

"I know you've been busy with the new job," Anne says as they walk toward the kitchen. "How's private practice?" Anne slides the pizza boxes onto the counter.

"Awful. Real estate law is not my thing. I'm thankful to have a job, but I miss being a prosecutor. I sure don't miss Harold though."

"Tell me about it."

"I'm glad you're here early. I need to talk with you." Kate pours two glasses of Chardonnay, and Anne perches on a bar stool while Kate sets out paper plates, napkins, and cups.

Anne takes a sip of wine. "Sure, what's up?"

"You know I've been bitching about how terrible the D.A.'s office has become since Harold took the helm. And I hear it's not getting better. It breaks my heart to watch things keep continuing to go downhill."

Anne nods.

"My dad keeps telling me I should quit complaining and do something about it. He's right. I'm seriously considering running for D.A."

"Yay!" Anne leaps up and high-fives Kate. "You mentioned a couple of months ago you were thinking about it. Tell me everything."

"Only two things to tell: One, I have no idea how to run a campaign. Two, I'll need lots of help. Are you in?"

"Sure. I know zilch about political campaigns, but I'll do whatever I can."

"But you do know all about managing volunteers. You did that for years at Victim-Witness."

"Yep, I can do that."

"And would you help with the communication pieces–news releases, brochures, and stuff like that?"

"I'm on it." Anne's mind kicks into gear: campaign slogans, news conferences, social media, and letters to the editor. Too excited to sit still, she pumps her fist in the air. "This is exciting."

"I've talked to several people who've run for local office. Of course, they tell me the first thing I've gotta do is raise money." Kate dunks a chip in the cheese dip.

Anne turns up her nose. "Don't count on me for that. I hate fundraising."

More women arrive with drinks and snacks.

"Hey, ladies. What's new?" Carol asks, plopping a box of chicken wings and a bottle of champagne on the counter.

"Well, a lot is new," Anne says, grinning in Kate's direction.

"I'm going to run for District Attorney," Kate says. Delighted squeals and chatter erupt.

"Perfect," Carol says. "I brought champagne because it was on sale, but now we actually have something to celebrate. This is the best news I've heard in ages." Carol pops the cork and pours champagne into plastic cups for everyone.

Maggie lifts her cup. "A toast to the next Chatham County D.A.!"

"Here, here, Sistuh!" says Anne, and they raise their cups.

Kate blushes. "Thanks, y'all. I'm probably a fool for doing this. I know it's a long shot. Harold is an incumbent who has already won one election. I'm a woman with no campaign experience, no supporters, no money, no nothing."

Maggie says, "Kate, don't sell yourself short. You're smart and an experienced, successful prosecutor. Surely the voters have seen what a horrible job Harold's doing. He has got to go."

"Yeah but voters have short memories." Kate fans herself with a paper plate. "I'll stick one of these pizzas in the oven. Then let's go out on the porch. I'm about to burn up in here."

"Well, take off that work dress, and you'll feel cooler," Anne says. "The rest of us changed before coming over. Liz isn't even wearing her pantyhose."

"True. I'll be right back." Kate returns wearing a Brooklyn Law School tee shirt and what appears to be a pair of her husband's boxer shorts. She shoos her daughter and son upstairs to finish their homework. The women all head out to the porch and sit around a big table.

"Thanks for coming over," Kate says. "I've missed y'all the last few weeks. Y'all keep me sane. And you realize I'm going to need you more than ever if I run for D.A."

A few months later, a different group of women assembles in Kate's den. Kate puts a tray of cheese crackers on the coffee table and thanks her campaign volunteers for coming. "Lots of work to do, so let's get started."

LaShay, who has a new job at S.A.F.E. Shelter, says, "Can we begin with prayer?"

"Sure," Kate says, closing her eyes.

"Dear God," LaShay says, "we pray you will always be the center of our campaign team. We ask for your guidance and blessings as we strive to do what's right for our community. We pray especially for Kate and her family as they have embarked upon this challenging and sometimes stressful campaign. We are grateful for your eternal presence in our lives. Thank you, God, for our many blessings. Amen."

Next to speak is Daphne Logan, a dynamic, middle-aged real estate agent who's agreed to chair the campaign. Her 17-year-old daughter,

Ashley, was robbed and killed in City Market four years ago after her high school prom. Kate successfully prosecuted the man who murdered her. Daphne's leadership skills, connections in the community, fundraising experience, and charm make her the perfect chairperson. She once raised more than a million dollars for The Children's Hospital at Memorial and has already collected thousands for Kate.

"Okay, ladies," Daphne says. "First we need to get out the invitations for the next Meet and Greet." These small gatherings, usually in people's homes, have proven successful in introducing Kate to folks, as well as getting volunteer and financial support. "The invitations are ready at the print shop. Who can pick them up ASAP?"

"I can," Anne says. "I'm getting more yard signs from there."

"Great. We'll get the invitations in the mail tomorrow," Daphne says, checking the calendar on her phone.

"It's almost a year til the election, but our social media blitz will launch next month. We're so lucky to have you on board, Brianna." Daphne smiles at the young Savannah State University student who jumped at the chance to be the campaign's social media chair after hearing Kate speak to her political science class.

A retired police captain serves as campaign treasurer. Another woman who met Kate at a Meet and Greet takes meeting minutes. A stay-at-home mom is in charge of distributing yard signs. This core group of women in Kate's den is the backbone of the campaign, but they're supported by many others to get all the work done. Anne stays in close touch with them, making sure they understand what to do and that their work is appreciated.

Anne is also responsible for media relations. But her most important role is as Kate's friend and confidante. She's the one Kate calls with good or bad news, who listens to her vent about frustrations and shares laughs about zany encounters on the campaign trail. Working on the election keeps Anne busy and gives her focus while still job hunting. She finds working for change empowering and way better than stewing about how bad things are in the D.A.'s office.

Daphne updates everyone on events scheduled for the next three weeks. Kate is to speak at the Downtown Neighborhood Association, civic clubs, and the Westside Senior Citizens Center. At the suggestion of one volunteer, Kate eats breakfast every Friday at various restaurants across the county and mingles with the patrons.

Daphne says, "I know we've been hearing people say they hope Kate wins, but she doesn't have a chance against an incumbent. She has no experience running a campaign and no base of support, blah blah."

"Yup," Anne says.

Daphne smiles. "I just tell them 'You're right. We have no experience running a campaign, so we don't know what our limits are. We just keep learning and growing and getting better.'"

Anne chimes in. "And some claim Kate is running only because she was a disgruntled employee. Pessimistic comments make me mad but also motivate me to work harder. Let the naysayers talk all they want. We're making inroads."

As the meeting winds down, Kate says, "I have a gift for y'all, just a small token of appreciation." She distributes refrigerator magnets with a quote from Margaret Mead: "Never doubt that a small group of thoughtful, committed citizens can change the world. Indeed, it is the only thing that ever has."

Chapter 64

Despite an early morning chill and drizzle on election day, Anne and two other volunteers stand at the corner of Abercorn and Derenne waving blue "Kate for D.A." signs. Many drivers honk. Anne grins and yells, "Thanks. Vote today. "When she sees a few cars with bumper stickers for Harold Carter, Anne squints to see if she recognizes the drivers, but usually doesn't. *Who could vote for that man after a sexual harassment lawsuit, a gender discrimination lawsuit, and out-of-control spending?*

Two more sign wavers, one for Obama and one for McCain, show up clad in bright yellow rain jackets. A few minutes later, a young man appears carrying a big Re-Elect Harold Carter sign. Anne's arms begin to ache from waving. She repeats to herself what she's been telling a weary Kate, "We're almost to the finish line. Gotta keep pushing a little longer; then we can rest."

By ten o'clock, the clouds part, and the drizzle stops. A new group of volunteers arrives, Anne returns to her car, grabs the towel she'd tossed in the back seat and dries off as best she can. Tired, cold, and hungry, she wraps the towel around her shoulders and starts coughing. *Why today, of all days, do I feel like crap?* She pops a cough drop in her mouth. *I don't care if I'm coughing like Typhoid Mary. I'm going to the election watch party tonight. After a year of campaigning, there's no way I'd miss it.*

Before leaving the parking lot, she looks up at the now empty sixty-foot globe on Derenne Avenue. Painted to resemble planet earth, the gas tank is a landmark for folks approaching Savannah from Lynes Parkway. *I wonder who painted the ocean and continents on that earth. And how?* She smiles, remembering Kate once saying, "You're so woo woo. I bet you go around singing 'Let There Be Peace on Earth.'" Turning right onto busy Abercorn Street, she thinks, *I'm praying for inner peace now. No matter how today's election turns out, it's all in Divine Order.*

Although other races are on the ballot, including the presidential one, Anne has focused all her energy on Kate's campaign and has been amazed at the massive amount of work involved. *Despite the odds, Kate has got to win. But if God forbid, she doesn't, the main thing to remember is we've all tried our best. Instead of just complaining about Harold, we took action.*

At home, she changes into dry clothes and makes cheese toast and hot tea with honey. She curls up on the couch with her snack, then emails her media contacts to remind them of Kate's watch party at The Hyatt that night. All three TV reporters reply, asking if they can interview Kate live on the six o'clock news. She replies Kate will be at the Hyatt at six but not available for interviews until later in the evening. *Hopefully accepting congratulations on her victory.*

Around two o'clock, Anne drives the few blocks to her polling place at the Tybee library. After clicking the box next to Kate's name, she grins. She's never felt so excited to cast a ballot.

When she arrives at The Hyatt that evening, the small ballroom is already packed with supporters. Although Kate's sister and brother live in Savannah, her other siblings and family members traveled from as far as New York. The room is filled with a cross-section of the community: conservative, liberal, young, old, black, white, Republicans, and Democrats. And there's Lily Davis. Anne rushes over for a hug.

"You look great," Mrs. Davis says. "Getting out of the courthouse agrees with you."

"Thanks. I'm poor but happy. Tell me how you're doing."

"Honey, I'm blessed. You know I enjoy serving on the mayor's crime prevention task force. I get to talk to young folks about the effects of crime. It's given me a renewed purpose since my son's death." A well-dressed man walks up beside them. Mrs. Davis smiles. "Anne, you remember Pastor Roberson, don't you?"

"Of course, I do," Anne says, grabbing his hand with both of hers. "You were one of the best speakers we ever had at our clergy seminar."

"Thanks, Anne."

Daphne Logan comes over. "Anne I hate to interrupt, but I want you to meet the editor of the student newspaper at Armstrong University. She has to leave soon."

"Sure. Excuse me, folks," Anne says.

Daphne escorts her across the room where a tall girl with long brown hair is waiting. "Tiffany, this is Anne Gardner who I was telling you about. Anne worked on her college newspaper and wrote for a daily paper in Alabama after she graduated. And, of course, she ran the Victim-Witness Program here for years."

Anne smiles. "Hey, Tiffany, great to meet you."

"You too, Ms. Gardner. I'm majoring in criminal justice, and I have a special interest in victims' issues. I wondered if you could come speak with our criminal justice club sometime."

"Sure. I'd love to."

Daphne says, "Tiffany was telling me they're expanding the criminal justice program and looking for an adjunct professor to teach a few victimology classes."

"Yes ma'am. It's a new position."

Daphne looks at Anne. "Hmm. I think I know someone who could do that."

Anne's eyes widen. "Interesting." She pats Tiffany on the shoulder. "I'm glad you came tonight, Tiffany."

"Me too. One more thing. Could I interview you for an article I'm writing about sexual assault?"

This kid reminds me of my college self. "Definitely. Let me find a pen to write my number."

"I'll enter it in my phone." Tiffany pulls her cell from her coat pocket, and Anne gives her the number. "I'll call you next week."

"Sounds good, Tiffany."

Maneuvering through the crowd to the refreshment bar and grabbing a bottle of water, she spots two volunteers at a table staring at their laptops. They're following results from the Chatham County Elections Board.

Kate, who must be exhausted, still looks fantastic in a blue dress the color of her campaign signs and brochures. She mingles, thanking everyone for their support.

The big-screen TV on the wall is tuned to a local station, and election results scroll across the bottom of the screen. Around nine-thirty, it says "Results from District 2 and 8 show Kate Phillips with 56% of the vote to Carter's 44%. The room erupts in applause. Anne's phone beeps, she answers, but can't hear a thing. She walks out into the hall with the phone plastered to her ear. It's a newspaper reporter, saying Robert, a photographer, is en route.

"That's fine. We're on the second floor." Anne heads back inside to tell Kate. Someone has written on a dry-erase board: "District 3, Kate leads with 51%." But the TV flashes "District Attorney's Race: Incumbent Carter leads in District 8 with 2,320 to Phillips's 1,436." A collective sigh permeates the room. Anne walks back out to the hall where a county commission candidate's supporters have spilled out from a nearby room. "We're pulling for Kate. I hope she's got it," one robust, semi-drunk man says. Anne nods and looks at the texts from well-wishers lighting up her phone.

Anne starts coughing again. She takes the escalator down to the lobby to escape the crowd, but when she sees Robert with his camera, she escorts him to the second floor. He says, "I've covered a lot of campaigns before, but that Harold Carter is one weird dude. He's so arrogant he won't return our calls. Then when I shot his profile picture for a Sunday feature, he acted like we were best friends. And I do mean best friends."

"Yep, he's a strange duck." *I bet he was hitting on you. You're his type--young, slender, and handsome.* As Kate whisks by them, Anne tugs on her arm, "Robert's here to take photos."

"Okay, hold on." Kate turns to check the whiteboard which has been updated. She's neck to neck with Harold. The next update has Kate lagging by about a thousand votes.

But by ten-forty-five, Kate is declared the winner with 53 percent of the vote. Amid shouts, hugs, tears, high-fives, and the flash of Robert's camera, Kate calls for the crowd's attention. "I truly couldn't have done this without all of you. Thank you from the bottom of my heart." She nods at her husband, who says a beautiful prayer.

Everyone follows Kate to the lobby where the TV stations are reporting live. The supporters squeeze in behind Kate as the camera pans the crowd. Kate beams. "I'm honored the citizens have chosen me to be their next District Attorney. During my campaign, I've had the opportunity to go out into the community and learn about their concerns. I promise to run the District Attorney's Office with professionalism and integrity. We'll not only prosecute criminals to make our streets safer, but we'll also ensure the rights of crime victims. That's my priority, to do both. Thank you, all."

The moment they've worked so hard for has finally arrived. Anne, teary-eyed, is filled with gratitude for having been a part of this grassroots movement.

Kate's supporters erupt into loud cheers, and Anne adds her hoarse voice to the celebration.

Sometimes justice does prevail.

Epilogue

Two months after the election, Anne collects test papers from her students in the Crime Victimology class at Armstrong University. "Don't forget," she calls out over the bustle of students leaving. "Next week we'll have a guest speaker discussing post-traumatic stress disorder." Anne finds her part-time teaching job a refreshing change from victim advocacy. It's an elective class, so the students have chosen to be there and seem eager to learn.

She puts on a sweater and heads to the parking lot. Inside her car, she checks her phone and sees a text from Melissa from WTOC. Anne calls her. "Hey, Melissa, what's up?"

"Hi, Anne. How's the new job?"

"So far, so good."

"Thought you'd want to know another victim of Harold Carter called the newsroom. He said he'd always thought he was the only one. He wants to talk to Jeffrey. Can you ask Jeffrey if I can give out his number?"

"I'll ask. What else did he say?"

"Not much, but he mentioned knowing Harold through juvenile court. I referred him to the attorney handling the class action harassment suit. If he joins the suit, it could bolster the case against Harold."

"True."

"This is my fifth call from a victim. Your speaking out made such a difference."

"Thanks. I'll let you know what Jeffrey says." Anne clicks off and starts driving to Tybee to meet Kate for happy hour. *I guess I did the right thing by spilling all to WTOC.*

Friday afternoon traffic is heavy, but Anne makes it to Tybee before dark and goes straight to Fannie's On The Beach. Kate waves to Anne from a table on the deck.

Anne sits beside her. "Hey, Kate, thanks for coming out to the beach. Since we're moving to Savannah soon, I wanna spend as much time here as I can. I'm gonna miss this place. I love it even on a cool January night."

"You'll only be twenty miles away." Kate slides a margarita to Anne. "I ordered one for you too. Drink up."

"Thanks." Anne takes a few sips. "You know I hate change, but leaving my career and moving to a new home might turn out to be all in divine order, as my mama used to say." Anne raises her glass. "Here's to new beginnings."

Kate rolls her eyes. "Good grief, that alcohol has already made you sappy." She leans closer. "I hate to break the spell, but I have some bad news."

Anne frowns. "What?"

"The police chief called this afternoon. Harold is dead."

Anne nearly chokes on her drink. "What?"

"The police found Harold unresponsive on his bedroom floor with a bullet wound in his chest after a hysterical Devin called 911."

"Oh dear god! What in the world happened?"

Kate shakes her head. "No idea... Of course, the police are questioning Devin. I heard Devin freaked out when he had to give a deposition in Jeffrey's harassment suit. Devin idolized Harold. It must have been hard to admit his lover was a sleaze."

Anne's eyebrows shoot upward. "Do you think Devin killed Harold?"

"Anything's possible. It could be suicide. The lawsuits have damaged Harold's reputation and his career. Everybody's talking behind his back."

Anne buttons up her sweater and stares at the ocean. "I can't wrap my head around this. Harold had some deep-seated issues. God bless him."

"Yup. It must have been hard for him to be closeted all those years. I guess he thought his family and church wouldn't approve. Sadly, after he was elected D.A., he became a different person. I couldn't trust him anymore. Disrespecting women, lying, alienating the police, and..." Her voice trails off. "Such a breach of trust."

They sit in silence until the bubbly waitress interrupts. "Hey, ladies. Y'all ready to order some shrimp or pizza to go with those margaritas?"

"No thanks," they say in unison.

Anne wipes away a tear. "Oh gosh, remember when we used to go to lunch with Harold? He was our friend long before he became our boss."

Kate rubs her index finger around the rim of her frosty glass. "I know. It's sad and bizarre and just friggin' awful."

"Whatever happened, I feel sorry for Devin."

Kate's phone beeps. "My phone is blowing up with people calling about this, but I'm not answering unless it's the police. I told them if they make an arrest, I won't be able to handle the prosecution. It's definitely a conflict of interest. I gave the state attorney general a heads up that he'd need to appoint a special prosecutor from another circuit."

"Oh gosh, I hadn't thought about that."

Kate scrunches her face when the women at the table beside them–bachelorette party–giggle as they hoist shot glasses. "Let's get outta here, Anne." She motions for the waitress and hands her cash. "Keep the change."

The two friends walk to the oceanfront parking lot. Kate looks up at the full moon illuminating the dark Atlantic in silvery light. "Mark Twain said everyone is a moon with a dark side they never show. But that's not true. We sure as hell have seen the dark side of a lot of people."

Anne puts her arm around Kate's shoulder. "Yup, and that's why we have to always look for the light."

ACKNOWLEDGMENTS

This novel would not exist without the extraordinary women in my writing critique group. Susan Earl, Beverly Willett, Judy Bean and Kim Evans offered invaluable insights about everything from pesky punctuation to plot structure and even the title. I was clueless about how to write a novel, but they believed in me when I didn't believe in myself. I'm forever grateful for their stellar writing skills, support, patience, and friendship. Thanks to past group members Charlotte Getz, Jo Dasher, Sarah Stroud, and Joyce Underwood who read the first scribbles of my manuscript and encouraged me to keep writing.

I'm blessed to have a close and loving family, due in no small part to my late parents Martha and Lewis Pitts. Much appreciation to wonderful siblings and their spouses for being so good to their baby sister: Lewis and Spoma, Paul and Karen, Margaret and Clyde. Special shout out to Margaret, the best sistuh ever who fixes everything from a broken computer to a broken heart.

One of the best decisions I ever made was to marry Jay Bradley. He's a gem. Grandson Joseph encouraged, um badgered me, to complete this novel. "Nana, are you *ever* gonna finish that book?"

Catherine Killingsworth offered advice that made my novel a thousand times better.

My publishing buddy, Dawn Major, is a steel magnolia whom I adore. And stellar author Robert Gwaltney didn't know me from Adam's house cat but answered every question I asked. Bless their hearts, and I mean that in a good way.

I'm beyond lucky to have the best girlfriends on the planet who have laughed, cried, and done life with me for decades. I'm talking about Amy McCaskill, Susan MacCrossan, Susan Lamb, Meg Heap, Kris Rice, Kim Rowden, Patty Morelli, June Fogle, Tina Smith, and the late Ruthie Anderson and Elizabeth Stewart.

My talented and hilarious friend Nancy Fullbright of Chickadee Communications expertly handles all the social media and publicity stuff that causes me to break out in hives. We unabashedly call ourselves the dream team.

Thanks to wonderful beta reader Laurie Milano and also to Kim McCoy who, during a quick lunch, suggested I change the ending.

Former District Attorney Spencer Lawton, Jr. championed the cause for crime victims long before it was the popular thing to do. I'm thankful he and Elizabeth Stewart hired me as a naive 23-year-old and I began a career I loved.

Rosemary Daniell was one of my first writing mentors. She continues to encourage writers through her popular Zona Rosa workshops.

Throughout the years of writing this book, I was inspired as I recalled all the courageous crime victims I knew.

I learned so much from middle school students I mentored in the Deep program. I helped them write their powerful stories and they, in turn, inspired me to write mine.

I'm grateful Gene Robinson of Moonshine Cove Publishing believed in my book and led me through the publishing process.